# Angel's Flight

## The Phantom Saga

Jessica Mason

Published by Murmuration Books, 2025.

ANGEL'S FLIGHT

**First edition. July 23, 2025.**

Copyright © 2025 Jessica Mason.

ISBN: 979-8-9986338-5-0

Written by Jessica Mason.

For Gaston.

Merci, mon ami.

# Author's Note

$A$ *ngel's Flight* is a dark, historical romance with adult themes and explicit content. This includes bondage and domination, sadomasochism, anal penetration, explicit language, violence, mental health struggles, discussions of infertility and content regarding the exploitation of teenage girls. For more detailed triggers and other information, please consult my website:www.jessicamasonauthor.com[1].

Thank you for reading.

---

1. http://www.jessicamasonauthor.com

# Foreword

S tories start and stories end. That is their nature. The curtain opens, then closes, and the tale is done, even though we know there is sadness to come after happily ever after or hope to be found after a tragedy. The story of *after* is a mystery; an immaterial, untamable thing. The unknown of what happened next is just an echo of a life that is done, even though there was so much left unfinished.

In other words: a ghost.

Some ghosts, however, are not what they seem. You, dear reader, of all people, should know this. Some ghosts are things of flesh and blood, of life and longing, behind the mask of a phantom. It stands to reason, then, that some endings are illusions too. Some stories go on because there is so much more to tell. They do not die, but find a new path, though it may be perilous.

Let us follow where it leads.

# Prelude

## Yville-sur-Seine, France

She had not been expecting visitors two days in a row, but the Baroness still managed to compose herself to meet the man from Paris. She did not, however, mind making him wait for three-quarters of an hour in the drawing room before doing so. The servants said she moved slowly because of her age, but in all her seventy-eight years, she had moved at the same pace: carefully and with poise. She was of the old nobility, from a family whose name went back centuries. Even though she had taken on a lower rank through marriage, Adelaide de Martiniac still comported herself with the dignity befitting her lineage.

So what if that appeared to others as moving slowly? They could wait. She was also very tired from the dramatic turns of the day before. Those shocks had been about lineage too, and she was proud of her old heart for enduring them.

Adelaide entered the drawing room with her head held high, her long skirts and petticoats whispering over the parquet floors as Jacques, her most loyal companion, tapped a path at her side. The small dog growled when he saw the man waiting by the fireplace, staring out the window.

"Good morning, Monsieur. I'm sorry to have kept you waiting," the Baroness lied as the man turned and raised an eyebrow at Jacques's threat.

"It is no trouble, Madame de Martiniac," the man replied. He did not use her formal title, pointedly so. Impertinent. "I realize the hour is irregular, but the news I bring could not wait."

"Everything can wait, Monsieur, when you are my age. Do have some chocolate," Adelaide replied as the maid entered with a silver tray bearing the Baroness's customary breakfast of *chocolat chaud* and apple pastries. She attributed her continued good health to her daily consumption of the drink.

"Madame, I am afraid this is not the sort of news to share over confections," the man replied with a scowl. He was of average height, this man, with neatly parted hair of pale brown. His moustache was equally tidy in a thin line above his lip. His posture was precise, and his pale green eyes were sharp behind his round glasses. He had the look of a man of business - a marked contrast to her guest yesterday.

"I have come to inquire of you about—"

"You must tell me your name before you bring up my grandson's disappearance, please," Adelaide said. The man at least had the decency to look surprised. "Come, come: what else would you be troubling an old woman about at this hour?"

"I am Monsieur Bidaut. I am in the employ of a firm in Paris."

"A firm that specializes in debt collections, I might guess?" Adelaide offered, but the man gave no indication she was right. "Antoine owed money to half of Paris. I would not have expected them to employ a lawyer."

"I'm not a lawyer myself, more of an investigator. Enough time has passed that at least one debtor has grown impatient and wishes to have your grandson declared dead."

The man waited a beat, as if he anticipated the words to hurt or shock the Baroness. They did not. She knew already that Antoine was rotting in the cellars of the Paris Opéra. The reaction this man had anticipated had come many weeks ago, and for a different grandson, when Adelaide had read the mysterious words in L'Époque: Erik is Dead.

The humble advertisement had shocked her. She believed she would know in her bones when her firstborn grandson died. She had dreamed of death for days before, and she felt something stop in her heart in the wee hours one spring morning. She had thought it was Antoine – for she had always known he would meet a bad end, just like his father.

It had taken until yesterday for her to be proven right when a man in a mask arrived on her doorstep. The ghost of her past had come, bearing news both dark and remarkable. The death of one grandson and the marriage of the other. Not to mention his resurrection.

"I don't see what the point would be in that," Adelaide sighed. "Dead or disappeared, your client won't get any money from Antoine. He had none."

"That's not necessarily true, now is it? A portion of your late husband's estate remains unclaimed, thanks to you." Bidaut said it plainly, with no guile or threat, which made it all the more impressive.

"Your client must be owed a great deal to have funded such thorough research. Who is it?"

"I am not at liberty yet to say," Bidaut replied. "The interested party has a substantial claim. One which they cannot pursue until Monsieur de Martiniac is dead in the eyes of the law."

"And you wish me to begin those proceedings?" Adelaide had to chuckle. Until yesterday, she had not even been sure that the awful boy was dead, but she couldn't tell the world how or why she knew.

"They have already begun, actually," Bidaut replied, much to Adelaide's surprise and interest. How could a debtor have managed that?

"So you are here to give me notice."

"And to try to persuade you to willingly pass over the inheritance that Monsieur de Martiniac was denied. I understand withholding it from him in life, as your grandson sounds like he was a less-than-honorable man."

"He was a monster," Adelaide corrected. "Like his father."

The father Antoine had killed. It had been a strange shift in her guilt to learn that it had been Antoine, not Erik, who had started the fire that killed her son. Erik had confessed it all in tight, tense words, gripping the hand of his beautiful new bride. She had been a wonder, his Christine – poised and kind, protective of her husband and assured of herself. It had been a balm to see that the grandchild she had failed over and over again had found a family, at last, that was worthy of him. Who loved him.

"Your words, not mine," Bidaut went on. "There is time now to undo some of the damage he did in life by making things right."

"What a strange way to characterize paying off his gambling debts."

"I never said the debtor I represent was such a person. Suffice it to say, my employer was done great injury by your grandson." Bidaut's face darkened, and Adelaide suppressed a shiver.

"Even if that is so, there is nothing to be had from me to make this person whole," Adelaide answered the man and the question in her heart. "The money you seek is gone."

"What?" For the first time, Bidaut seemed surprised.

It had been a gift as much to Adelaide's conscience as to the young couple to finally bestow Erik's rightful inheritance upon him. She had insisted he take the sum, even if it was blood money of several sorts. He deserved it more than any de Martiniac did, and it would help him to start his new life, wherever that might be.

"I released it into the care of a charitable order," Adelaide lied easily. "I can't tell you the name, for it was an anonymous donation.

It was done, as you said, to undo some of the evils my son and grandson brought into the world. Seek all you want, but there is no money left. I have retained enough to keep myself comfortable until I die, but that is all."

"Are there records of this transaction?" Bidaut asked, taking a notebook from his pocket and jotting something down.

"That is a question for my solicitor," Adelaide shrugged. "Before you ask, he has recently gone to Geneva."

"How convenient," Bidaut muttered, annoyed at what he assumed was a lie.

It was not. The transaction was taking place in Geneva, where banks didn't ask questions and where new names and lives could be easily procured for the inheritors of this not-so-small fortune. It was there also that Adelaide had been assured she could write to them, and that they might, when they were settled, send some word to her.

"Is there anything else you need of me?" Adelaide asked coolly.

"I would give my condolences on—"

"They are unneeded. The de Martiniac name will die with me, but not for a long time."

"I may be in touch," Bidaut answered.

"I do hope not. Good day, Monsieur." Adelaide busied herself pouring a cup of chocolate as her maid showed the detective (or whatever he was) out of her house. She watched out the window as he made his way down the garden path, among the blooming tulips and hyacinth. It was a perfect spring day, and she wondered if Erik and his love, wherever they were now, were enjoying it.

They had seemed happy when they looked at each other, full of relief at their dark tale having reached its end, or rather, finding a new beginning. There had been such love in their eyes, love that reminded Adelaide of what she had shared with her own late husband. The man who had given her the ring which Christine now wore. Love to the stars and beyond.

The memory of her late husband pierced her heart like a knife, the pain so sudden and fierce that it made Adelaide gasp. Grief was strange like that. It could leave her for months, or even years, then suddenly it was there, to remind her that the other half of her heart was gone and buried.

She hoped it was a long time before Erik and his love had to feel that pain before fate ripped them apart. Despite the stability of one sort that Adelaide had been able to provide, there were so many more obstacles in their way. Erik's face and past, their lack of any friends in the wide world into which they now embarked. That world itself was a cruel place.

She hoped they found happiness, but the visit from Bidaut worried her. Already, someone was asking about Antoine, seeking to uncover the mystery that protected Erik. He wore a new mask sometimes, her grandson, a strange thing with glasses and a beard that let him pass more easily for a regular fellow if you didn't look too closely. This contrivance with Antoine (to have died for Erik and 'provide the body in the Opera Ghost's grave' as had been vividly described) was such a mask and could just as easily be snatched away.

She would write to them of Monsieur Bidaut's visit, Adelaide decided. They deserved the warning that someone wasn't content to let Antoine sink into obscurity and be forgotten. It wasn't surprising that his crimes would have consequences and echoes that were hard to evade. Some scars never fully healed.

# 1. Sunrise

## Florence

Late August, 1881

Florence felt empty in the summer, and more so at this early hour. The August heat had not abated in the night and sat heavy on the quiet streets, humid from the moisture of the Arno running through the ancient city's heart. Christine liked the quiet of the dawn, as shadows receded from the winding streets, and the Florentines began their work for the day.

There, sweeping the front steps, was Signora Genco. The fierce old woman unquestionably ruled her son: a great, burly man named Vito. Signore Genco and "Mama" (as he called her affectionately) had rented Erik and Christine the flat above his for the month and asked no questions about their strange new tenants. Christine liked the elderly woman who insisted on feeding her every time she came within five feet of the kitchen. Said kitchen was near the inner courtyard of the building, and the walls were lined with beautiful Italian pottery that Mama Genco took more pride in than her actual son.

It had made Erik nervous to live in such close quarters with another family after months of discrete inns, hotels, one rented house, and years alone below ground before then. Christine had argued it was not so different than sharing a home with a thousand artists and musicians. At least here, the walls and floors would be thicker than previous lodgings. They had only received scornful looks from a dowager in a neighboring room once after a particularly enjoyable night.

The streets of Florence were narrow and crooked, paved in worn cobblestones that had known the footsteps of Botticelli and the Medicis. It was a stark contrast to the order and modernity of Paris, the calm precision of Geneva, or even the sprawl of Milan, where they had so recently stayed. The centuries-old buildings seemed to hang onto the heat like it was a treasure as Christine wended her way through them. Barely dawn, and she was already sweating under her linen dress, her skin prickling with irritation. Of course, it wasn't just the stifling air that caused her discomfort. There was also the fact that she had awoken alone. Again.

Erik's note had said he couldn't sleep because of the heat. There was truth to it, for sure. It was quite a thing to go from living in a perpetually cool cellar to enduring the warmth and hurry of the living world. Still, she knew it was more than that. He'd been anxious for weeks, his agitation growing day by day as the temperature increased and his mood darkened. She wished she knew how to lighten it.

Christine slowed as she passed two nuns in quiet conversation and gave them a nod. She tried to make out their exchange, but only a few words made it through, something about food, perhaps, and a father. Maybe a priest. Christine had been disappointed in her progress in Italian so far. It turned out singing it for years wasn't a substitute for formal instruction, and though it had some similarities to French, Christine had still spent many a day in Florence, barely able to communicate, especially with her translator and tutor not always available.

That meant she couldn't ask anyone now if they had seen said translator. Not that Erik would have let himself be seen. He reminded her of a cat sometimes, always disappearing on some adventure whenever the fancy took him or retreating into some secret world where mere mortals could not follow. She knew the things he would seek out to ease his restless soul – solitude and beauty in the form of art, music, or architecture.

Unfortunately, they were in a city filled to the brim with such things, more so than any they had visited in the past months, and Christine wondered if that had been their mistake. Or hers. Maybe Erik didn't like being in a city full of immortal art when his creations were unknown to the world – some of them locked up in a safe in Geneva, others under the care of a patient friend in Paris who had not answered her letters of late. Christine missed both cities now, but she missed friends like Julianne even more.

They had drifted east for months. From Paris, they had gone to Rouen, then paid their respects at the home of the Baroness de Martiniac. It had been right to visit the only living relative Erik knew to inform her of his half-brother's death. Less so to come away from that encounter with the promise of an inheritance awaiting Erik in Geneva if they contacted the right man at the right bank.

It had been unbelievable to discover that, not only did they have the not-insubstantial fund Erik had hoarded from fleecing the Opera to support them, but half of a fortune he had never thought to lay claim upon. They had made their way to Geneva and stayed there for a few weeks seeing to their financial and legal affairs – the least of which was finding a means to make Erik even exist under the law, a condition he had resisted for days until Christine had – in his words – fucked the resistance out of him. It had been blissful, in its way: ensconced in a private, well-appointed room in the city's best hotel. Nothing to do but read and talk and make love and play music.

Now it seemed like a dream, as she wandered the hot streets of the latest city that was supposed to give them sanctuary. After weeks in Geneva, the kind solicitor working on behalf of the

Baroness – poor Monsieur Tissot – had made Erik Gilbride a person with papers and accounts who might receive correspondence through Tissot wherever they traveled. And they did need to travel.

Through Tissot, they had received correspondence that someone wanted to declare Antoine legally dead and claim the funds that they had just acquired. That revelation had led them from Geneva into several villages tucked among the Alps, taking in the mountains and lakes as summer set in. It had been another honeymoon of sorts among the hills and woods.

The village of Lungern, where they had found a quiet house near the woods, had felt like somewhere they could stay. More of a home than the hotels and inns, it had been humble, but Christine had loved the little garden, and there had been a piano there for Erik to play. They had thought they were far enough from anyone else that no one would hear them singing.

Christine had expected that time to be easy, once they were finally free to be together and alone. But what they had experienced in the cellars of the opera wasn't easy to leave behind, despite the joy they found in one another. It wasn't easy to forget the injuries done to friends or the hearts broken along the way. Or the bodies they had left behind.

The nightmares had begun in that little cottage. Erik had grown restless, and Christine had started to face why they were there. She still dreamed sometimes of Antoine de Martiniac, only this time, he killed more than Philippe de Chagny. Some nights, she still saw the great chandelier of the Palais Garnier fall at her feet, engulfing her in flames.

Christine could feel them still. The heat of them, rising around her. Turning her skin to crackling meat...

"*Signorina, ha bisogno di aiuto?*"

Christine jumped at the words and the hand on her elbow. When had she started leaning on this wall? Why was her head spinning? She was breathing fast and felt hot and cold at the same time. A Florentine woman with a kind face was asking her something again.

"I'm fine," Christine muttered in French, and the woman frowned. "*Son... Sono bene*," she tried again. She was sure she didn't look fine, and she felt like a fool for having such an attack on a public street, but the woman was either satisfied or frightened enough to let Christine go.

She quickened her pace, though she wasn't even sure where she was going. She wanted Erik – her damn husband – not some stranger she couldn't understand to console her. She had slept poorly too. She was more alone than him in a city she didn't know, full of people she could barely communicate with. This flat was the fifth place they had stayed since Lungern, after Erik had come home one night to their cottage and declared it was time to leave. Christine had not argued because she had hoped that leaving would end the nightmares and attacks of memory.

It hadn't. At least in Italy, the music and the heat were good distractions.

The street spat her out into a piazza, one of a hundred such squares in Florence, where merchants were opening their shops as the pale blue sky brightened above. This place she knew. Here she could breathe and find her bearings. On cue, bells pealed from a church nearby, scattering pigeons from the rooftops like a beacon.

"Signorina Christina!" a warm voice called from a shop, and Christine turned with a smile to see a bright, round face peeking from behind a display of fresh breads and sweets.

Patricia was in her sixties at least, but she moved behind the counter of her bakery on the square with the speed and energy of a woman half her age. Her skin was tanned and warm, and it reminded Christine of the bread and pastries she offered hot from the ovens to grateful customers. She had worked for a time in France, learning from bakers there, and sold confections with names and flavors Christine recognized. That had been why she'd come to the shop in the first place, and she'd been happy to find someone who spoke a language she knew.

"*Buongiorno*, Patricia," Christine tried. The woman smiled and began fussing with a tray of croissants dusted with almonds. They smelled heavenly, as did the whole shop, though Christine wondered how Patricia could stand the heat of her ovens in this oppressive weather.

"You are early this morning! I am barely ready for you."

"I have lost my husband, and I'm trying to find him," Christine replied. She tried to make the words sound like a joke, but the truth of it smarted.

"Ah, *si*, your husband that very surely does exist," Patricia replied with a wink. Erik never went with Christine to Patricia's shop, though he did eat what Christine brought back from her excursions when she made him. Patricia was convinced that Christine had invented a husband as an excuse to wander the city freely as a liberated woman. Or to order extra bread and pastries.

"He couldn't sleep in this heat and went off somewhere."

"You should find a man who escorts you places," Patricia said. "Or who has a name at least."

Christine scowled. She had been afraid, since they left Paris, of speaking Erik's name at all. It felt dangerous, even though there were many Eriks (and Eriques and Erics and Enricos in the world) and the infamous Erik who had haunted the Opéra was dead, according to most who knew that name. She was still paranoid about saying it and revealing him. Maybe it was habit, or maybe it was a sense that they were still not safe. Running for months would do that to the mind.

"I'm content with the one I have," Christine sighed. "But I will only be getting breakfast for myself today, as his punishment for leaving so early."

Patricia handed Christine the croissant wrapped in wax paper and happily took the few *lire* that Christine provided in exchange. "There is a cafe, down near *Santa Croce*, that many of your people go to. You will find yourself a good Frenchman there. It is called *Les Halles*."

Christine's heart didn't jump because she wanted a new husband, but because the idea gave her a glimmer of hope that there was a place in Florence where she could perhaps find another person she could at least talk to. She had never been to *Santa Croce*, though she had heard it was even more beautiful than *il Duomo*. She had also heard that the church had an excellent organ, and it was as good a place as any to search for her spouse.

It made something ache in her. For a few weeks, they had been human and normal, they had lived in the sun and forgotten the past. Now, here she was again, searching for a ghost.

# Paris

Meg had not been below the stage in months.

Most of the Opéra had recovered, though slowly, from the devastation wreaked by the Phantom. First had been the public areas. The Grand Foyer had opened for a small dinner and then a party in the name of raising the funds to reopen the Opéra fully and replace the shattered chandelier. The artists had not been invited. At least, not the ballerinas.

Next to reopen had been the rehearsal rooms, then the offices and studios, their doors unlocked after weeks of hibernation. The wood had creaked and stretched like an old dancer struggling out of bed in the winter, but slowly, the rooms warmed again and people began to pretend everything was normal. Meg couldn't though. She still remembered.

She avoided the *Salon du Danse*, even when it reopened. The room was adorned with gold butterflies and portraits of great dancers looking down on their young successors. Meg didn't like it. She didn't like the hidden balcony above those portraits, where men would watch and pick out nubile girls to support.

Finally, months after the horrible accident with the chandelier and the death of the Comte de Chagny, the Palais Garnier had reopened. And with a new chandelier too! (Or at least the old, ruined one had been rebuilt and rehung above the auditorium.) The burned and crushed seats had been replaced, and you had to look very carefully from the stage to see the difference between the old and new red velvet.

It was there though: a subtle scar on the beauty of the auditorium. Meg's mother clucked her tongue at the sight as she escorted Meg to rehearsals and classes. She was here to learn to be a great ballet dancer, one in a long legacy of French art, but it all felt like she was merely preparing for doom. One that started in the *Salon du Danse*.

Meg remembered how Rochelle had tittered and giggled before her debut among the patrons, then the way she had blushed and flirted with the man who had taken an interest in her. She had seemed so happy, but when she returned to rehearsal the next day, the light had gone from her eyes. Meg didn't want to be like her. Ever since then, Rochelle had been careless and fearless in that tragic way that girls are when they decide they have nothing left to lose.

Rochelle was the one who had told Meg about the secret meeting in the cellars. Meg had balked at the very idea of it. No one went into the cellars. They were haunted. She'd said as much, and Rochelle and Marie had laughed at her. Blanche had called Meg a ninny. No one had seen the ghost in months, they said. He had died.

How could a ghost die, Meg wondered?

Meg, inquisitive as she was, wasn't brave enough to defy her friends. So after a respectable time waiting after rehearsal, she snuck away from her dozing mother and made her way down the cold, gray steps to the secret world under the stage. She stood out in the gloom with her golden (perpetually unruly) hair and white ballet skirts catching every whisper of light that reached those hidden halls.

There were many places to hide here, whether you were a dancer, a stagehand, or something else. Meg passed by a knot of workers smoking and sent them a scowl. Their cigars were forbidden both backstage and here, where everything was wood and rope, and an errant piece of ash could bring the entire opera to ruin. Just in time, a fireman on patrol caught the group and began berating them as Meg descended lower, smiling at their comeuppance.

She was less glad when she heard the voices of her friends further off in the dark, snickering. When she found Blanche, Rochelle, and Marie, they were huddled around a letter Blanche was holding, their faces full of shock and delight.

"What's that?" Meg demanded.

"It's a love letter," Marie squealed. "To Victoire from an American."

"Why do you have it?" Meg asked, trying to see if the paper was, indeed, some fabulous confession of adoration.

"She left it out," Blanche replied with a shrug that made her pale blonde curls bounce. "After bragging that a rich railroad heir was in love with her."

"So she wanted you to find it?" Meg pressed, a little confused.

"We wanted to see if it was true," Rochelle shot back. She was the darkest of the trio, with sleek black hair and deep brown eyes that reflected the darkness. "And see if he's bored with her yet."

"It sounds like they haven't even done anything other than eat," Marie added with a sigh at the letter. "Though he does say he wants to taste her oysters."

"I didn't know Victoire was a fishmonger," Meg said lightly, and the other girls burst out laughing. Obviously, she had missed some vital, secret meaning. "Don't you have anything better to do than read people's personal correspondence?"

"Not since the Opéra reopened," Blanche sighed and leaned against a stone wall. "And he disappeared."

The words made a chill go up Meg's spine.

"Do you really think he's gone?" Marie asked, voice small and sad. She had grown pale beneath her ginger hair and freckles.

"Mother says they've been selling his box. Monsieur Moncharmin assured her it would be fine," Meg answered, both proud and dismayed. Her mother had taken immense pride in being the Ghost's box keeper, and the Phantom himself had seen to it that they were protected. Now that he was gone, Meg felt more helpless than she had before. And she had been quite helpless.

"No voices? No disturbances?" Blanche asked.

Meg shook her head. "Nothing. No notes either."

"Damn, I was hoping he'd have me promoted too," Blanche sighed.

"I saw something."

They all turned to Rochelle, who had spoken in a blasé, matter-of-fact tone. She looked satisfied by their curiosity and attention, raising her chin defiantly.

"When?" Marie demanded.

"Two days ago. I was walking alone backstage, and I saw someone in a mask," Rochelle replied. "And a cape."

"This is a theater. There are always people in costume," Blanche scoffed, but her voice was shaking. "It could have been anyone."

"It felt like him," Rochelle countered. "For the first time in months, it didn't feel like the Opéra was empty."

Something a little like hope surged inside Meg, but she tamped it down. It was too fantastical. "I heard Jammes telling someone that Christine Daaé carried the ghost away with her when she ran off and jilted the Vicomte de Chagny," Meg stated. She'd been holding onto that one.

"How does one carry a ghost off?" Rochelle asked with a sneer.

"She was a witch, that one. Maybe she trapped him in a crystal ball or something," Marie suggested. The little dancer had always been vocal in her disdain of Christine, maybe because she had taken some of the spotlight from others. Marie herself had enjoyed a brush with fame when she had posed for a scandalous sculpture by Monsieur Degas.

"So she put him in her pocket and ran away, so he could torture and enchant people for her?" Blanche said. "I doubt that."

"It isn't a coincidence that everything happened around her, and the chandelier fell while she was singing," Meg offered. "My mother says—"

"Do you have any thoughts of your own?" Rochelle snapped. "Your mother says this. Your mother knows that. All because she claims she waited on the ghost for years."

"She did!" Meg protested.

"Well, I saw something that looked like him and I believe my own eyes, not some doddering concierge," Rochelle hissed, and Meg's cheeks burned.

"But everyone—" Marie began, and Rochelle shot her a glare.

"If you're so certain the ghost is gone, go down to the fifth cellar and see." Rochelle issued the challenge with a crooked, cruel smile.

"I will then." Meg turned on her heel and strode to the closest staircase. She didn't look back at her aghast friends (though she had no idea if they were aghast, or even if they were really friends or just cruel girls she worked with and knew). Meg's bravery was like the flare of a match, and she knew it would burn out quickly.

All she had to do was go down to the lowest cellars, look about and see that there was no ghost there and come back up. That was all. There was no reason for her heart to thunder so. There was no need to be afraid. Her mother assured her that the ghost had departed and Meg herself had felt the emptiness in the building for weeks.

She could feel it now, couldn't she?

She found herself in a dark corridor with walls of cold, gray stone, like a castle or a prison. It was incredibly quiet, like all the noise of the world was shut out here, and the dim light of the gas lamps left so much in shadow. Perfect places for a specter to hide. For something to watch.

Meg shivered, despite herself.

The Phantom was gone, and she knew that. So why did she feel like the dark was alive once again? Why did she feel the air vibrating as if a predator were waiting in the dark, preparing to strike? Meg moved further into the dark, crossing herself as she did.

This was stupid. She was letting her imagination get away with her. Mother would tell her to laugh at the dark. It wasn't shadows that could hurt you, but people.

Had it been a shadow that killed Philippe de Chagny when he drowned that night? The question made Meg shudder again. The tulle of her skirt rustled in the dark and then seemed to echo right behind her...

Meg spun. Expecting – or praying – to see a rat or one of her friends come to antagonize her. But there were no rats of any kind.

Just shadows. Shadows that moved quickly across the corridor then disappeared.

Meg yelped as she saw it: a flash of white, the same color as the infamous mask of the ghost. She spun and ran as fast as she could, terror and shock driving her out of the fifth cellar like the devil was on her heels, all the way back to her friend's secret hiding place.

"Well, did you—" Marie's mockery was cut off when she saw Meg's face. "Oh no."

"I'm sorry, Rochelle," Meg nearly sobbed, wishing one of these girls cared enough about her to embrace her. "You were right. There's..." Meg swallowed. She didn't want to say it or believe it, but it felt true. "There's something down there."

"That's impossible," Blanche said.

Rochelle at least had the decency to look worried by the confirmation.

Marie was shaking, looking over her shoulders in fear. "I knew he wouldn't stay gone. He belongs here," Marie whispered,

"I don't understand," Meg whispered, looking around them towards the dark corners which once again seemed full of dangerous power and potential. "Maybe I was dreaming."

She had to talk to her mother or someone who knew about these things. Meg had to learn if anyone else had seen anything in the Opéra's depths these last weeks. The legends had remained, of course, in the months since the strange affair of the chandelier and Christine Daaé, but those were just stories. Stories that had a neat, if mysterious, ending.

Now, Meg had seen something with her own eyes to show her that the story wasn't over. Not remotely.

## Florence

E rik had come to see the tombs. The *Santa Croce* basilica was famous for its funerary monuments, mainly to men the church had condemned or outright expelled in life, but whose fame in death had been so great that even God's bureaucrats had been forced to pay attention. Erik had wanted to be alone when he looked at the statues of Dante, Machiavelli, and Galileo, because he didn't want Christine to see the regret and shame in his eyes when he regarded their legacy.

The huge church was pleasantly cool compared to the sticky, suffocating heat outside. The white, pink, black, and green marble arranged in perfect symmetry inside and out of the building held on to the cold of the earth, and the high vaulted ceilings shaded the pews and chapels as Erik stole through the emptiness. To be in a place like this, alone and silent, sneaking among art and beauty so intricate and grand, reminded him of his opera. Here he was again, a ghost among the tombs, fleeing from mortal sight.

He didn't know if that made him nostalgic or ashamed.

The Opéra was full of monuments too. The loges were all flanked by busts of greats of French music and art, from the infamous to the obscure. The entrance foyer held statues of Lully, Gluck, and Handel, and the outside of the building was adorned with even more faces of celebrated musicians of the past. All preserved. All remembered.

The former ghost looked up at the face of Dante Alighieri and sighed. Dante had thought very highly of himself. He had been right to do so, but even so, it had been bold of him to place himself in the company of Vigil as an equal to walk through hell. Erik wondered what hero he would be assigned if he were to wander the circles of the afterlife as a tourist. Maybe Mozart...

"He's not even in there, you know."

Erik spun, his hand darting to an empty pocket on reflex. There was no Punjab lasso waiting for him there to defend him from the young man who had spoken to him in Italian. Who now looked at Erik with undisguised curiosity.

Erik had taken the precaution of wearing his special mask today, though the false beard that hid its nature as a mask and the spectacles were cumbersome. It was safer for when he walked in the world, though not perfect. Even so, his height and thin frame made him a unique sight, as did his black clothing and untrimmed hair. He was a stark contrast to the interloper now staring at him, a younger man with a square jaw, keen eye, and a rather ostentatious moustache that matched his deep brown hair.

"Didn't mean to startle you, friend," the man said with a cautious smile. Erik tried to relax. This man was not a priest, clearly, which meant he had as much of a right as Erik to be in the church so early in the day, which was to say, no right at all.

"I didn't think anyone was here," Erik replied slowly, and the man's eyes widened subtly at the musical lilt of Erik's voice.

"Neither did I, but when I went to use my key, the door was already open. I didn't know Padre Navone had given access to someone else to practice." The man glanced down at Erik's shoes meaningfully. They were his organ shoes, narrow and sporting sturdy heels. He'd grabbed them first this morning when he'd dressed in the dark to avoid waking his sleeping wife. A vain hope that he might use the great organ in the Basilica had perhaps been one of his reasons for breaking in.

"Oh. Yes. He didn't tell me anyone else was given permission," Erik lied.

"It's no great trouble. Perhaps we can practice together. I need some critique from a fellow musician. The Padres here are kind, but they do not know music, and since Signore Barbieri has been ill, I have had no compatriots."

Erik regarded the cheerful young man with interest. He had not met many musicians in Italy at all, though it was in many ways a more musical country than France.

"You may reconsider that. I'm a very harsh critic," Erik muttered, and the young man grinned.

"Excellent. I need it. I'm Jack." The man held out his hand.

"Unusual name for an Italian." Erik took the offered hand and shook it carefully, noting how Jack looked at Erik's long fingers with interest.

"It's a nickname. An English friend at the University started calling me that because he said there were too many boys with my given name. I liked it, so I've kept it for use with friends. I can tell you'll be one." Jack seemed quite proud of himself for such a compliment. "And you are?"

"Erik." He didn't know why he gave his true name to this man. Maybe he trusted him as a fellow organist. Or he remembered the many admonitions from Christine that making friends wasn't so bad an idea.

"A pleasure."

"What did you mean?" Erik asked, nodding to the monument beside them. "About how he's not there. Did you mean Dante?"

"Yes. He's actually buried in Ravenna, where he died," the young man grinned. "He was exiled from Florence for writing the wrong things. But he was a famous Florentine, you see, so they built him a tomb, even so."

"One might say a man is lucky to be remembered in so many places."

If Jack heard the bitterness in Erik's voice, he ignored it. "The latest edition is Rossini's tomb, across the way. As a musician, I'm sure you've seen it."

Erik shook his head. "I was waiting to see him last and pay my respects."

"I avoid him," Jack confessed. "He reminds me too much of all I will never be."

"That makes two of us," Erik replied, surprised by his honesty. "You are a composer too?"

"A poor one," Jack said with a shrug. "You?"

"An unaccomplished one," Erik echoed, and Jack narrowed his eyes in interest.

"Such is the way of it, I suppose. Come, let's wake the great lady from her slumber." Jack headed towards the back of the church and the small door that Erik knew would lead them up to the organ.

Tightly coiled, narrow stairs took the two of them to a hidden compartment filled with keys and stops that smelled of old wood, paper, and oil. Jack lit a small oil lamp to add to the meager light that made its way into the chamber from outside.

Erik liked church organs for many reasons. It was thrilling to create such a huge, powerful sound as one person, but there was also the fact that organists in many churches, such as this one, were almost completely hidden from the congregation below. The music of the organ was meant to evoke the choirs of heaven, to emanate from the walls like the voice of God.

"Now, who shall reveal themselves first?" Jack said, taking Erik aback for a moment. Had he noticed the mask? "I confess, I'm not used to seeing the audience. Though I did learn to play at the church where my father and grandfather played, so I have had harsher critics."

"I promise not to be critical for at least five minutes," Erik reassured the younger player. That seemed good enough for Jack, who took his place at the instrument and began setting the stops and pipes to his liking. There was already music on the stand, open to a complex canon. "Will you be playing the Pellegrini?"

"I'll be trying," Jack sighed and began to press the keys.

Erik smiled despite himself as the music began. It was one of those canons that began simply with a single line of melody, then bloomed into more and more lines of harmony and counterpoint until it was a tapestry of sound echoing through the church below.

Jack was competent, but not a great player, just as he had said. He lacked a certain ease and comfort that was hard to achieve on such a complex instrument, and it was clear he had learned to play in a church, just as he said. Still, Erik couldn't help but be moved to hear another musician. It had been weeks since he and Christine had been entertained by anyone but themselves, and while it was always a joy to sing with her and play himself, there was something freeing about being in the audience.

Up here, hidden away, listening to music with a critical but appreciative ear, he once again remembered the Opéra. He thought of his box, of his seat tucked in the private corner, and the carved column. The music of the orchestra and voices ringing out... To the chandelier.

The memory sent a sensation not unlike a shock through Erik. A spike of anxiety and guilt that went from the base of his spine right to his heart. It was a cold, guilty feeling, spreading into his veins like ice and taking his breath away. His vision blurred, and he grabbed the wall as Jack played on, insensible to his companion's sudden attack.

He had to breathe, like Christine reminded him to do when this happened. It had happened before, more times than even his kind wife knew. It happened more and more since coming to Italy, but she didn't need to know that. He had to handle this himself and just. Breathe.

He tried to listen to the music and push away the fear that this young musician had heard of the disaster at the Paris Opéra months ago. Even if he had, there was no way he'd know that the strange man he played for was the one responsible for it. The one that had so nearly caused so much more bloodshed and pain.

Another breath pushed back a fresh spike of fear as Erik steadied himself. Jack wasn't his enemy. Jack wasn't some member of an angry mob. This wouldn't be like Lungern. This wasn't some child.

*Let the fear pass,* he heard Christine say in his memory, and he tried to.

Breathe in. Breathe out. Listen to the music.

Slowly, the world steadied, and Erik's heartbeat slowed. He wished he weren't wearing this awful mask so he could feel some fresh air on his face, even if it was still hot and stifling. God, he hated summer.

"I think it would have been better in C sharp, down a third," Jack remarked. Erik realized he'd finished playing and was scowling at the music. "He barely uses the foot pedals, and really, what's the point of an organ piece without them?"

"It's less tiring to play," Erik offered, and hoped Jack didn't notice or remark on how exhausted he sounded.

"Would you like your turn? Oh, you don't have any music."

"I don't need it." Erik had not meant to sound as arrogant as he did, but Jack just chuckled and let Erik take a seat at the keys. It was as instantly comforting as taking Christine's hand or shutting the door on the outside world. Erik's fingers touched the keys, and he took a moment to get the feel of the instrument. It was like meeting an old friend in a new place. Or he assumed it was – he didn't have that many friends.

He began to play. Bach, of course, because it only felt natural, and it comforted him in times of turmoil to return to the precision and near scientific complexities of the organ's greatest master. He heard Jack give a slight intake of breath and it made something new flare in his heart.

How long had it been since he'd played for someone other than Christine? He used to make money on the streets with his music, reveling in the attention and money from the crowd, but that felt like that was another life. To play for a fellow musician, but also an unknown, was new and thrilling in its way. Erik didn't need to impress this young man, but the showman in him wanted to. In truth, he just wanted to play. He wanted to be home.

Music carried him to a secret paradise, as it always had. A place of sound and feeling without vision and judgement. It was safe there, a place where his fear and guilt could pass like so much dissonance, where things made sense and feeling was pure. It was where he was most himself, even when it was another man's work. It was a balm and a joy, and he had missed it.

He wished he could tell the one person that mattered how it felt, how he needed this, but he didn't want her to worry. He hoped she was still sleeping soundly, where he had left her, and when he returned, the music would stay with him.

Just seeing a bill of fare in French (next to the Italian one) displayed proudly at the door of Les Halles put Christine at ease. She wasn't even hungry after her croissant from Patricia, but she ordered at the counter nonetheless just to speak her own tongue.

"A *chausson au pommes*, please," she said in French, and the man behind the case smiled broadly at her.

"You're French?"

"French enough," Christine replied. She didn't need to tell this man that while her mother had been French, her father had been Swedish and Romani, or that she had spoken three languages as a child before moving back to France after her mother's death.

"Of course, welcome to a piece of home," the baker replied warmly. "Where are you from?"

"Paris most recently." Christine took her flaky pastry filled with apples and cinnamon.

"I have just been to Paris," a voice in French cut in and Christine turned to see another man behind her. He looked to be in his twenties and had the same sort of cheerfully vacant expression that Christine had known upon the face of another young man of the same age.

"It's a wonderful city," Christine replied carefully. Despite what Patricia said, she didn't need or want male attention.

"In fact, you look familiar," the man went on. Awkwardly, Christine turned and paid the baker, her pulse speeding up. "Might we know each other?"

"We do not." Christine would certainly have recognized such a face. She turned to go, and the man stepped in front of her.

"Wait, did you perform? An actress or—" Christine gulped as recognition flared in the man's face. "At the Opéra!"

"I don't sing anymore." Christine tried to pass, her spirit falling as she realized she would not be spending a pleasant morning in conversation with her (almost) countrymen in this café.

"Oh, that's a tragedy – what was your name again?" The man demanded, again blocking Christine's exit. "I know I've seen you!"

"She does not wish to see you." The voice that interrupted was female – measured and calm. Christine looked to see that her savior was a woman slightly smaller than her with mouse brown hair. She wore a dress made to look something like a man's suit, with a high collar and a tie, and she wore delicate spectacles. "Please leave the lady alone."

"I was only trying to be friendly," the man grumbled as he sulked away, leaving Christine to smile gratefully at her savior.

"Thank you. That was very kind."

"Men can be so entitled when they think they deserve our attention," the woman replied, flexing her brows behind her round, brass glasses. "Were you staying or going? I was about to walk around the piazza if you would like some company."

"I would like that very much," Christine said. The woman opened the door and they returned to the rising morning heat, but it, at least, was less lonely with another woman by her side. "My name is Christine," she offered, almost tripping over the words when it occurred to her that she had just almost been recognized and might want to keep things to herself.

"Pauline," her new companion replied, offering a hand to Christine. Her grip was strong and confident. Reassuring, even. "I have come to Florence only recently from Rouen, where I was a student. I'm studying art."

Christine could not help but smile at that. "I was a student in Rouen too. At the conservatory of music."

"So you are a singer, like he said? Are you in Florence to perform?"

Pauline surely meant it well, but the question cut deep. Christine had chosen to leave the stage. The applause had been empty, and the backstage politics were too cutthroat for her. Even so, she missed it lately. Not just the music, but the community of the Opéra; the camaraderie that grew when you spent days and nights together in rehearsals and hidden in the dark backstage.

"I... No. I'm just travelling."

"Alone?" Pauline asked, her expression more impressed than scandalized at the possibility.

"No. I've come here with my husband." It was still such a strange thing to say. Even though she wore Erik's ring and had taken his name, it still felt like such a secret, intimate thing to confess. It didn't help that her husband preferred to disappear so often.

"Oh, how lucky," Pauline said.

They made their way slowly around the piazza, the great façade of *Santa Croce* rising before them in white accented with the Florentine colors of teal, brick red, and black. The churches here were like nothing in France, with their gray, Gothic spires and vaults. Here, the marble glowed and gleamed with color. This church had a window in the shape of a six-pointed star as well, setting it apart from others in the city. Erik would love it.

"He is a musician too," Christine sighed, answering a question she had not been asked. "A great one."

"Then it's his work that has brought you here?" Pauline asked innocently, and Christine stopped herself from scowling. His previous work was the reason they had run here, and the reason she had no idea how long they would be staying.

"Not really, he—"

Christine stopped in her tracks as they came closer to the church door. She had meant to make up some lie about her husband seeking work as a teacher, but the muffled sound of the organ from inside the church stopped her. It wasn't just the beauty of the music that captured her attention: it was the melody. She knew it but had never heard the old Irish folk tune transformed into a rhapsody on organ. If the melody had not given him way, the perfection with which it was being played would.

"He what?" Pauline asked.

"He is meeting me soon. I apologize, I must go," Christine said.

"I will be at the café again tomorrow at the same time. I go every day! I'm happy to meet again. I have been looking for more friends here," Pauline said in a sad and sweet way that affected Christine. She wasn't so different from her.

"I will try to be there. Good day for now." Christine scurried away to the front door of the great church, where a priest was just unlocking it for the day. He looked as entranced and confused by the music emanating from inside as Christine was.

"*Buongiorno, Padre*," Christine said with a polite nod. "*La musica... Molto bella.*"

"*Et misteriosa*," the priest muttered, and Christine certainly understood his meaning. It was all the confirmation she needed. She didn't wait for more conversation from the priest, simply strode inside and blessed herself from the font before taking a place in a pew close to – she hoped – the exit from the organist's cubby.

She had spent many nights and days of late listening to her Angel of Music play for her, either on the violin or piano, or even the guitar when he had found one. Not since Paris had she heard him play the organ. She knew it was him. The melody Erik had sung her so many times of wild mountain thyme and purple heather was perfection in such a setting, but it was the feeling behind the old song rendered in this way that resonated the most deeply in Christine's soul.

There was joy in the music, and gratitude, but also fear and regret. She understood it and didn't at the same time. When had this adventure of theirs become something that scared them? When had it become more about running than about really starting a new life? She had felt so alone lately, and this music told her that so had Erik. But how? Why? They had each other now, and they had fought so hard for that. Was it not enough?

She wasn't surprised to feel a tear escape down her cheek as she listened, her soul soaring and smarting at the same time. When it ended, she rushed to wipe her cheeks and compose herself. She was still annoyed at being abandoned in the dark, and that was an easier feeling to live with than the mysterious sorrow lurking somewhere in the corners of their life.

She waited patiently until a plain door opened and Erik emerged, masked as she had suspected... And in conversation with a young Italian man.

"I see you found a predictable diversion to avoid your wife," Christine drawled in French, and her husband froze in his steps. The man next to Erik looked between them, bemused.

"I came to look at the art, and this kind young man offered me a chance to play," Erik replied sheepishly. The 'kind young man' narrowed his eyes.

"I thought Padre Navone invited you?" he said in French, clearly to Erik's shock. Christine didn't bother suppressing her smile. Served Erik right for giving in to his more larcenous tendencies.

"I... may have misstated," Erik muttered.

His companion merely laughed. "Well, I'm glad then. I was saying goodbye to my job entirely when you played. No one would keep me on even as a guest organist when they could have you." The man gave a warm grin from beneath his moustache and held out his hand to Christine. "Signora – or perhaps I should say Madame? – I'm Jack. A new friend and admirer of your husband."

Christine took Jack's hand carefully and shook it. He was obviously a musician, and he spoke French. He could perhaps be a friend to both of them. God knew they needed it. "He is a remarkable musician, my husband. Perhaps we all can speak of music or your fine city over supper soon?"

"I'm free tonight!" Jack replied excitedly, and Christine saw Erik's eyes widen in subtle horror behind the spectacles attached to the mask. "I know a quiet place; they won't bother us. It's on the *Via Spoleto*. Sandro's. It will be perfect!"

"We don't need to take up more of your time," Erik sputtered, but it was clear Jack had made up his mind.

"I will meet you there at nine o'clock," Jack declared, then seemed to realize that time still existed in the moment and grabbed his pocket watch. "Damn. I'm going to be late for my maestro. I will see you tonight!"

With that, the young man bounded off, leaving Christine to stare down her errant beloved. Erik sighed contritely, shaking his head.

"I guess I'll deserve this punishment," Erik muttered.

"Dinner with a new friend is hardly a punishment." Christine approached the person who had become her entire society in recent months and took his hand. "It will do us both good. Until then, your actual punishment for absconding again is to spend the day with me."

"Oh, how will I bear it?" Erik smiled back. Or Christine was fairly certain he had smiled; it was hard to tell with the bearded mask.

"Come home so you can take that thing off and I can see you properly," Christine ordered. She could hear Erik grumble in his mind and smirked. "I would say more, but we are in a church."

"Quite a lovely one, isn't it?" Erik replied as he fell into step next to her.

She nodded. It was a remarkable building, like so many they had seen in their weeks in this country that was both young and ancient. It had its own character, like Florence itself. Proud and gaudy yet indisputably refined. It felt like being in a mosaic.

"Maybe we can light a candle and pray for relief from this heat," Christine suggested as she took Erik's hand. It was warm, either from playing or from the weather. Either way, she didn't entirely mind.

"Fire to dispel heat seems counterproductive." Erik glanced at her, and she felt it like a breeze against her skin. How was it that just his gaze could still affect her that way? "Maybe I'll light one to ask forgiveness for abandoning my wife."

"Again," Christine corrected, but his mere presence was already having its usual effect on her. Her anger was fading, like night to the dawn, with her love as the sun. "I do not think I could stay cross with you for very long. Who would I talk to?"

The warmth of the day hit them as they left the great church, at the same time as Erik's smile spread, as visible as could be.

"I'm sure you would find someone."

"Yes, but why would I want to?"

# Paris

Meg had not felt this important in months, and that had been her fifteenth birthday. Even that had not been greatly noted. In all truth, she had not been so popular since she had been promoted to the head of her row thanks to the charity of the ghost. Maybe it should have worried her to be the center of attention because of the ghost. What if he punished her? What if she was wrong?

No matter. She felt like a queen surrounded by all the young dancers asking her over and over again to retell her encounter until the ballet master had shooed them away. Even then, everyone whispered to her at every spare moment. She didn't want rehearsal to end, but after several hours, her legs and toes were tired from hours of practice. She also needed to tell her mother about what she had seen.

Or maybe she didn't. Her mother didn't really need to know. She didn't need to invite her scorn or her admonition that Meg had just been seeing things and was losing what little mind she had. She'd already had her hands full with Meg's sulking since the Opéra reopened, and the young flautist whom she had kissed at the masquerade had not returned to the orchestra. Meg knew in her heart somehow that Pierre wouldn't have been impressed by her encounter with the ghost.

Meg lingered as long as she could in the rehearsal salon in case anyone else wanted to talk to her. Maybe Rochelle would have something to say about it all. She had been sour all morning because no one was interested in her old story. A smug smile was about to form on Meg's face as she looked over at her sometimes friend, but it fled when she saw the patron arrive.

She didn't know the man's name, but Meg knew his sort. He had a cruelty about his smile as he accosted Rochelle and took her by the elbow.

"Sorry to be late," he muttered. Rochelle didn't seem disappointed that he had not come to watch rehearsals.

"Patrons aren't allowed here for these sorts of practices," Rochelle said, looking sidelong at Meg, as if for help. How could Meg help her? And why?

"I shall have to talk to – ah, here is the man himself," the patron said cheerfully as none other than Armand Moncharmin entered the room. The manager looked as unhappy to see the patron as Rochelle.

"What is the problem?" Moncharmin asked the young dancer and the man who had to be twenty years older than her.

"I was informing Monsieur Tremblay that rehearsals such as these are closed to patrons," Rochelle said.

"Indeed, they are," Moncharmin replied before Tremblay could argue. Meg noted how incensed the older man looked, but his ire was focused on Rochelle, not the manager.

"Well, we shall see," Tremblay muttered. Meg wasn't able to see how he left with Rochelle – she was too distracted by Moncharmin turning his attention entirely to her. In a heartbeat, he was a foot from her, looking discerningly over his half-moon spectacles.

"Monsieur Moncharmin, how can I help you?" Meg stammered. Why did she feel like she was about to be in awful trouble?

"It has come to my attention that you had some sort of encounter this morning in the cellars?" His question was pointed. Meg found herself gulping and shrinking into the floor.

"I saw the ghost," Meg replied, her voice small. "In the cellars, out of the shadows. I saw him."

"No, you did not," Moncharmin countered smoothly. "There is no Opera Ghost. Not anymore."

"I'm not lying! I know what I saw."

Moncharmin frowned at her, clicking his tongue. "I have no doubt you saw something, but it was most likely a fireman. Maybe a rat catcher. They lurk down there sometimes and have a habit of frightening people."

"Rochelle saw something too!" Meg tried, looking at the empty corner where her fellow ballerina had just been. "I'm sure others have."

"They have," Moncharmin replied, much to Meg's shock.

"What?"

"I make it my business as the now-sole manager to keep abreast of all the rumors that circulate, especially given the colorful reputation this opera has gained in recent years," Moncharmin explained, sounding exhausted. "There are always people telling stories about seeing things in the dark or their costumes mysteriously disappearing or someone sabotaging their music."

"Because the Opéra is haunted!" Meg was perhaps surprised that in one day, she had gone from believing the Opéra was once haunted to knowing in her very soul that it always would be.

"Because artists in all theaters have vivid imaginations and love a good story. It's more amusing to believe a ghost stole your tutu than to accept the truth that you left it in the dressing room," Moncharmin smiled, the gaslight reflecting off his spectacles and brown hair. "Just as it's more exciting to have an encounter with a phantom in the cellars than to see a shadow from an old set piece."

"It wasn't a—" Meg began to doubt herself. What had she seen?

"I came here to assure you, as I do all employees who have such encounters and stories, that you are safe here," Moncharmin went on, sincere and kind now.

Meg didn't feel safe, though. She felt ignored and dismissed. "The ghost never threatened me. Or anyone good," Meg added. The ghost had gone after cruel people like Carlotta or Joseph Buquet... The man he had killed. How had Meg forgotten that?

"Who is good or bad is a hard thing to judge, so we will leave that to God, not ghosts." Moncharmin looked at the other door to the studio. "Ah, your chaperone is here. Good evening, Madame Giry."

Meg's mother looked thunderous. She held her shawl about her shoulders with white knuckles, and her chignon was mussed, as if she'd rushed here. Meg wanted to become a wood panel on the floor.

"Meg, what is going on?" her mother demanded. "We need to get home."

"Nothing untoward, Madame. I was just assuring Meg of the Opéra's continued safety after the incidents this spring."

"Wonderful. Come along, Meg." Meg scurried after her mother, casting one last look at the manager. He appeared pleased with himself, as if he'd successfully doused another fire of rumor and everything would be alright now.

"I know what I saw. The ghost is still here," Meg declared, as much for herself as for her mother (who clearly had heard the tale at this point).

"The ghost is not for us to meddle with or understand." The response surprised Meg. She had been expecting Mother to act like Moncharmin and tell her she was a silly child, seeing things. "If you want to stay safe here, don't spread stories. True or false."

"But—" Her mother silenced Meg with a glare, and the conversation was over.

They said no more as they left the Opera through the back entrance. It was significantly less grand to go out this way than through the grand foyer with its mosaics and marble and statues. Yet, even here, as they passed offices and empty halls, Meg felt a chill. A familiar chill.

There was something in the Opéra. She knew it not merely because she had seen it, but because she could feel it now that she tried. The sense of the place breathing, of the building holding in pain like a bandaged wound. It was still there. Maybe it had left before, but something had returned.

Meg shivered at the thought as they crossed the threshold. She looked to her mother for comfort, only to find her distracted, hand thrust into her pocket. What was she reaching for? Meg couldn't entirely see, but when her mother withdrew her hand Meg caught the slightest glimpse of something white. Like paper.

Like a note.

# 2. Webs

## Florence

"I've always wondered how a country can function when the entire population sleeps half the afternoon," Erik remarked as he peered through the slats of the shutters. He liked this style of window: able to let in the light from the sky, but also maintain the privacy of, say, a hideous man who wanted to look out at the world and not frighten anyone on the street.

"Can you blame them, in this heat?" Christine sighed, slipping her arms around Erik's waist and resting her head affectionately against his back. He let out a long sigh, the tension leaving him with his breath as he savored her easy, gentle affection.

"Not really. It's miserable," Erik replied. "Maybe we should have gone to Sweden instead."

"You'd hate the summers there. It's light until past ten o'clock, and then the sun rises at four in the morning." Her voice was warm, like the sun itself. "There would be no night for you to run away into. Now that I say it, maybe you're right."

"I'm sorry. I've just been restless lately." It was a half-truth, the only kind he could tell her that wouldn't trouble her.

"At least you made a friend," Christine offered, and Erik scoffed.

"You're really making me go to this supper?"

"Yes, and I won't let you escape before then." Christine turned him around to face her. She looked at him with soft, gentle eyes, an expression that still awed him when it was bestowed on his unmasked face. "Until then, we should do as the locals do and rest. Come to bed."

It was an enticing prospect, Erik had to admit. His wife (how remarkable that he could call her that) was in nothing but her chemise, her dress, petticoats, and corset discarded hours ago. He could make out the curves of her body through the linen and her skin was glowing with warmth.

"How can you be sure I won't run off again? Sleep is hard in the heat if one isn't relaxed," he said, flirtatious, and a spark kindled in Christine's eyes.

"Then I simply won't allow you to move," she replied with a cool composure.

Erik followed her to the bedroom in their little rented flat with the obedience of one in a trance. The room was cooler, with only a few bars of sunlight sneaking in through the shutters to paint the stucco walls. Their bed, with its wrought-iron frame, was still unmade, and the nest of linen sheets met them with a whoosh of air as Christine pulled him down into an embrace.

Gods, what a wonder it still was to kiss her. What a joy it was to taste her lips and savor her tongue as it darted against his. He surrendered to her as easily as ever, letting her strip off his shirt and caress his scarred skin. He followed her eagerly as she scooted upwards, right to the center of the bed, and pulled him into her arms and between her legs. He liked it there.

He liked it as well when she surprised him and flipped their positions so that she straddled his hips, drawing back to show her sly, dangerous expression as she began to undo his belt. He did not simply like it when she took control like this. He loved it. He made sure she knew, twisting his hips beneath her so she could feel his hardness growing.

"Not yet," Christine chided, his belt sliding free.

"But you're right here," he argued cheekily, sweeping his hands up her thigh and under the chemise to grip her round, perfect hips. He ground his cock against her, winning a jolt of pleasure before she seized his arms and pushed them away.

"You're impatient and defiant," Christine purred, taking him by the wrists. "Even after running from me in the night. I shall have to teach you a lesson."

The words only made Erik harder, as did the careful pressure of her hands on his wrists, forcing his arms above his head. His eyes fell closed as Christine pressed her body ever so softly against him, from his groin to his chest. The fleeting pleasure made the feel of his belt looping his wrists come like an electric shock.

Erik's eyes flew open in time to see his wife smirk triumphantly as she lashed his bound hands to the bed frame, trapping him. To be constrained like this was always something that had filled him with terror, and now he felt his heart beating from dread as well as with desire.

Darkness edged on his thoughts. The same suffocating fear that had seized him back at *Santa Croce...*

"Breathe, my love," Christine commanded.

He did. He tested the strength of his bonds and the rush of fear became something else. Something utterly intoxicating.

They had not done this for a while. Yet it felt right to be subject to her, to this goddess above him. He was helpless as she drew off her chemise, revealing the perfection of her body. He loved every inch and wanted so badly to touch and taste her rosy nipples or tender thighs. His bondage assured he couldn't, and that made him want her even more.

"Still so eager," Christine remarked with a sigh as she bent and freed him from his trousers, nuzzling his cock with a soft teasing touch and swift kiss that offered no relief to his need. "All this energy and nowhere to go."

"There is nowhere I'd rather be," he sighed in return and earned a smile.

"It gives me quite a thrill to see you like this." She slunk up his body again, his flesh burning each place hers touched him, tempting and gentle. "Let me show you."

He groaned as her thighs bracketed his bound arms and she gifted him with her wet cunt against his mouth. He had no choice but to serve her, and he lost himself in the ecstasy of bringing her pleasure with his lips and tongue. She moved her hips in rhythm against his face as she gripped the bedframe, matching the movements with sweet, strangled moans of delight.

"Yes. There. Make me come... Right there," she commanded, and Erik obeyed, his mind fogging with desire and something more as the leather of his belt cut into his scarred wrists. He was confined by her, being used for her pleasure, unable to escape, and he adored it.

She came with a shudder, moisture slipping down his cheek as she did. Erik drank her in, ready to give her more. In an instant, she was gone, then her thighs were on his hips and...

"Oh God," he moaned as she encased him in warmth. He was so desperate for her, so hard he could feel every inch as she engulfed him. He looked up with unfocused eyes to watch her as she began to ride him, chasing more pleasure. He rushed to meet her, thrusting as hard as he could, even as his soul and his mind were transported to a place of pure feeling.

The bed creaked and strained as they moved. His wrists and arms screamed as he tensed with something like pain, but also beyond it. He felt delirious, and there was nothing but Christine above him, thrashing against him as she used him and tightened around him. She was so beautiful, even when she doubled over and grabbed him, her nails digging into his chest as she found her climax. The pain and the pulsing were all too much, sending

Erik over the edge with her. He climaxed into her in hot spurts, spasming and straining against his bindings.

He was safe and free, and it was good. He could be good if she ruled him.

His mind swam with color and contentment, time starting and stopping in an irregular rhythm. He was barely aware of her untying him, then kissing his moist brow.

"Rest now, my love," Christine commanded, and he draped her in his arms. Sated and safe, he slept at last.

# Paris

S haya would not have chosen this bistro if it were up to him. The Marais was painfully bohemian, and a substantial walk from the *Rue de* Rivoli, but Armand had been insistent about the quality of the beef stew at the place, and Shaya had learned that the opera manager couldn't be dissuaded on matters of cuisine. At least he had committed to pay, as usual.

"There you are," Moncharmin called from a table outside on the street, in the typical Parisian style. Good, they were to dine outdoors, which Shaya much preferred on summer evenings.

"I hope I'm not too late," Shaya said, looking about as he took a seat. "I assume this is some highly sought-after establishment with the urgency of your invitation."

"Oh, not exactly," Armand replied sheepishly. The man had looked harried and exhausted every time Shaya had seen him in the recent months, but he was particularly sweaty and rumpled today. "I needed to talk to you about an important matter. Or I think I do. If it's nothing, we can still have a good meal."

"What's going on?" Shaya asked, anxiety prickling the back of his neck.

"Have you heard from… him?" Armand's voice was unsteady, and Shaya knew why. To even speak the name Erik was a dangerous thing, after all they had gone through to save and send off the infamous Phantom.

"Not for a few weeks. He wrote to me through a solicitor in Geneva, via, I think, Milan? He didn't say so, of course, but the postmark and the paper were easy to track, if you know what to do." Shaya tried not to sound too proud of his detective work. In truth, it had been a diversion – a little puzzle to solve. Life had become considerably more boring since the Phantom had fled his opera and city.

"And no indication he wished to return?"

"None at all. I don't think he intends to come back to France for a long while. Though it doesn't sound like they've settled anywhere," Shaya added with a smile. It was quite a thing to think fondly of the man he had pursued for so long, then stood next to at his wedding to the most remarkable of women.

"Oh. Good. That's good to know," Armand exhaled. "Should we get some wine? Though – a month, you said? That could be enough time to travel."

"What do you mean?" Shaya asked, concern growing.

"It's nothing. I mean– I think it's nothing."

"I was a spy and a detective for a long time, Armand. I know when someone is lying."

Armand scowled. "It isn't anything, I promise. It's just that in the last – well, it must be the last month – there have been a few incidents at the opera."

"Incidents?" Shaya didn't like the sound of that. He didn't like how green about the gills Armand looked either. "What sort of incidents?"

"Nothing of great note. The usual stories and superstitions of the artists. They still blame everything that goes wrong on the ghost." Armand sounded like he was reassuring himself as much as he was Shaya. It was not comforting.

"Erik told me that most of the ills and accidents attributed to him were just that – normal mishaps that people called the work of a ghost because it was amusing."

"Exactly! That's what I thought. Think. Whatever people have seen in the cellars—"

"Seen?" Shaya echoed incredulously. "What do you mean?"

"A few ballet rats and a fireman glimpsed a figure in the shadows in the lower cellars. They swear it was the ghost," Armand confessed, trying and failing to sound untroubled. "I know, as you do, that he is gone. So they can't have seen him. It's concerning, nonetheless. And some of the– the mischief has felt different."

"There's been mischief?"

"Tickets mixed up. Keys missing. It's most likely the staff getting their sea legs after all the disruption." Armand looked to Shaya for reassurance, but Shaya had little to give.

"You should be wary. It could be something else – some*one* else – who decided to fill the open position of opera ghost." Shaya shook his head as he said it. "Though no one but us and a few others are aware that the ghost was a man. I could see no reason for anyone to take up his mantle."

"We're probably just being paranoid," Armand said with a forced ease. "I've heard about men coming back from wars and going into a panic when a broom falls because they hear the sound of a gunshot."

"You're probably right. When I left Persia, I checked for spies and eavesdroppers everywhere I went for months, even though I knew none had followed me."

"Yes. Exactly." Armand gave a weak grin that brightened when the waiter arrived. "Ah, yes! We'll start with the Côtes-du-Rhône..."

Shaya didn't listen to the complicated order: he was too lost in thought. There was no way in hell that Erik could have returned to Paris and the Opéra without Shaya's notice – or without letting someone know the reason. Such a move would need to have a reason. Erik wasn't technically a wanted man in Paris, but he would be hunted if he came back to the city. Especially if the Comte de Chagny had even the slightest hint that the man he blamed for ruining his life and killing his family was alive. To return would be suicide.

# Florence

T he hole in the wall on the *Via Spoleto* could barely be called a restaurant. That made it all the more charming to Christine. Erik didn't seem to mind either. He seemed far more relaxed after their *riposo*, as the Italians called it. Though Christine didn't believe that most who enjoyed the afternoon nap did so after tying up their lovers and riding them to climax.

In the candle-lit shadows of the restaurant sitting in the back with Jack, Christine blushed at the thought. She really should have been paying attention to the debate Erik and Jack were having about the merits of Bellini in comparison to Rosini, but Jack had become so passionate about the subject he had switched (perhaps unknowingly) into Italian, and Erik had followed him right over. For her part, Christine was full of incredible food and comfortable in the shadowy cellar, so her mind was relaxed. All she could do was listen and try to catch a few words out of context while admiring the skill of her husband's tongue.

She blushed again, thinking back to a different skill and how she had demanded it of him. Claimed it. She didn't know what had come over her. She had done such things before, but not since Paris. Controlling and containing her dangerous lover had been both a heady drug and a vital need, but their lives were different now. She didn't need to keep him in check, so why had she felt such a deep urge to do it again? Why had it increased her pleasure and desire to such a shocking extent?

Erik's hand covered hers on the table, bringing Christine back to the moment.

"You should hear her sing Casta Diva," Erik was saying, in French now, with immense pride. "No one has sung it better."

"You're a flatterer," Christine muttered and looked up to see Jack beaming at her in interest.

"I would like to be the judge of that myself, Signora Christine," the young musician declared.

Jack, she had learned, was an aspiring composer who claimed he was good at all the minutiae of being a musician – finding work and patrons and crafting orchestrations – but had, as of yet, failed to find his compositional muse. He was a great admirer, like Erik, of the legato of the *bel canto* composers, the innovation of Wagner, and, of course, as an Italian, would give his life in the name of Verdi, but he wanted something new.

"Indeed, all this talk of opera and your skills makes me wish I could hear either of you sing anything," Jack went on.

"We don't perform. Or I don't. Anymore," Christine demurred.

"But you haven't said why!" Jack pushed. "Nor even said where you were a diva."

He meant it well, Christine knew, but it still made her stomach churn to think of her brief and tragic career as a prima donna. It reminded her of the pain one felt for a lost friend. Something she had longed for and nurtured – that had been part of her for so long – was gone. Her life went on, and she survived now because she had given it up, but there was still a hole in her heart where it had been. It was taking much longer to heal than she had anticipated.

"We– she sang in Paris. Nowhere you would have heard of," Erik half-lied.

"You'd be surprised how much I hear about Paris. Though they care more for ballet than opera there, do they not? I heard about the controversy with their mounting of Don Carlo. No offence intended," Jack said.

"None taken," Christine sighed.

"The Opéra in Paris had the potential for greatness, but—" It was Erik's turn to fumble for words. He had tried, in his way, to advance a musical cause, and now even that power and connection were gone for him.

"But you have come at last to the home of real opera and know better now," Jack finished for him jovially. "Let us not linger on useless comparisons that will embarrass France. I assume you two met in some musical fashion. Tell me the story of your love. How many years have you been together?"

Christine tensed. It wasn't that the answer itself was incriminating, but it did give her a jolt to recall that she had not known Erik for more than a year. God, this time last year, she was still fighting to keep her place at the conservatoire. The speed with which her life had changed and changed again made her dizzy.

"Erik was my teacher," Christine began unsteadily. "It's not a complex tale. I... fell in love with his brilliance."

"Despite his wounds from some terrible war?" Jack replied with a sigh. Erik stiffened. "Oh, I'm sorry, my friend. I didn't think it would be untoward to mention it." The young man gestured towards Erik's face. Or more accurately, his mask.

"I hoped you hadn't noticed," Erik muttered.

Christine grasped his hand. She could feel his panic and tension. He had been hurt so many times by so many strangers and people who were supposed to be friends. All because of his face.

"I had an uncle. Well, we called him Uncle. My town is small, and everyone is a relative of some sort. He served in the wars of independence in the sixties against the Prussians. Those brutes with their bombs and shells. One took off half his nose and all of his left eye. He wore a porcelain mask to conceal the wounds. You are French and you remarked on the Germans earlier. Was it the Prussians who wounded you too?"

Erik stared at the man, and Christine's mind raced. They had made excuses before about the mask, along similar lines, but never with such detail.

"Yes, I was in the siege of Paris," Erik replied quietly. Once again, not entirely a lie. "It was brutal. I don't like to talk about it or..." He gestured weakly towards his face. "Or this."

"Then we shan't!" Jack said cheerfully. "Let me tell you about my home. Lucca is a wonderful city. Though I guess 'city' is a relative term compared to Firenze or Paris. It's small by comparison. My forefathers have served as *Maestro di Capella* and organists at the cathedral of San Marino for over two hundred years! I would have taken the position when my father died, but I was only six."

"My father was a musician too," Christine said with a smile. "It's wonderful how love of song and harmony can flow through blood."

"I'm sure your heirs will be prodigies when you have them," Jack replied. "Though I do not wish you as many as my mother. I have eight siblings, on earth and in heaven."

It was Christine's turn to quietly wince, and for Erik to squeeze her hand. Each month, she wondered if something would be different and she would discover that no, she wasn't barren, thanks to a childhood illness. She hated how she wished for it in her heart, over and over, in the days before her blood came. Erik had no desire for children and was glad they wouldn't have any, and it would be such a terrible complication to everything, but she wanted it, even so.

"She sounds like a brave woman," Erik offered. "I have heard of Lucca. It must be beautiful to be so near the ocean. Is it cooler than this in the summer?"

"A bit. You must visit if you can. How long will you be in Firenze? I must go home in a few weeks. Someone is having a birthday or a christening. Or was it a wedding? I can't recall, but my attendance is required."

"We don't know how long we'll be here," Christine said with a mix of sadness and hope. Things were looking up after a poor start to the day. They were making friends, and maybe that could give them the confidence to put down some roots.

"We could not think to impose," Erik added.

"Nonsense. You're my friend now, and my house is open to you... for a price." Jack gave a playful grin and looked around the nearly-empty restaurant.

"A price?" Erik echoed. "I don't—"

"Play for me again. Something old or something you have written," Jack prompted. Christine realized he had been looking at the decrepit piano tucked in the corner. "I would offer a trade of one of my compositions, but it would be a poor exchange, so I offer friendship and hospitality instead."

Christine caught Erik's eye as he looked to her for reassurance. He had played for Jack this morning at *Santa Croce*, but this was a far more intimate setting where Erik was exposed. There were two patrons eating in another corner, and the cook and waiter were chatting through a door. Yet, Christine could see the spark of interest in his eyes. Despite being a man who hid in the shadows, Erik loved an audience.

"Go ahead, my love," Christine said sweetly. "Though we must warn our new friend that all other music will seem lacking after he hears yours."

"Glad you aren't setting the expectations too high," Erik grumbled, but Christine knew he treasured the compliment. "If you both insist."

"We do," Jack chortled.

They moved to the piano, Jack and Christine taking seats at an empty table as Erik settled himself before the keys. Christine wondered what was going through his mind – was it a tangle of all the different melodies she knew were constantly playing there? Was he plucking one from the bunch to improvise upon, or would he be choosing a composition he had explored before?

Erik began and it was indeed a melody Christine had heard in his compositions. A song of sweet, sad hope, filled with longing. Erik changed it from the last time Christine had heard it and sung along without words. Now it sounded like Florence itself; like the soaring cathedrals and crooked old streets full of life and tragedy, a river of love flowing through the center, like a vein from a breaking heart.

Christine tore her eyes away from the sight of Erik losing himself in the music to look at Jack. He was entirely overcome, his mouth slack beneath his moustache, and tears in the corners of his eyes. She had suspected he was the sort of musician who cared not for honors nor spotlight, but who truly and deeply loved music. And so he was. The young student watched Erik with nothing short of awe, and Christine couldn't help but beam with pride. She only wished she could sing too, but it was not her moment.

Erik finished too soon and turned to his meager audience. To Christine's delight, all the people in the room, strangers and friends alike, burst into applause. She saw the way Erik drank it in, and it filled her with the same bittersweet pride as before.

"You were right, Signora Gilbride," Jack said, breathless as he clapped. "I will never be the same after this."

"Erik has that effect on people," Christine agreed, though the way Erik upended lives and transformed all he met wasn't always a blessing. It had been for her, but it had come with pain.

They ambled back to their flat through the nighttime streets of Florence. The heat had faded at last, and the air was sweet and warm. Christine felt content and confident enough to lace her arm through Erik's, take his hand, and rest her head on his shoulder as they walked.

"That was nice, wasn't it?" Christine asked hopefully. "I like Jack."

"Do you think I should meet him again as he asked? I worry if I critique his work, I'll be too cruel," Erik mused. "And I don't want to leave you alone again."

"I have made a new friend too," Christine said with a smile, proud to finally share her secret. "Her name is Pauline. She's French. Someone I can talk to."

"That's good," Erik replied, but didn't sound like he meant it.

"If you can trust Jack, I can trust her," Christine chided, and Erik gave an assenting sort of grunt as they reached the entrance to their flat. Signore Genco was there with his mother and another man, conversing over pipes in the night.

"*Buona sera*," the mother said, then asked Erik something else in Italian that Christine didn't understand. She wished she had because it made her husband and the other men laugh.

"She said, 'The night makes everyone beautiful, until a real beauty like you comes along to outshine us all,'" Erik whispered in her ear.

Christine blushed and sent the old woman a smile. "She is too kind."

"She is right. Let us go up, my wife," Erik went on, tugging Christine's waist.

She was happy to return to their little rented flat. It had come with furnishings, and though they were older and worn, they were welcoming. Christine liked them and the stucco walls and the painted tile by the fireplace they hadn't used yet, and the windows looking out onto the streets.

There was a courtyard at the center of the building that she wanted to spend more time in. It had a little fountain, and Mama Genco (Christine really had to learn the woman's proper name) and her son had filled it with plants and lemon trees that were heavy with fruit.

"We could stay here, you know. In Florence. Stop running for a while," Christine said aloud as the thought crossed her mind. Erik regarded her as he locked the door behind them and took off his mask. There was a sheen of sweat on his poor face, and Christine, for the thousandth time, pitied how uncomfortable it had to be to wear the thing day in and out. "The heat will pass, and the people here are good."

"The people everywhere are good. They are not the problem," Erik countered. "In every city and village, there are normal folk living their lives, happy and content and good. I fear I'm always a wrench thrown into the works to disrupt everything and reveal the bad in everyone."

"Maybe before, but it's different now. You're not alone." Christine approached her strange husband and snaked her arms around his waist. "Everything has changed now."

"I hope you're right," Erik sighed.

Christine smiled back. Some of the weight of all the questions Jack had asked that she could not answer lifted from her soul. That was the past, and this was their future. There was hope for them, and she would hold onto it.

# Paris

M eg couldn't stop shaking all day, and thus, couldn't stop falling in rehearsal. She had been reprimanded many times and moved to the back of the formation in the *Salon du Danse*. How could she contain herself, though? After days of sneaking about her own home, trying to get into her mother's things, she had finally achieved a triumph this morning and snatched the note from her mother's vanity.

Meg had never seen one of the infamous notes her mother would sometimes find in box five and deliver to the management, though she had asked a thousand times. Now Meg had one, tucked into her bodice and waiting to be read. She had to wait, of course. It wasn't right to read it alone. She needed her friends with her.

Meg looked to the front of the formation to watch Rochelle do an elegant *rond de jambe*, the skin of her back that was exposed by her white practice costume taut over flexed muscles. Next to her was Cécile Jammes, who had not smiled for many months, and beyond her was Blanche, who kept looking up at the patrons and losing her footing.

Blanche had not secured a patron, though she was eager to. Rochelle, who had Monsieur Tremblay, didn't look at the patrons. Good for her. Meg disliked the feeling of being on display as the wealthy men talked too loudly over the rehearsal pianist and flicked their cigars so that ash fell on the ballerinas below. They surveyed the crop of women and girls with the same detachment as Meg's mother used for selecting produce from the market stalls by the Seine. Meg didn't like feeling like a tomato that wasn't quite ripe.

"That's enough for now," Charles LaRoche sighed with a bang of the cane he used to keep time for the dancers. Meg could have sworn that it was usually an ostentatious ebony thing, but today it was a boring, worn brown. Maybe the usual one had broken. It didn't matter – at last, it was time!

"Marie!" Meg hissed, rushing forward from her place of punishment to seize her friend. Marie looked shocked by the ambush. Meg couldn't blame her.

"What's gotten into Giry?" Blanche asked with a superior sigh. "You were dancing like a drunken elephant."

"I was distracted!" Meg squealed. "I have something—" She stopped herself as Rochelle and Jammes joined them. Jammes hated any mention of the ghost ever since she had been the first one to find the body of Joseph Buquet.

"Did a patron finally send you a love letter, little mouse?" Jammes asked Meg, then turned to Rochelle. "I was sorry not to see your paramour in the crowd today, Rochelle. Maybe he's grown bored of you."

"I pray for that every day," Rochelle hissed back.

"I wanted to show you something." Meg paused. How could she get rid of Jammes? The girl had no friends.

"What a lovely bouquet of flowers," a voice declared, and Meg swore internally. They had missed their window to escape, and now the patrons had come down. The one who had spoken approached their group with an oily smile and oilier hair. The man with him had blondish brown hair and an overly complicated goatee that didn't suit his face. They both towered over the small dancers, which made Meg straighten up. A sparrow puffing out its feathers to scare off a hawk.

"Good day, Monsieur d'Amboise," Jammes smiled. "And..."

"Monsieur Clermont," the blondish man said and extended a hand, not to Jammes but to Rochelle. "My condolences, Mademoiselle Moreau. What happened to your dear friend Monsieur Tremblay is so awful."

"What?" Rochelle asked, looking around the circle of girls and men.

"We haven't heard anything about Monsieur Tremblay," Blanche confirmed. The men gave them pitying looks, though d'Amboise also looked delighted to share whatever the news was.

"Monsieur Tremblay was assaulted last night! Beaten black and blue and robbed!" d'Amboise exclaimed and looked to Rochelle.

Perhaps he was hoping she would gasp or begin to weep, but her face was blank as she digested the information.

"That's terrible," Marie finally said. "Was he in some dangerous part of town?"

"He was on the *Boulevard des Capucines*, just leaving the Opéra!" Clermont lamented. Now that was shocking. The Opéra was the very heart of Paris, in a respectable and well-travelled area. Thieves and cutthroats didn't usually prowl here.

"Perhaps he should not have been walking alone at night," Rochelle said with a shrug. "Thank you, Messieurs, for the information."

"We are happy to console you," d'Amboise pushed back, oozing toward Rochelle and Blanche.

"We are needed in the costume shop!" Meg piped in, and the crowd turned to her. "Well, I am. They asked me to bring Mademoiselles Carcaux, Moreau, and Van Goethem too."

"I was supposed to see my sister," Marie argued, as Jammes looked daggers at Meg.

"She'll still be in class. Come along," Meg said and took the small dancer's hand to lead her away before anyone stopped them. She sometimes forgot that Marie also had family at the Opéra, an older sister who worked as an extra in large crowd scenes and a younger one who was a junior student at the school of dance where all the *petits rats* started.

Meg hurried through the halls with Marie in tow, the other girls following close behind, until she found a secluded corner for them to hide.

"Meg, have you forgotten where the costumers are?" Blanche asked.

"I don't think young Giry here really meant what she said," Rochelle replied, looking somewhat amused. "She wanted to get us away from those two vultures and Jammes."

"So I could show you what I found!" Meg squealed as she pulled the note from where it had been hidden in her bodice all day. "My mother had it – it frightened her. I haven't opened it yet, but it has to be from him!"

"Him who?" Blanche asked, and Rochelle groaned.

"Do you mean the ghost? He's sending notes through your mother again?" Marie demanded, utterly breathless.

"Or your mother received some bill or a note about some sick relative that you've stolen from her," Rochelle countered.

"Let's see it then," Blanche said, her blonde ringlets shaking at the side of her head. Meg's hands shook as she unfolded the note. Maybe Rochelle was right – maybe it was something personal her mother didn't want her to see. Something from her father's family, perhaps, or...

"Red ink," Marie gasped.

Meg's eyes finally focused on the paper in her hands. Indeed, the words were scrawled in a jagged handwriting that was hard to read, in ink red as blood.

"*Remove the following, or I shall:*" Meg read, voice unsteady. "Then a list of names."

"Names of whom? Dancers? Am I on there?" Marie squeaked. "I knew I never should have taken the offer to pose!"

"There's no Van Goethem," Blanche reassured her as she looked over the list. There were six names scribbled on it. "None of these are dancers or even singers, as far as I know."

"Orchestra, maybe? Or stagehands?" Meg suggested, before Rochelle gasped.

"They're patrons. Look." Rochelle pointed a quivering finger to the final name on the list. "Tremblay. And now he's been assaulted."

"You think the ghost did that?" Marie asked, grabbing Meg's arm for protection. "Like he did to Buquet?"

"No, that can't be," Meg exclaimed.

"He's already killed one patron. Poor Philippe de Chagny," Blanche sighed. Only recently had La Sorelli returned after her period of mourning, but Meg thought her wearing a black veil still was a bit much. She also didn't believe that the ghost had done the Comte de Chagny in.

"That was an accident in the lake," Meg protested weakly. "This might not be about the patrons. It can't have been a threat to your Monsieur Tremblay."

"I thought you were convinced this was from him?" Rochelle asked, her thick black eyebrows high in judgement and disbelief. "Don't tell me you still think he's benevolent! Not after the chandelier."

"No," Meg protested, the awful sound of the chandelier crashing into the audience echoing in her memory. "But he's the Opera ghost – he doesn't go outside the Opéra!"

"Says who?" Rochelle asked, raising her chin like a duchess. "I heard that—" The dark-haired dancer stopped herself.

"Heard what?" Meg demanded. She very much didn't like not knowing every story and rumor of the ghost.

"Antoine de Martiniac didn't die in the opera," Rochelle smirked.

"Antoine de Martiniac isn't dead," Blanche countered, blinking in confusion. "Is he?"

"No one has seen him in months, and he was best friends with Comte Philippe. The Ghost killed them both, is what I think." Rochelle explained. "So does Jammes."

"Are you friends with that sour sack of frowns now?" Marie piped up as Meg shook her head and tucked the list back into her bodice.

"Still, why these patrons?" Meg asked. "Do you know why anyone would want to hurt your Monsieur Tremblay?"

"I can think of several reasons, but none that a ghost would care about," Rochelle replied, face darkening. Meg turned from Rochelle to the other girls. Blanche looked guilty, and Marie dubious. Meg felt pity.

"We care," Meg said softly. "We didn't do or say enough, but we care."

"It's too late," Rochelle said, waving her hand. "At least he's dealt with now. Please have your mother send the ghost my thanks."

"Rochelle—" Meg began, but the bang of their ballet master's cane interrupted the conversation.

"Get back to rehearsals, all of you," LaRoche declared, and the ballerinas rushed to comply. LaRoche caught Meg by the arm, holding her back from the others before they went in. "I hope you improve your performance for the rest of the rehearsal, Meg Giry. To be a troublemaker is one thing, but a troublemaker who doesn't know her steps with no patron to protect her is another."

"I understand, sir," Meg muttered, feeling small and helpless.

"A few of them were interested today, so you know. Monsieur d'Amboise thought you were quite intriguing if you'd like to change things."

"Perhaps," Meg whispered, and it seemed to satisfy LaRoche. She rushed back into the *Salon du Danse*, shivering as she did.

She'd had a protector, once. Now, she was sure he was back.

## Florence

It felt good to have a routine, Christine mused as she made her way to Les Halles to meet Pauline for the third day in a row. It was good to have something regular to pursue daily to give one a sense of normalcy, even in an uncertain time.

There were, of course, rhythms to the days she shared with Erik. They rose late more often than not, and someone would eventually decide it was time for food, and then they would fall into some diversion. Reading was a popular pursuit, though as much as that was a routine, so was Erik muttering about how he missed his library. He missed having a piano at hand too, but he hadn't needed to complain about that of late, as he had been regularly meeting with Jack while Christine visited Pauline.

They would do other things, of course; or had done other things in the days and months of their travels. Exploration and invention and simply talking for hours. They would eat late and make love, though last night they had not for reasons that also made Christine happy she would see Pauline today.

"There you are, right on time," Pauline called when Christine arrived at Les Halles. The other woman already had two pastries in front of her, and cups of strong Italian coffee as well.

"Old habit," Christine muttered as she sat.

"From the theater?" Pauline asked with a curious smile.

"Oh yes. Early is on time, and on time is late," Christine replied, quoting so many maestros and conductors. "There are a hundred other people who want the same job; if you're late, they'll give it to one of them."

"That sounds quite cutthroat," Pauline said with a laugh.

"Oh, it is." Christine took a sip of coffee as Pauline looked her over.

"Did you ever have any great rivals?" she asked with a grin. "I'm sure there was competition for the roles you wanted. Did you ever have to fight someone for it?"

Christine nearly choked on her drink but covered it with a cough. Pauline couldn't know how many people's lives had been destroyed at the Palais Garnier in the name of rivalry, and how much Christine was responsible for it. "A few."

"Oh my! Do tell!"

"Oh, I'm sure it's nothing more interesting than what you encounter among artists," Christine said, strained.

"I stole a girl's oils and threw them in the river for looking at me wrong," Pauline said with an utterly calm expression that chilled Christine to the bone – until she broke into a smile and laughed. "Or not."

The joke put Christine at ease. "There was one woman who tried to have me fired, more than once. Because I was better than her."

"What a bitch," Pauline grinned. "I can't imagine wanting to take away someone's livelihood over something as silly as a stage performance."

"Indeed." Christine looked down at her untouched pastry, nauseous guilt rising inside her. Sometimes Carlotta featured in her nightmares, screaming for vengeance. Christine had earned her grace in the end, but it didn't undo the things both of them had done. It didn't bring back Joseph Buquet or...

"Are you alright?" Pauline asked, and Christine realized her distress must be showing.

"I'm fine," she lied, plastering on a smile. "It's all in the past, and I had my triumph over her. Well, with help."

"From whom?" Pauline asked, eyebrows raised. "Your mysterious husband and teacher?"

Christine forced herself to take a bite of food so she wouldn't have to answer. She'd been incredibly careful with what she had told Pauline about Erik, not even revealing his name. Of course, that had made her more curious. "He was a great advocate for me when I was performing," Christine said carefully.

"I'd love to have a man like that," Pauline sighed. "Someone who would commit unspeakable acts if it meant making me happy."

"I don't know about unspeakable," Christine sputtered around her mouthful.

"Well, you are married, and I have heard things," Pauline chuckled. "You have to get that sort of thing in before all the babies come along."

Christine swallowed before she choked this time, but it didn't stop the sadness that welled up in her so powerfully that she couldn't look Pauline in the face.

"Oh no, what did I say?" Pauline asked, reaching over to grip Christine's arm.

"It's nothing. It's just that..." Christine sniffled and tried to compose herself. "We've been married for several months, and nothing has happened in that respect. I thought this month it might, but yesterday... I'm sorry, this isn't polite conversation."

Christine didn't want to think about finding blood on her petticoats or the cramps in her gut. She didn't want to think about Erik's relief.

"I'm so sorry," Pauline said, and it sounded like she meant it. Christine let out a little huff of a sob because it was what she needed to hear.

"It's so stupid, really," she began. "I know it's not the time. We're not settled, and I'm still young, but I don't have a career to nurture anymore, so there's part of me that thinks I could have more meaning if I had a child. I know that's not a good reason to want a baby, and my husband certainly doesn't want the complication, so I should be relieved, but—"

"It's still a disappointment. I understand." Pauline's eyes were soft when Christine met them, warm and comforting enough that Christine let out a sigh of relief to simply be seen in her secret grief. "But you're also right – you're young and there's a whole world out there to explore and see before you're tied down. I think it's wonderful that you get to do whatever you like and go wherever you want. You're so free."

"Yes, that is true," Christine said, though her voice quavered. She wanted to tell Pauline that she had grown up with this type of freedom and so had Erik. They had both wandered so long without a place to call home until they found the Opera. Then they had given it up, to have each other, and returned to the freedom of open roads and vast skies.

Christine could not say aloud how tired she was becoming of that kind of freedom or how a life without a home sometimes felt like a prison too. Maybe that was changing, she told herself, as she looked at her new friend. Maybe this was where they would finally land.

# 3. Refuge

## Florence

It was a habit for Erik to walk in the shadows and alleyways. Even though his mask concealed him, he still didn't like crowds and strangers and preferred longer but safer routes through Florence that avoided the main roads. Jack had remarked that morning on how Erik had appeared in the university courtyard like a ghost, and the young man hadn't understood why that made Erik laugh.

Erik didn't know what to call his meetings with the young musician. They were not lessons; Jack had already studied the principles of theory and had an excellent grip on orchestration and harmony. It wasn't collaboration (though, to be fair, Erik had never had a collaborator). He and Jack exchanged melodies and pored over things they had written, mainly arias for operas that did not yet exist, and discussed how they could be improved. Jack had a great ear, if not a great creative spark of his own, but in a few sessions, he had helped take Erik's melodies and harmonies to a higher level, something that shocked Erik. He had, of course, thought there was no room for improvement, but he had been humbled.

Maybe it was collaboration? He would have to ask Christine. She knew the intricacies of human friendship and interactions. It was thanks to her encouragement that he had continued these sessions at all. It made him feel exposed to have a real acquaintance again, after he had lost so many and been betrayed by others.

Maybe that was why he'd been more careful in recent days when journeying about the city. That, or the memories of not being hidden in Lungern.

It was thanks to this precaution that Erik could do something else he had been denied the pleasure of for many months – watch his beloved from the shadows. He had come to their street via a hidden alley just in time to see Christine approaching and would have revealed himself to join her had he not seen the other woman beside her.

This had to be Pauline. From what Christine told him, she and this unimposing woman had much in common, almost surprisingly so. Pauline too had lost her mother when she was young and her father when she was a teenager. Pauline knew and liked so many of the same places in Rouen that Christine had frequented; it was a wonder that they had not met there.

Now Erik finally had the chance to take in the woman for himself. She was shorter and stouter than Christine, with a softly mussed quality. She wore glasses and a brown dress with a high collar and black tie, cut like a man's suit, but her hair was feminine. It was styled very much like Christine's, and their hats were at the same angle. Christine, of course, looked beautiful in her dress of pale green, her cheeks pink as the little flowers on her hat. Her smile towards her friend was kind, then knowing as she paused and looked up around her.

She'd sensed him watching, as she always did. Remarkable.

He snuck closer to listen to the conversation, now that she knew he was watching. Pauline was in the midst of a lament.

"—Beginning to think your husband is a mere fiction to keep your dignity and drive away suitors," the smaller woman laughed. "Surely there is no other reason not to let me meet him."

Erik stiffened. He didn't like anyone prying.

"He is a very private man," Christine explained, and Pauline narrowed her eyes.

"You will be in Florence for a while, yes?" the other woman asked. "You will have time to prove he's real."

"We haven't decided if we're staying," Christine countered.

"Can I at least see your flat? If he is not home, I'd love to see how someone else lives in this city." Pauline's smile was bright as she asked. Too bright for Erik's taste. He knew Christine enjoyed having a friend, but this young lady was incredibly nosy, and he didn't like nosy.

To her credit, Christine shook her head and politely stepped towards the entrance to their building. "I'm afraid not. I think he may be resting and, as I said, he is very private. Have a good afternoon, Pauline."

"Will I see you tomorrow?" the young woman asked, a bit too eagerly.

"We may travel to a neighboring city tomorrow, actually. My husband had been talking about seeing some of the architecture. I'm sure I will see you the next day," Christine said with a smile. The statement surprised Erik because he had said no such thing. Was she trying to avoid her friend?

"Of course! I will see you then." The woman kissed Christine quickly on both cheeks and took her leave.

Erik waited until the street was empty to emerge from his alley and approach his scowling wife. "Did you lie to her because I was here?"

"No. She asks so many questions," Christine sighed. "I wanted some reprieve."

"We can do what you said and go to one of the Tuscan hill towns and explore tomorrow, if that's what you would like."

Christine looked dubious, her smile unsteady. "You have an appointment with Jack that I'm sure you don't want to miss, and I've barely seen this city."

"Let's change that then, right now," Erik said before he could think better of it.

Christine looked at him like his hair had caught fire, disbelieving and suspicious. "What on earth do you mean?"

"Let's see Florence, right now. As much as we can until our feet ache. I'll take you to the Uffizi to see the Botticellis and the Medici tombs and—"

"Don't give it all away," Christine laughed, taking his hand. "Show me."

Erik wasn't sure what it was that had made him bold. Maybe he was jealous of another person potentially showing Christine this city (for she had mentioned exploring the shops on the Ponte Vecchio with Pauline). Maybe he was warming up after a week in pleasant company with Jack. Maybe he felt guilty that he had dragged his wife across the continent for months, and they had barely had time to enjoy it.

"Come, this way," he said to her, squeezing her hand.

It made him feel immeasurably braver to be out in the wide world beside her, her fingers laced with his. When he walked the streets with her on his arm, she was the one strangers saw – a perfect beauty, outshining the beast beside her and lifting him up from the dark with her light. She deserved all the world, his wife, and he'd give it to her.

It was their most pleasant afternoon and evening together in weeks (at least, one that involved them leaving their bed). Erik took her to the Duomo, which they had seen before, but this time, he let himself become a teacher and storyteller, as his nature demanded. He told her of the competition to build the dome, how Brunelleschi had created a marvel of architecture that was also art itself. They walked through the naves and apses, and then across the square to take in the golden, Byzantine splendor of the Baptistry.

But that was only the beginning. Erik guided her to the palace that once housed the great patrons of the Renaissance and now held their greatest art. They marveled at the Birth of Venus, La Primavera, and more wonders at the Uffizi, walking among others speaking foreign tongues. Young men and women on their Grand Tours of the continent, perhaps, or older couples who were Florentines long before they had become Italians.

Christine reminded him near sunset that they had to eat, and so they did, finding a dark corner in a café and filling themselves with pasta and crumbling Tuscan bread. Everything was fresh, straight from the summer fields, and Erik didn't even mind the awkwardness of eating through his false beard.

They wandered the streets long after dusk, and it felt like the whole of the city was with them: musicians played on the corners, friends called to one another from windows, and the strange French couple ambled together, content as could be as they made their way home.

They approached their secluded street, hand in hand, enjoying the night together in amiable, loving silence. Erik looked at Christine in the flickering lamplight and smiled. Today reminded him of when she had first come into his world, wary and fearful, when he had shown her the underground roads of Paris and the secret wonders of the Louvre. Then, no piece of art they had looked upon had been as beautiful to him as the woman at his side... Now, they were in a different nation, and so much pain and joy had passed between them, but Christine was still the most wonderful thing he could ever see.

He wanted to tell her. He wanted to take her upstairs as soon as they reached the Gencos' door and show her how much he loved her. Back in Paris, after the Louvre, he had wanted so desperately to kiss her and make love to her. Now he could, and it would be in a flat with windows and gentle night breezes, a place they had started to call home.

Erik began to speak as they rounded the final corner, but a crash interrupted him.

"Please! No one is here!" came a pained cry in a female voice. It was Signora Genco, Erik was sure of it. Instinctively, he grabbed Christine, pulling her close to protect her.

"What's happening?" Christine hissed, trying to make out the shadows moving at the door of the Gencos' building. Their building.

"We know you're lying!" a rough man's voice replied, and there came another crash. He was throwing pottery on the cobblestone street, right next to where Mama Genco was cowering on her knees next to the prone body of a man. It had to be Vito.

Another man emerged from the door that led into the courtyard and tossed his compatriot another vase. The one who had caught it was wiry and fair, with a bowler hat perched on his head. He would be easy to take in a fight, though he would be fast. The other man was huge. He nearly filled the doorway, and he had a cruel look about him. They had subdued a bear of a man like Vito, which meant they were extremely dangerous.

"Tell us where they are, or the next one we crack will be on his head!" the wiry one declared, holding the urn aloft.

"What are they saying?" Christine demanded in a fierce whisper, shaking in fear beside him.

"They're looking for someone or something," he replied hastily, his pulse racing. These thugs were clearly professionals when it came to intimidation and hurting people. Did Vito owe money to some unsavory character? Or perhaps...

"He's not hard to miss, we've been told," the large one mumbled just as the terrible thought occurred to Erik. "Tall and bony. Black hair and a mask. Who can miss that?"

"No one who lives here wears a mask! The husband – he is a veteran!" Mama Genco protested, her voice thick with tears. Erik's heart seized with rage and guilt. This woman was suffering because of him. Either through ignorance or charity, she was trying to protect him.

"Did they say mask?" Christine gasped, grabbing Erik to hold him back now. "Oh God, are they looking for us?"

"They pay their rent and do not bother us!" Mama Genco cried, and the brute hurled the vase to the pavement next to her, missing Vito's head by inches. Vito groaned and tried to move, but the wiry one pressed a foot to his throat.

"Oh, you're awake?" the assailant sneered, leaning down. "Did you know you're renting a flat to a monster?"

The word was like a spark to the dynamite inside Erik. In the word, he heard echoes of hundreds of voices – his parents and his victims and those he had thought friends and those that knew him as an enemy. Women and children, screaming at the sight of him, running away through the woods to summon the village to drive out the monster.

"Erik, no!" Christine cried, trying to hold him back, but she couldn't contain him. She was wrong to even try.

Erik sprang from the shadows and seized the smaller man, unbalancing him and using momentum to hurl him against the wall.

"If he is a monster, then you should be more careful," Erik hissed, meeting the man with a fierce kick when he rushed at him and sending him to the ground. Mama Genco screamed, and Erik looked up to see the larger of the two barreling towards them. Erik braced himself, driving his shoulder into the center of the huge man's chest and knocking him back at the cost of the man grabbing at Erik's face as he tore off the mask.

Good. It was easier to fight this kind of vermin when they were scared. Erik reared up, and the large attacker stumbled back, breath knocked from his lungs and face filling with horror as he looked on Erik's deathly countenance.

"Devil!" he gasped and crossed himself.

"No, but I will be happy to introduce you to him," Erik growled.

"Oh God!" Signora Genco cried as Christine rushed to her side and helped her away from the fray. Erik made the mistake of looking at the old woman's terrified face and not Christine's, and the horror he saw there sickened him. "What is he?"

"Erik!" Christine cried. He saw the movement out of the corner of his eye in time to catch the lithe man by the throat as he charged again.

Erik's rage poured into his hand as it tightened around the man's neck. This man was the real monster. A common criminal sent to track him down like a dog. Erik squeezed, and the man scrabbled at his hand and arm, trying to get away even as the air left his lungs. Erik wanted to see the light leave his eyes...

"Erik, no!" Christine screamed, and he made the mistake of looking at her. He saw the fear and devastation on her face.

He couldn't do this again. He would lose her.

The first blow struck him in the ribs, and the second one in his face. It was the other man, breath and bravery recovered. Erik ducked the third punch and forced the victim still in his grasp between them as a shield. His friend knocked the other aside and out of Erik's grasp, so that he fell unmoving on the ground. Someone screamed as the brute struck Erik, and he finally hit back, using his speed against the larger opponent.

The man wound up for another blow, then howled in pain as the women screamed. It took Erik a half second to see that Vito had recovered on the ground, grabbed a jagged shard of pottery, and drove it deep into the man's thigh. The assailant crashed to his knees, and Erik had a choice. He could end this and kill him now or help the man who had just saved them when he had no reason to.

Erik rushed to Vito and heaved him up from the cobblestones, carrying him to the entrance. His mother helped him in as Christine slammed the door behind them and bolted it shut. They were safe, but it wasn't over. Erik watched through the peephole as the men in the street struggled to their feet and glowered at the locked door.

"It's not over, monster!" the huge one cried. "There will be more coming for you! The one who wants you pays well and won't be denied a prize!"

Erik let out a shuddering breath as he watched the men retreat. He didn't want to look away even when they were no longer visible. He didn't want to turn to the people cowering next to him in the entryway who had seen him for what he was in all the most terrible ways.

"What did they say?" Christine asked first, voice small and shaking. Erik turned to her and met her eyes, ignoring how Mama Genco winced when he did.

"They were here for me," Erik replied grimly. "We have to get out of Florence."

## Paris

"You're late," Darius scolded the moment Shaya opened the door to their flat.

"I told you I planned to observe as long as I could after the performance," Shaya countered, and Darius shook his head, ever tolerant. Shaya didn't mind the concern. Darius's fussing came from a place of love, and his admonition was as welcoming as the smell of tea brewing and the cozy furnishings of the home they shared.

"Was there anything to observe?" Darius asked as Shaya removed his coat and Astrakhan cap.

"There is no love lost for Halévy among the audience, which I can't blame them for. The talk in the salons was mostly of business and politics and who was sleeping with whose wives."

Darius squinted at him. "What else are you not saying?" Of course he knew. He always knew.

"There was also discussion of the robbery and beating of a patron by the name of Tremblay. It's shaken everyone," Shaya confessed with a sigh. "It happened close to the Opéra, and Tremblay has been unable to describe the attacker because he was surprised from behind."

"That doesn't sound like Erik. And robberies happen even in the posh neighborhoods."

"That's what I keep telling myself, and why I was late."

"You lingered in the street around the Opéra, hoping to catch this assailant at work again," Darius surmised, and Shaya nodded. "And you were unsuccessful."

"I'm probably just being paranoid." Shaya shook his head and sank into a chair by the fire. "You're right about me needing some other pastime. Though I refuse to write a memoir – that's for old men."

"And you are, of course, young and vital," Darius chuckled. "Maybe this is something to keep you occupied." He produced an envelope from his pocket and handed it to Shaya. It was a telegram.

"What on earth?"

Shaya didn't receive a great deal of correspondence. His few friends were in Paris and his remaining acquaintances in Persia didn't often write. He only knew of one person who might be contacting him. A person he had immediately tried to contact a week ago.

He tore open the telegram and read:

*From the offices of Tissot and Garibaldi, Geneva*

*Dear M. Motlagh,*

*Your letter and the enclosed letter directed to the client of M. Tissot were received today. We regret to inform you that no correspondence to M. Tissot or his clients can be managed or answered at this time, as M. Tissot has taken unexpectedly ill.*

*Regards.*

*T. A. Martin*

Shaya reread the missive, trying to control the twisting, suspicious feeling in his stomach.

"What is it?" Darius asked.

"I wrote to Erik last week – or attempted to. I sent a letter to the solicitor in Geneva."

"I know, you wouldn't stop complaining about how much it cost to get it there quickly."

Shaya scowled. "The office replied to say that the solicitor has taken ill and no letter can be forwarded. I'm sure it's nothing."

"You used to say that, with Erik, nothing was a coincidence," Darius replied slowly. "This means he can't be reached to answer any questions, and we don't know where he is."

"It wouldn't be like Erik to harm his solicitor or avoid me now," Shaya argued automatically. "I have a terrible feeling that someone else is looking for him, and the list of people who want to find him is very long."

# Florence

C hristine finally began to cry as the carriage rounded the bend, and the place that might have become a real home left her sight. Signora Genco and her son had been kinder than they had any right to be in helping them pack and summon transportation but had also made it clear that the two of them were no longer welcome under that roof after all the evil they had brought. Neither she nor Erik had argued.

"Why didn't you tell the driver to go to the train station?" Christine asked, trying not to let her voice crack.

"We're not going to the train station," Erik replied, the same darkness in his voice that had been radiating from him since he attacked those men. They had deserved the fight, Christine knew that, but it still didn't make seeing Erik like that again any easier. She had thought they were done with the violence they had left behind, but it had found them.

"What do you mean?"

"We're going to see Jack."

Christine dared to meet Erik's golden eyes. They were as deadly and determined as ever. "For all we know, Jack was the one who led those men to us," Christine protested.

"Exactly. If he is, I will find out who he told." Erik's tone made it clear he wouldn't be arguing this point, but after a beat, his eyes behind the mask softened, and the tension in his body dissipated. "If he wasn't, then we need him as a friend."

"What if it was someone who followed me?" Christine whispered back, sickened. "Pauline or Patricia or—"

Erik grabbed her hands as she began to shake. In her mind, she saw it again: the chandelier falling. The bodies. She heard the screams and then the gunshot...

"Christine, don't do this to yourself," Erik commanded, forcing her to look at him as he tore off his mask. He breathed slow and deep, making her match him. "The evil of others is not your fault," he told her as the queasiness ebbed and her heart slowed.

She wanted to argue, to ask if that applied to him, but she couldn't. She had married him, knowing all he had done, and forgiven him. Because he had changed, he had chosen life. A real, free life for them that seemed unreachable now.

She embraced him instead, taking comfort in his solid form against hers and the familiar weight of his arms around her. The only consistent thing in months of wandering was him. He was all she had, and that had to be enough.

The carriage lurched to a stop, and Erik pulled back to look at her. She had to be a mess, with her hair falling from its bun and cheeks red from crying. She envied Erik the mask as he replaced it on his face.

They left the carriage waiting and made their way into the ancient building where Jack lived. The hall was barely lit this time of night (or technically early morning) and the paint on the door was peeling, but it opened quickly after Erik's knock.

"What in the devil—" Jack stopped in shock. Christine knew what he saw: Erik in his old mask, mouth uncovered and set in a grim line, gold eyes blazing with danger as he stood at his full, imposing height. Then there was Christine next to him, with tear-stained cheeks, looking as if she had just run for her life.

"I would like to know, my friend, if you are surprised to see me alive and free," Erik demanded slowly. "Please think carefully before you answer."

"I'm surprised to see you at my door in such a state," Jack answered, not obeying the order to think at all. He was rumpled and in shirt sleeves, with ink stains on his fingers. "What is this about your life? Are you in some sort of trouble? Signora, are you alright?"

Jack leaned forward, but Erik stopped him, eyes locking with Jack's and boring into his soul to determine what Christine already knew – that this was not the person who had betrayed them.

"Men – paid thugs – came to our flat and assaulted our landlord, trying to find us," Christine explained, and Jack looked appropriately astonished by the revelation.

"Why would someone be trying to find you? Is it a debt, or have you done someone some greater offence?" Jack asked, more concerned than suspicious. "Can I help?"

The menace left Erik, like shadows driven away by a flame. "Thank you. May we—"

"Yes, of course, come in." Jack ushered them into his untidy bachelor's flat, and Christine shook her head at the state of it. There wasn't a clear surface in sight, with every table covered with music, books, and a few unwashed wine glasses. There was no carpet and hardly enough furniture. "The maid has not come by this... month," Jack muttered.

"We won't stay too long," Christine said politely (and hopefully).

"You can't go home if someone is looking for you," Jack countered, meeting their eyes. "May I know why my friends are being pursued?"

"It's a long story," Erik said. "One that I fear will diminish your regard for me. If this arrival has not done so already."

"There was a reason we had to leave Paris," Christine cut in, sighing at her husband's dramatics. "We made many enemies there."

"I made enemies there," Erik corrected. "We can't tell you more and risk harm coming to you by knowing too much. Just being here..."

Christine could tell that Erik was beginning to regret this. She could read the thoughts racing through his head clear as day – that he was cursed and knowing him brought only sorrow and suffering to those around him. That all of this was what he deserved.

"My husband is a good man, despite what he may think or imply," Christine said, taking Erik's hand and turning to poor, bewildered Jack. "He has endured many cruelties and abuses and done dark things to survive, but he – *we* – are trying to leave that behind."

"I know," Jack said to their surprise. "I can hear it, I mean. In every note you write and play. Erik, I haven't known you for long, but I know your soul in your music, and it strives for the light. Yours is a gift worth protecting. You are a man I am glad to know."

"For now," Erik muttered, looking away to hide that he was moved by Jack's words. Christine squeezed his hand. One day, she would make him believe fully in why she chose him each day. "We need to get out of the city—"

"And you can't risk a nosy landlord or a long passage. I have the perfect solution for you," Jack said with a grim expression. "You will go to my house in Lucca."

"Where your family still resides?" Erik scoffed.

"I'll have you know I have a respectable set of rooms that are mine alone," Jack said, puffing up in pride. "That I inherited. The quarters are close, but I will send a letter explaining that you're a friend in need, not to be disturbed! And I'll be there in a few days!"

Christine looked to her husband, letting hope flare in her heart again. "We can rest there, hope whoever is looking for us loses the trail, and then decide where to go."

Erik's shoulders sagged in agreement. "Fine. It will be temporary, and..." Christine watched as a new flare of fear filled Erik's eyes, his gaze darting worriedly about. "You must warn them about the mask and not to ask about it."

"I will, of course," Jack said quietly. "Am I allowed to ask?"

"No," Erik almost growled, and Christine stepped between him and Jack.

"Erik. He has told you he is your friend," she chided. "He will understand."

"It's alright," Jack said with a weak smile. "Whatever injury or scars you bear, this is what has kept such a brilliant talent from taking its place among the greatest of our generation. Something beneath that mask has forced you to hide, and that seems to me a great tragedy. For music, and for you."

"I..." Erik stammered.

Christine was pleased to see him surprised by someone. It happened so rarely. "He also detests the politics and people of the musical world," Christine added, and Erik looked at her in consternation. "It's true. You're opinionated and quarrelsome."

Jack shrugged as Erik looked to him for support. "She said it, not me."

"When can we depart for Lucca?" Erik asked with a sigh. "We have a carriage outside and a driver greedy enough to take us that far."

"Let me write a few letters, and then you can go immediately," Jack said with a smile. "While you're here, look at what I have on the piano and make your quarrelsome opinions on it known. Please eat if you're hungry: there's bread and oil in the kitchen."

Christine gave Erik a nod. It was alright to indulge his friend. She wouldn't be taking the offer of food, however. All the fear and anxiety from the past hours had taken up residence in her stomach, leaving no room for hunger. At least now they had a place to go.

Was this what it had been like for Erik all his life? Moving from place to place when things went wrong? She knew his tale now, from beginning to end. He had told her on their journey to Geneva in the long hours on the train. It had felt then as if they had reached the end of that story, the happily ever after that so few found and fewer deserved.

But it hadn't ended. Their life had gone on and on. There had been good days and there had been terrible ones. Today had been both. Christine could barely comprehend that before sunset, they had marveled at the beauty of the city and reveled in possibility together. Now, they had to leave it, and even with Erik right there, she felt so alone.

# Paris

Meg was a poor detective, but in her defense, she had received little training. And she had no place to work outside of, well, work. She couldn't very well compile her findings at home, where Mother might find them. To that end, she had decided to keep her notes and anything else she found hidden at the Opéra. She had a perfect spot – an old prop room where no one went except to occasionally steal a nap on a decrepit old bed (scenery from some bygone production back at the old opera on the *Rue le Peletier*).

Meg had told her mother she needed to practice alone as her excuse for going to the Opéra so early. Now, she was tucked in a corner with her little oil lamp and the papers she hoped would help her understand something.

*Remove the following, or I shall.* Meg read the note again. She had memorized the names in red ink: *de Lancey, Goncourt, de Montier, Tremblay, Sabran.* All patrons.

Meg had never been terribly good with names. She didn't know the name of every girl in the corps de ballet. Some days, she could hardly tell them apart in their identical white tulle skirts. The same was true of the patrons. They all looked the same in their black suits, top hats, and silk cravats. Their heights, hair colors, builds, and ages varied, yes, but there was a sameness about all those men that went beyond even that of the ballerinas. They all looked at girls like Meg the same way, with the same cold calculus in their eyes. Meg had grown accustomed to ignoring them years ago.

Now she regretted that. She needed to know what Messieurs Goncourt et al had done to earn a ghost's ire. A few of them did have paramours among the dancers, as Tremblay had with Rochelle. De Montier was often seen with a pouting, aloof girl named Anastasia (a name everyone knew was a fiction), and Sabran, a garrulous older man, was smitten with a talented dancer named Hermine, who had received great prominence since Sorelli's star had begun to fade.

What of the others? Meg had circled the patrons' names on the page in her little notebook where she had copied them down. As far as she knew, nothing had happened to the remaining four after Tremblay's incident. Last night had been uneventful in the *Salon du Danse*, but Meg didn't know about outside.

Meg tucked her notebook behind a box of old helmets and blew out the oil lamp. She could see well enough to get through the mess in the near darkness, thanks to the light from the hall. She wondered how soon the gas lights would be replaced. The process of converting the Opéra had already begun with the chandelier, which glowed brighter than ever now that it had been outfitted with the new electric light. Meg hoped not too soon. The modern illumination was so harsh, and she feared it would take away some of the magic of the great building.

It felt haunted, Meg mused as she climbed the steps from the cellar up to the dance studio hidden under one of the small domes on each side of the building. It felt the same as walking in the cemetery when they went to visit Father, or when she had gone to the crypts at *Saint-Denis*. There was a weight to the air in the Opéra. It left for a while, but now, it felt heavier than ever. Maybe he was mad about the new chandelier.

"I'm afraid to walk alone now!" a voice said from inside the studio before Meg could enter. It was Sorelli herself, sounding put upon and pathetic. "I don't know if I can stand all this stress."

"So you've said." That was Jammes speaking. Meg peeked through the door at the group. They were gathered around the person Meg had hoped to catch practicing early with the other soloist – Hermine. "But this is not about you."

"Her patron was attacked just like my Philippe!" Sorelli yelped, and Meg's heart seized. There had been another attack.

"Monsieur Sabran is nothing like your Philippe," Hermine sneered. She didn't look as upset as Meg would have assumed at hearing such news. "He's half-deaf and drinks too much. He probably fell on his face and blamed it on a robber."

"I heard his arm was broken," Jammes said darkly. "And right after you said the other day you hoped he'd end up like Monsieur Tremblay and never touch you again."

"What are you implying, Cécile?" Hermine growled. "I was with Sorelli and our friends last night at her flat. You remember friends, don't you? You used to have them."

"And Jammes wouldn't know much about what some must tolerate to please a man," Sorelli added, which made Meg blush on Jammes's behalf.

Meg herself had never spoken to anyone of seeing Jammes in the arms of another woman at the masquerade months ago – but rumors had a way of spreading in the Opéra. Maybe Julianne had said something, though it occurred to Meg for the first time that Christine Daaé's former dresser had not returned to the Opéra when it reopened. Sorelli's barb set a fire in Jammes's eyes, and she spun away from the other dancer, making for the door.

Meg had no time to hide as Jammes wrenched the door open and revealed her. "What are you doing lurking out here, you little sneak? More secret business I'm not needed for?"

"I..." Meg met Sorelli's eyes over Jammes's shoulder. "I heard about poor Monsieur Sabran. I wanted to make sure Hermine wasn't too upset."

"In hopes of getting in a soloist's good graces to advance yourself?" Jammes accused.

"Cécile, calm down," Hermine chided. "Meg was just being kind. You should try it sometime."

Jammes gave them all a final huff and stormed past Meg.

"What is wrong with her lately?" Sorelli sighed. "Of all the people to be put upon, with all this violence."

"Unlike you," Hermine sighed.

"I loved Philippe," Sorelli crowed.

"And I hated Georges," Hermine countered. "What matters is that this is the second time one of our patrons has been attacked: this time, right outside the Opéra on the *Rue Auber*! Next time, it might be one of us. It might be worse than a robbery."

"So he was robbed?" Meg asked. The other women looked at her suspiciously. "I heard it was just a beating."

"Why would someone attack a rich man and not rob him?" Sorelli snorted.

"Maybe he was on someone's list," Meg said before she could stop herself. "Of enemies! I mean. Men like that – of influence, like him and Tremblay – they make enemies."

"Everyone enjoyed him," Hermine replied. "Except his wife and I and whoever came before me, I guess."

Meg was about to ask more when she heard it. A soft sound through the dark from far down the hall: laughter.

"Who was that?" Meg squeaked, spinning around to see the source of the sound. She found nothing but shadows.

"Who was what?" Sorelli asked.

"I have to go," Meg said and rushed towards where she had heard the sound. There, rounding the corner, was a shadow – she was sure of it. She saw it for only a moment but it was there. Meg sped up, pursuing the phantom but came to an empty dead end. He had disappeared, like always.

Meg knew what she had seen, though. She knew what she had heard. More importantly, another of the men on the ghost's list had been attacked. She needed to warn the others. Who knew if they were destined for a fate like Tremblay's or one like Philippe de Chagny's? Meg certainly didn't want that on her conscience.

## Lucca

E rik wished, more than anything, that he could take the mask off and feel the fresh air on his cheeks. They had been in Lucca for three days, keeping to Jack's rooms in his family's house and trying their best not to be seen until it started to drive them mad. Christine had begged him to come with her on a walk along the old walls of the city.

The walls were wide and easy to walk. Laid out in a jagged pattern, the old fortifications had once protected Lucca from enemies from the land to the east and the sea to the west. Now, as the sun set and silence stretched between him and his wife, Erik did not know if any place would ever feel safe for them again.

"Jack should be there when we get back," Erik sighed as he looked out over the darkening landscape.

"And that will make a difference for us?" Christine asked, not disguising the hopelessness in her voice.

"I hope he will have a telegram back from Tissot with answers." It wasn't safe to contact the solicitor from Lucca, so Jack had done it for them in Florence. "It might give us some idea of who is after us. Me."

He dared at last to look at Christine. Her auburn hair was half-loose, strands wafting in the evening breeze. Even now, her beauty was devastating. Such sadness and worry filled her forest eyes, and it was there because of him.

"Then what? Where will we go?"

"I don't know," Erik answered sadly.

"When we began this, it felt like the whole world was ours to explore," Christine went on listlessly. "I thought I would be able to wander with you anywhere; that as long as we had each other, it would be fine. I thought it might be like life with Father before he got sick, but, Erik..."

"It's not enough, I know," he finished for her, and the regret in her face at the truth of those words rent his heart. "You deserve a home and a life. You always have."

"We deserve that. Both of us," Christine argued. It was useless to tell her how little he agreed. "We swore vows to one another to walk this road together. Do not forget that, Erik."

Erik forced himself to nod, trying to claw back his reason and faith in her from the dark place in his mind to which it had fallen. "We could go to England, put a channel between us and the continent."

"You hate England."

"I hate the English, but I could cope," Erik muttered, but he knew that it wasn't convincing.

"America then. There's enough room there. Though the crossing would drive you mad."

"It's only a week, we would be fine if we kept to our rooms," Erik argued. Why was he arguing for a place he didn't want to go? "But then we'd be in New York."

"Another huge city where we know no one and I can't understand a word that's being said," Christine sighed. "Though I guess that would be the case anywhere. We can't go back to France. It's too close to whoever it is."

"America is a great land with great opportunities," Erik mused. "Though I have heard that the powerful are not fond of those who aren't like them. Half the country fought and died in a war so they could keep human beings enslaved. Not to mention how they've treated the Irish and Italians that have flocked there."

"It might be better than running for our lives forever," Christine countered, but her energy had flagged. "I guess there's Ireland. Your home by blood."

"Absolutely not," Erik spat, surprised at his vehemence. "We are to leave the past behind, and I have tried Ireland. There's nothing for us there, and it's the absolute opposite of a great city."

"It could be different with me," Christine tried again, and Erik found himself wincing as she went on. "Or is Ireland like Vienna? Or Venice and Prague? Another place you've seen and suffered, so I am not allowed to decide if we could try again there."

This was a familiar argument. He had left a trail of pain and enemies and destruction over Europe for decades before settling in Paris. There were few places left he hadn't been run out of or eventually run from.

"America then, I guess," Erik sighed. He hated arguing with her. It made him so afraid. Afraid he would say the wrong thing or that her rightful anger would finally make Christine realize what a mistake she had made, yoking herself to him.

"Let's get back. We'll talk more after we hear from Jack," Christine muttered, clearly seeing his acquiescence for the surrender that it was. "Maybe he knows someone who has made the journey."

"Maybe."

The idea of such a journey nagged Erik the whole way back to Jack's home. Until now, it had been a quiet little house, located near the cathedral where his family had served as music directors for generations. There were others there, of course, including Jack's widowed mother and grandmother next door, but they had left Erik and Christine entirely alone to recover and rest after their flight from Florence.

However, Erik realized as they approached: the house was no longer quiet. The windows were full of light on the bottom floor, and people teemed inside. He could hear the raucous chatter down the street, and on instinct, he froze.

"Jack must be home," Christine said reassuringly, taking Erik by the arm. "Everyone has come to greet him, it seems."

"I didn't realize he was related to the whole city," Erik muttered.

He wasn't in the mood for this. He wanted nothing more than to retreat to their room (or even better, a nice dark cellar where no one would find him) and lose himself somehow, be it in a book or a composition, or even making love to his wife for the first time in days. There was a need for her that had begun to skitter under his skin, and not merely for her body. Erik's mind had returned at the most inopportune times to what she had done the day he met Jack. How she had dominated him and how much he wanted her to do it again...

Erik shook himself from the thought as they caught sight of Jack in the sea of relatives and neighbors that had flooded his house.

"There you are! Come in, we have enough food to feed an army!" Jack called.

Erik dearly wished he were back in the Opéra with a wall to disappear behind. There was nothing he wanted to do less than mingle with strangers. He didn't have the energy right now to even find the darkest corner where he could hide so that no one would look too long at his face and discover it was a mask. He didn't want to make up lies or avoid questions. He just wanted silence.

"You can say you're ill, if you want to," Christine murmured beside him.

Of course she knew. Of course, she understood how anathema this situation was to his very nature. Even so, guilt fell on Erik's heart like an avalanche at the words. Guilt that she had known immediately what he was thinking, shame that he even had to think it, and more guilt in knowing that he had no will or power to stay. He hated to disappoint her, but she would be fine.

"I already ate, and I need a rest," Erik lied to Jack when he reached them. He didn't like the sad way Jack's face fell, but the young man couldn't possibly ask this of him. "Give your family and friends my regards."

"Of course," Jack muttered.

"You will still have me," Christine said with a smile, and that certainly brightened Jack's expression. It soured Erik's mood further when she put her arm through Jack's, and he swept her away into the festivities.

Erik became a shadow as he maneuvered through the house and up to their rooms, where he closed the door tight behind him before tearing off his suffocating mask.

He could still hear the party downstairs. Christine's sparkling laughter cut through the din and Erik imagined her smiling at Jack and all those strangers that could make her happy. Was this what it would be like for them when they found a place to settle as Christine wanted? Would he always be locked away somewhere, leaving Christine to her friends, while nature denied her a real family of her own?

Erik shook his head. They never talked about the fact that, month after month, her courses came and nothing quickened in her womb. Erik hated how grateful he was that at least he had been saved from passing on his cursed blood, but he knew how sad it made his wife. She had grown up dreaming of a family like the one she had shared so briefly with her own parents. Happy and loved, together in the sun.

Now, here they were, lost and frightened, separated in the growing dark.

C hristine felt as tired as she ever had after a performance as the celebration of Jack's return to Lucca finally began to ebb into the night. At least she had been able to practice both her Italian and some of her English. The man who had given Jack his non-traditional moniker had come with him from Florence and was named Howard. He was from Cornwall. This had delighted Christine, given Cornwall's proximity to Brittany and thus Perros. Hearing him speak the Celtic language that the two locations shared, even if she didn't understand it, sounded like a bit of home.

Howard was a student of language, and he had met Jack not in Florence, but in Milan, where Jack was set to return as a student in the fall. Howard, however, had completed his studies and was currently seeking a position "doing something somewhere pleasant that wasn't too strenuous," according to him. He had gamely translated for Christine whenever some member of Jack's circle came to greet her and feel her out. Eventually, he just answered for her when asked about her husband or if she had children and where she was bound next, and he didn't comment at all about the sadness that he surely could see growing in Christine's eyes at each question.

It was Christine and Howard who remained in the courtyard as the crickets buzzed and the stars twinkled above. Christine could see a candle burning in the room she shared with Erik, and part of her wanted nothing more than to go to him and weep for how upended and confusing everything was. Another part of her was angry at him for leaving her alone again to face questions she couldn't answer.

"Where's Jack gone?" Christine asked Howard, in French, thankful that he spoke the language.

"Oh, I saw his mother pull him off for a lecture," Howard drawled, taking a puff from a cigar. The smell reminded Christine of the balconies and salons of the Opéra. She was glad Erik was too protective of his throat to ever touch them. "I think she heard at last about Jack's assignation with a married woman. In Jack's defense, his lover is married to a horrible man."

Christine raised an eyebrow. "Was that really your business to tell me? Or do you just like being salacious?"

"The second, of course," Howard said with a devilish smile. "Though, perhaps, it's a bit of a warning. Half the people who meet Jack fall madly in love with him, and I wanted to save you any trouble."

"I'm quite in love with my own husband," Christine grumbled. Howard shrugged in an insouciant way that intrigued her. He reminded her of a friend she missed very much. "Are you among that unlucky, lovestruck number, Mr. Ashe?"

Howard took another inhale from the cigar and looked Christine over. "You're a lady of the theater – or were. I think you understand me."

"I do," Christine smiled.

"My infatuation with Jack was a passing thing," he went on with a shrug. He was fair in his coloring, almost pale, and his water-blue eyes looked nearly gray in the night. "I shall recover. Will you?"

"Recover from what?" Christine asked lightly.

"Whatever it is that has sent you fleeing here with your mysterious husband, who Jack can't stop praising as the greatest musical mind he has ever encountered. I was utterly jealous on the ride here. Yet, there seems to be some great tragedy following you."

Christine froze as rending metal and gunshots echoed in her mind. She saw blood. Broken bones and scars and snapped necks. She forced herself to breathe and focus on Howard's apologetic face.

"I can't talk about it. I should go to bed," Christine managed and stood without letting Howard see she was shaking.

"Signora Christine!" Jack's voice called before she could escape, and the young man bounded into the courtyard. "I'm so sorry we haven't had time to speak alone. I have the telegram for Erik that he was waiting for."

"I'll take it up to him," Christine declared, grabbing the missive. "We can talk in the morning."

"I'll see you then too," Howard called as Christine rushed away, paper clutched in her hand.

It was a relief to see Erik hunched over papers at the small desk by the window. He jumped up and turned to her, an expression of contrition and worry visible behind the mask he had not taken off. Because he didn't feel safe. Neither did Christine.

"I'm sorry I was..." Christine began.

"I don't begrudge you enjoying the party," Erik said immediately.

Christine wanted to argue because she had not really enjoyed anything. She had played her part and watched as an outsider as a community had come together in familiar joy. She'd listened to people joke and argue in a language she didn't know. She'd watched old women clutch Jack's face and poke his ribs and knew they were telling him he wasn't eating enough. She'd watched mothers with children hanging from their skirts gossip and help each other wrangle little ones. Men had smoked and discussed who knows what, speaking in serious tones of serious things that Christine had no chance of affecting or being a part of.

"I met Jack's English friend," Christine said instead of all of that. "You'd like him, I think. He speaks French as well as Italian, and I think he mentioned Greek. And Cornish! Have you ever heard Cornish? Of course you have."

Erik had her wrapped in his arms before the tears could escape her eyes. He knew, perhaps not the cause of the wound, but that the pain was there. He was the consolation.

"I'm sorry, I should have—"

"I can't stop thinking about everything that happened in Paris the night..." She couldn't even say it. *The night we all nearly died. The night I saved us, but not everyone. The night I chose you and the new world we would find.*

"Me too," Erik confessed against her hair, then kissed her forehead. "That and everything else."

"I chose you," Christine whispered, gripping the fabric of his shirt tight as something roiled inside her. "I married *you*. I need you with me."

"I know." Erik didn't protest as Christine removed his mask. It felt so good to kiss him. It felt right. It always had. He was the one who made everything feel distant, and for a few moments, the little world they shared felt safe.

"I love you," Christine whispered against his cheek. "I think sometimes you still forget that."

"I love you too," Erik replied, the disbelief in his voice all the confirmation of his doubt she needed.

"Undress me," Christine ordered, and Erik obeyed with no hesitation. He kissed her and touched her as he did so, taking care with her buttons and laces. She wasn't as patient with him, tearing off his shirt and trousers when it was time, then sighing as he lifted her to the bed. "Make love to me," came another command, and she wrapped her legs around him.

"My love," Erik breathed in her ear, nuzzling against her neck and kissing her racing pulse as he slid home inside her. Whatever was left of the world melted away as they began to move together, finding a slow, delicious rhythm as their desire took hold. Christine's eyes fluttered open and shut, the cracked plaster above them filling her vision and then disappearing as her mind burst with golden stars that reminded her of his eyes.

"Look at me," Christine pled, threading her fingers into her husband's dark hair. He made a sound of protest, and she knew this was one of those nights he wanted to hide from her – hide his ugliness and shame even as his body merged with hers. "Look at me," she commanded again and yanked his head up so that he had no choice.

"Christine," he moaned, eyes wide and awed. She knew him and his body, the things he liked, but didn't ask for. She knew what this hint of pain did to him. She tightened one hand in his hair, pulling hard, and he responded with his hips, increasing their speed. "More," he barely whispered.

Christine gripped his shoulder with her free hand and dug in her nails, forcing him all the while to look at her and be seen. His face was inches from hers, his sunken eyes and the collapsed nose that made him look like a corpse above her. Christine forced him closer to her and licked along the jagged scar on his cheek, then bit his earlobe. "Harder," she gasped as the ferocity of his thrusts increased.

"I'm so..." Erik protested as he drove into her. "So close."

"Not yet," Christine heard herself hiss and drove her nails deeper into his flesh. She pulled his hair again, forcing him to meet her eyes. "Not yet. Make me—"

"Yes, my love," Erik whined and grabbed her by the thighs, pushing her legs up so that he could fuck her so deeply she felt it in her bones. Christine could barely breathe with the force of it. Her body was all coiled heat and need. She felt her pleasure rising, chasing his as he served her. As he waited and obeyed.

She froze in a silent cry as the climax hit her, her eyes wide as they locked with his in a final silent command to follow. He did, careening over the cliff of their pleasure as all vision and strife and noise left her. There was no difference between them in that moment, as he poured himself into her, hot and sweet. He was hers, and she was his, and that was all that mattered.

They held each other after, cradled in one another's arms. Erik sang to her, knowing what she needed without a word now, the old Irish song he'd serenaded her with long ago. For a while, she was at peace. For a while, she was safe with him.

Until the dreams came. They were familiar now. Dreams of the Opéra, opening her mouth to sing, and no one hearing her. She tried to scream too, and no one heard her warnings as the chandelier crashed down. Bodies hung around her, and the gunshot was so loud, she felt it in her bones. She turned and saw Erik falling to the ground, a gaping wound in his chest, his heart torn into pieces because of her...

Christine gasped awake, drenched in sweat. Erik stirred beside her, gold eyes cracking open. "Are you alright?"

"No," she whispered. "And I don't know why. Why can't I forget it all?"

To his credit, Erik didn't ask what she meant. He only rose to hold her. "Living with our pain does not mean we forget it. We cannot erase our scars, only accept them."

Christine wished she knew how to do that. Erik didn't seem to know the secret either, only that it was possible, somehow.

She looked out the window and saw the first traces of dawn on the horizon, much to her relief. She didn't want to go back to sleep. She wanted to do something to move them forward at last. With a start, she remembered her last interaction with Jack.

"Jack had the message – the telegram from Tissot," Christine exclaimed, jumping from bed and wrapping herself in a blanket as she searched for the paper. She found it on the floor next to her skirt and handed it to Erik. She didn't like the frown that appeared on his mangled face. Not one bit.

"This says Tissot has been ill. He can't handle any correspondence at all." Erik looked up at her, realization dawning.

"Maybe someone went to Tissot and found out where we were from him?" Christine murmured.

"I need to go to Geneva immediately."

"We," Christine countered, her heart falling again. "We need to go to Geneva and find out what happened to Tissot."

"No, my love, I have to go alone. It will be faster, and I need you here to make arrangements."

"Arrangements? For what?"

"For passage to America," Erik countered calmly. "Jack can help, and I just—"

"Want to keep me safe because someone could be lurking there that could hurt you," Christine finished for him, annoyed at his coddling. "I can protect myself. I'm not an idiot."

"I know you're not," Erik argued. "But I also don't want to worry about you the whole time, and if anything were to happen..."

Christine frowned at his tone and expression. She, by her very presence, could endanger him because he would think only of her and not himself. She'd already been taken once and used against him; who knew if these new pursuers had similar ideas? "I hate this."

"I know. I do too," Erik sighed. "But if I can move our funds and discern what has happened with Tissot, it will make the next part so much easier."

"The part where we truly start a new life," Christine asked, that old hope kindling in her again. She wanted to believe that it would be different this time. It had to be.

"Don't be long," Christine sighed.

"Three days. That's all I need."

# 4. The Cost of Living

## Paris

Shaya never planned to find himself in the *Faubourg Saint-Germain* again so soon. He had not intended his feet to take him to the place of his great failings: when he had fallen in with the Vicomte, now Comte, who had determined to destroy Erik. Shaya had helped Raoul de Chagny and Antoine de Martiniac do terrible things, and they still weighed on him daily. Adèle Valerius had suffered the worst because of him, and the fact that Shaya had killed her abuser didn't alleviate his conscience.

The neighborhood was lovely in late summer, trees heavy with green only now showing a tinge of yellow on their leaves. The last time he had dared show his face here, they had just begun blooming. It gave him comfort to see how reliably the seasons changed here, though the thought of the deep cold that awaited in winter made a pang of homesickness for Persian heat prick his heart.

The fashionable crowds were up and about for their morning walks and visits. Shaya strolled at the same pace, watching from the corner of his eye and catching fragments of conversation. Were any of them talking about the attacks on men of their number at the Opéra? Did they know? It had not been in the papers, and Shaya would know.

He read the society papers every week, scanning them for mention of Raoul or his sister, Sabine. The de Chagny siblings were all alone with their fortune now, and they had retreated from the fashionable scene. Raoul had withdrawn the family's patronage of the National Academy of Music, understandably, and given up the family box. There was no way he would know what was going on in the Opéra now, and Shaya certainly wasn't going to tell him.

He slowed his pace as he approached the entrance of the Chagny manor. It was much as he remembered it, but somehow more austere. Any light and joy that had been in the place were gone, and the curtains were drawn in the windows, keeping out the sun. All the windows but one.

Shaya didn't falter when he saw the figure looking out onto the street from the second story of the house. He was proud of that, because what he had glimpsed might have made a less experienced detective trip or pause. But he didn't. He simply kept walking, noting to himself that there was a potential new complication in the story.

# Geneva

Erik exhaled in relief as he exited the train in Geneva. He had come to hate rail travel in recent months. He hated the noise, the shaking of the cars, and most especially, the crowds. Even with the luxury of a private compartment, there was no avoiding the hordes of people in the stations and corridors. It made his skin crawl to be so confined with his fellow man. He was exposed, always being watched, and as a creature who preferred solitude and shadows, this discomfited him in the extreme.

At least it was dark now, he told himself as he made his way through the massive, modern station, wincing at the noise of steam and steel. The last time he had arrived in Geneva, Christine had been with him, her presence a balm in the crowd. They had celebrated her birthday here, after Erik had forced them to leave the Alps. It had been a good distraction, and he had attempted to be a dutiful, doting husband who showered his wife with new dresses and gloves and whatever else she had wished for, thanks to the small fortune they had accumulated. Christine had never admonished him for keeping the money he had extorted from the Opéra, nor had she encouraged him to refuse the blood money that was his 'inheritance.'

Maybe she should have, Erik thought, finally escaping the station and stepping into the cool, Swiss night. The money felt like such a weight, even though it gave them freedom. It was complicated to have it held in a bank, to have to deal with lawyers and bankers and all this nonsense. If he had his way, he would have simply sewn the cash into some garment and kept it hidden in a trunk... Where, Christine had told him many times, it could easily be stolen or set on fire, and then where would they be?

They could be free.

Free to wander the world as God intended, on their feet with only the sky above them and the road before them. No one could drive you out of your home when your home was the entire world, Erik mused as he looked up at the starless sky.

Tissot's office wasn't far from the train station. Erik assumed it would be closed this late. That would make it easier for Erik to enter undetected, find Tissot's residence, and then go to question him. This was not, of course, strictly legal, but it didn't matter if he wasn't caught. It wasn't like he would be stealing.

It gave Erik a thrill he wasn't proud of to take stock of the offices of Tissot and Garibaldi. Locked doors were just puzzles to be solved, and he relished that none yet had defeated him. He waited until the street was empty to make his move, and he was so quick picking the lock and letting himself inside that anyone passing would think he had his own key.

Erik laughed quietly as he entered, the only sound he made as he stepped through the shadows. Last time he had been here, it had been broad daylight. It had felt so wrong to be doing business like a regular, pedestrian man with his wife beside him. This – creeping through the dark like a specter – this felt far more familiar. In some ways, he would always be a ghost.

Tissot's office wasn't locked, which was concerning, but at least convenient. More concerning was the state of the place as Erik could make out in the dim orange light from the gas lamps outside: it had been ransacked. The drawers were ajar, papers strewn on the floor, and ledger books were cast all about. The desk, however, was perfectly orderly, with piles of correspondence arranged next to a silver letter opener. The miniature knife had been carefully set parallel to the letter. Someone had found what they were looking for, and it was right here.

Erik drifted towards the desk, nervous energy thrumming in his veins. He knew who these papers concerned. As he reached for a match in his pocket to light the oil lamp, he saw the name: Gilbride. The name he had chosen to be a real man with real accounts, who could now be tracked and discovered. Erik reached for the oil lamp and froze as his fingers grazed the brass base. It was warm.

"I must say, your timing is impeccable," a voice spoke from the dark.

The man who emerged, lighting a match as he did, was painfully ordinary. He had neatly parted brown hair, a thin moustache, and keen eyes behind his spectacles.

"So, you've been waiting for me?" Erik asked, leaning forward on the desk and spreading his hands on the papers that concerned him. "It's an intrusion to read a man's mail, you know."

"Does that apply to ghosts and criminals, Erik? May I call you Erik?" the man replied politely, as he lit a gaslight on the wall.

"Only if I know what to call you." Erik held the man's gaze in a challenge. He hadn't produced a weapon, but that didn't mean he was unarmed. Erik hoped his opponent was thinking the same thing – wondering what means of death Erik had concealed beneath his long cape.

"I am Monsieur Bidaut. It is a pleasure to meet you at last."

Erik narrowed his eyes. "You were the one harassing the Baroness de Martiniac."

"Your grandmother, yes," Bidaut replied with a sigh. "It was her information that led me here, though it did take time to put together the pieces to suss you out in Florence. Where, of course, you had to cause a scene."

Erik waved a hand. "Merely self-defense. What do you want from me?" The fingers of Erik's other hand had wrapped around the hilt of the letter opener on the desk while Bidaut was distracted. It would have to do.

"Oh, I thought that would be clear. The money that should have gone to your half-brother, on which you have a dubious claim at best." Bidaut said it with a polite smile. "But which you have quite a firm legal grip on."

Erik sighed in disappointment. "Money? This is all about money – not revenge or something more interesting?"

"That I am not at liberty to divulge," Bidaut said with an amused smirk.

"How boring." Erik looked over the man. "That explains why you haven't threatened my person yet."

"Indeed. I need Erik Gilbride alive to transfer the funds we want from a very stodgy Swiss bank." Bidaut looked at his nails and shook his head. "Which you shall do at our appointment tomorrow."

"Why on earth would I do that?" Erik didn't like where this was going. There was something dangerous in Bidaut's calm demeanor.

"Because it is the easiest way to avoid harm from my associate in Italy to one Mademoiselle Christine Daaé, whom you have been claiming is your wife."

Erik's heart stopped, a hundred visions of Christine in peril racing into his mind. "Christine is no longer in Florence," Erik whispered, praying their precautions had been enough. "Your associate there won't find her."

"My friend arrived in Lucca yesterday," Bidaut replied. Erik couldn't breathe. "And located your dear Christine quickly. If you do not come to the Augsburg bank at eight o'clock tomorrow and sign over your misbegotten fortune to my employer, then I will not send the telegram telling my associate to spare your lover. They are waiting to strike at noon. Violently."

"I could kill you right now," Erik growled. "Better – I could make you bleed until you send that telegram."

"With only a letter opener?" Bidaut chuckled. "That would be impressive. I think my pistol will be faster."

Erik grimaced as the man withdrew the gun from his coat and aimed it at Erik. The man had considered everything in laying this trap, and Erik was rusty. "I will make you pay for threatening her."

"You will be the one paying, Monsieur. I look forward to doing business with you tomorrow," Bidaut said and turned his back on Erik with the confidence of a man who couldn't be struck down. If Erik tried, it could mean doom for Christine. How could he have been so stupid to leave her, thinking that was what would keep her safe?

Erik stood in the dark as Bidaut retreated, leaving him to the prison of his thoughts. No train would take him the three hundred miles back to Lucca fast enough. How could he get a telegram to Christine this late at night? Would warning her put her in more danger? How could he be sure of her safety or the threat to her either way?

Erik *could* do as he had been told, of course. He could throw away the money and the easy start at a new life it represented. They had barely touched it for the very reason that he seemed incapable of actually putting down roots anywhere that he might be forced to live as a real man and not a shadow. Life was so much harder that way.

## Lucca

C hristine was grateful to see the first light of dawn against the sky. She had not slept at all. It had been impossible to rest without Erik beside her. All night, she had told herself he would be fine, but her fear had whispered back that he was in danger. She had hoped that the light of day would return her sanity, but no; she was as afraid as before, if not more so.

She stared out the window to the hills of Tuscany to the north and prayed. She prayed for her husband's safety. She prayed he could hear her, wherever he was.

"Erik, something is wrong," she whispered to the brightening sky. "I can feel it, my angel. I wish you could hear my prayers."

Only silence and the wind answered. At least it was acceptable now to get up and dress. Christine took as long as she could, but it was still only seven o'clock when she finished. Her stomach was growling, and her eyes were heavy with exhaustion in a way that only the strongest Italian coffee could cure.

It was a relief to find that the kitchen wasn't empty, though it surprised her to see Howard there in shirtsleeves, adding fuel to the stove with a kettle already in place.

"I hope that's for coffee and that you intend to share it," Christine said.

The man turned to her with a smug smile, eyes twinkling. At least one person looked rested. "Of course, my dear Madame."

"What are you doing here?"

"I have a key," Howard replied. "I'm sorry if Jack didn't tell you. I came to berate him for abandoning me last night."

"Surely he's not awake yet," Christine laughed, seating herself at the table while Howard busied himself with the coffee grinder and set out three cups.

"Oh, he is. He probably didn't sleep at all last night. If I know my friend, he'll be slinking back from sweet Elvira's in mere moments. Ahha."

Perfectly on cue, the door that led out back from the kitchen opened to reveal Jack looking tousled and sheepish. "Both of you? Really?"

"I was just here for coffee," Christine said with a shrug.

"I'm the one here to keep an eye on things," Howard added with a wicked look. Jack hid his blush and shook his head.

"Are we meant to take you to the – *come dici*? The office for the ship?" Jack asked Howard.

"You don't both have to come," Christine muttered as Howard placed a fresh cup of coffee in front of her that smelled heavenly. "I could probably manage."

"These agents will take advantage of a lady alone, I fear," Howard said. "I have nothing else to do, and Jack doesn't want you to go. Or at least your genius husband."

"Ah, *basta*," Jack groaned. "I said I don't want him to go so far away. Your rainy little island is the most I will tolerate if they want to punish themselves with that language."

"English is the tongue of Shakespeare and Milton," Howard huffed.

"Do not listen to him, Christine," Jack interjected. "You're a singer. Tell me one great opera written for that bastard tongue! There is no music to it! It's worse than German!"

Christine burst out laughing. "I don't mind it. I've been studying it so I could read Shakespeare," she countered. "I'm sure Erik will be flattered to hear you will miss him."

"What is there in America?" Jack pushed back. "Everyone is going there! I can't understand. At least all the Italians on their way lately know each other – you will know no one."

"Perhaps it will be a good place for their careers," Howard offered.

Christine avoided answering by taking a scalding sip of coffee. She had no career anymore. Perhaps she could find a new one doing... something? Somehow, she had to fill the time, but there was only so much a woman like her would be allowed to do. She hated that she was so limited.

"What about my career?" Jack whined.

"You'll be fine," Howard sighed. "One day the muse will strike."

"The Angel of Music," Christine murmured. "My father said the angel blesses musicians with inspiration. Erik was mine."

"See? He's a gift from God," Jack argued, and Howard rolled his eyes.

"What if you go west? Jack is obsessed with all the stories of cattle thieves and train robbers in the desert out there."

"That doesn't sound too hospitable," Christine said with a grimace. She had read some of those stories, too, and other tales of the vast lands America had claimed for herself in recent years. It felt wrong to expand so violently into the wild.

"How far is the ticket office?" Christine asked. "I would like to have all this arranged as soon as possible."

"It's on the other side of town, alas," Jack replied.

"Then we should leave," Christine declared, gulping down the rest of the coffee and springing from the table, much to the shock of the men. It served them right for making her question this choice of America (as well as her entire purpose in life).

The men followed her as she made her way to the front of the house and stepped into the street. No hat or gloves, which would mark her as very unladylike, but she didn't want to search for them. Someone must have been shocked because Christine noted a female figure dart away as soon as she was outside.

"Which way?" she asked, breathing in the scent of the morning, still moist with dew.

"Right, my dear," Howard chuckled, and Christine took off down the street. She had to keep moving or the gnawing anxiety inside her would catch up to her and swallow her whole. She had to accomplish something today that was meaningful and move them in some direction, even if it wasn't the right one. She had to—

"Christine?" The female voice was not one Christine expected to hear, and she spun in shock to look at the speaker.

"Pauline?" Christine balked as the young woman embraced her, much to the chagrin of the men with her. "What are you doing here?"

"I came to see the architecture," Pauline replied with a smile as she withdrew. She was in her customary sort of dress, collar buttoned high and her little cravat tidy, but her spectacles were askew and a few wisps of brown hair had escaped from under her hat. As if she had rushed to reach Christine. "I was inspired when you said you were visiting the hill towns. I didn't expect to see you here!"

"I – we—" Christine glanced at Jack and Howard. "We decided to meet a friend here, instead."

Christine's mind raced back to her last encounter with Pauline, right before Erik had spirited them off for their beautiful tour of Florence. When Pauline's questions had become too much for her, and she had lied about leaving.

"Isn't it a lovely city?" Pauline said, looking between Christine and her male companions and clearly expecting an introduction. Christine made a decision and twined her arm with Howard's.

"It is. We have adored it. Pauline, I know you wanted to meet my husband. Your wish is granted," Christine said with a smile. She watched Pauline's face, and for a second, her smile faltered before she extended her hand.

"It is a pleasure," Pauline said. "I would say that Christine has told me so much about you, but that is unfortunately not the case. You must be Jack."

Jack extended a hand, and Pauline took it, as Christine's stomach twisted. "Indeed. Though only my friends call me that. You can call me Signore—"

"We really must be off," Christine cut in. Pauline blinked, and if Christine hadn't been an actress herself, she wouldn't have seen how she struggled for a moment to keep her mask up.

"Where are you headed? Perhaps we are going in the same direction," Pauline asked sweetly.

"I'm escorting my friends to the navigation office, much against my will," Jack replied, and Christine wanted to throttle him. "Perhaps you can convince them that America is a terrible place."

"America!" Pauline gasped. "Oh dear, that is too far! Monsieur Gilbride, you can't be serious."

"I think it will suit us," Howard said slowly, looking at Christine for some guidance.

Christine let go of Howard's arm and advanced a step toward Pauline. The woman's smile wavered again. "You're right. I never told you much about my husband. Including his name."

"Surely you did," Pauline tried to laugh. "Or yours."

"I did not tell you about Jack either," Christine replied, cool and calm. "Jack, who you could have followed here to Lucca yesterday."

Pauline made a scoffing sound that was immediately cut off by the force of Christine's fist driving into her jaw. Pauline stumbled back, gripping her face as the men gaped at Christine's show of violence.

"What on earth?" Pauline whined.

"My friends, would you be so kind as to seize this woman? I would like to have a discussion with her about who she is working for and what she wants with me and my husband."

# Paris

Meg wanted to review her notes before the large rehearsal today, but the Opéra wasn't as quiet as she had hoped. There were always people in the Opéra right at dawn: firemen on their patrols, the janitors burnishing the floors. Today, a gaggle of singers passed Meg in the halls on their way to review the score of *La Juvie*.

Meg didn't know any of them except Rose Carron, the newest leading lady, now that La Carlotta and Christine Daaé had destroyed one another. Carron was talented, surely, but she didn't burn with holy fire from within the way Daaé had. At least she was an improvement from Carlotta, whose shrieking Meg could never stand. There were other new singers since the Opéra's reopening. The mezzo who had replaced Adèle Valerius was making waves – she was rambunctious and bright but didn't have Valerius's gravitas. Carlos Fontana and Robert Rameau were still the premier men of the company, but Moncharmin kept talking about adding more artists in every voice type so more performances could be possible. Meg wondered what chaos an opera with multiple divas would beget.

Seeing Carron and thinking of Daaé brought Meg's thoughts, once again, to the night the chandelier had fallen, when it was claimed Christine had disappeared right off the stage. Meg had not seen it herself, and most assumed Daaé had merely run away in the chaos. Maybe it was because Daaé was gone that the Phantom had returned with such violence...

Meg finally made it to the prop room, her heart racing as she entered and picked her way through the old furniture and debris to the corner where she had hidden the note and her detective's journal.

The journal that was sitting on the floor, not hidden where Meg had left it.

"What are you doing there?" Meg asked, gooseflesh rising on her skin. She had been careful to put it away. And the note – where was the note!?

Meg rushed to the hiding place and riffled through – nothing. She picked up the journal and shook it. Maybe the note was in there? No, there was no trace. At least she had copied down the names. She flipped to the page she knew held the ghost's list, and her stomach dropped. The list had been torn out, and on the page beyond it, a single word was scrawled in the same blood-red ink and jagged hand that had been in the note:

*Stop.*

The ghost knew she was trying to discover his plans. Meg, for the first time in her life, not only felt seen and important: she felt as if she were in terrible danger.

## Geneva

Erik was tired down to his bones in a way he had not been for months. Not since he had terrorized the Opéra had he endured such an eventful and fraught night. Even then, there had not been so much whining from his – what to call them? Victims? Errant employees?

As if on cue, the man next to him groaned. Erik rolled his eyes.

"You're being rather dramatic," Erik sighed. "Your hand will feel fine in a few days."

"Yes, Monsieur," the man whimpered. Erik had no patience for his misery. How was he to have known the little solicitor had bones the consistency of toast? Erik checked his watch for the tenth time in as many minutes and exhaled in relief. At last.

"Now. Go. Do as you've been told and you will never hear from or see me again," Erik told Martin (he had not bothered to remember the Christian name of Tissot's associate).

"Yes. I understand," the little man said, nodding so hard his body shook. He made a move to leave and Erik grabbed him, pulling him close with one hand while raising his mask with the other. The man yelped.

"I hope you do, because I do not make threats lightly," Erik growled before pushing the man away. He rushed down the street, fully in view as he entered the bank. Once he was out of sight, Erik tried to breathe. Now for his part.

He adjusted his bearded, cumbersome mask, the sweat on his brow causing the papier mâché to scratch horribly against his skin. He hated this thing. He hated that he felt people looking at him as he crossed slowly to the bank, keeping his hat low and his collar high. He hated everything about this, from the fear for Christine in his heart to the ache of violence in his hands, to the itch for death in his blood. If something happened to her, there would be no end to the carnage. He swore it.

The sight of Bidaut waiting at the appointed spot, genially regarding the morning traffic and crowds in front of the Augsburg bank, only made Erik angrier. He wanted to have his hands around that neck, but he could do nothing until the telegram was sent.

Bidaut noticed him quickly and had the audacity to give a polite smile as Erik approached.

"Ah, you were almost late," Bidaut said. "Shall we?"

"Are you in such a rush to take everything I have?" Erik asked, as cool and cruel as he could manage. "Surely, you've waited this long; a few questions won't ruin your schedule."

"I wouldn't stall long if I were you, Erik," Bidaut said with a shrug. "My associate has a strict deadline."

"Is your man on orders to simply kill Christine in broad daylight?" Erik asked back, hating the images that filled his mind.

"You would know how easy it is to eliminate someone before those around them can even guess there is an assailant close," Bidaut shrugged. "A sharp knife, a passerby on the street who bumps into a lone woman. Accidents happen."

"She is not alone, you know. I wouldn't leave her unprotected," Erik countered. All night he had gone over the locks on Jack's house and the many people in the residence. Jack himself wouldn't let harm come to Christine if he could manage it. "This could all be a trick."

"You know in your heart it's not," Bidaut said plainly. "It's just money, anyway. Money you don't need or, let us be honest, deserve."

"What do you know about what I deserve?" Erik drawled. He didn't like this conversation, but he wanted to keep it going as long as he possibly could. If he could glean some clues from Bidaut, all the better.

"Don't you think it's a bit uncouth to use an inheritance from a father you killed, that you kept from a brother whose life you ended," Bidaut asked as if he was discussing the weather.

Erik was grateful for the mask now because it hid any shock that might have shown on his face. So, this man thought he knew the circumstances of the death of Alfred and Antoine de Martiniac. Very few people were aware of Erik's involvement in his father's death, and even fewer knew for sure that Antoine was dead. No one but Erik, Christine, and Shaya knew it was Antoine who had killed their father, and that Antoine's body now rested in Erik's makeshift grave below the Opéra.

"Who told you that fascinating story, Monsieur Bidaut?" Erik replied, his mind filled with the hateful face of the one noble who had any chance at spreading such a story, but if de Chagny was aware of Erik's continued survival, he would have been employing much blunter methods. He certainly wouldn't care about the money. "It's quite outlandish, I must say."

"Antoine had, if not friends, those invested in his financial affairs, whom he kept apprised of certain matters. That is all you need to know." Bidaut was smart, not giving Erik any confirmation either way. "Now, I think we can stop stalling."

"Why? This is such a fascinating conversation," Erik quipped, but Bidaut laid a hand on his side, above where his pistol rested. The threat was clear, and Erik could only hope that he had given poor Monsieur Martin enough time. "Lead on then."

Erik walked slowly behind Bidaut into the cavernous front hall of the bank, where they waited. He watched as Bidaut scanned the quiet lobby, taking stock of the men behind their brass bars opening up for the day, looking for someone specific...

"Is your accomplice sleeping in?" Erik asked, but it didn't rattle the other man – assassin or paid detective, Erik was unsure of what to call him. Just in time, a harried-looking banker with a white beard appeared at the back of the lobby and waved to Bidaut. His bald head was shining with sweat, and he was out of breath, which Erik hoped indicated the sort of morning he was having.

"Good day, Monsieur Bidaut," the man said in French, with a slight German accent. "And is this Monsieur Gilbride as promised?"

"Yes, Herr Knopf," Bidaut replied. Knopf looked terrified as he surveyed Erik. He didn't attempt to make himself look natural under Knopf's gaze and fixed him with his more withering stare.

"Yes. I'm here, as promised," Erik hissed.

"The paperwork is all ready," Knopf said in a quavering voice. Erik and Bidaut followed the quivering man into the back of the bank, past accountants and clerks beginning their days amid quiet conversation. The place smelled of metal and paper – money. Erik detested it.

Knopf's private office was small, and a desk with papers was set out already and prepared for them.

"This should be quick and simple, but you are free to read over the transfer paperwork, Monsieur," Bidaut said.

"Oh, I trust everything has been done correctly," Erik said casually, but made sure to fix Knopf with one more long look as he spoke. The man went even paler under his sodden beard. "Forgive me. I should take this off to make sure you know everything is above board."

Knopf gave a cry and looked like he might faint when Erik removed the mask. Sometimes the fear and horror his face evoked was worth it, Erik thought. So too was the relief of fresh air against his skin. He turned to Bidaut, who didn't seem shocked at all by his visage.

"Please sign," Bidaut said, indicating the papers.

Erik did make a cursory read of the contract as he took up the quill and dipped it into the inkwell. All his assets held by the Augsburg bank were to be transferred to the care of a separate bank, where only the account number was listed. How very mysterious.

Erik marked the page without hesitation, though it was still odd to sign his full name. He imagined Christine's face upon discovering that they had gone from having the means to go anywhere and do anything to having nothing. Would she still want him if that were the case? He hoped not to find out.

"There, easy," Bidaut said cheerfully. "Herr Knopf, would you summon someone to send a telegram for me?"

"Yes, Monsieur," Knopf said and rushed from the office. Erik replaced his mask before looking back at Bidaut. He was holding out a telegram for Erik to examine.

"As promised," Bidaut said as Erik took the paper. The message was short, in French: All is well. Go Home.

"This will ensure your agent in Lucca won't harm my wife?" Erik asked, just as calmly as Bidaut. The other man nodded as Knopf returned with a young man in tow. Erik watched, holding his breath as Bidaut handed the boy the form and money to send the telegram.

"We need never see one another again," Bidaut declared. "Our business is done. I bid you good day, gentlemen."

Erik wanted to follow as Bidaut left, but he knew it would be suspicious.

"And my accounts are closed?" Erik asked lightly of Knopf when they were alone. The man nodded vigorously.

"Yes, good Monsieur, exactly as Monsieur Martin explained they were to be."

Erik let out a sigh of relief. "Is London the farthest institution that could be reached?"

Knopf nodded vehemently. "And the safest. Monsieur, all of this is so irregular, I would ask that—"

"Don't worry, I'm leaving."

Erik was quick about it, moving through the lobby, where he finally saw Martin cowering in a corner. Erik met his eye, to which Martin responded with an indication of *left*. Erik nodded in thanks, and the man bolted. He went, Erik noted when he exited, as fast as he could to the right. Erik went left, and soon enough, he saw Bidaut's brown bowler hat moving down the streets.

Once again, Erik was a ghost. He slipped like a shadow through the crowds behind the man who thought he could beat him, following down streets and alongside the river through the heart of

Geneva. It became clear where they were going: the other bank that was supposed to soon receive Erik's money... Had he not already sent it elsewhere, thanks to Martin. It would be a while before Bidaut discovered the truth: he would be bleeding too profusely.

Erik was quick about it, rushing through the narrow back alleys and even scaling a building that got in his way. He arrived just ahead of Bidaut as the man rounded the final corner, and Erik made his move. Bidaut didn't see Erik coming, not until it was too late and the blade was in between his ribs. The man gave a soft grunt as Erik seized his arm and looked him in the eye.

"What was it you were saying about random collisions on the street?" Erik whispered. The man seemed to be trying to talk through the pain. "Please try not to die. That would be terribly inconvenient and break a promise to my wife. Though I also made a promise to you, and I'm a man of my word. I couldn't have you well enough to send another telegram or make any more trouble."

"I won't be the one to make the trouble," Bidaut gurgled, something mad in his eyes that sent a chill down Erik's back. "She will. She'll take any excuse to hurt your whore."

Erik twisted the knife in Bidaut's side, and the man grimaced. "And you thought I couldn't accomplish anything with a letter opener."

Erik encountered no resistance as he hauled Bidaut from the street (it looked as if he was guiding a friend to talk in an alley). He walked him further and further back until Erik pushed the man against a wall.

"Maybe I shouldn't let you live," Erik whispered and gripped Bidaut by the throat. For the first time, Bidaut looked afraid, and it was intoxicating. Erik squeezed, watching the fear spike even as the man struggled for air. He saw so many other faces as he kept choking: the boy's. His brother's. That villager in the Alps who had barely passed childhood.

Christine's.

Erik let Bidaut go as soon as consciousness left him, allowing him to fall in a heap on the ground, the silver hilt of the letter opener still protruding from his side. He'd be fine. Probably. Erik didn't have time to worry. He had a train to catch.

# 5. Imposters

## Lucca

Christine had never kidnapped anyone, so she was unsure if what she was doing to Pauline counted. It was rather thrilling to have someone under her control, but it was also terrifying. What was she supposed to *do* with the person who had chased them down to the ends of the earth?

"This seems rather excessive," Jack whispered nervously, glancing at Pauline's restrained form in a chair from the corner where he and Christine were conferring. "My family will have questions if they walk into the kitchen and see a woman tied to a chair."

"Then keep them out," Christine snapped.

"For how long?"

"Until Erik returns," Christine declared.

"What can Erik do that you can't?" Jack asked uneasily.

Christine gulped. The old Erik would not have paused in hurting this woman for information, but Christine had to believe he was different now. Though he had not been different when fighting with those men in Florence. He had been brutal, and Christine hated to think that they needed that brutality. "He's more versed in these things," she answered tightly.

"In tying up strange women and extracting confessions from them?" Jack looked extremely worried. Christine was, again, left to wonder how much he regretted making their acquaintance.

"What do you think I should do instead? Call the police?"

"The police here only care about what they are paid to care about, and you can't afford the debt it would entail to put her in jail, even for a night," Jack said with a grimace. "I don't even know what you'd tell them—"

"That wouldn't get me arrested first," Christine finished with a sigh.

"You could just talk to me."

They turned to look at where Pauline waited, bound to a kitchen chair with Howard glowering behind her. She looked distressingly pleased to have their attention.

"I may have some insights for you. You seem overwhelmed by all this, my friend," Pauline went on.

"You're not my friend," Christine replied, stalking towards the smaller woman.

"No, I wasn't." Pauline shrugged. "But you were so easy to turn into mine."

Christine squinted at Pauline. All her softness and warmth were gone, so different now than when Christine had first encountered her. "You helped me when that man was harassing me."

"I paid him, yes," Pauline replied proudly, "And then became all a lonely, gullible girl who once believed in fairy tales and ghosts could want in a friend."

"Ghosts?" Jack echoed. Howard also looked perplexed.

"Oh. They don't know your whole story, do they?" Pauline said with a wicked grin that made Christine queasy. "Gentlemen, are you aware you're harboring the wife of a dangerous criminal?"

"He is not dangerous," Christine snapped, more to Howard and Jack than to Pauline. She couldn't risk losing the only allies she had left.

"Such a naïve fool, sweet Christine," Pauline sighed. "When I began to study you, I almost admired you. Such an independent woman, so talented, able to bewitch such an unparalleled beast. Then you tossed it all away."

"I made my own choice," Christine protested. She hated this. Hated how it felt like all her mistakes had suddenly turned into a thing of flesh made only to mock her.

"Have you heard her sing, gentlemen?" Pauline went on, ignoring Christine in a way that made her feel utterly powerless. "I saw her in Paris, at her last performance, no less. She was brilliant. Truly brought the house down. To think such a voice will never be heard again except by a murdering monster."

"You know nothing about my husband or me," Christine seethed, her cheeks burning as she avoided Howard and Jack's eyes.

"I know everything about him. And you," Pauline smirked. "I have made myself an authority on all the secrets you tried to leave behind at the Palais Garnier – where your dear Erik spent years terrorizing people."

"What is she talking about?" Howard asked. Christine stared at the man who had been so quick to help her, unable to explain why she and Erik were being hunted.

"We simply want to live our lives in peace," Christine whispered, panic rising along with her memories.

"Peace? After he brought down that chandelier?" Pauline scoffed.

"The chandelier that fell during the performance in Paris?" Jack asked, face paling in horror. Christine couldn't meet his eyes.

"That's enough," Christine ordered, but it sounded like begging.

Pauline continued to smile. "You don't want them to know about the monster you married and all the awful things you've done?" she asked, nodding towards the men who had foolishly helped Christine. "Have you seen the creature yet, young sirs? I've only heard stories, but I'm amazed she can keep her stomach when he takes her."

"Careful, Signora," Howard warned. "You're talking about our friends."

"They are killers," Pauline whispered, holding Christine's gaze as she did. "They ran from France to escape their crimes. I am only on their trail to exact justice."

"You have been misinformed," Christine hissed. "I have made mistakes, but I'm not—"

"Don't waste your excuses," Pauline sneered.

"Who told you all this?" Christine asked, trying to keep calm as her heart pounded. She couldn't look at Howard or Jack. She didn't want to see them judge her. Is this what Erik felt like when he was unmasked? "Tell me why you've done all this."

"Our services have been procured on behalf of the estate of one Antoine de Martiniac," Pauline replied lightly. "You do recall your husband's last victim?"

Christine did recall – vividly. She heard the shot that ended Antoine's life over and over in her nightmares. But it hadn't been Erik that killed him, and Antoine, rapist and killer himself, had deserved his fate. Of that, Christine was certain, and that certainty gave her strength.

"Then you have been lied to," Christine exhaled. "It's you who serves a monster. Or the ghost of one."

"Keep telling yourself that."

"You said *our* and *we*. You work with whoever it was harassing the baroness," Christine went on, trying to steady herself. "That was months ago."

"We did lose you for a while after that," Pauline sighed. "But a recent uptick in correspondence from Paris changed our fortunes. The delay allowed us to learn about you and Monsieur Gilbride.

Such an interesting choice – his mother's name. Rare in France, but so common in Ireland. Especially around – what was her backwater village called? Coolaney - that's right."

"You will not involve any more innocent people in this," Christine growled, and Pauline laughed.

"Like the sweet family of dear Jack here? Or whoever this useless lout is?" Pauline nodded backward towards Howard. "Mark my words, gentlemen, this strumpet and her phantom aren't your friends. They are using you like they've used all the others they've hurt and discarded. I wonder, Christine, did Erik offer you to them as payment for their help? I'm sure you're quite the obliging whore since you can't—"

Christine's slap echoed through the room, leaving a red welt on Pauline's pale cheek. "How dare you?" she breathed, shaking in anger and shame at what she had done. What she was. What Jack and Howard would see her and Erik as now.

"So, the angel has a spine," Pauline muttered. "I still don't know what your Erik sees in you. What sort of caring wife doesn't even ask after her husband when he's in danger?"

Christine launched herself at Pauline, only to be caught by Howard.

"Madame Gilbride, a word," Howard admonished. He was strong for his size, and Christine couldn't resist as he guided her away from the woman she very much wanted to strangle. "Jack, *guardala.*"

"*Felicemente,*" Jack replied, stepping in front of Pauline with a frown. "See. Not useless."

Howard hauled her out of the kitchen, letting her go once the door was shut. They were in the bright summer sun in the courtyard now, and Christine had never felt so exposed. Everything she had tried to hide and run from for months had found her. Jack and Howard were going to believe Pauline because half of what she had said was true, and the rest was so easy to believe after all she had done...

"I'm sorry," Christine whispered to Howard and the sky. She was sorry for everything, but it didn't matter.

"Take a breath. She's upsetting you on purpose, Christine," Howard said, calm and soothing in a way that shocked her. "She wants you off guard so you'll let her go."

"She wants you to turn on me," Christine argued, shaking her head. "What she said about Erik and me... I'm not..."

"I know," Howard said simply, and the storm in Christine's heart suddenly subsided.

"What?"

"I said I know," Howard repeated with a lopsided smile. "You're not the monster she says."

Christine stared into his pale eyes, her panic receding. "You barely know me. You've never even met Erik."

"Christine, the first night I met you, I knew I could trust you with a confession I've made to very few friends," Howard said, taking her hand. It was remarkable how much the simple contact grounded her, as did the sincerity in Howard's eyes. "Men like me must be careful, as I'm sure you know. I have a sense of who I can trust – who I can tell is kind. I trusted you because my heart said to, and I was right to do so. I can only assume a man like your husband who has charmed you and Jack, is just as remarkable. I don't see why the ravings of an obsessed lunatic who has been hired by some other villain to pursue you should change that."

Christine sniffled, noticing the tears on her cheeks for the first time. "I've been so afraid to be found out."

"I can understand that too," Howard replied with a shrug. "But you must ask yourself: who are you? Are you the version of Christine that she wants you to be? The one she can hurt and manipulate? Or are you more?"

Christine felt like some restraint on her soul that she hadn't known was there had suddenly been released. A weight lifted as Howard smiled at her. "I know who I am. You're right."

"Good girl." Howard squeezed her hand. "Let's deal with this harpy. Have you any ideas other than slapping her again? I don't think that will make her talk, despite how satisfying it might feel."

Christine laughed weakly and shook her head. "I guess we will keep her here until Erik comes back. I can't make this sort of decision without him. I don't want to endanger you or Jack though. I'm sorry to involve either of you."

"We are helping you because your goodness is clear," Howard replied with a reassuring squeeze of Christine's hand. "I also don't want to see your life destroyed before I can hear this music of your husband's. It's made Jack brave enough to get involved, so it must be quite impressive."

"He'll be delighted to share, I'm sure. Until then, is there a cellar here?"

"Where else would they keep the wine?" Howard asked back with a wink.

The scene was unchanged when they entered, save for Jack sporting a deeper frown.

"Have you talked her out of her hysterics?" Pauline purred as she caught Christine's eye.

"Help me with her," Christine ordered Jack and wrench Pauline up by the arm, holding her tight enough to smart. At least she could make her hurt as they dragged her to the door down to the cellar. God, Erik wasn't supposed to be back until tomorrow – did she need to find this creature a bucket? Food? How was she to eat if she was bound?

"Having second thoughts, Christine?" Pauline asked. "You look ill."

"I'll make you look worse if you keep talking," Christine spat back. Her captive only laughed as they shoved her into the dark.

"You would know about monstrous looks, wouldn't you, dear?" Pauline called as they shut the door on her.

Christine leaned against it once it was locked, sighing and looking at Jack. "I need to get tickets as soon as possible for New York."

# Paris

"**I** need to talk to someone," Meg blurted out as she and Rochelle left rehearsals. Blanche and Marie were ahead of them, talking amongst themselves, and Meg had seized the opportunity to confess to her friend.

"You seem quite capable of that," Rochelle replied, cool and calm as ever.

"About the—" Meg lowered her voice, "the ghost."

"Are you still on about that?" Rochelle laughed. "Do you think he handled Sabran like he did my dear Tremblay? Again, we should be grateful."

"I do think that, and I think there's more to this," Meg countered.

"Then go talk to them," Rochelle said, nodding at Blanche and Marie.

"I don't want to endanger them and you—" Meg gulped as Rochelle gave her a withering look. "I need help in this from someone strong," Meg countered. "Someone else who has seen him and knows he's... more."

"I saw a shadow, Meg." But Rochelle looked dubious, and she had stopped walking, allowing Meg to draw her into a quiet corner. "But I guess this is more interesting than gossip about who will be cast in the new productions."

"Do you remember the note I showed you? That I took from my mother?" Meg asked, her heart beginning to speed up. "Sabran was on it, and he was assaulted just like Tremblay."

"Yes, that was curious," Rochelle muttered.

"I hid the note in a prop room, and it was taken," Meg hissed. "The ghost wrote to tell me to stop!"

"And why haven't you?!" Rochelle squawked. "Dear lord, Meg. Two grown men far stronger than you have been seriously hurt. If the ghost has warned you to stop interfering, you should listen."

"It doesn't feel right!" Meg protested. "I need to know what's happening and why now. I need to talk to someone who knows more than me."

"That's a long list," Rochelle sighed. "Why not ask your mother? She's his box keeper."

"She'd only scold me," Meg sighed. "Do you think Jammes might know more than she lets on?"

"Why Jammes?" Rochelle asked. "Because she's been even more horrid since we reopened?"

"She was close friends with Julianne Bonet – and she was Christine's dresser."

"Then talk to her, you ninny."

"She quit, don't you remember?" Meg said. "No one has seen her since the night the chandelier fell. If she were around, she'd be my first interview."

"I didn't realize she was gone," Rochelle muttered, and Meg glared at her. "Oh, don't be dramatic, costumers come and go as fast as choristers. Though now that you mention it, I heard a rumor about her – she was seen talking to the Persian. So was Jammes, I think. Why not talk to him?"

"The Persian?" Meg echoed. Everyone knew of the strange foreign man who came and went throughout the Opéra. He had not been seen backstage for a while, but he had a new box, which had been a topic of gossip for a brief period. Monsieur Gabriel had even seen the ghost and the Persian talking together in the hall once.

"Mademoiselle Giry!" Meg nearly jumped out of her skin at the sound of her name in such a deep voice. "I was hoping to find you. Good day, Mademoiselle Moreau."

It was d'Amboise, the patron who had told them about Tremblay. His hair was slick against his head, and Meg could smell the cologne wafting off him in waves.

"Why were you hoping to find me?" Meg asked, blunt and bored.

"To invite you to dinner after the next performance. I have learned that no patron has ever taken you out," he said with a wicked smile.

"Meg is not available for dinner," Rochelle said, placing a protective arm around Meg. "She's fifteen."

"What does that have to do with anything?" Meg asked as Rochelle unceremoniously hauled her off.

"But Monsieur Goncourt would like to meet you too!" d'Amboise called, and that made Meg's stomach drop even more as Rochelle rushed them down the hall, away from the flummoxed patron.

"Goncourt was on the list!" Meg whispered to Rochelle. "I could warn them!"

"It's not worth the risk," Rochelle answered with a dark glare. "Trust me. If the ghost is going after patrons, it's best to stay away."

"Is that all?" Meg dared to ask. She remembered the night the light had gone from Rochelle's eyes. She had hoped it would begin to return now that Tremblay was gone, but there was no such luck.

"You're naive, Meg, and a fool. Keep out of all of this," Rochelle said flatly.

"But the ghost—"

"Maybe it's not him," Rochelle shrugged. "Spirits move on, don't they? Maybe something else took his place."

# Lucca

E rik made no attempt at subtlety getting off the train. His mind was on fire with worry and rage, in no small part thanks to the letters retrieved from Tissot's desk that he had finally been able to read. Thank heaven he had more important things to do than rush back to Paris and rip apart whoever it was using his name to some mysterious ends at the Opéra. One fool at a time, he told himself as he ran from the station and through the darkening streets of the city. What if he had taken too long? What if he was too late and Christine...

No, he couldn't think like that. He would feel it, Erik told himself, if something horrible had happened to her. He had always believed in the unseen world, in spirit and magic, if only as a comfort in his darkest hour. What he shared with his Christine felt like that – a connection that went beyond mere love to something transcendent. She could feel him when he watched her, and he knew in his soul that if harm came to her, he would feel it too.

That was what he told himself over and over as he rushed to Jack's house, his lungs burning with the effort, each stride on the cobblestones shaking his teeth. He had to be in time. There was the door, and there was light in the upper windows of the house. There was no crowd looking over a bloody body, no commotion. That was a good sign.

Erik burst into the courtyard, and the trio sitting there sprang up in surprise. Erik didn't care who the other man was beside Jack. All that mattered was Christine standing there, whole and healthy, as she rushed to him.

He embraced her fiercely, kissing her to make sure she was real and feel her breath. She knit her hands in his hair, knocking off his hat, and Erik thought he might weep. He had made it.

"What are you doing here so soon?" Christine demanded as she pulled away. She looked pale and worried, and her eyes were rimmed with red.

"It was a trap. There was a man in Geneva, he—" Erik didn't even know where to start. "Someone was sent here to hurt you! Have you seen—"

"I know," Christine cut in, gripping his arms.

"You know?"

"I caught her. It was Pauline. She's in the cellar." There was a tone of embarrassment in Christine's voice. "I know I shouldn't have taken her, well, captive, but it all happened so fast and—"

"Did she hurt you?"

Christine shook her head, bemused. "You seem to know more about this than I do. Could you do me the favor of explaining?"

"Yes, I'm sorry," Erik replied and finally became aware of the two men staring at them. "I hate that I've involved you in this mess, Jack, truly. And?"

The other man held out his hand with a kind smile. "Howard. I'm a great admirer of your wife's fortitude and your melodic prowess. Jack has played me some of the songs you've helped him with."

"And that made you willing to help my wife take a would-be assassin captive?" Erik replied dubiously. He did shake Howard's hand, though he was glad he had gloves. He still detested touching strangers.

"Well, I signed up to help her get tickets to America, but this was far more entertaining," Howard replied with a shrug. "Though I really haven't been much help."

"You've been essential," Christine replied with a smile to the man that almost made Erik jealous before she turned back to him with utter devotion in her eyes, curdling Erik's envy to guilt.

"I'm glad you weren't alone," Erik forced himself to say. "I went to Tissot's office in Geneva, and there was a man there, Bidaut. The same one who—"

"Accosted your grandmother," Christine finished for him, much to his surprise. "They were waiting, watching and studying us."

Erik sighed. "Finding us in Florence was all part of a scheme that I walked straight into. Bidaut accosted me and..."

Christine looked at him gently as Erik paused, the fear he had held back in those moments finally hitting him and gripping his heart. "Erik, what happened?"

"He informed me that he knew where you were – exactly – and that he had an accomplice who was ready to kill you or at least harm you horribly if I didn't comply with him." Erik gave a bitter laugh. "Once again, it was all about the bloody money. The inheritance. He wanted me to sign it over to whoever was employing him."

Christine's eyes widened, and Erik could practically see the progression of thoughts through her mind as she imagined their life and plans (pathetic as they were currently) crumbling in her hand. "Did you do as he asked?"

"Not entirely," Erik replied, shame spiking in him again. How had he ever considered it? "I dragged one of Tissot's clerks out of bed and forced him to help me move the funds before Bidaut could have me sign them over. We only just barely made it, and only because our adversary didn't think I would ask for help."

"Hauling a poor man from his bed to perform some arcane accounting for you is hardly asking for help," Christine chided.

"How much money is this all about?" Howard asked lightly.

"Enough that I don't feel entirely secure telling you the number," Erik muttered back before returning his attention to Christine. "The money is safe, but Bidaut will find out eventually that he was tricked. So I—"

Erik wanted to crawl out of his skin remembering the violence he had done. He had promised her that was behind him, and he could see in her eyes already that she knew he had betrayed that vow.

Christine glanced at the men beside him, her face grim. "*Is he alive?*" she asked in Swedish, for it was not the sort of thing one said in polite company.

"*Yes,*" Erik replied in the same tongue. "*Hurt enough to slow down.*"

Christine looked at him with a mix of emotion Erik couldn't read, though it didn't stop his shame from winding up from his gut like a living thing to choke him and whisper in his ear that it was all over. It had all been for nothing, and now Christine would see the mistake she had made.

"Pauline was outside waiting for me this morning and accosted us," Christine said instead, stepping back and gesturing to Howard and Jack. Erik didn't like the new space between them, but he deserved it. "She knew Jack's name and yours. She followed him here."

"I'm sorry, my friend," Jack added. "I didn't know that this was all so dramatic."

"How could you have?" Erik shook his head, focus still on Christine. "So you took her captive in Jack's cellar?"

"We questioned her in the kitchen," Christine countered. "It went poorly. She knows all sorts of things about us. We couldn't go to the police, so we just kept her here."

"And you want me to find out what's behind all of this?" Erik asked grimly. He felt the ghost of heat on his palm; the memory of gripping Bidaut's neck, like he had so many others.

"No," Christine said, firm and calm. "If anyone gets to hurt her, it will be me, but I don't think that will get us much of anywhere."

"What you need to do is get somewhere safe, where they can't follow," Jack said.

"How to do that has been the subject of debate for much of the day," Howard added, with a wry smile that made Erik entirely too suspicious. "Now we have a plan."

"You will need to trust me," Christine said softly.

"I trust you more than anyone," Erik replied. "Myself most of all."

# Paris

Shaya crumpled the paper and threw it into the fire. It was stupid to try to write to Erik again, especially with only the barest of conjecture. He had to confirm his suspicions before he made more trouble. Anyway, there was no knowing if the letter could even reach Erik or where the man was.

"Your tea is cold," Darius chided as he came to stand over Shaya's desk. "Shall I make you more?"

"I can make it myself."

"Can you? In twenty years, I think I've seen you boil water three times," Darius teased. "I don't think you even know where the tea is."

"I know my own kitchen," Shaya scoffed, and Darius raised an eyebrow.

"Your pension may pay for it, but it's my kitchen, and I will make the tea."

Shaya opened his mouth to spout another useless argument, but a knock at his door stopped him. A rather frantic knock at that. "Make it strong," Shaya muttered to Darius.

Shaya opened the door to reveal Armand Moncharmin looking pale and clammy. Not an entirely unexpected sight, given the circumstances lately, but still a worrying one.

"I'll make extra," Darius said before disappearing into the kitchen.

"What's going on?" Shaya asked as he let Armand inside. The man's answer came in a piece of paper he pulled from his pocket.

"Someone has taken up our old friend's manner of correspondence." Armand thrust the letter against Shaya's chest before flopping into a chair by the fireplace.

Shaya looked down at the ghost's note. For that was what it was... Yet it wasn't. The handwriting was jagged and the ink was red, just as Erik's old notes had been, but it was not exactly his old friend's hand. The contents were even curiouser.

*My earlier note has been ignored, so I write again with my warning. Remove the following patrons from the positions, or there will be severe consequences for them.*

*De Lancey. Goncourt. De Montier. D'Amboise.*

There was no signature.

"This isn't Erik," Shaya muttered.

"I know, but it's something or someone making trouble," Armand sighed. "And hurting people. These men are next!"

"Can't you just warn them not to walk alone at night?" Shaya knew the futility of that suggestion the moment it left his mouth, and Armand gave him a withering look. Men like these didn't take such warnings seriously. "Can you just do as you've been asked?"

"Those men represent tens of thousands of francs of funding for the Opéra that we desperately need right now. Things are bad, my friend. I can't just cut them off!" Armand whimpered. "Though they are all rather odious."

"Who could be doing this?" Shaya wondered aloud. "Everyone who knows Erik's secret knows that you know it."

"I'm sure that sentence made sense to you."

Shaya scowled. "Whoever is doing this knows that the opera ghost is a fiction, one that can be adopted by another, as it seemingly has been."

"None of this makes sense," Armand sighed. "You're the only one who has any idea how to go about this. I can't bloody well tell the police. They barely let the incident with Comte Philippe go, and I can't have them snooping in the cellars."

Shaya closed his eyes at the words, darkness falling in his heart. It was a sin to take a life, and yet he felt so little remorse for killing Antoine de Martiniac, and that troubled him.

"What about the correspondence being ignored? Have you received other notes?"

"You think I wouldn't have told you if that were the case?" Armand scoffed. "I came as soon as this reached me."

"How did it reach you?" Shaya pressed. Erik had sent his notes through box five's concierge, Madame Giry, or when he was feeling especially dramatic, just left them on the manager's desk.

"It came in the mail," Armand replied simply, blinking at Shaya.

"In the mail? That's far from ghostly," Shaya scoffed. "In fact, perhaps this character is not trying to be a ghost at all. The attacks have happened outside of the Opéra."

"So what do we do?" Armand asked, just as Darius returned with two fresh cups of tea.

"Well, we have four names and two of us," Shaya said and received an incensed look from Darius as the words left his mouth. "Three, I mean."

"I can ask Robert for help, perhaps... then we might follow all four of these men after the next performance and see if someone comes for them?" Armand looked green at the idea, but Shaya nodded.

"Until then, I will do some exploring," Shaya sighed. "Though I must admit, I won't be happy to be back in those cellars."

## Lucca

Christine took a deep breath as she braced herself on the door. She could do this. Erik was here – though he had brought more complications than solutions. That was a fight for a different time: they had a prisoner to deal with now.

"Are you sure?" Erik asked softly as he arrived beside her, eyes wide and worried behind his plain mask. Christine nodded.

"It's the only way." She'd had this discussion with herself several times in the last hour and was almost convinced. She hoped he was.

"Then let us begin." Erik opened the door to the cellar and charged down into the dark. Christine rushed after him, her heart already pounding.

"Erik, wait!" she cried as he rounded the corner to where they had left Pauline.

The chair was empty, which was very much not part of the plan.

"Where..." Erik began, casting about as a figure moved behind him.

"There!" Christine yelled. Erik spun fast as lightning, catching Pauline by the wrist as she launched herself at him and forcing her to drop the broken wine bottle she had been wielding like a knife.

"Would killing me really do you any good?" Erik sneered, twisting Pauline's arm back painfully. "Your firm wouldn't like the mess."

"I had to take the chance," Pauline laughed, then gasped as Erik increased the pressure. She didn't seem to be in pain though. In fact, she looked rapturous. "I almost had you. Disappointing. I expected more from a phantom."

"Well, I don't want to fail to meet any more expectations," Erik replied, voice low and deadly. He caught Pauline's other hand easily as she swung at him, then in an instant, he twisted her around, trapping her wrists behind her so she was facing Christine. "My dear wife, would you hand me that cord Pauline here left on the ground? I'll make sure it's tight this time."

Christine didn't let her eyes leave the two of them as she knelt to comply. When Pauline finally winced as Erik forced her to move, Christine knew she should have worried about the state of her husband's soul, but she only felt satisfaction.

"We want you to tell us who employed you and Monsieur Bidaut," Christine demanded, her voice unsteady as she handed Erik the frayed rope that Pauline had somehow escaped from. Pauline only stared at Christine defiantly as Erik forced her back into her chair and bound her tightly and viciously.

"My wife asked you a question, Mademoiselle – what was your surname, by the way? Is Pauline your real name at all?"

"Topilina," Pauline said, her voice taking on an interesting lilt as she said the name.

"Interesting," Erik muttered. "Now, my wife's question."

Pauline sneered at Christine as Erik loomed behind her like a great raven ready to strike. "You calling her your wife doesn't make her any less of a failure," Pauline spat, looking Christine up and down with pure disgust. "Just like forcing some poor priest to mutter magic words won't erase what she's done."

"I was hoping you'd say something provocative," Erik sighed, and in a flash of movement, he had a second length of cord around Pauline's neck.

"Erik!" Christine screamed, watching as the woman struggled fruitlessly to breathe, her face turning red and her eyes bulging with terror. "You can't kill her!"

"Why not? I killed Bidaut. Probably," Erik replied lazily as horror filled Pauline's face at the words, and spittle dripped from her mouth. "This ties up a loose end. Pun intended. We throw her in the river, and we'll be done with this."

"Then they'll just send someone else!" Christine cried, tears stinging her eyes.

Erik gave a dramatic sigh and let the dark-haired woman go. Pauline took a gasping breath and looked up at Erik with a terrible, hungry smile. "That's more like it."

"We'll let you go if you go back to whoever sent you and tell them to leave us alone!" Christine begged. "This money isn't worth your people suffering or dying. Please, let us live our lives in peace."

"My employers don't care about that, you idealistic little fool," Pauline laughed hoarsely. "They don't care about your love or whatever fictions you concoct to sleep at night. After this, they'll be even more determined. There's nowhere you can go where we won't find you."

"Well, if that's the case," Erik said, coming around in front of Pauline at last and leaning in close. "I would like to know who would hunt me in such a way, so I can eliminate them."

"No!" Christine screamed and grabbed Erik by the shoulder, hauling him back out of the cellar while Pauline cackled behind them. "Erik, we can't do this!"

"We can't leave loose ends, you have to understand that!" Erik shot back, echoing off the stone wall. "Not if we want to start fresh."

"Did you not hear her?" Christine replied, equally fiercely. "She practically promised that they will follow us to New York! Killing her will only make it worse and – dear God, you said things were different now!"

"Things will be different the moment we get on the ship, I swear."

"Erik, please! Let me try to reason with her one more time before you..." Christine couldn't even get out the words. Erik sighed in something like disgust.

"We have to be on the way to Naples by dawn. I will give you an hour," Erik rumbled. Erik huffed and disappeared back into the dark, to where Jack and Howard hopefully waited to do their part. Christine rushed back down the stairs. She had to be quick about this.

"So the dog is back in his cage, and you've come to try and sway me?" Pauline mocked as Christine returned to the little circle of light she sat in, cast by an old oil lamp. "But sway me to what? To change my heart? For you?"

"I thought we could be friends once," Christine countered. "You were kind. You made me feel so much less alone."

"Because you were a fool then and you're a fool now if you think I'm going to tell you who I work for out of the goodness of my heart."

"I don't care who you work for. I care that you live and leave us alone. And you'll do that if I let you go," Christine stated, and for once, Pauline looked shocked. "I don't want another death on my hands or his."

"So you admit what you've done?" Pauline asked carefully.

"We did not kill Antoine, if that's what you're asking." Christine braced herself at the way the memory of his body hitting the floor still made her sick. How his corpse became a falling chandelier in her mind. "But we... He has done things and is capable of horror. So, I'm saving your life and we are leaving this damn continent."

"You think an ocean will be enough to keep you from the past?" Pauline spat as Christine approached.

"I'm going to let you out, and you're going to run out of here. Erik and the others are busy with our things. You have to go quickly," Christine ordered as she stepped behind Pauline and began untying Erik's tight knots around her wrists. "Please."

"You think I'll care that you saved me," Pauline asked, fascinated and cold.

"I want to think you have a soul capable of compassion," Christine replied and meant it. Even so, she was not surprised when Pauline sprang up the moment the bindings were loose and struck Christine hard in the face with the chair as she pushed it back. She added a vicious kick straight to her stomach that took the wind out of Christine's lungs.

"You're more of an idiot than I thought," Pauline chuckled.

Christine shut her eyes tight and braced herself for another blow, but it didn't come. Instead, she heard the sound of Pauline's steps retreating up the stairs. Christine held her breath, scant as it was, and listened to the distant sound of a door slamming. Then nothing.

She waited in silence, her jaw smarting where the chair had struck her and her guts aching. She was glad her corset protected her somewhat, but it was still a chore to move. Luckily, a shadow appeared and helped her.

Erik was there, right where he said he would be, helping her to stand.

"Are you alright?" Erik asked, touching her face gingerly. She could see the concern in his shining eyes, and it warmed her heart. It made her feel cared for and seen as only he could.

"Do you think it worked?"

"She ran out into the street, like we hoped," Erik replied. "And she saw the tickets on the table in the kitchen, in case she didn't hear our destination."

"She heard it," Christine sighed. "She wouldn't have left me in one piece if she didn't know where to find me again."

"You hardly seem in one piece."

"I've had worse," Christine replied with a shrug. "Or maybe it's you who's supposed to say that."

"I'd encourage you to get some rest, but I don't think either of us will be able to sleep tonight." Erik still pulled her into his arms, and Christine melted into them. Part of her wanted to recoil; it recalled the violence he had unleashed on Pauline with fear and disgust, even knowing it had been a ruse. What he'd done to Bidaut hadn't been, but that was the price they paid, wasn't it?

"We'll sleep on the train," Christine murmured against his chest. "It will be a long journey."

"I love you," Erik whispered in her ear, somehow knowing she needed to hear it. "I love you, and I'm sorry for all of this. I truly am. I'm sorry we can't go to America now."

"It was too far, anyway," Christine replied, and let another dream wither in her heart.

## Paris

S haya meandered through the Tuileries as dawn broke, mired in indecision. He had promised Armand he would look about at the Opéra, but he had a nagging instinct that his suspicions about the de Chagny manor were more important. How this new phantom and the secrets that the family kept were related, Shaya had no idea, but he knew there was a connection.

For the hundredth time, he wished he could speak to Erik about it.

Shaya slumped onto a bench between two manicured trees and tossed the last of his breakfast roll to a horde of waiting pigeons. They were all over the gardens, outnumbered only by the crows who roosted there at night, close to the cool air of the river.

Shaya cast his eyes to the trees just in time to see a murder of birds explode from the branches in a great cawing cloud. Something must have disturbed them. Yes – there. A figure was standing by a tree trunk in the shade... looking at Shaya.

Another man would have thought nothing of it. Another man would have assumed this other was merely out for a walk, the same as Shaya, enjoying the last gasps of summer before the trees shed their golden leaves and left the gardens like a museum of skeletons.

But Shaya wasn't another man. He had been raised among spies and treachery; he had spent years in the secret police, observing the Persian court and years after that tracking a ghost. He knew when he was being watched.

The hair rose on the back of Shaya's neck as he regarded the spy across the park. Shaya couldn't make out any details except that he was a man of average height and build. Had he noticed Shaya watching him back? He hoped not.

Shaya rose, making sure to look casual and calm as he wandered out of the gardens to the *Rue de la Paix*. The streets were quiet and uncrowded this time of day, with only a few shop owners and waiters outside sweeping steps and cleaning tables before the workday began. Shaya made it to the *Place de Vendôme* before pausing, making a show of looking up at the triumphal column Napoleon had erected in the square. His gaze followed the spiraling line of figures on the green bronze as they ascended, telling the story of old battles.

Or that's what he made it look like. In truth, his focus was on his peripheral vision, taking stock of anyone who might follow him into the square. It took a moment, but he wasn't disappointed. The same figure from the Tuileries entered the square, his gaze falling on Shaya before retreating to a newsstand.

Shaya walked nonchalantly from the square, checking his reflection in windows along the avenue as he meandered. He didn't catch sight of the other man until he reached the Opéra and went left on the *Rue Scribe*. Perhaps the man knew where Shaya was headed, for he drew closer, to see which entrance Shaya made for. It wasn't a simple thing to enter the Opéra alone when one wasn't a patron or employee. The backstage entrance at the rear of the building on the *Boulevard Haussman* had an imposing gate, but the guard there knew Shaya – and had been paid well by him before.

So did the clerks by the door, who opened it for Shaya. He smiled at them in clear view of the glass-paneled door because he wanted the spy to see. He wanted whoever was following him to know he was in the Opéra and nowhere else.

The dark figure waited across the *Boulevard Haussmann*, watching the door. Shaya watched him in return. He waited, observing from a hidden corner for a quarter of an hour, then made his move. It was thanks to Erik that he knew one of the secret ways out of the Opéra – the stables. The groom was asleep in a stall when Shaya shuffled by, and soon enough, he was back on the *Rue Scribe*. Soon enough, he found his pursuer, seated in a door frame, watching the Opéra.

Now it was Shaya's turn to watch. The man looked bored, and after ten minutes, he took a notebook out of his pocket and jotted something down, exactly as Shaya would. What Shaya wouldn't have done was leave his post so quickly, but this one was young. His gait was easy and spry as he headed away from the Opéra down the *Rue Auber* and towards the *Saint-Lazare* train station. Thankfully, the man didn't enter the crowded station but turned right and towards the shops at the new *Galeries Lafayette*. He went beyond that too, with Shaya trailing all the while until he turned down a small street and entered a nondescript building. Offices of some kind.

Shaya wondered if he should wait to see what kind of building this was or come back some other time. His impatience won out, but he was careful about it. He waited for another man to walk along the street and then followed a little beside him, only glancing at the names on the plaques by the door before moving on. One look was all he needed.

Pomeroy and Associates: private detectives.

# 6. In Plain Sight

## Genoa

E rik could barely make out the port from the window of their room. There were a few boats moored at the docks – flimsy wooden things meant for fishing or pleasure – and they seemed like toys in comparison to the great steel hull of the steamship waiting in her berth. Even though it was past midnight, men were at work loading the holds with goods to be transported along with the throng of people that would board in the morning. Most of them were bound for America. But not them.

Because of what Erik had brought upon them, they would disembark in Dover, England, and fumble their way onward from there. He didn't like the idea. He resented that they had to sail through the Mediterranean for days to avoid setting foot in France. He detested that he still couldn't sleep, even next to his wife. He didn't like any of this. He hated it. And he hated himself for bringing it all upon them.

She doesn't deserve this, a voice whispered in his ear.

A breeze rose off the sea, heavy with the scent of salt, cool against his bare face as he stared out into the night. He had loved the sea when he first saw it as a child when he had thought it meant adventure. Now it was a mystery, like everything else.

"Why are you awake?"

Erik turned to look at Christine, propped up on her elbow in the bed. The watery moonlight cast the room in shades of black and blue, making her skin look ghostly pale where it peaked out from her white chemise. Pale as a ghost.

"Bad dream," Erik answered. "I remembered the horrors of English food."

"As if you'd remember to eat without me," Christine smiled in reply. "What is it, really?"

Erik braced himself. He didn't want to say it, but he couldn't lie to her. Maybe confessing his sins would help. Maybe if she knew the depth of his shame, she would forgive him.

"I shouldn't have acted so rashly," Erik confessed, shoulders sagging under the weight of his guilt. "Hurting Bidaut. Going to Geneva at all. I went too far with Pauline."

"It was part of the plan," Christine consoled him, voice gentle as night. "We had to convince her, and I wanted to see her hurt."

Erik dared to move to the bed, kneeling on the floor so he could look up into Christine's pensive face. "It's normal to want to hurt the people who hurt us. That betray us."

"It's normal, but it's not good," Christine countered. "You were right to trick Bidaut, to save us, but not to give in to that violence."

"I'm sorry," Erik repeated as if it would matter. A fresh pang of shame bloomed in his chest. He didn't deserve the kindness in her eyes, and soon, she'd realize that. "I can never say it enough."

"Erik," Christine whispered, placing her hand against his bare cheek. "I forgive you. That is the promise I made to you because I love you."

"I don't deserve forgiveness," Erik said before he could stop himself. "At least, I don't feel like I deserve it tonight."

"Would you rather I punish you?" Christine scoffed, but it made something strange prickle under Erik's skin as he bowed his head.

"Sometimes, I think I would," he confessed in the barest whisper, his mind drifting back to the last time they had made love and the way she had yanked his hair and clawed his skin. How the pain he deserved had become pleasure and peace.

"What are you talking about?" Christine asked, voice tense.

"Things feel better, sometimes, when you..." Erik began, unsure of how to articulate this. "When you're in control. When you give me what I deserve."

"What you think you deserve, you mean," Christine finished for him, clearly aghast, sitting up in the bed and boxing him in between her legs as she took his hands. "I don't want to hurt you. You've already been hurt enough in your life."

"That's..." Erik dared to look up at her, imagining his ruined face in the moonlight. Did he look contrite or horrific? Or both? "That's what makes it better. To feel pain or to be bound by you. Somehow, it makes the past hurt less. It makes me feel safe to be controlled and—"

"Punished." Christine finished for him, soft, but not disgusted. Her eyes were unreadable as she looked down on him from high above him. "You don't..."

"Please," Erik begged, dropping his head to kiss the hem of her chemise and then the cool skin of her calf. "Please, let me serve you. Give me my penance. Make me your dog and teach me to be gentle, after all I've done."

"I don't know how," Christine breathed back as Erik laid his forehead upon her foot. He could feel her trembling. Or was it him?

"Command me. Please."

He held his breath, eyes closed as his shame and need warred within him. He needed her to do this; dear God, he needed it or he would tear himself apart.

"Get up. Now." Christine's voice was entirely changed – husky, confident, and unquestionable. Erik scrambled to obey, standing before her in the watery blue moonlight. "Take off your trousers."

Erik was quick to comply, once again, exposing his fully naked body to her eyes and the chilly air of the night. Christine looked at him with hooded, lustful eyes as he did. She drew off her chemise in turn, exposing the ivory contours of her body to his eyes. Round breasts and hips, soft belly, and the thatch of hair below it. Utter perfection before his eyes, in perfect contrast to his scarred, ruined flesh. He couldn't help but reach for her.

Christine slapped away his hand.

"I didn't command that," she chided. Erik's pulse quickened and his blood began to move in one specific direction. Christine smirked as she looked him over. "Does that make you hard? To be reprimanded like an errant boy?"

"It does."

Christine's eyes darkened further as she advanced on him until she was an inch away. She lightly tapped his cheek with her open palm. It wasn't a slap. It was a test. Or a warning. "I didn't say you could speak, either."

Erik nearly groaned at the word, but he bit his lip and nodded in turn. He would obey.

Christine leaned towards him, her cheek against his, her breath jagged against his ear as she exhaled. "I will stop if you say to stop."

Erik nodded again. He understood.

Christine nuzzled against his neck, dropping gentle kisses along his collarbone, lulling him into a haze. Before she bit. Her teeth sank into the meat of his shoulder, not hard enough to break the skin, but hard enough to hurt. The pain was brief, but it hit Erik like the first swig of liquor, deliciously clouding his mind.

Again, soft kisses, and another bite on his bicep. Then along his chest, before she grabbed him and held him close as she sucked a brutal mark right above his heart. Erik was fully hard now, his cock pressed between them and leaking for her. It was hard to stay standing as she kept up the random patterns of pecks and then pain, but she was holding him, her elegant nails driving deep into his skin and that was bliss too. His hips moved of their own accord, seeking the relief of friction for the organ trapped between them.

This time, the slap was real.

Erik blinked at his mistress, his cheek smarting and his head spinning. Her expression was one of delight and power like he had rarely seen, yet it was amazing. He almost wilted as she seized him again and clamped her teeth on one nipple, sucking and worrying it with her teeth so that he had no idea what to feel. She pinched the other between her fingers, twisting it and sending electric pulses of sensation all through him.

"Oh, God, that's so good," he whimpered.

This time, the slap left him reeling, the pain and punishment hitting him like a beautiful wave come to drown him. He fell to his knees, unable to stand, and Christine grabbed him by his long hair, hauling him to where she wanted him to be as she tumbled back on the bed.

"Serve me," she ordered and pressed his face between her thighs. With delirious joy, he obeyed.

She tasted like honey and spice. She was wet and hot against his tongue and lips, quivering with desire for him – for this – as he devoured her. She tugged his hair hard and steered him exactly where she wanted him as he licked and sucked.

"Fuck, yes, there! Use your hands. Fill me up," Christine panted above him. Erik did as he was told, penetrating her with three fingers that slipped so easily inside as she writhed, thighs clenching upon his shoulder. His cock was so hard and untouched that it ached, but the pain melded with the delight of her pulling hard on his hair and then driving her nails into his neck. God, he might come from this. Just from the ecstasy of being hers. Giving her his submission and penance.

She came with a long moan, her body freezing and then convulsing with the orgasm as Erik looked up from his place between her thighs. Nothing had ever been more beautiful. He would crawl over hot coals and broken glass to be with her if she commanded it. He would suffer however she would let him.

"On the bed," Christine gasped when she released him and Erik scrambled to comply. She straddled him the moment he was prone, drawing his arms above him and to the brass frame of their rented bed. She guided his fingers around the smooth metal, looking down at him from within the curtain of her falling hair. "Do not let go. If you do, you won't come tonight. And do not come until I command it."

Erik bit back a protest and tightened his grip. His brain was a fog of need, his body singing at every touch Christine gifted him with, from her nails raking down his chest and legs to the hungry kisses and nips at his thighs and then her mouth engulfed his cock.

He groaned and gripped the bedframe so tight he was sure he'd bend it, but he didn't let go. He wasn't allowed to let go and... Dear God, what else was he not allowed to do? He couldn't think. He couldn't do anything but submit as she swallowed him down. Her tongue and teeth were perfection, her lips and throat, everything. He was going to explode or die or...

"Not. Yet." She grasped the base of his cock hard, holding back the peak of his pleasure. Erik nearly screamed in frustrated need, but he didn't let go and he didn't come. He wouldn't disappoint her again. He would be good. For her, he could be good.

"I love the way you taste," Christine whispered, licking the entire length of him as she played idly with his balls, squeezing just hard enough to make him shudder on the edge of agony. "Do you know what I love more? Seeing you like this. Watching you work so hard to do as you've been told. It's so beautiful, Erik."

He shut his eyes, but the tears still came. He wanted to beg her to stop saying such lies or to hurt him again. He should let go to show her that she was wrong. He was shameful, cruel, and impertinent...

"Can you hold on for me a bit longer, my love?" Her voice broke through his spiraling thoughts like a song. "Can you obey me?"

Erik nodded so hard it shook his whole body.

"I knew you could," Christine purred. "Now open your eyes and watch me."

Erik forced himself to look, his muscles screaming and his heart pounding. Christine loomed above him, gently caressing his cock, and then...

"Don't look away, my love, watch me take you in. See how we fit. See how you fill me." Christine stifled a gasp as she lowered herself onto Erik's length, and he watched himself disappear inside her.

It felt like heaven, like absolute paradise, to be sheathed within her. It was torture too, for she moved so slowly, tense and tight around him. She gave him everything and yet kept him at bay, holding back his peak. God, how he loved her, but how wrong and broken he felt to be subsumed by such a divine creature...

"Don't go to that place," she commanded, somehow reading the shame in his heart. "Look at me and see the one who loves you. Who chose you. Who chooses you still."

Erik gave a strangled, guttural sound of assent. He wanted to move; to let go of the bed, grab her by the hips, and fuck her so hard the walls shook. He was so close he could barely see, but he still obeyed. He stared up at her perfection as she rode him, steady and smooth, and he held back. It was so hard, but he held back.

"There, yes, you're so good for me," Christine whimpered, speeding up her hips. Did she truly enjoy this – to rule him and see him at her mercy? If she did, even a bit, that made it worth this agony on the precipice of joy. "Erik, you are good. You're mine and you're good."

He couldn't breathe or even make a sound but he could hold back. He could obey.

"Come for me," Christine cooed, and Erik shattered.

The climax took away everything. All thought and guilt and pain. There was nothing but light and pleasure, pulse after pulse, as he poured himself into her. Into the goddess of ecstasy above him as she joined him in the perfect, quiet place. He was forgiven and absolved, his pain and obedience transmuted to absolution. He was whole and safe, thanks to her.

He didn't know how long the pleasure held him and was barely aware of Christine prying his fingers from the bed frame and returning his aching arms to his side. She was there beside him, mopping his body and brow with a cloth, to clear away the sweat and tears and seed before she kissed him.

She kissed him and he let himself love it. He let himself deserve it and savor it because he had done as she said. He had been good and he could do it again, all for her. His arms smarted with scratches and stiffness as he wrapped them around her, but the echoes of pain weren't shameful anymore, or frightening. They reminded him of exactly who he was: hers.

## Paris

M eg knew she was being stupid, but that didn't stop boys, so why should it stop her? Every instinct told her she should not be in the Opéra cellars, and yet, as she descended the stairs into the cool, quiet dark, she couldn't help but feel excitement. She had always been sweet and accommodating; always did what Mother or the other dancers told her to do. She was a good student because she never argued with her ballet instructors or tried to get too much attention. Now she had an order from the ghost himself to stop.

Meg would be expected to go along with all of that, but she wasn't. Whether it was spite or rebellion or idiocy fueling her, she didn't know and didn't care. She was making her own choice for once, and it was thrilling.

"You can do this, Meg Giry," she whispered as she made her way through the dim maze of set pieces and backdrops. Some were old, taken from the previous National Opera House on the *Rue le Pelletier* before it burned down, and the collection gave the curious experience of walking from a painted forest to a Turkish seraglio to a crumbling castle in a few steps. If Meg had not been so nervous, she would have been fascinated.

"I know you're around here somewhere, steps," Meg muttered. This was the third cellar though and Meg was determined to reach the fifth.

A shadow moved, far down the long corridor of sets, and Meg nearly screamed. Somehow, she kept her feet moving towards where the figure had gone. It had been far too big to be anything but a person... or a ghost. Meg drew up onto her toes, using every muscle in her dancer's body to be silent as she turned the corner to follow the shadow – only to crash into a very solid male form.

Meg screamed and the man jumped back in as much terror as she. Looking at him stole the sound from her throat and she stared up in awe. It was the Persian.

"What are you doing down here?!" Meg demanded, clenching her fists in what had to be the least intimidating display the man had ever seen. "Are you working with him again?"

"What?" The foreigner looked utterly confused.

"I will call a fireman!" Meg squeaked, though she wasn't entirely sure how she would do that. "Or the management!"

"I'm here with personal permission from Monsieur Moncharmin," the Persian sighed. "I assure you, young lady, there is nothing for you to fear from me."

"So it's just a coincidence you're here now that the ghost has returned?" Meg demanded then covered her mouth. She'd said too much.

The man looked at her curiously. Now that Meg was really looking at him, he didn't match the image of 'the Persian' she had in her head. He had copper skin, and a beard, and wore a grey fur cap that came to a peak – all marking him as different from most men at the Opéra. But he was also different in that his eyes were keen and kind, and there was something in his demeanor that made Meg think he respected her, at least as a young woman.

"What are you doing down here, Mademoiselle?" he asked, almost amused. "Not looking for ghosts, I hope."

"If I am, it's none of your business," Meg declared, hoping to sound haughty, but only coming across as guilty.

"Then we have something in common," the Persian replied with an incongruous smile.

Meg frowned at him. "You're looking for him too? I thought—"

"I have great knowledge of the Opera Ghost, this is true, and it has been my mission in the past to make sure the Opéra was safe. I have undertaken that mission again," the Persian said. "Imagine my surprise to see the daughter of the Ghost's box keeper wandering the cellars looking for something."

"She's not his box keeper anymore," Meg exclaimed and wanted to kick herself. Why did she keep talking?

"Yes, I heard that box five was being sold again."

"It's not a very good seat, to be honest, so it's still empty," Meg muttered.

"Does she still get notes from him? Is that why you're here?"

For once, Meg held her tongue. "Why should I tell you? Or believe you're on a mission for the management?"

"You're right to be cautious. Let me start again," the Persian said before giving Meg a small bow. "My name is Shaya Motlagh, former Daroga to the Shah of Persia. That means I was a policeman and detective in the palace."

"A detective?" Meg echoed, fascinated.

"And you are Meg Giry, whom the ghost had promoted to leader of her row as a favor to your mother for her loyal service," the Persian – no, Monsieur Motlagh – went on. "I promise, Mademoiselle Giry, that you can trust me. If you know anything about the incidents lately, I need to know. More people may be in danger."

To Meg's shock, the man pulled a note from his pocket and showed it to Meg. "*My earlier note...*" Meg muttered as she read.

"Do you know about this?" Monsieur Motlagh asked, voice cutting through the rush of blood to Meg's ears.

"My mother," Meg replied softly. "She received at least one note and I took it. She didn't want to bring it to Monsieur Moncharmin."

"Why?"

"I don't know, sir," Meg replied, looking at her worn-out shoes but still feeling Motlagh staring.

"But you have a suspicion."

Meg took a deep breath. He truly was a detective, to be able to read her so well. "I think she knows this is different. The notes are different, I'm sure, and these attacks on the patrons–"

"Are entirely new. Yes," Motlagh muttered.

Meg squinted up at him. "What about the Comte de Chagny and the disappearance of Antoine de Martiniac?"

"The ghost wasn't behind those," Motlagh replied with surety that gave Meg a chill. How did he know? "You're a smart girl, though, to think of that."

"Thank you," Meg said, fully earnest. No one had ever given her such a compliment. "I wanted to find out more about the note I stole – borrowed, I mean – from my mother. I was trying to suss out what these patrons had in common, but then it was taken. Replaced with a note to me telling me to stop."

"And you came down here in defiance of that?" Motlagh chuckled.

"Not very smart, I know," Meg sighed.

"Perhaps not, but it was brave."

This made Meg stand up a little straighter. "Did you find anything?"

"No. His door is sealed and closed like it's supposed to be," Motlagh said as if it made sense.

"His door? To where? Hell?"

Meg wasn't sure she liked that the man laughed at that, but his laugh was warm and comforting in such a dark place. "It's complicated."

"I'm smart and brave, like you said. I can handle complicated," Meg declared, raising her chin proudly.

"There are some secrets that are not mine to tell," Motlagh said in turn, though he sounded regretful. "But perhaps, if you earn my trust, I will tell you what I can. I would need, well, a favor from you first."

"I'll do it – whatever it is," Meg said so fast she was embarrassed.

"Excellent," Motlagh smiled, perhaps impressed. "Meet me at the back of the Opéra tomorrow after rehearsal. Which you are late for right now."

"Damnit," Meg said under her breath. "Are you saying that so that I'll go away and you can look around without me interfering?"

"I also truly don't want you to be late."

Meg looked the man over one more time, then gave a dramatic sigh. "Fine. I will meet you tomorrow."

"If you figure it out on your own, I'll be impressed," Motlagh said, mysterious and polite at the same time.

"Figure out what?"

"Why a ghost would need a door. Or a salary. Or write notes."

With that, the Persian turned and left Meg alone, disappearing behind another set piece like a ghost himself.

Meg wondered absently what she looked like as she turned and rushed away through the cellars and up to the studios, praying she, indeed, wasn't late. Motlagh couldn't possibly mean what he had implied. The mystery of the ghost could not be so simple and yet so bizarre...

What about Red Death, though? That thought kept coming back to her. Everyone had believed Red Death was the ghost come to punish them all, then the woman in black had danced with him like he was a man. Meg would never forget the captivating sight of Red Death and his Dark Lady. The woman who had convinced them all that their macabre guest had been a man, not a ghost.

Unless they had all been right. Unless the ghost needed doors and money and boxes and obedience because he had never been a ghost at all.

## The Adriatic

Christine had not been on a ship in a very long time, and her body objected to it. Her seat on the promenade was relatively comfortable, and the fresh air out here eased her stomach, as did looking out at the ocean so she could see the way they moved with the waves. She dreaded going back to her and Erik's little room with its small window, where the rocking would feel so much worse.

Maybe there was another reason she didn't want to face him. It had been so strange to board a ship and talk about luggage and complain about the food after the night before. The things she had said and done...

Her cheeks heated to think about it, which she hoped at least made her look a little less green. She had never been shy about the pleasure Erik gave her. The way he made her abandon herself carnally had always amazed and enticed her to him. She had commanded him before – the first time she had made him come she'd bound him, as payment in kind for how he had restrained her when she had believed he was an angel. He had deserved that, she'd told herself, just as last night he had claimed to deserve what she had done to him.

But how had she done it? How was she able to bring herself to strike him? To mark him with her mouth so forcefully that he was covered in red bruises today. They had been vivid against the scars on his pale skin, marks of other violence that Christine had added to because he had begged her for penance. She didn't understand, and worse, she didn't know why the thought of it – of her fearsome ghost kneeling or bound beneath her – made her insides quiver and warmth bloom between her thighs. Why did that power bring her peace? Last night she had slept untroubled by nightmares for the first time in weeks...

"Still getting your sea legs?"

Christine nearly fell out of her deck chair at the sound of Howard's voice, barely saving herself from humiliation by gripping the handles as she looked up at her new friend.

"Didn't mean to alarm you," Howard said with a smirk that would have been irritating on anyone else. "Are you alright?"

"Not remotely," Christine replied with a forced smile. "But life goes on."

"It does." Howard took the deck chair beside her and handed her a glass of something.

"I don't think a drink will make me feel better," Christine lamented. The beige color of the liquid didn't look appealing.

"It's mainly ginger. I have the stewards make it for me when I sail. Helps the seasickness. I could tell you were suffering earlier." Howard gave an encouraging smile and Christine took a careful sip of the concoction. It was spicy and effervescent and settled her stomach immediately.

"Thank you. You didn't have to," Christine said before downing another draught. "You didn't have to do any of this – or accompany us to London."

"Of course I did. You're the most fascinating people I've met in an age," Howard replied with the wry humor he always seemed to exude. "Jack might murder me if I let you go, and one day, I hope you will tell me your full story."

"You wouldn't believe most of it." Christine sighed.

"Oh, don't be so sure. I've met many interesting people. Including myself!"

Christine chuckled. "You are quite charming."

"I know," Howard grinned. "Though, you have told your husband that you're not my flavor, haven't you? He seems the jealous type. Some men don't like finding that out either."

"I have, and Erik would never mind that." Christine smiled, recalling Erik's many adventures. "He likes your flavor as well as mine, if you understand me, but I shan't be sharing him."

"As I said: the most fascinating people I've met in ages," Howard murmured. Christine took another sip of his potion, rather pleased with herself. "You'd be a sensation in London, you know, if you wanted to be. There's a whole underbelly of the city full of fascinating people with unconventional stories and preferences. Your husband's talent alone—"

"Would attract more attention than we need right now."

"Perhaps," Howard shrugged. "Anything is possible, I like to think. You two can decide who to be and what to do. What do you want your future to be?"

Christine's nausea returned. She'd been asking herself that for months, trying to produce an answer that was more than 'be with Erik wherever life took them' because that wasn't an answer at all. That wasn't a life.

"I don't know," Christine confessed softly. "I spent my life training to be a singer. I achieved all my dreams faster than I ever could have hoped, but they didn't make me happy. They made me miserable."

"Dreams can be like that," Howard replied, and he looked wistful. "I had plans that were made for me and that I made for myself, and all of them have either failed me or disappointed me since I finished my studies. So here I am now, assisting fugitives on the run from murderous spies."

"We're not fugitives," Christine scowled. "At least, I don't think so."

"It delights me that you have to ask," Howard grinned. "But back to my question. What do you want to do or be, if you can be anything? And don't say happy. Everyone wants to be happy. I want specifics. What do you like to do?"

How dare he ask such a question in such a way that made Christine feel so unmoored.

"I like to... learn," Christine offered uneasily, for it was true. "I like to play and sing, even if it's not for a crowd. I used to like to help people when they were hurt."

"That's something!" Howard grinned. "Though, it sounds awfully messy and exhausting. I was hoping you'd say something like painting. I knew a few painters."

"As if I'd even be able to converse," Christine lamented.

"Well then, let's focus on the first thing and get you another lesson in English. Right now. We won't even have to go inside."

Christine appreciated the distraction, as well as the lesson. English was easier for her than learning Italian, because it was so different, though parts of it were miserable, with its muddy vowels and nonsensical rules. At least she didn't have to remember if a chair was male or female in that tongue.

She returned back to their cabin once the sun began to set and the sea breeze had picked up. Her stomach was still uneasy, and so were her nerves, but it still was a relief to enter the cabin where Erik waited, looking out to the sunset with a book open in his lap.

"Where did you even find something to read? I don't remember packing that one," Christine chuckled when he looked at her with the sweetest of smiles. It might have been because she was carrying food, but she liked to think she had some part in bringing him such joy.

"I borrowed it from... somewhere," Erik replied innocently. "I'll be sure to give it back."

"If you can remember where you stole it from," Christine sighed. "I shouldn't give you dinner as punishment."

"I can think of better ways to keep me in check," Erik smirked, eyes sparkling behind his mask.

Christine had never blushed so fiercely in her life. She couldn't even look at him with such ideas in her mind. She busied herself with the food instead, setting out the bread, cheese, and meat on the little desk in their cabin. "I... Never mind."

"I didn't mean to scandalize you, Madame."

Christine jumped because, of course, Erik had materialized right behind her. He laughed warmly at her shock, peering into her face as she attempted to glare at him. "I'm not scandalized. I'm simply confused about..." Christine swallowed, her mouth going dry as she tried to name what had happened.

"What I needed last night?" Erik asked softly, and Christine was unable to look away. Even so, she didn't want to do this with his mask on. Gentle as ever, she lifted it from his face and set it aside.

There was her husband, the man she loved with all his flaws and failings. The man she wanted to protect and heal.

"I don't understand why you would want me to hurt you," Christine said at last. "After all you've been through – all that pain – why would you need more?"

Erik's golden eyes were thoughtful, but not scared or ashamed. "I'm not certain myself, but pain is different when it comes with pleasure from you. It feels liberating. Safe in its own strange way."

"Safe," Christine echoed, thinking back to how Erik had been the night before. A calm that had overtaken him in his desperation to obey and repent to her that had been beautiful and intoxicating. "I made you feel that way."

"How did you feel?" Erik asked, touching her cheek and pushing back her hair in that soothing, entrancing way of his.

"I felt powerful," Christine confessed, letting go of her shame. "Like there was one thing, at last, I could control. I guess that felt safe too, but..."

"But what?" Erik pushed, not allowing Christine to look away from him, even though she tried to.

"It still feels wrong to have enjoyed hurting you," Christine whispered. "It feels cruel."

"I know you would never really hurt me," Erik breathed back. "I know you would stop if I asked. I know you know the difference between inflicting a sensation upon me I ask for and pushing me into the darkness. I trust you."

"I don't know if I trust myself," Christine half-laughed.

"We don't have to do it again if you're not amenable to it," Erik said with no judgement in his tone, but Christine was still sure he was disappointed. Perhaps because she felt a pang of panic herself at the possibility of closing that door.

"I didn't say I didn't want to do it again."

Erik raised an eyebrow, or what he had that passed for one.

"I just need time to consider and adjust," Christine went on, even as a terribly wicked thought whispered in the back of her mind. "Or plan."

"Plan?" Erik asked, so soft and awed Christine blushed again.

"Well, we won't be doing anything on this damn ship, so don't get too excited," she chided, playfully pushing him away.

"Are you still feeling ill?" Erik took up a piece of bread to offer her. "Something plain may help."

"Howard helped – with the seasickness, I mean. He had some concoction with ginger."

"He's an interesting man," Erik muttered. "I still can't comprehend why he's helping us. He must value Jack quite dearly to aid his friends."

"He also thinks we're very interesting," Christine said as she and Erik sat on the creaking bed that took up much of their cabin. "I didn't have the heart to tell him how truly boring you can be."

"How dare you." Erik gave her a playful glare. "I'm the most unconventional passenger on this ship."

"Perhaps," Christine shrugged. "But I haven't heard any of them go on for hours about the failings of English architecture or, God, what was it the other night? Some chemist obsessed with milk?"

"Pasteur is doing amazing things," Erik squawked. "As I was saying—"

"You're not helping your case, you know."

Erik gave her another scowl. In his face, to anyone else, the expression might have been terrifying or horribly ugly. It only made Christine laugh, because he was as harmless as a lamb right now, her terrible phantom. He was hers to tease and adore and needle, and she loved him. It brought her joy, even as they rolled along the sea to destinations unknown, just to love him. To hold him close as long as she could before he strayed again.

# Paris

S haya had made sure that he wasn't followed today. It had not been easy. He'd had to go all the way to the Marais and waste his entire morning reading the paper at the Place des Vosges, driving his shadow to boredom before disappearing into a library. After that, the detective had slunk off and Shaya had finally made his way to the Opéra.

Shaya had begun to piece together a story about the man assigned to follow him. He was young and impatient. He thought himself an expert at tracking his prey. Perhaps he'd been a hunter in his youth, then become a soldier because he wanted to keep playing with weapons. That didn't pay well, so now he had found work for a firm of private detectives. He was new at the job though and had been assigned the tedious job of following a foreigner throughout Paris day in and day out.

Of course, Shaya didn't know how long this man had been watching him. Maybe he was so accustomed to Shaya's comings and goings that he didn't feel the need to put in the extra hours. Maybe he had already seen something.

There was an increase in the sound of movement, signaling an exodus of dancers and singers from the stage and the end of rehearsal. Shaya stood from his seat beside the window and turned to survey the crowd. He was unobtrusive, but little Giry's reaction to Shaya almost gave away the entire game.

Her eyes – which were already permanently wide – somehow grew larger and her face fell into an almost comical look of dread when she made eye contact with Shaya. He stifled a chuckle and nodded before turning and walking out of the building. He trusted the young dancer to follow, which she did. At least her footsteps were quiet: that was promising.

He walked a little way down the *Rue Auber* before stopping at a café and looking at the young woman who stopped beside him. "Are you hungry, Mademoiselle Giry?"

"Always," Meg replied, looking suspicious and annoyed.

"Excellent. I find it's a bad idea to discuss important matters on an empty stomach." Shaya entered the café, and Meg rushed after him, sitting quickly when he found a table.

"Do we have to eat before we talk?" Meg leaned in close. "I need to know if you really meant if he is... Or was..."

"You can say it aloud, Mademoiselle. No one is listening here."

"How do you know?" Meg asked in a furious whisper as a waiter appeared. She looked at him like he might have been a gendarme – while he looked at Shaya and Meg the way all waiters in Paris looked at customers – like utter nuisances.

"Two hot chocolates, please," Shaya said to placate the man. Meg continued to stare at him. "I know we are safe because it's my job to know and the man who has been following me of late is not here. He wouldn't come this close."

Meg gasped. "Someone has been following you?"

"We'll get to that later," Shaya smirked. "Tell me: what have you discovered about the ghost?"

"I haven't discovered anything," Meg snapped back, then frowned. "I finally saw the truth. I think. There is no ghost. There's always just been a man."

"You sound disappointed." Indeed, the young woman's face was somber, as if she was speaking of some sort of heartbreak.

"It's one thing to have a ghost in your theater – all proper theaters do have one, I've been reliably told – but the Opéra's was the most interesting. It was all rather magical. To think it's all been a man is so disappointing. And frightening." Meg shuddered, and Shaya wondered if she was remembering Joseph Buquet.

"It was all quite the tragedy, that's true," Shaya sighed. "I regret my part in making it worse."

"Your part?" Meg's eyes went wide again, not leaving Shaya's for a moment as the waiter deposited their *chocolats chauds*. "Do you know him? Is that why you came here from Persia?"

"I knew him, yes," Shaya corrected.

"You speak as if he's dead, but you just told me he's not a ghost."

Shaya had to consider his next word carefully. There was a fine line between revealing that the ghost was a fiction created by Erik and revealing Erik himself. "He is. The man who became the Opera Ghost died soon after the chandelier fell."

"I don't understand," Meg whispered. "So is the Opéra truly haunted now? No. It's too different. Something has changed."

"Follow that line of thought, Mademoiselle," Shaya said as he watched Meg's mind work.

"It's someone else? But who?" Meg asked in awe of the revelation.

"I do not know, but I mean to find out. More importantly, I mean to discover why."

Meg opened her mouth as if to answer then shut it quickly before taking a sip of her chocolate. Shaya wondered what her theory was and if she would share it with him at some point, but he didn't wish to pry right now. He had other business.

"I told you I needed a favor. I need your help to help me solve this – a woman on the inside," Shaya explained. "And I also need help with another mystery that may or may not be related. I'm not sure."

"Does it have to do with whoever has been following you?"

Shaya smiled. "Like I said, you're a smart girl. Yes. I need help to find out who has hired detectives to spy on me. Since I can't walk into their offices and ask, I need an assistant."

"And you want that to be me?" Meg let out a rather undignified guffaw. "I don't know the first thing about detective work or subterfuge!"

"Perhaps not, but are you willing to learn? I know you do not know me well, but I promise I'm a trustworthy teacher." Shaya took a sip of the thick, rich chocolate as he regarded Meg.

"Why would you trust me?"

"The ghost trusted your mother," Shaya confessed. "And in the end, I trusted him. I wish to continue to honor what he saw in your family."

"And you have no one else to ask," Meg finished for him, sitting up a bit straighter.

"That is also a factor."

Meg Giry gave him a long, discerning look before a sly smile spread over her young face. "Well, I've always been a good student. Start teaching."

# 7. New and Old

## London

E rik wanted to collapse on the bed as soon as the hotel room door closed, but Christine beat him to it. She flopped on the mattress, making the frame creak, and gave a groan of delight.

"Usually other things have to happen first before I hear those sorts of sounds," Erik sighed as he sank down next to her. She burrowed into his arms immediately and he let out a breath he had been holding for a week. They had made it somewhere safe. For now, at least.

"Swear to me we won't travel again for at least a week," Christine muttered against his chest as they relaxed into the stiff (but thankfully clean) mattress.

"I swear to that and another after it."

The journey by sea had been claustrophobic, to begin with, but rough seas and the crush of people throughout the boat had made it worse every day. Erik had detested large ships before they embarked and now was sure that he would hate them forever. There had been no place to go where there weren't hordes of strangers, all staring at him even though he had his special mask. So he had stayed in their cramped cabin, tripping over their trunks and his wife every moment and trying not to go mad being unable to play or sing or compose. At least they had been safe at sea.

The only relief from the boredom and confinement had been Christine and her insistence that Erik 'get to know' their traveling companion. His few hours conversing with Howard had been light points of the trip. He was an amusing man with a biting sense of humor that Erik very much appreciated, but there also seemed to be something secretive about him – a louche mysteriousness that reminded Erik too much of the dilettantes that frequented the Opéra.

He had to be grateful to Howard for his help, no matter what. They had arrived late last night in South Hampton and the man, by some miracle, had procured tickets on the first train to London before Erik and Christine could even find their bearings or worry that someone was waiting to find them. That had meant trudging through the port city in the wee hours of the morning and then waiting for hours at the station. It had been exhausting in a way that left him feeling like he'd been hollowed out and cast aside like a piece of used fruit. Or something else. He was too tired to think of a decent metaphor.

The train voyage had been no better than the boat, but at least Christine had been beside him all the while. Even all these months later, Erik still found himself in awe of how she made him strong and calm. To hold her hand, to lean against her as they tried to rest... It was wondrous. Yet, even so, Erik felt as if the journey to London had rattled his very bones.

All he wanted to do was sleep. He closed his eyes, breathed in the familiar scent of Christine next to him, and let himself rest. Just for a moment.

A moment apparently meant several hours. When Erik opened his eyes, the room was dark and the noise from the street outside was far more subdued, though someone was knocking at a door in the hall.

"Did we fall asleep?" Christine asked with a yawn as she rose.

"So it would seem," Erik replied. The sound of knocking came again, louder this time... from their door. "Only to be awoken."

It was an unspoken agreement between them that Christine would always be the one to deal with people. She spoke to attendants and porters and maids. She had been the one to procure their room here after Howard had left them to take lodgings with a friend. So she was the one to crack the door to see who had disturbed them. Erik stood back so he wouldn't be seen, retreating to a corner on instinct.

"Oh good, you're awake," came Howard's jovial voice, and Erik's tense shoulders relaxed.

"Barely," Christine muttered as she let the man in. "What time is it? I thought you were getting dinner with a friend."

"I did, and now it's time to show you London!" Howard laughed as the door closed behind them. He looked Erik over and shook his head. "You haven't even changed from your travel clothes. How unfashionable. Our hosts won't be amused."

"I don't plan on being placed in a position where anyone will judge my fashion," Erik grumbled before Christine sent him a warning scowl.

"You don't need to wear that bearded monstrosity either," Howard added, much to Erik's annoyance. The man had been clear in his hints that he wanted to see what was behind Erik's mask that was so terrible, and Erik had been adamant in his privacy.

"I think what my husband means to say is that we appreciate the invitation, but we just want to find some food and go back to sleep," Christine said, kind and warm as always.

"There will be food there – the finest in London. Not that our food is particularly of note, but it will be edible," Howard laughed. "I've missed this specific little salon for months, and I didn't think I'd make tonight's, but here we are. I won't show up without my fascinating new companions who will enthrall everyone. You're in the greatest city in the world and no one is after you at the moment – enjoy the freedom!"

Howard couldn't see Erik glowering behind his mask, but Christine laughed softly at his obvious displeasure. "I enjoy freedom away from crowds. And Paris is the greatest city in the world, just so we're clear," Erik muttered.

Erik looked to Christine for support in the argument, but there was interest in her eyes that caught him off guard. "You have been complaining about feeling cooped up," she said.

"Because I wanted fresh air, not to go to a party," Erik snapped back.

"What if I want to socialize?" Christine demanded, her voice cool and challenging. "You wouldn't make me go alone?"

"I would still be there," Howard quipped, but Erik couldn't hear or see anything but his wife. There was an unmistakable look of power in her forest green eyes, and it made a wonderful shiver run up Erik's body.

"You'd make me go?" Erik asked, trying to sound dismissive and only marginally failing.

"I would command it," Christine said in such a tone that Howard had to awkwardly cough after a moment to break the spell she cast. The message was clear. They were going and Christine wanted him to enjoy it. Erik wasn't sure he could, but if nothing else, he would enjoy her.

"I'll let you change then. Don't be too long," Howard said and exited the room. Erik couldn't help but laugh at his speed.

"I think you may have proven he's indeed an Englishman," Erik said.

"Does he think I'm going to have you right now while he's waiting outside?" Christine did indeed step extremely close to him and slid her hands up his chest with a smile.

"Is he right?"

"No." Christine said it with the most wonderfully wicked smile. "We're going to do as he said and change, then we are going to have a delightful time among Howard's eccentric friends. Only after that – and only if you behave – will we come back here so I can have my way with you."

Erik threw his mask to the floor and kissed her, savoring the taste of her laughter as he did. Christine pushed him back and batted his arm with a playful frown, and his satisfaction only increased. "I promise to be as docile as possible."

"Only at the party," Christine countered. "I'd like you to be exceedingly forceful after."

"Yes, Madame," Erik grinned.

He floated on the joy of her commands as they changed, trying not to be too distracted by the sight of Christine's pale skin and round thighs. Soon enough, he was in a suit of pristine black with a fine shirt to match, and Christine had dressed in a gown of midnight blue that they had purchased in Geneva. She was glorious.

"Here, you can match me," Christine said as she pulled a sapphire-toned cravat out of Erik's case and approached him. It made his head fuzzy when she pressed herself to him and drew the vibrant length of silk around his neck, fastening it tight. Like she was binding him again. Keeping him safe. Keeping him hers.

"It will be my honor," Erik exhaled and went easily as Christine took him by the hand to guide him out into the night.

Howard had a carriage waiting for them (closed, thankfully) to take them through the city. Erik had not made much of a note of the buildings or landscape when they had arrived; he had been too tired. Now he looked at the city through Christine's eyes as they rambled along among the gaslights.

Where Paris had been forged by Baron Hausmann into perfect, symmetrical order, bisected by grand avenues rebuilt in a symphony of limestone and slate roofs, London was a maze cobbled together over centuries. There was no rhyme or reason to the streets, and the buildings were a hodgepodge of ancient and new. It was charming, in its way, Erik had to admit. London didn't hide what it had once been, the way Paris tried to. A thousand years of history was on display on every street, if one could make it out through the soot and grime from the coal fires and factories. It was hard to breathe here, compared to the salt air of the sea or the humble streets of Florence, but it certainly was lively.

"Where are we headed? Pretend like I know," Christine asked as they passed through a large park.

"Belgravia, but the bad half of it," Howard replied. "My friend is an itinerant Lord, or he was when last I left him. He's probably bumbled his way into becoming a Baron by now."

"That's right, your nobles here have titles that matter," Christine remarked.

"They don't matter here either," Erik sniped, and Howard gave him a look.

"Do you hate the upper class for a respectable reason or because you grew up playing with toy guillotines like a good Frenchman?" Howard remarked.

"I hated them in France because they took everything they wanted and left nothing but grief in their wake," Erik hissed.

"Maybe they're better here," Christine said gently, stroking his arm and reminding him that he had made a promise to behave.

"Oh no, they're not. Mostly," Howard smirked. "But they're English, so they're quite polite about it all. The people you're about to meet though aren't for all that – the manners and decorum and propriety of our dear queen. We've made our own little Bohemia."

"Where a man in a mask won't stand out?" Erik asked tersely.

"You'll be the least interesting person there," Howard assured him, but what truly calmed Erik was Christine entwining her fingers with his.

The manor they arrived at wasn't ostentatious, but it was still grand, with walls of white stone and dozens of windows shining with light. Erik braced himself for stares as they entered, giving their coats to a footman. He had no idea what he had been expecting – perhaps a formal supper or ball – but that was not what awaited.

The best way to describe what they walked into was a salon. There were groups of people filling the parlors, taking food from laden tables, and engaging in idle conversation and debate. But there was more than that. A woman was doing a painting of a man holding a monkey in a corner. Two men who were clearly a couple were draped together across a divan, laughing with a woman in silken robes with ebony skin. In another room, a professorial character stood in the corner with a turbaned Sikh. People laughed and mingled, and no one gave Erik and Christine more than a lingering look.

Erik... did not hate it. Christine smiled next to him, her arm entwined with his, and it occurred to Erik that they had never done anything like this.

"Let me introduce you to our host. Or hosts," Howard said in French, and led them to the largest parlor. There was a small man there lying on a chaise longue with his head in a beautiful woman's lap as she fed him grapes. "Dear God, Bernard, you're going to choke eating that way," Howard remarked.

"Is that Howard Ashe back from the continent?" the little man exclaimed, scrambling to sit up and blinking at Howard. The woman who had been feeding him laughed warmly and handed the man a pair of thick spectacles. As soon as they were on his face, he grinned. "It is! How are you, old chap?"

"A little worse for wear, like all of us," Howard replied.

"Speak for yourself, Sir," the woman purred. She was more than buxom, with breasts so robust her neckline could scarcely contain them. Her hair was blonde, styled in a mass of beautiful curls, and decorated with bangles that didn't look like real jewels. A character if ever Erik had seen one. "Some of us are thriving."

"My dearest Letitia, you are Venus herself descended to earth," Howard said as he took the woman's hand and bowed to kiss it. She smiled like a gracious queen.

"Introduce me to our new friends," the blonde commanded.

"Voilà," Howard replied, waving Erik and Christine forward. He spoke in French: "New acquaintances, discovered in the most delightful corners of Florence. Erik and Christine Gilbride: musicians, among other things. This is Lord Bernard Chumley and Letitia Trumbull."

"Delighted to meet you," Letitia said in perfect French, rising to embrace Christine and kiss her swiftly on the cheeks. "I love musicians. Have you been to the Opera at Covent Garden yet? I have a lover with a wonderful box who took me the other day to see their new production of Don Carlo. Their Eboli was a revelation."

"What are they saying?" the Lord whined in English. "Howard, I do hate it when you do this."

"We have only arrived today," Christine replied in French with a smile. "Is Lord Chumley here not your lover?"

"Oh, he is, but I have many. My Lord here keeps me the most comfortable, but the affections of a woman such as I can't be exclusive." Letitia gave a provocative wink.

"You're in the presence of one of the great courtesans of London," Howard explained, and Chumley gave an annoyed huff.

"Do you really use that word?" Erik asked and noted the way both the Lord and lady of the night looked at him when he spoke, and how they finally took in his mask. Erik switched to English. "Do not worry, sir, we have not said anything about you."

"Whatever you want to say, keep saying it, my dear," Letitia replied and reached for Erik with fascination on her face. "What a voice you have. What sort of musician are you?"

"Any kind I like," Erik replied, letting his pride puff out his chest a bit, even as he shied away from the woman's touch.

"His skills are unmatched," Christine said proudly.

"Will you play for us later?" Letitia asked. "After you have some refreshments and enjoy the night, of course. I wouldn't put you to work so quickly."

"Perhaps I can be persuaded," Erik murmured.

"Tell us more of the Opera here first," Christine went on cheerfully. "It has been a long time since I have attended. Who was this Eboli you saw? Perhaps we know her name."

"Adèle Valerius. She was transformative," Letitia answered.

Christine jumped in excitement, gripping Erik's arm. "Adèle is in London! I have to see her!" Christine cried and turned to Letitia. "She is an old friend. One of my dearest."

"Is she? I have an appointment to call on her tomorrow. You must join me," Letitia replied. "I'm desperate to add her to my circle."

"Oh, I would love that," Christine sighed.

"Would that be wise?" Erik asked softly and received a truly chilling glare in response. "Never mind. I won't attempt to keep you from your friend."

"And I can't keep you two from the crowd much longer," Howard interjected. "I think more people would like to meet you."

Erik sighed and allowed himself to be led away from the hosts, giving them a bow as Christine promised she would return. Howard introduced them to a professor, a poet, and several other interesting sorts that soon overwhelmed Erik with conversation and questions. It was a relief to lean into Christine and translate for her, as well as a pleasure to watch her practice her English with new partners.

However, Erik was more than relieved when he finally found the music room. There was a lovely piano, inlaid with floral designs of lacquered wood, and next to it, a case of instruments, including a violin.

"Use anything you like." Erik turned to see that Letitia had entered, with Chumley trailing behind her like a loyal pet. "I can tell you want to."

"Can you, now?" Erik asked.

"In my profession, it is imperative to be able to see what people want," Letitia said with a shrug that made her décolletage ripple. "Go ahead."

"I'll accompany you. We'll play the piece you were working on before we left Florence," Christine suggested brightly. It would be easy to forget, given his wife's operatic skill, that she was also accomplished at the piano. Erik's heart swelled with pride to stand beside her as she tested the instrument.

The room quieted as they began to play, sweeping the crowd of strangers into the embrace of melody. The violin and piano danced together, trading phrases and unspoken stories as easily as lovers would trade kisses, and it filled Erik with the same delight.

Their audience didn't know exactly what their entertainers were thinking or feeling as they played, but they knew what the music made them feel, and that was nearly as intimate. It reminded Erik of why he loved her – how special a thing it was to be able to share this secret language with his wife – he could tell them through the notes from his bow how he needed and adored her.

The thrill of playing with her carried Erik through the rest of the night – beyond conversations and pleasantries and promises to meet again – all the way back to their rooms, where he was finally granted his reward and lost himself in the pleasures of the flesh as easily as those of music. He hoped the walls were not too thin here, for the performance they gave was far more vocal.

# Paris

**M**eg very much liked being a spy. This surprised her, given that she had always been bad at lying – or assumed she was. Now, she was on her way to her greatest test of subterfuge yet, sneaking along the *Boulevard Haussmann* to meet a master detective, and she was more excited than frightened. Who would ever have thought it of little Meg?

Meg had managed to fool even her mother into thinking she wasn't up to anything out of the ordinary, thanks to her tutor in deception and detection. Shaya had given her the simple advice to say something true that was somehow also a lie. She had told her mother she was helping a new friend with errands at the Opéra – and that had been true! She had helped.

In the week since entering the Persian's employ, Meg had prevented another attack. Or at least delayed it. She had seen Monsieur Goncourt drunk and stumbling out of the Opéra alone after watching his dancer reject him after a performance. The man had been a prime target, but Meg had saved him in the best way she could: by sweetly encouraging Monsieur d'Amboise to take care of his ailing friend. Meg had not liked that part – d'Amboise had continued to pay too much attention to her, but the man had reported the next day that a shadow had followed them into the street but fled away.

He had not called it a ghost. Why would he? It had been a man of unknown purpose. Thinking about it made Meg shiver even in the waning warmth of the day. It was what they didn't know about this new phantom that Shaya thought was most dangerous. The man who had worn the mask before – the one Shaya assured her was dead now – had been dangerous, but his purpose had been known. Now they knew so little.

Meg darted down the alley where she was set to meet her mentor, frowning in frustration about how little they had learned even though she had spent the last week listening to every story and exploring every nook and cranny of the Opéra. There had been more sightings, she knew that now. Tales of a masked shadow were increasing, shared in hushed tones among trusted friends...

"Careful, Meg: someone could sneak up on you."

Meg jumped at the admonition, spinning to see Shaya behind her wearing his accustomed wry smile. "I expected you to come from the other way!" Meg protested. "I was watching."

"You have to watch all ways at all times."

"You make it sound so simple." Meg scowled but tucked the lesson away in her head. "I was wondering what we're going to learn about the ghost from me going into a detective's office."

"As I told you: I'm not sure my spy is related, but I have a feeling it might be and that's as good a reason as any to pursue more information."

"Is it?" Meg balked. "I have feelings about lots of things and I don't get nosey about them."

"Don't you?" Shaya chuckled, and Meg made a face. "What are you feeling right now?"

Meg regarded the man. She had quickly come to like him over the last week. He was kind, intelligent, and spoke to her like an equal, but he was clearly keeping his own secrets. "There's something you're not telling me about the old ghost."

"There's a great deal I'm not telling you about him, that's correct."

"How did he die?" Meg blurted out, and Shaya raised his brows in surprise. She had been bold, but she hoped it would be rewarded.

"Of a broken heart," Shaya replied, voice soft and sad. That had not been what Meg was expecting. She had thought, perhaps, some sort of duel between him and poor dead Philippe de Chagny or the presumed-dead Antoine de Martiniac.

"He loved Christine Daaé, and she left Paris."

Shaya nodded. "She loved him in return."

She had been the woman in black at the masquerade. She had sung down the chandelier. Now she was gone, disappeared off to who-knows-where. "That's so sad."

"Are you ready?" Shaya asked, changing the subject. "Do you remember what you're to say?"

"Yes, I've rehearsed it. Much easier than a pas de deux," Meg smiled. "Now give me the money. I always wanted to say that."

Shaya smirked as he handed Meg the envelope holding several hundred francs. She hoped it was enough. "Good luck. Leave immediately if anything feels wrong or dangerous. You won't be able to see me, but I'll be right here."

"You're a strange sort of guardian angel," Meg quipped and wasn't prepared for the quick flash of emotion on Shaya's face. "Oh. Do you not believe in those? I thought that your people – I mean – your faith isn't Christian, but—"

"There are angels in the Quran," Shaya answered warmly. "I was thinking about something – someone else I once knew who had a keen interest in them."

"Oh. I'm sorry." Meg didn't know why she said that, but it felt right. Shaya seemed to take it to heart. "I – thank you. I hope I won't disappoint you."

"You could not, Mademoiselle Giry."

That made Meg swell with pride. It meant something for a person such as him to believe in her. She could do this, she was certain of it. She wouldn't disappoint him.

Meg straightened her dress and hat as she made her way out of the alley and across the boulevard. She was wearing her Sunday best – a nice dress of blue that contrasted with her blonde hair, and a smart pair of shoes with white and black leather, newly cleaned. She felt more like a lady than usual and hoped the costume would be adequate.

The offices of Pomeroy and Associates were pointedly unobtrusive. It made sense to Meg that a business that relied on secrets would have such a plain storefront and nearly unreadable signage. The only people who came here were the ones who really needed these services, or who had heard of them from someone else. Meg and Shaya had decided she was the former because she didn't want to be caught in a lie claiming she was the latter.

Meg braced herself as she walked inside and the little bell over the door rang. The front office was small and taken up by an empty desk. Beyond that was a hallway leading to other offices. It took a moment for one of the hallway doors to open and for an older man to emerge. He looked at Meg and then the empty desk and gave a powerful sigh.

"I should never have sent her off," he muttered, then turned his attention back to Meg. "Good day, Mademoiselle, may I be of service?"

"Yes, I hope so," Meg said with her most charming smile. "I need a detective for a delicate matter involving, well, a man of means."

"Really?" The man huffed. He was almost what one would call burly, with a greying beard and a keg of a belly, but his eyes were bright and thoughtful as they looked over Meg. There was a small scar on his cheek, just below his left eye, and Meg wondered if he was a former soldier of some sort, or if his past was even more intriguing. "You look too young to have that sort of business. Where are your parents?"

"Well that's what I need to find out," Meg replied. "This man of means may be one of my parents, but I don't know for sure and I was hoping you and your firm might help me confirm that. If that is the sort of thing you do. I assume you're Monsieur Pomeroy?"

"I am. And we attend to all sorts of matters here." He looked Meg up and down. "For the right price; a high price for the utmost in service. You need to know that before we waste each other's time."

"I can pay. I assure you." Meg patted the pocket of her dress. "Perhaps there will be more if the result is to my liking? Is that something people do?"

"It is, indeed," Pomeroy replied with a circumspect squint.

"Would you be handling this, or..." Meg made a show of looking around the empty office. "It says associates on the sign, but I don't see anyone else here. Not that I would mind being assisted by the man in charge."

Meg surprised herself with the way she said it – she was sweet and flirtatious. She usually hated making a show of being small and feminine and vulnerable for old men, because the patrons of the Opéra needed no encouragement, but there was a spark in Pomeroy's eyes when she spoke.

"Yes. Well," Pomeroy sighed as if this was an ongoing annoyance. "Many of my agents are in the field and working today. I do have one who specializes in female troubles, but she's abroad at the moment."

"Abroad?" Meg asked, batting her eyes. "Your agents travel so far?"

"Indeed," the man said, puffing up proudly. "Our network is not as extensive as the Pinkertons, but it will be one day. My agents are willing to go to the ends of the earth for our clients. Though I can't imagine your case will take us so far."

"It must be thrilling to travel on such errands," Meg smiled. "Shall we discuss more in your office or were you waiting for the rest of your staff? I'm sure there are many of them."

"They are due back any moment," Pomeroy replied, looking out the window and widening his eyes at something he saw. Meg moved to look, but the man stopped her – seizing her by the shoulder and herding her back down the hall. "Yes. You should wait in my office. I will deal with this."

Meg was fascinated to see the man so flustered. What had he seen and who was coming inside that had upset him? The bell over the door rang just as she was shut in the office. Meg froze, listening. She was supposed to see if she could find any files or correspondence that might reveal who had hired these people to spy on Shaya. But that gut feeling – the one Shaya himself had told her never to ignore – wanted her to listen.

"What in God's name are you doing walking in here looking like that?" Pomeroy growled.

"Thank you for your concern. I'm healing well," a male voice replied with acid in his tone. "I thought you'd be happy I'm alive to keep doing my job."

"You'll only use this to ask for a raise," Pomeroy replied. Meg dearly wished she could peek out the door and see what sort of state this other man was in.

"It would be a one-time bonus for being stabbed," the man replied. Meg bit her lips so she wouldn't gasp.

"Well, you won't get a damn thing from me or Madame de Martiniac after how badly you bungled," Pomeroy hissed. "I had to personally advance the money for Pauline to get a ticket to America only for it to be a dead end. You're both useless."

"He's a wily devil. Any luck here?" the other man said as Meg's brain started to feel like a kettle at a high boil. Had he said the name de Martiniac? How could that be?

"Nothing of note with the foreigner. Pierre is sick of following him," Pomeroy answered. Meg nearly whooped in joy. She hadn't had to riffle through files at all.

"Pauline has a plan, but it's mad. We should check in with the client. This is getting expensive, not to mention dangerous," the injured man said with affected boredom. He was pretending, and a man like Pomeroy would know that.

"Oh, you can't fool me. You want to catch them as much as she does, don't you? For pure revenge now," Pomeroy said after a beat, proving Meg right.

"Do you mean Pauline or the client?" the other scoffed.

"I will discuss it with you later. I have someone in my office now who may have something simple for us that doesn't involve a wild goose chase across Europe."

"Or a fortune and a trail of dead bodies."

"You didn't die, for God's sake. Pierre is at the Tuileries. Find him and bring him back so we can strategize."

Meg once again heard the tinkling of the bell above the door. She barely had time to rush back to her seat before the desk and compose herself before Pomeroy reentered.

"I'm so sorry to keep you waiting, Mademoiselle. Please, tell me more about what we can do for you."

Meg smiled sweetly, as much to herself as to the older man. He had already done more for her than he could possibly know.

# London

Christine's excitement at meeting Letitia for tea before calling on Adèle had faded to anxiety. Erik's clear worry about the encounter had not helped at all. She told him, and herself, that this was not another Pauline. This was a woman who was known (infamously) throughout London. She wouldn't betray them. It could be dangerous to see Adèle, yes, but hopefully, Pauline was halfway to New York by now.

London felt different, Christine had decided. Or maybe it was better to say she felt different in London. Her nightmares had started to fade, replaced by dreams of green hills and empty libraries. She didn't know what those visions meant, but she welcomed them, along with her waking fantasies of other ways to discipline her husband that were quite pleasant as well. Would a woman like Letitia know about such things or would that be too forward to ask about over tea? She would have to see how the friendship evolved.

This was a good thing, Christine assured herself as she fixed her hat and looked around the ornate interior of the tearoom to which she had been directed. It was filled with palms and fine China on display, as well as lamps of colored glass and ornately carved wood paneling. It screamed of riches, but in a subdued, English fashion. It was a sharp contrast to the simplicity of Paris bistros, and Christine doubted she would be able to get a good cup of coffee here.

"There you are, Mrs. Gilbride!" a trilling voice called, and Christine rose to greet the gorgeous woman. She was in a dress of pale yellow satin edged with lace, carrying a matching parasol. It didn't escape Christine's attention that most of the eyes in the room turned toward them as she rose to greet Letitia.

"It is so very good to see you," Christine said in her rehearsed English, and Letitia pouted and placed a hand on Christine's cheek. "Was that bad?" she asked in French.

"Not at all, my dear," Letitia replied in French as well. A woman at the table next to theirs gave a quiet huff of disapproval. "I just love to speak French and scandalize stuck up English harpies." Letitia turned to the woman and smiled.

"I like you," Christine laughed as they sat. "I do need to practice my English though. If we are to stay."

"Do you intend to linger in London or somewhere else on this dreary island?" Letitia asked with delight.

"I honestly don't know. I don't dislike it so far."

"But you were in Florence before? And Paris! Oh, I adore Paris."

Christine knew Letitia meant it kindly, but it only made her heart ache. "It's a wonderful city. What did you do there?"

"Why, it's where all the best women of my persuasions learn their skills," Letitia said with a wink, and Christine suppressed a guffaw. There were still women looking at them from all around the room.

"Do these ladies here know your... gifts?" Christine asked. It had been Letitia's idea to come here, but they had not been served at all yet.

"Oh, yes. Their husbands even more," Letitia replied. "Though they would never admit it. I like to come here once in a while to remind them all that I'm still here and still thriving."

"How delightful. I think you'll like Adèle and she you."

Christine stopped. Adèle had once been brazen in her pursuit of lovers who could advance her career and keep her comfortable, until one such lover had turned on her in the vilest way because of Christine. Adèle said she forgave her, but would she want to see Christine after everything?

"Did you know her as a musician? Were you a singer too?" Letitia asked.

"I was. I performed at the Opéra with her," Christine confessed, and Letitia looked adequately impressed. "I met my husband there. He was my teacher, but I decided I wanted a different sort of life."

"What sort is that?" Letitia asked kindly, only for Christine to sigh.

"You see, that has been our problem. We needed a different life, but we weren't specific in our petitions to fate of what exactly that meant. So we wander." The honesty was a relief. Erik had never been one to plan ahead far, and while Christine had nurtured many dreams before, they had not been solid, realistic things. Just dreams.

"Well, now you're in the land of practicality and propriety. I'm sure it will encourage some realism," Letitia laughed. "Though that would be a shame, I think. Magic and mystery are so much more fun."

"One can't live on those," Christine murmured.

"You'd be surprised. Come, it's time for our appointment. I have my carriage – well, Bernard's. He's quite accommodating."

"Don't you want to wait for tea?" Christine asked, but as she looked around, the disapproving looks sharpened.

"They'll never serve me here. And I'll tell you a secret," Letitia replied, and took Christine by the arm. "I hate tea."

"So do I," Christine giggled so loudly that one old woman looked ready to faint.

Letitia whisked them away to the waiting carriage, smiling all the while. She was like a beam of summer sun with her yellow dress and blonde hair, and it made Christine feel warm to be near her.

"Erik loves tea. He makes some himself," Christine volunteered when they began to roll along.

"What an interesting and mysterious man your husband is. A Frenchman with the name of a Viking and an Irishman."

"His mother was Irish." Christine wondered if that information was wise to volunteer in this city.

"So was mine," Letitia replied, and Christine relaxed. "Though I keep that quiet among the upper crust. A whore they can tolerate, but an Irishwoman enjoying life in their midst is something beyond the pale."

"Is the prejudice really so bad?" Christine knew there was no love lost between the nations – one occupying the other – and that had been why it was such a shock to find herself here with him.

"Certainly. Worse in America though, I've heard. I have friends that went there for a fresh start and it's been a struggle. Everyone seems to be leaving Éire," Letitia said with deep sadness. "But here I am, in this lovely town, trying to make it as wild as I can, bringing a bit of Dublin and Paris to the mix."

"Tell me more about your life here?" Christine asked hopefully. She didn't want to think about America and all the places she couldn't be. Only the place she was. "Are all your parties as exotic as the one last night?"

"Far more so," Letitia grinned. "I have various circles of friends and acquaintances. Some, I invite to salons to bare their minds and souls in music and conversation, but the genuinely interesting ones I invite to enjoy bare asses and rare entertainments from other friends."

"My goodness," was all Christine could say, blushing to imagine such an event.

"It's very much the opposite of goodness," Letitia replied. "The other month, we had the most expert flogger in attendance. Men were lining up to have a go under her whip in front of everyone. She punished them quite fitfully for begging."

Christine didn't even try to keep her jaw from dropping. "Oh."

"Dear me, have I shocked you? I assumed a singer from Paris who runs in the same circles as dear Howard would know of such things!" Letitia grasped Christine's hand comfortingly. "You are married to a man who goes about in a mask."

"That's only because—I mean, I'm not offended! I—" Christine didn't have the words, so she only laughed.

"Intrigued then?" Letitia asked with a sly smile, and Christine's cheeks burned.

"I was not expecting such conversation," she finally said, and it was Letitia's turn to laugh.

"When you meet a courtesan for tea, you must adjust your expectations."

"Apparently," Christine muttered.

"Ah, here we are," Letitia blessedly exclaimed.

They exited the carriage and beheld a handsome townhouse, far more luxurious than the flats in Paris. Adèle was doing well for herself here. A quiet maid let them in and showed them up to the door of a parlor, letting Letitia in first.

"Miss Ryan, a delight to meet you," came a voice Christine had not heard for months. She wasn't prepared for how the familiarity struck her heart. It had been so long since she'd had anyone she knew besides Erik with her.

"Madame Valerius, thank you for receiving me. It's an honor to even share a room with such an artist," Letitia was saying. "I hope you don't mind, but I have brought you a very special gift to celebrate your success here in London."

"A gift?" Adèle asked as Christine stepped into the room.

For a moment, she froze, looking as if she could not believe who she saw before her. The last time Christine had seen Adèle was at the wedding before she and Erik had fled Paris forever. Now here Christine was, standing before her friend like an errant child come home to a parent after running away.

"I believe you two know each other," Letitia said, breaking Adèle from her stupor.

"I hope you don't mind me joining—" Christine's apology was eclipsed by the sudden power of Adèle's embrace as she hugged Christine so tight she could barely breathe. Christine's fear evaporated, replaced by overwhelming affection and gratitude for Adèle's grace.

"Dear God, girl, I thought I might never see you again," Adèle whispered into her hair. Christine drew back, sniffling and trying to keep her tears at bay.

"I wrote, but—"

"I left Paris only a few weeks after you," Adèle explained. "I didn't let anyone know where I was. I assumed you were too busy getting ravished from here to Calcutta by your infamous husband to worry about me."

Somehow, that was what broke Christine and she gave a laugh that was half a sob. "I missed you," she whispered.

Adèle smiled. "And I you. Oh, Miss Ryan. I'm sorry, I nearly forgot you," she added, turning to Letitia and wiping her eyes.

"It's alright. When Mrs. Gilbride mentioned last night that she was a friend of yours, she didn't explain how close," Letitia said with no judgment.

Adèle looked at her curiously. "How did you come to be invited to one of the most infamous and exclusive gatherings in London – one I myself have tried to attend?"

"You're welcome any time," Letitia countered as Christine fumbled for her own answer.

"We... made a friend in Italy who helped us in a difficult patch. He's acquainted with Letitia." Christine wanted to cry again at reducing the dramas of the last few weeks to so simple an excuse.

"Italy? My goodness, I'll have to hear all about it. I assume you aren't travelling alone, *Mrs. Gilbride*?" Adèle asked with a twinkle in her eyes.

"No, of course not. Erik and I are here together," Christine said, and the happiness in her voice was genuine. She hoped the relief in Adèle's face was too.

"You know Mr. Gilbride too?" Letitia asked, and Christine winced. She didn't want Adèle questioned about this. She knew more about Erik than almost anyone and had paid the price for that before.

"Only in passing through my dear Christine. I'm surprised you met him, but I'm glad to hear he is being sociable," Adèle replied, smooth as ever.

"Only when I force him, which I think he enjoys in a strange sort of way," Christine said. "But Letitia didn't bring me to her visit to hear my tales. Tell me about you! I didn't think you would leave Paris so soon. How is Julianne? She's not with you, is she? I haven't heard from her at all."

"I received very good care from Julianne, but I'm too old for her. I knew it was time for a new start. Your departure was really what inspired me," Adèle answered with a twinkle in her eyes.

Christine had never been entirely sure what had happened between Adèle and Julianne – brief love affair or a deep friendship. It wasn't her place to pry, but if it had helped Adèle, she was grateful for it.

"Why London?" Christine asked.

"Why not? It's quite the city, and so different from Paris. I needed a change." There was sadness in Adèle's eyes for only a moment. "And I had an excellent offer from the Opera at Covent Garden, thanks to a recommendation by Armand Moncharmin. The journey was a chore, however."

They all sank into seats in Adèle's well-appointed parlor as they relaxed into conversation. It was comforting to talk of everything and nothing – to hear the predictable tales of rivalries and affairs at the London Opera House that were so similar to what had gone on in Paris.

Adèle was doing well, receiving great acclaim by the audience, but had yet to be welcomed into polite society in the city – being a singer and French were two sins too many. Letitia assured her that it was of little import, and that she would see her acquainted with the underground of artists and creatives that she knew. Apparently, she had recently met a man claiming to be a sorcerer and member of a secret society of magicians, something Erik would be fascinated by, and she felt comfortable saying as much.

Soon enough, an hour had passed and it was time to go – at least for Adèle, who had to prepare for curtain.

"You will visit again soon? I'm free tomorrow," Adèle asked as Christine rose. "Tell me all the things you can't today."

"I don't want to take up too much of your time," Christine muttered and received a gentle glare for her trouble.

"I want to see you here tomorrow, for luncheon. Bring your husband, if he can bear it."

"If I can tear him away from whatever dusty tome or composition he's engrossed in, I shall."

"Good," Adèle said, and pressed a friendly kiss to Christine's cheek. "I'm so glad you are well."

"And I you," Christine said with all the sincerity she could muster. She was grateful, truly, for old friends and new. It made her feel like more of a complete person to go out and about, even as, at the same time, it made her eager to get home to Erik.

Home was a strange thing to call their rooms in the hotel, but as she had sworn to him and kept reminding herself, there was no home for her but him.

# Paris

"How many more churches will we be going to?" Darius demanded the moment Shaya stepped into their flat. He looked as frustrated and exhausted as Shaya felt, which was saying quite a bit. "I'm one more record room away from converting."

"No luck for you either?" Shaya sighed. Perhaps it had been a stupid idea to look through parish records for any note of a marriage between Antoine de Martiniac and the mysterious

Madame that had hired men to spy on Shaya and traipse around Europe hunting a ghost on the same person's whim.

"None. She could be lying, whoever she is," Darius offered.

"If my hunch is right, then she'd want a paper trail, at least to give things legitimacy."

"What sort of things?" Darius asked with narrowed eyes. "I know there's something you're not telling me."

"It's just a suspicion. I might not have seen what I thought. I can't always trust these old eyes," Shaya muttered. "But if you insist—"

The revelation was cut off by furious knocking at the flat door. Shaya and Darius exchanged looks before his former servant answered it, perhaps out of habit.

"Who are you? Where is—" Meg Giry demanded as she craned her neck to look into the flat. "Oh, there you are. I've been knocking on doors and I think I may have upset one of your neighbors."

"You were following me?" Shaya balked, more impressed than annoyed.

"Well, you haven't contacted me at all since I solved your case!" Meg cried, entering without invitation as Darius stepped back.

"The case, as you call it, is far from solved," Shaya stammered. "And I was allowing you to observe goings on at the Opéra."

"Someone stole money from the box office," Meg sighed, much to Shaya's surprise. "It's apparently been going on for a while in small amounts."

"Armand would have told me about that," Shaya said, more to Darius than Meg, worrying what it meant that he hadn't known about it.

"He doesn't know! One of the clerks has been trying to have an assignation with an alto from the chorus – which says a lot about him – and he ran to her today in a panic over the discovery and I heard it all."

"And that's what you ran here to discuss?" Darius asked, garnering Meg's attention once again.

"Who are you?" Meg looked the man over, surely noting that he was Persian like Shaya, but smaller and softer around the edges.

"Darius Veyssi," Darius replied with a bow of his head.

"He is my—" Of course, Shaya was the one at a loss for words. It wasn't easy to describe what Darius was to him. No longer a servant or a vassal, not a lover of the normal sort, but still family. Still his heart in this strange land. He settled on the simplest title. "My companion."

"Oh. That's lovely. You know, my great aunt had a companion she lived with until she was ninety. Lovely women, both of them. So strange they never married," Meg remarked and Shaya saw Darius holding in a chuckle. "But I didn't come to tell you about the money! Well, I did. I had no idea where to find you yesterday or this morning, so I went to the agency to see if you were lurking about on some off chance."

"I do not lurk," Shaya huffed.

"You do. Technically," Darius interjected, much to Shaya's dismay.

"I like him," Meg grinned. "Anyway. I went to Pomeroy's, but you weren't there, so I waited and then I saw him!"

Meg was nearly vibrating from excitement as she gripped Shaya's hand. "Who?" Shaya asked, utterly at sea now.

"I didn't think I had seen right – is that the term – and maybe I recognized him wrongly. I mean, I only ever saw him from a distance at the Opéra. Before I could check, Pierre – your man, the one who hates following you – went off and I followed him to see if he'd lead me to you and he went to the Tuileries and soon enough, you came by and I followed you here."

"You had two people following you here and you missed it?" Darius scoffed.

"I knew he was there and I lost him when I went into *Saint-Eustache*," Shaya sniped back.

"But not me!" Meg piped up. "Because you told me to be patient. So I was, though I did stop for a crêpe, and by the time I was done, you were far down the street and I ran after you – to here!" Meg paused breathlessly and grinned. Darius cleared his throat, prompting Shaya without words.

"Yes, you did an admirable job," Shaya sighed, and Meg grinned. "But who did you see at Pomeroy's?"

Meg's face was instantly dire as she leaned in to explain. "Firmin Richard!"

Now that was unexpected enough that Shaya had to take a moment.

"He's the old manager," Meg added softly.

"I know who he is," Shaya muttered and looked at Darius. "Why would he be involved?"

"He was de Martiniac's partner in his endeavors," Darius replied darkly, because, of course, he was faster than Shaya or Meg in these connections.

"What endeavors? Is this why you've been avoiding me?" Meg squawked. "You know things about de Martiniac and this Madame that you don't want to tell me, don't you?"

"You've taught her well, Shaya," Darius said with a smile that Shaya answered with a frustrated glare.

"You're not helping," Shaya muttered.

"But you have, and I know as well as you that this is all connected. Your spy and what's going on at the Opéra and the ghost." Meg looked up at him (for she was nearly a foot shorter) with piercing, impatient eyes in her innocent face. A face that he could not lie to.

"It is, but some aspects must be kept secret. I must ask you to trust me about it," Shaya replied at last. "There are things that even I do not understand, and what you've revealed today makes it all the more confusing."

"What were you doing in *Saint-Eustache*? I thought your people went to a different sort of place?" Meg asked, directed to both of them.

"It's called a mosque. I wasn't there for worship, but to examine their marriage records," Shaya answered with a sigh, making his way to his seat by the fireplace. It was too warm still to light it, but he missed the glow.

"Trying to discover who married de Martiniac?" Meg asked, again earning an approving look from Darius.

"It's a fool's errand, you're right," Shaya said.

"Especially when one of your secrets is that you already have someone in mind," Darius said. "Someone who was engaged to him perhaps?"

Shaya cast the other man a toothless glare even as realization dawned on Meg's face. "I need to be sure, and it's a very dangerous thing to investigate that family."

"For you," Darius corrected softly. When Shaya looked at him, there was a dangerous spark in his eyes. Meg saw it too.

"Me?" Meg gaped. "Seeing a detective about a made-up case is one thing, but you want me to spy on the de Chagny family? Why?"

"Because if Firmin Richard is involved now too, we must know how dangerous this case has become," Shaya replied. "And how much they have at stake."

# 8. Delights

## London

Erik looked despairingly at the letter before him on the desk. He wasn't used to writing correspondence not meant to threaten or compel, and his penmanship really was as awkward as Christine teased him for. Still, he needed to update Shaya and assure his old nemesis that the real Opera Ghost remained retired.

It was disquieting to think of someone else in the place Erik still longed for. He woke up most days looking for the familiar sight of his canopy or his organ, longing for the simple feel of the Palais Garnier, only to remember he'd never see any part of the Opéra ever again. How dare someone haunt that place when he couldn't?

"Who is that to? Didn't you write to Shaya days ago?" Christine asked as she slipped her arms around his chest and rested her chin on his shoulder. Instantly, he was warmer and more relaxed, comforted by her touch. The sun had set hours ago and the damp, foggy cold had begun to creep in, whispering of fall around the corner.

"It's to Moncharmin. Adèle mentioned that she was going to contact him, and offered to slip a note in," Erik muttered.

Their visit to the erstwhile Madame Valerius had been both strange and amusing. It had felt so normal to just go somewhere with his wife and hear tales about Adèle's time at Covent Garden. Of course, the normalcy had fled as soon as they had begun their narrative.

The story of the last few months was as notable for the things they said as for what they didn't. They had remained vague about the money, agreeing beforehand to not bring up Antoine, lest it upset Adèle. Erik had also been obtuse about leaving the Lungern because the reason was something not even Christine knew nor needed to know. It seemed so insignificant now, after their dramatic departure from Italy. At least Adèle had not heard any rumors of hauntings from the Opéra, the subject of Erik's letter.

"It's too bad you don't have your red ink," Christine teased, and Erik tried to laugh.

"I miss it, sometimes," he confessed instead, fingers tracing over the uncharacteristically kind words he intended to send to the office he had once lurked beneath. "Sending my notes. Having an impact on something, even if it was just to frighten a bureaucrat."

"I miss it too," Christine agreed, much to his surprise. Erik turned to her curiously. "Not you being a terror to those poor men, but the Opéra."

"Is that why you declined Adèle's invitation to see her perform?"

Christine gave a sad smile and nodded. "I don't think I'm ready yet to..." She bit her lip, unable to find the words, but Erik knew them.

"Be reminded of what you've lost," Erik whispered.

"What I chose to give up," she corrected him. "I could have stayed if I wanted to. Or at least I tell myself that."

"You can always adopt a new name and sing wherever you like."

"Someone would recognize me and word would spread and questions would be asked," Christine said, shaking her head. "And I would find myself exactly where I was before – deaf to the applause and caught in despair. I'm not meant for fame."

"You're meant for more than this, though," Erik said again without thinking, guilt seizing him at the regret in her voice.

"More than to be caught in a constant flight from ghosts and horrors."

"I don't miss you being morbid and self-effacing." Christine took his hands and clasped them to her heart. "I chose you, knowing it wouldn't be easy. We face this all together, and that is what I am meant for."

"It is the greatest honor ever given a man – to be loved by you, my Christine," Erik whispered as he twined his hand into her hair. "I can only hope to be worthy of it. Perhaps tonight, I will be."

"What do you mean?" Christine asked, curiosity rising as he had hoped. "You've already taken me to see the city more than enough times."

"Twice counts as more than enough?"

"For you. In London."

Erik laughed at how well she knew him. It had been a strain on him to go out and about with her to the great museums and for a carriage ride in a park, his paranoia and pain always lurking at the back of his mind. For Christine, he had endured it as he had endured dinners with Howard and tea with Adèle. He wanted nothing more personally than to shut the curtains and spend a few days in their expensive room, but that was not what a good husband would do.

"I have something more intimate planned," Erik said with a smile, hoping internally that this might bring relief to them both.

"This isn't one of Letitia's private parties, is it? I don't know if I'm ready for that either." Christine was blushing, which fascinated Erik.

"It's not," Erik said carefully, pulling Christine up into his lap and enjoying her warmth and weight. It was steadying. "But now I'm quite intrigued as to what she's been saying that has you, of all people, blushing."

"It was nothing! I'm sure she was joking about events where, um..." It was highly amusing to see the woman he had done many unspeakably carnal things with sputtering over something scandalous.

"Are they orgies?"

"No!" Christine yelped in a tone Erik would place somewhere near a high B flat. "They're a sort of salon, I guess, and she mentioned there was a woman at one. Who men lined up to be attended by. With a whip. Or flog. Something like that. I didn't ask for details." Christine's face was nearly crimson now as she hid it in the crook of Erik's neck.

"Oh, I wish you had," Erik chuckled. "That sounds delightful."

"Don't play with me!" Christine exclaimed, looking up at Erik with a gentle sort of annoyance. "It does not... Does it?"

Erik gave the slightest of shrugs and Christine's eyes went beautifully wide. He had to fight the urge to think more on the subject, given his lover's position so close to the organ that might respond to a fantasy of her wielding such punishment.

"Perhaps something to discuss later. We do have an appointment," Erik said as he rose, though the admonition did nothing to dispel the suspicion in his wife's face.

"What – when did you make an appointment for something?"

"I do go places without you. Though it's generally miserable, I must admit," Erik sighed as he searched the room for his mask, coat, and hat. "You may need a shawl: there's a chill in the air."

"Are you going to tell me where we're going?"

Erik smirked at her over his shoulder. "No. It would ruin the surprise."

"Ever the showman," Christine muttered and shook her head.

Soon enough, they were in a carriage with the curtains drawn: both for privacy and to keep up the suspense. Christine stared at him with a mix of consternation and amusement that he deeply enjoyed.

"What part sounded delightful?" Christine blurted out, increasing Erik's good humor.

"Whatever do you mean?" he asked back with a simpering tone which earned him a delicious glare.

"You know what I mean. What part of watching a woman do that to men at a party was delightful to you?"

Erik took a long moment to stare at her. He was far more interested in her thoughts on the matter than quickly revealing his. "Not the watching part, which I don't think should surprise you."

"But you—"

"Here we are," Erik exclaimed as the carriage jerked to a halt. Christine looked just about ready to murder him, which made her all the more beautiful. "Come along. We're going around the back."

"Where are we?" Christine demanded as she joined Erik on the street.

"Not far from Trafalgar Square," he answered, though he knew that wasn't what she wanted to hear. He waited for her to look up at the building beside them. It was hard to tell what it was from the street, with its rows of windows adorned with classical decoration and the filigreed roof above. Luckily, the plain, wooden stage door was a giveaway.

"Are we at a theater?" Christine asked. "It's far past time for curtain."

"Indeed, it is. And this theater is dark tonight," Erik replied, taking his wife's hand to guide her to the door. "There is at least one person keeping tabs. Who should be here..." On cue, the door opened and a yawning man in plain worker's clothes looked them over. "Right now."

"You Howard's friend?" the man asked in a cockney accent, wariness in his expression.

"Indeed. Thank you for your assistance. Here." Erik produced several pound notes and the man grinned. "For your trouble and discretion."

The man stared at Erik, perhaps not comprehending, though Erik's English had been impeccable.

"Leave us alone."

"Right. Get on inside and I'll lock the doors, so they'll be shut when you go out," the man said, gesturing for them to enter. Christine looked thrilled and Erik felt the same, especially when the door shut behind them and they were alone in the quiet theater. Erik took up the oil lamp the stagehand had left and lifted it to guide them.

"I've never been here before today when I made these arrangements," Erik mused as they moved through the corridors. "But it feels so familiar, doesn't it?"

"When I first came to the Opéra, it felt like home," Christine murmured, squeezing Erik's hand as he led them (hopefully) up a flight of stairs and to the stage. "It felt like all the theaters and concert halls I'd been to with Papa."

"A theater holds the same magic, no matter where it is," Erik confirmed, a chill running up his spine. In the distance, he saw a light and headed towards it. Sure enough, the ghost light awaited them, burning in its iron cage on the stage to ward off the unquiet dead (or to give stagehands a light when they began work for the day). "Only the ghosts change."

"Why did you bring me here?" Christine asked softly, voice thick with emotion. She looked out on the darkened auditorium. It was much smaller than the Palais Garnier. The seats were still red velvet, but the walls were plastered with ivory paint, and their decoration not nearly as ostentatious. A row of unlit candelabrum adorned the overhang of the balcony, and high above hung a dark chandelier. Best not to think too much on that. What concerned Erik more was the rehearsal piano remaining on the stage.

"Because it has been too long since I have heard you sing for me in a place like this," Erik confessed. "That is what I miss most of all."

"The acoustics?" Christine joked, but Erik could see she was moved by the gesture.

"The magic," he countered. "What would you like to sing, my love?"

Erik sat at the piano, waiting. There was no aria that she could choose that he wouldn't know. She looked at him from the center of the stage, her eyes bright with love. "The Bellini we were working on in Florence, please."

"An excellent choice," Erik said, and began to play. He didn't have to look down at his fingers, so he could watch her. His goddess of love and song at whose feet he worshipped.

"*Casta diva...*" Christine began, becoming Norma and calling to an ancient goddess of the moon. Her voice spun out in glorious sound, smooth and bright at the same time, like moonlight itself. It wasn't perfect, not polished as she had been months before on the Opéra stage, but it didn't have to be. It didn't matter if a trill was missing there or a note was flat here, his angel sang out of love and joy, and it was utter perfection to Erik's ears.

She sang for him and for herself, letting her voice rise to the heavens, filling the dark theater with a different kind of light. It was magic he had sorely missed, but he was so happy to share with her once again.

When her aria concluded, it was Erik's turn to choose and he began the accompaniment to a sweeping duet, a confession of love and devotion by Bizet. Then another song. And another. Their voices rang out for no one but each other and the ghosts that might watch from the shadows.

# Paris

"Tell me again why I'm about to humiliate myself?" Blanche demanded for perhaps the seventh time.

"I'm solving a mystery," Meg replied, yanking her friend across the bridge as they approached the *Faubourg Saint-Germain.* Meg didn't know this arrondissement well at all. Her kind of people (poor, young, performers – take your pick) were not welcome in the neighborhoods of the wealthy and well-to-do.

"That makes no sense! You're a dancer, Meg Giry, not a—whatever else you're trying to be." Blanche trotted after Meg, trying to keep up with her frantic pace.

Meg didn't want to waste too much time on a conversation she didn't want to have. Was she supposed to tell Blanche that, since she was the only one who had a passing friendship with Sorelli, and thus the de Chagny family, she was the most convenient accomplice?

"If it works, you'll have a delicious rumor to spread: how about that?" Meg muttered as she stopped and checked the blue and white street signs mounted to a wall. "Here we are."

"If what works? I don't even understand what you're trying to discover with all this!"

"You'll know," Meg countered. "Do you recall your part?"

"It's not that complicated to attempt to return a watch," Blanche sighed. "More so to keep someone entertained while you do something stupid."

"I'll only attempt the stupidity if I have a good chance." Meg's stomach grew uneasy thinking about the plot and the possibilities.

"You're mad. I'm looking forward to telling you I told you so," was all Blanche offered with a shake of her head.

"Noted." Meg took a steadying breath as they reached their target.

The de Chagny manor was not notable among the other houses of the Faubourg. If anything, it was rather austere and old-fashioned, and the hedges looked like they needed a good trim. The gate was open, at least, and they didn't have to wait long for a butler to open the door.

He looked annoyed at Meg and Blanche's very presence, which Meg thought was unfair. They were nicely dressed, with clean gloves and hats. Blanche's even had a lovely flower tucked into the band.

"Good afternoon," Blanche began, as planned. She was older and prettier than Meg, which made her the natural focus of the man. "We don't have an appointment but we were hoping the Mademoiselle la Vicomtesse or Monsieur le Comte were in. We think we have something that belonged to their family."

"Give it here; I'll show them," the butler replied.

"No offense, Monsieur, but we'd like to take it to them personally. It's too precious a thing to risk it going astray," Meg piped in. She knew it was rude and, indeed, the butler's eyes widened in offense, but it was better to have him off balance.

"Mademoiselle la Vicomtesse is occupied today," the butler grumbled. "And her dear brother is also quite busy with matters of business."

"We won't be long!" Blanche said sweetly, trying to be charming but arriving at simpering.

The butler sighed powerfully and gestured for them to enter. Meg's heart jumped in private triumph. She had completed one step. Onto the next.

They were shown into a parlor with a handsome fireplace that remained unlit. It was still summer, of course, but the room was cold and a certain darkness lurked in the corners.

"Wait here. He'll see you when it's convenient," the butler said and shut the door behind him as he left.

"Well, this is nice," Blanche murmured, looking around at the books on the shelves and a dusty globe. "Nicer than Monsieur Tremblay's flat at least."

"He had a flat?" Meg asked, aware the moment she said it that the flat wasn't the worrying part of that statement.

"I think he had a house too. Somewhere around here." Blanche's face was impassive as she spoke, her eyes staying to the windows and the street beyond. "But he keeps a flat close to the Opéra for convenience. I went with Rochelle once before she was relieved of him. Come to think of it, it might not even be his alone. Just a place the patrons use when one of them needs it."

"For seduction," Meg whispered, scandalized.

Blanch scoffed and gave her a withering look. "Seduction is not the word for it."

"Do you know what happened to Rochelle there?" Meg asked fearfully, but Blanche waved the question away.

"Nothing of the kind would happen here. Raoul de Chagny is a better man than the other patrons. And not just because he's younger and handsome," Blanche giggled, and Meg rolled her eyes. She didn't want Blanche distracted. "Do you remember how mad with jealousy we all were when the Vicomte – at the time – was so enamored of Christine Daaé? And after she laughed in his face, the lunatic."

"Maybe he's seen the light now," Meg wondered aloud. "I mean, after she broke their engagement and went off wherever."

"Do you think he's ready to love again?" Blanche mused. "He's so handsome."

"Please don't throw yourself at him," Meg sighed. "He's sworn off the Opéra entirely now that his lady love is long gone. He probably won't be interested in artists."

"Well, maybe not you," Blanche shrugged. "How rich do you think they are?"

Meg looked around the parlor. It wasn't gilded in gold like the grand salons at the Opéra, seeking to be another Versailles, but it wasn't crumbling either. It was simply empty.

They jumped when the door opened and the man of the house entered. Meg had only ever seen Raoul de Chagny from afar, and that had been months ago. In less than half a year, he seemed to have aged five. He had a beard now, of the same fair brown color as his hair. There were circles under his eyes and a somberness to his expression that was entirely new. Perhaps losing a brother did that to a person.

"Good day, Monsieur le Comte," Blanche said first, making a rather awkward curtsey that Meg was sure was unnecessary. "Thank you for seeing us."

"I'm terribly busy. What is it?" the Comte replied tiredly.

"Busy with what?" Meg asked, hoping she looked as foolish as she was making herself sound. Shaya had told her to use the fact that everyone would underestimate her as a weak, silly girl to her advantage, and she meant to. "Surely you don't need to work like us."

"My family owns many business interests and lands, as all nobles do, and they do not manage themselves," Raoul replied tightly.

"Philippe never mentioned that," Blanche said, oblivious to the way the words darkened Raoul's face.

"Yes, I know intimately now how much my late brother assumed, as you seem to, that we needed only to spend money and not worry about the maintenance of it," Raoul grumbled.

"It's your brother that brings us here, Monsieur," Meg piped up and received a doubtful frown. "I found this, you see, in the cellars."

Meg produced the gold watch from her pocket. It was a lovely piece; she would have to ask Shaya where he had procured it.

"And she showed it to me and I recognized it, I'm sure," Blanche added. "I'm Blanche Carcaux. You may remember me. I was a friend of Philippe's."

"You mean of Sorelli's." Raoul corrected, unimpressed. "You do look vaguely familiar." He looked over Meg with a combination of boredom and disdain.

"Margaret Giry. I'm called Meg," she answered with a polite smile.

"Giry. I know that name from somewhere," Raoul muttered, peering more intently at Meg. She had to ball her hands into fists to keep herself from squirming.

"Her mother was the ghost's box keeper," Blanche interjected, to Meg's horror. It was a mistake for Blanche to say that because the Comte's expression changed from annoyed to thunderous.

"Your mother ran errands for that horrid demon, and you come to me with a watch you conveniently found in the Opéra?" he asked, a threat in his tone.

"Only because Blanche encouraged me!" Meg squeaked. "She recognized the watch!"

"So you were going to keep such a treasure for yourself before an honorable young woman forced you to return it?" Raoul shot back. Blanche looked horribly pleased by the backhanded compliment.

"No, Monsieur! I knew it had to belong to someone important and I showed it to friends to see if they recognized it," Meg protested. "Which brought us here. We would have sought you out at the Opéra, but I was given to understand you have withdrawn your family's patronage."

"Yes, we've had to cut a great many frivolous expenses, but that one was a pleasure to eliminate," Raoul replied. There was something truly vicious about the way he said it.

Blanche wasn't deterred. "Oh, that's such a tragedy, Monsieur le Comte! We all so enjoyed your visits."

"Show me the watch, girl," Raoul snapped.

Meg handed him the timepiece, proud that her hand remained steady as she did. He took it and examined it carefully, eyes narrow.

"This does look familiar," the Comte said, much to Meg's shock. His eyes fell on her again, scornful. "I supposed you're expecting some sort of reward. I know they don't pay you anything at your level in the corps."

"We couldn't—" Meg began.

"But we accept, that's so very generous of you," Blanche interrupted.

"I have money in my office: come along," the man ordered, placing the watch in his pocket. Meg was flummoxed. It wasn't his brother's, but he had taken it – why? She looked around the house as they made their way through to a study. There were very few ornaments decorating the place – no fancy vases or candlesticks, and not even many pictures, but space remained where Meg knew in her gut those things should be.

He was going to sell the watch for money like they had done half the furnishings of the house.

The Comte's study was chaotic, with piles of ledgers and papers all about. At least it lent credence to the idea that he was untangling some financial mess his brother had left them.

"Will five francs be sufficient?" Raoul muttered as he rummaged in a drawer. As soon as he rewarded them, he would see them out, and Meg had not learned enough.

"May I use the washroom?" Meg blurted out.

"Meg! How improper!" Blanche chided, swatting her on the arm. "Monsieur le Comte, I apologize for my companion. She's young and has never learned manners."

"It's true, Monsieur," Meg lamented. "But there's no public places anywhere in the Faubourg and—"

"Jesus. It's upstairs. Be quick about it," Raoul sighed.

"I'll make sure to keep you entertained," Blanche said and shot Meg a wink.

Meg wondered how blatant Blanche's flirtations would be and if they would get her anywhere. Hopefully, they would keep the Comte amused and distracted while Meg got to work.

She sped up the grand staircase of the manor and onto the upstairs level. To be fair, Raoul hadn't told her where exactly the powder room was, so it was completely understandable for her to open all the doors to look.

The first door was a bedroom with all the furniture covered in sheets. They looked like shrouds – ghostly, sad things – and Meg guessed that this was the late Philippe's chamber. The next room was practically empty, save for a bed that was half disassembled, and the next door was locked.

The fourth door she tried was the powder room, and it was impressive in its size and appointments, but Meg ignored it for the door next to it. It opened to a room that smelled of perfume and femininity.

"What are you doing? Who are you?" a female voice demanded from the bed. Meg froze as a woman rose from behind the curtains of the canopy and came around to confront Meg.

"I'm sorry! I was looking for the washroom!" Meg stammered as she looked the woman over, taking in every vital detail. She looked like a darker, colder version of her brother, this Vicomtesse.

"Who the hell are you?" Sabine de Chagny hissed, pulling her robe closed too late.

"I'm Meg. I was returning a watch to your brother that I found in the Opéra. It was your brother's – other brother's. God rest his soul," Meg said all in one breath.

"Get out of my room and out of my house, little rat," Sabine growled.

Meg rushed down the stairs to obey. She found Blanche and Raoul still in the office, with Blanche leaning towards the Comte in a way that someone might find seductive if they were lacking their spectacles.

"I'm ready to go!" Meg said as she grabbed her friend. "You have our reward?"

"I do," Blanche grumbled, fighting Meg's attention. "But we can stay!"

"We will talk some other time, Mademoiselle Carcaux," Raoul said with a tone and expression Meg couldn't discern. "Good day to you both. I trust you can find your way out."

"We can," Meg smiled and dragged Blanche to the front door through the sad, empty hall. "Goodbye!"

As soon as they were through the gate, Blanche shook her off. "What is wrong with you? I was having a lovely conversation."

"I didn't bring you here to flirt."

"Yes, you brought me here on the promise of five francs and good gossip. One of which I now have and will be keeping." Blanche jangled the coins in her hand. "Now, where is this scandal I was promised? I didn't see anything of immediate note."

"That's because you didn't see the sister. I did," Meg smirked. She wondered if it was a useful thing to tell Blanche what she had confirmed for Shaya. It would cause a scandal indeed, and the family would know exactly what the source of the rumor was. It was risky, but if Sabine was already using a married name, this was why.

"What's wrong with his sister?" Blanche pushed, and Meg exhaled. Better to know where a fire started if she was going to watch the flames.

"Nothing is wrong with her, she looked quite healthy. I'm sure her baby will be healthy too."

# London

C hristine had not wanted to dine alone. Alone, of course, was a relative term. Letitia had been there, and Adèle, and a score of other people in the smoky pub, but it had left Christine feeling alone because Erik had not been there. She didn't blame him, of course; it wasn't the sort of place he enjoyed. It was too loud and packed too close. She wouldn't have wanted him to come, but she had still been left offended to be in a crowd alone again.

Letitia had sensed her melancholy and engaged her in conversation. Perhaps it had been loneliness that had made Christine mention the things she had and therefore learn more than she could have imagined. There was no unlearning it, however, and now, here Christine was, walking back to their room at the Reubens with a fire in her brain and something altogether unexpected in her hand.

Erik had also wanted to stay back because he had fallen into a new fixation in the last few days. Christine didn't understand completely why he was so excited about the English texts of electricity and currents that he had acquired, but they had engrossed him for days. Christine wasn't sure, but it seemed to be his method of coping with the continued limbo they found themselves in.

It had taken Christine a while to not take offense at the way Erik's mind would put its entire, impressive power behind one new pursuit or obscure idea. She had become used to being that idea, but even a man who loved her as much as Erik couldn't keep his focus on her entirely every hour of every day. Nor should he have to, Christine told herself as she rushed quickly through the lobby, holding her shawl in front of her to conceal her dangerous prize.

Tonight, she wanted to be that obsession again. She wanted to feel – or more accurately, be reminded – that his devotion was hers and she could make his attention hers too. If she could get up the spine for it. She was still unsure, but her discontent was morphing into need that pushed her along, all the way up to their room and through the door.

Erik had not budged from his chair by the hearth, the only change in the way she had left him being that some of his books had moved.

"Did you even eat?" Christine asked without ceremony when he looked up at her. He was wearing his old, white mask. He did that when he was alone in places like this, where some maid or concierge could come in with a key. It made him feel safe, but it made Christine sad that he needed it.

"I... don't think so," Erik answered, and she could hear his brows furrowed in contemplation even though she couldn't see them. "We did have a large lunch."

"You would die without me," Christine sighed. "Not from a broken heart, but of starvation."

"It could be both. Did you enjoy your evening?"

Erik had not noticed her shawl, which was good, and Christine exhaled as she set it on a chair near the bed.

"It was amusing. They sang pub songs," Christine said, moving towards her husband. "You might have liked it. Everyone was building their own harmonies to sing about the glory of brown ale."

"Before or after they ate that mush made of peas?"

"At least they ate."

"Fair enough," Erik chuckled, but it faded quickly as he looked at Christine. "Are you alright?"

"I missed you is all," Christine replied, her mood warming just to be close to him again.

"I'm sorry. I shouldn't have been so distracted." Erik was instantly contrite, as she knew he would be. Almost too much so.

"I don't ever want to make you do things that don't agree with you," Christine countered. "I can understand what you need and still miss you."

"I should be better though," Erik sighed and looked to his book, now with guilt. "I was distracted."

"I know you were. I'm not angry." Christine said the words, but knew he didn't really hear them. It had been like this, off and on in their marriage. She would tell him one thing, but the dark voices inside his head were often louder than her words. She hated those voices. She wished she could cast them out forever and make Erik believe her. They were like weeds in a garden that constantly had to be removed, so tonight, she would be a gardener.

"You should be. You deserve—"

"If you dare say again that I deserve a better husband or some other such nonsense, there will be consequences," Christine admonished, surprised at the steel in her voice.

"I'm sorry," Erik whispered, but there wasn't contrition in his voice. There was something like excitement. A breathlessness she knew, and it made her smile.

"Stand up," Christine ordered, a thrill rising inside her as well. "Take off that mask and look at me."

Erik obeyed, silently and quickly, but Christine could see the tension in his shoulders and the questions in his eyes.

"Do you believe me when I say I love you?" Christine demanded, firm and calm. "Answer out loud."

"Sometimes," Erik replied. While Christine was annoyed at the answer, she was at least comforted by his honesty.

"Do you believe you deserve that love?"

Erik opened his mouth to speak, but no sound came out.

"That's answer enough," Christine sighed.

"Christine, I—"

She stopped him with a raised hand. "No excuses. I want you to..." Christine swallowed. The will to command was easy to find, but there was still a part of her that cringed at the brazenness of it. It wasn't proper for a woman to order a man around, but it felt so good, and the anticipation in Erik's golden eyes made her brave and breathless. "Go to the bed, turn your back to me, and undress."

Her heart pounded as she watched Erik comply. She loved how he moved – his grace and elegance. She loved the sight of his skin – the way his taut muscles were visible on his back as he took off his shirt. She even loved it when he exposed the rest of himself, including the pleasing roundness of his ass and long legs.

She took her time just to look at him as she unbuttoned her jacket and then slipped out of her skirt and petticoats. She wanted to see what it did to him to listen to her movements. What was he thinking? What was he hoping for? Were those dark voices telling him he was flawed and loathsome, or was there anticipation rising in him?

She tended to the curtains and locked the door, methodical in her steps through the room. She doffed her stockings and shoes, remaining in her corset and pantalets. She wanted to be wearing something for this, to make the imbalance between them even more askew. There was one more thing, though, that would tip it. That would take this to somewhere new. Somewhere they had never been.

"Would you like me to remind you who you are?" Christine asked as she opened her shawl on the chair. "You can say no. We can just make love or go to bed. If you want this, I need you to choose it."

"I want it," Erik said without a moment of hesitation. "I... I need it."

"Tell me to stop and it ends. No judgement or punishment," Christine went on, repeating what Letitia had informed her was the most crucial element of these kinds of encounters, no matter who they involved. She had been very firm that Christine understood that above all before giving her the object she now took from the folds of her shawl. "Do you understand?"

"I do."

He sounded calm, but tense. Christine was anxious too. This could be a disaster. This could shock and horrify him or send him spiraling into some terrible memory. Christine stepped closer to him and caressed his bare back, tracing the long lines of his scars with gentle fingertips. Erik sighed at the touch, relaxing.

"Do you think these are proof? That you could not deserve me?" Christine asked, barely more than a whisper. "Don't lie or tell me what you think you should say or what I want you to say. Tell the truth."

"I do," Erik breathed back. "All of me is proof."

Christine shook her head and braced herself. He did need this and she needed to do it.

She brought the crop up and aimed. It was smaller than a whip, this stick wrapped in leather and crowned with a wide panel just smaller than her palm at the end. Letitia had shown her how to use it if she so desired and had not asked any intrusive questions, nor had Christine pursued knowing why she had it with her. Now it was hers, raised and ready to be a reminder of her love.

She brought it down on Erik's back, not too hard, but not gently either. It landed with a sharp smack and Erik gasped, the speed of his breath increasing. But he didn't react like it was pain of the normal sort.

"You believe I have made some sort of mistake?" Christine asked, the quaver in her voice fading now.

"Yes. Every day I wonder when you'll see the truth." Erik's voice was the one shaking now.

Christine breathed deep and waited a beat, until he began to wonder what awaited, then struck again, harder this time, on the meat of his thigh. Without hesitation, she delivered another strike against the other. The sound her lover made was not one of pain, and it made her skin begin to heat as soft redness spread where the crop had done its work.

"Why do you not trust the words I say?" Christine asked, trailing the crop over his ass.

"I—" His hesitation was too much, and Christine struck again, provoking another low groan.

"Go on."

"Because everything in my life says it can't be true," Erik answered at last and earned another thwap to his back, and another over his shoulder. His head fell back, his eyes falling closed as if he was sinking into pleasure. That was what she was giving, Christine was sure now. It was a kind of pleasure she had never thought possible. She felt it too and it was intoxicating.

"I say it's true," Christine stated, her voice as firm as the strike she landed against his hindquarters. She peeked around to his front, nuzzling his shoulder and delivering a kiss. He was hard, his cock leaking and flushed, even though it had not been touched. She gave him another playful hit on his thigh, then a harder one on his ass. He groaned again and a fresh bead of moisture emerged. Christine was wet too, her desire seeping down her thigh.

"Do you believe you're good, my love? Good enough for me?" Christine whispered in his ear and he shook his head violently. She struck again.

"I can't," he almost moaned. Another hit, another gasp.

"You can." Another strike from the crop and his hips shuddered forward like he was desperate to fuck, but he only had the air.

"I..."

Another hit, so hard against his back it echoed through the room. "Say you're good." Another. "Say it because it's true." Another blow, another moan of ecstasy. "Say it because you are so good right now, taking what you think is punishment. So good for me."

"I am. I am good... for you."

That wasn't enough, and the blow against his ass let him know it. Christine was leaving marks now, red and vibrant across his pale skin. The sight of those marks and the way her victim shuddered at each touch made her cunt *ache*. She wanted to devour him and defile him at the same time, but more than that, she wanted to break the chains he kept himself in. She wanted to shatter his hatred and build him anew without it.

"You're good as yourself," Christine panted, hitting again. "You are good and you deserve love."

"Yes. I do," Erik moaned, doubling over, his arms bracing himself on the bed. His whole body was shaking with the effort it took him to stand, to keep being good. It was an obscene sight: his ass presented to her, raw and striped with marks from her crop. It made Christine dizzy to look, delirious with thoughts of what else she could do, but she had to stay in the moment, had to savor this.

"You're so beautiful," Christine said aloud. "Do you believe me when I say that's how I see you?"

She struck again before he could answer and he arched his back into the blow. "Yes, my angel," Erik groaned. "I believe you."

Christine didn't know any longer if the strikes from the crop were punishment or reward, she only knew how Erik responded, how his hips bucked and his body shuddered with each blow. With something like... delight.

"Could you come this way? Just from this?" Christine asked, her voice a mere rasp as she delivered another delicious hit.

"I... I don't know," Erik muttered as if his mind was far away. "If you... If you will it."

"But then where would that leave my poor cunt?" Christine said, shocked at her own words as she trailed the crop over the marks she had left. The beautiful evidence of her love etched onto his skin.

She was kissing his back before the thought was even complete in her mind, dropping the crop to the bed and fumbling with her bodice as her lips traced the inflamed skin. Erik made a noise that might have begun as her name but melted into a guttural, wild sound. She was wild too, desperate for it to be her lips and teeth and hands and nails against his flesh, not a piece of leather.

He whimpered so beautifully as she bit and scratched, flattening her now bare body against his back. It was torture of another kind, this time for her. It was pure agony to see him so lost and not have him within her.

"Fuck me, right now," Christine panted, and it was all her desperate lover needed to hear. In a heartbeat, he had her on her back, lifting her by the hips as he knelt on the bed and driving into her so hard and deep she had to scream into a pillow so she wouldn't alarm the neighbors.

That might have been the last civilized thought she had before he began to drive into her, fast and frantic for release. It was rough and relentless, his cock filling her so completely and touching her so deeply she could hardly comprehend it. In mere moments, she was rushing to her peak, her body quaking as they gave into pleasure.

"Yes. That's so good. You're so good, my love. You're—" The climax stole the words from her throat and the breath from her lungs. Erik gave a perfect cry above her, joining her and filling her with hot seed. He pumped and shuddered even as Christine went limp, her body no longer subject to her commands.

But he was. He always would be.

They collapsed onto the bed, together and his lips finally found hers. He tasted of salt – of tears or sweat or both – and he kissed her long and deep, pure love in the embrace. Finally, after what felt like forever, she opened her eyes to meet her husband's. They were glowing with adoration.

"I believe you now," Erik whispered, forehead against hers. "Dear God, I believe you."

"For now," Christine sighed back. "I fear I may have to remind you again at some point."

"It's highly possible," Erik replied with laughter in his voice. He looked so unburdened in that moment, so free and full of joy. Christine had given him that, somehow, with a crop and commands; she had driven back the dark from his heart and mind. And hers too. There would be no nightmares tonight for either of them.

"I think another such lesson would be a true delight," she whispered back and kissed him again.

# Paris

S haya wondered as he glared out of his window across the *Rue de Rivoli* and to the Tuileries if he should have offered to meet young Margaret Giry at the Opéra instead of his home. It wasn't that he minded having guests – it was that Meg wasn't adept at taking hints when it was time to leave. The night before he had assigned her reconnaissance at the de Chagny manor, she had stayed long past supper, chatting with Darius about all manner of things from vegetables to their travels. They seemed to enjoy it, but it made Shaya sympathetic to Erik's choice of life in a secluded cellar.

Shaya frowned at the thought of Erik. He had been a recluse in his way in Persia when Shaya had first known him. It had only been thanks to Ramin that Erik had socialized at all, and grudgingly so. Shaya tried to imagine him now, out there in the wide world, with Christine beside him. What were they doing? Had they settled anywhere? Had he truly changed? Shaya knew the last answer in his heart but doubt still nagged at him.

The man Meg had overheard had been injured. Had it been Erik? Had he meant to kill?

Shaya recognized Meg's knock and scowled as he went to open the door.

"Did you see me on the street?" Meg asked without ceremony, barging right inside. "I was trying not to be seen, like you suggested. It's not hard if you walk along the galleries. Where is Darius?"

"Making the tea," Darius said as he emerged from the kitchen with a tray of cups and a pot.

"Do you have those biscuits again? With the nuts?" Meg asked with wide eyes.

"You ate the last of them, but I'll make more soon." Darius smiled and gave Shaya a look. "I'm glad someone appreciates them."

"I appreciate them," Shaya crowed. "Pistachios are just bloody expensive and impossible to find."

"Of course," Darius smiled. "Now, Mademoiselle Giry, don't keep us waiting. What did you discover?"

"It's as you suspected," Meg began, and Shaya felt a rush of pride mixed with dread. "Sabine de Chagny is with child. It's probably why she hasn't been seen."

"She wants to avoid a scandal," Shaya muttered. "She cares about her family name, even though she will claim she wed de Martiniac before he... disappeared."

The lie in the word was bile on Shaya's tongue. He remembered the certainty in what he had done, the justice in it. But he had still taken a life and left this unborn child without a father. Then again, knowing everything about Antoine de Martiniac, Shaya had perhaps spared the mother a marriage to a monster and the child being raised by one. Not an easy thing, either way.

"But she still wants his fortune, I think," Meg went on, and Shaya could see her mind working. "That's what the man Pomeroy was talking to said they were after: a fortune."

"That doesn't make sense, de Martiniac was broke," Darius mused aloud.

"He was, but when he had plans," Shaya bit his lip. There were things that Meg couldn't know about Antoine's plots. "He was close to claiming one."

"He and his wife – I guess we can call the Vicomtesse that – have that in common. Her family is struggling."

"The de Chagny family?" Shaya asked. This was new and vital information. "They always lived so richly."

"Philippe, I think, was good at spending money and not at keeping it flowing," Meg answered knowingly. "The house has been stripped of valuables and the Comte made remarks about his brother's bad hand for business."

"So you spoke to Raoul?" Shaya asked, and Meg nodded.

Shaya wanted to ask how the man was – for he certainly was a man now, not the naïve boy who had been twisted by all this calamity into a creature of hate that bordered on madness. But what would be the point, when he knew the answer would be that any light that had been in him was snuffed out now.

"Was he well?" Shaya asked at last, and Meg cocked her head.

"Do you know him? Through the affair with Christine Daaé and the Phantom?" Meg asked back. Shaya didn't need to say anything for the answer to show on his face. "He wasn't in good spirits, to say the least. And he kept the watch."

"What?" Shaya huffed.

"Probably wants to sell it," Darius muttered. Shaya understood the impulse, but he had wanted to sell it back and get a refund of his money. "If he's selling things from the house and watches that don't belong to him—"

"And working to repair whatever financial mess his brother left," Meg added.

"That means he doesn't anticipate some great fortune being found," Shaya finished. "That makes sense. If Raoul knew—" He stopped himself and met Darius' eyes. If Raoul knew Erik lived, he would have gone mad with it and made far more violent and vociferous contact with Shaya than sending a spy.

"Sabine is doing this on her own," Meg said, then furrowed her brow. "Trying to find her husband and his fortune?"

Shaya and Darius exchanged another look. "Who else could it be? He's disappeared." For a moment, Meg seemed to take the story as Shaya hoped until the line between her brows deepened, reminding Shaya that she was smarter than that.

"But then why watch you?" Meg asked aloud as Shaya swore silently in his head. "What would that avail her? What does any of this have to do with the haunting of the Opéra? Though our new ghost wants money too..."

"Firmin Richard," Darius answered. "He's involved. Visiting Pomeroy. Helping Sabine. We can't forget him."

"He had dealings with Antoine, he wants that debt repaid," Shaya mused aloud.

"Could he be our ghost?" Meg asked, eyes brightening.

"I had not considered that, to be honest," Shaya replied, looking between the other two. He had not considered any suspect too deeply when it came to 'their' ghost. The ghost and Erik were so deeply entwined in his mind it was hard to think of some other man behind that mask.

"He knows the Opéra and he – did he know of the truth about the ghost?" Meg demanded, her energy rising as she stood and paced in front of the fire.

"He did," Shaya confirmed. "And he knows of me."

"He has a reason to hate patrons too, if he feels they forced him out!" Meg went on. "We should pursue it!"

"How will we do that?" Shaya asked, unable to stop himself chuckling. "I could speak to Armand."

"I could keep looking around the Opéra," Meg mused.

Shaya frowned. "I hope it doesn't involve blindly looking through the cellars."

"Well, you could come with me."

"There's nothing to be found there," Shaya replied, and that was entirely honest. Darius gave him a look that was also a question, and Meg seemed skeptical. "All the doors I knew of down there are sealed and locked. I've checked."

"Even the one in the third cellar?" Darius asked.

"Where we met?" Meg added.

Shaya nodded, though the thought brought him little comfort. Erik had assured him that the torture chamber was sealed and dismantled as well as it could be and that there was no getting into his secret home now. Shaya was loath to check. It was too close to the secret place where Antoine de Martiniac's body lay, wearing a match to Erik's gold ring.

"Well then, I'll keep asking around and listening like a little mouse. Or rat, I guess," Meg said with a guileless shrug, before frowning. "There's a patron who has been asking me to dinner. I could talk to him and see if he knows if the other victims had a grudge against Richard. Though he's a bit odious."

"Be careful, young Meg," Darius said before Shaya could. "People have been hurt gravely in this drama, and the patrons are their own sort of danger."

A dark expression overtook Meg's young face. "People are hurt every day. Most of us don't get any justice. Anyway, there may be one other complication that might nudge things along."

"What have you done?" Shaya asked. The look Meg gave him reminded him profoundly of the sheepish expression he would find on Ramin's face when he caught him sneaking back home some nights: guilt mixed with hope that the one who had been caught was too innocent and liked by Shaya to be put into trouble.

"I needed help with the Comte, someone that knew him, like I told you. Well, she knows now. About Sabine de whatever-she's-calling-herself-now." Meg confessed.

"And your friend is a gossip," Shaya sighed.

"Rumors might spread. If we're lucky, the de Chagnys are so isolated now they won't hear," Darius offered.

Shaya shook his head and sighed. "We can only pray," he lamented. He didn't want this blowing up. He didn't want the Comte or his sister to know they were being investigated and spied upon right back. He wanted no reason for them to come anywhere near the Opéra.

If this new ghost was Firmin Richard, that was one thing. It would be a relief, in a way, for the source of this confusion to come from within that house. Because if it was some other phantom who could make Raoul de Chagny think his work was not done, Shaya shuddered to think of what chaos would fall.

# 9. Damnation

## London

Erik had become accustomed to the streets of London, but he still didn't know his way exactly, a status he found frustrating. In his youth, he had learned a city in a matter of days, pouring over maps and wandering the streets (usually at night). Apparently, that skill required practice or the energy of youth to maintain, or at least a willingness to amble about alone. London herself was a sprawling city made up of villages and neighborhoods that had been slowly devoured by the beast of progress, shrouded in the veil of fog and dust from coal factories and gray clouds, which made navigating it even harder.

For Christine, though, Erik would try. An evening walk didn't appall him either. As well-appointed as their rooms were, with their view of the Queen's stables and prim blue wallpaper, Erik was beginning to feel confined and anxious. It was good for him to get out and make his way to Christine. He had promised to meet her at her friend's, even if part of him wouldn't mind being punished for being late...

Erik's steps sped up through the winding, gaslit streets. His spine straightened as he recalled what they had done two nights before. What she had done to him and for him. There were still moments when he stepped outside himself with confusion and disgust, aghast that he had enjoyed such humiliation and pain.

There was more wrong with him than he had ever thought, and he had spent his whole life aware of his monstrousness.

The shame had manifested the morning after, when Erik's skin had smarted against the sheets as he awoke. The comfort of holding Christine had become arousal at that feeling, but his desire had felt different in the cool light of morning and an awful shame had hit him like a wave. Within minutes of waking, he had found himself fighting for breath as panic enveloped him.

She had known, of course; his Christine always knew when something was wrong. She had broken through his panic and reminded him that there was nothing to be ashamed of if what they had done had been what he wanted. It had been, he assured her, reminding her and himself that she could never really hurt him. They had enjoyed it, both of them, and they were not alone in enjoying such pursuits. More importantly, she had assured him of his goodness.

That was the word he still couldn't understand. His Christine loved him and redeemed him and that was so hard to believe, but he did believe it when she commanded him and demanded his submission. She had punished him so beautifully for not believing that he was worthy of her, she had to be right. She had made him into someone good and that wasn't a crime. It was a miracle.

Erik turned down a street, reasonably sure it would take him the right way. He couldn't afford to be this distracted walking alone at night, even if the memories dimmed the edges of the world most pleasantly. It felt so good to be hers, and yet it felt good to be free and unencumbered on the streets of a great city, his fate safely his own.

London was dark, and he was a dark figure within it. He was in his accustomed cape and wide hat, and it was foggy and cool enough here to justify a scarf around his chin, obscuring the edges of his mask. He could have worn the special one, but the spectacles and beard were so cumbersome and he wasn't going somewhere where people would care.

He wanted to be ignored, but alas, he wasn't alone. There were steps behind him. Steady on the cobblestones and in pace with his. Erik tensed. How long had a stranger been behind him? Was it a thief or another agent like Bidaut? Or was it nothing?

Erik took the next turn down a narrow alley and found a shadowed doorway in which to disappear. He still knew how to be a ghost. In a heartbeat, he was concealed in the safety of the dark, waiting for the steps to turn.

His pursuer was a man. Short and stocky with a workman's cap upon his head. The man paused at the entrance of the alley, sniffing the air like a predator. He had been following Erik, but what for? He peered into the dark for a few moments longer before moving on. Erik waited several beats before he emerged, but soon enough, he was on his way again and it was he who was following. The man ambled along slowly, observing people as they passed while Erik remained a silent shadow behind him.

It wasn't until Erik saw the man take notice of a woman walking alone that he understood. This was no spy or an assassin. He was merely a common criminal who had seen a man walking alone looking wealthy enough to rob. Now he had a better prospect.

Erik continued to follow, wondering what the thief intended. Was he a pickpocket? Erik doubted that. This man didn't display the skill needed for such work. As a master pickpocket, Erik would know. Relieving someone of their purse or watch was best done in crowded places, where no one noticed when one nudged by and slipped a hand into a coat. No, this man moved with aggressive audaciousness and he was getting closer to the woman. She was older, above working class, and unaware of her danger.

What was Erik to do? He had gone on a simple walk to meet his wife, and the universe had seen fit to present him with a test for which he did not have an easy answer. Christine told him to be good, that he was good, but what would a good man do here?

Stopping the thief was the obvious answer. But how far did stopping him go? Should he wait for the man to strike, or descend first, like a nightmare setting upon the unsuspecting assailant? What would a good man do with a thief in his clutches then? Erik couldn't very well haul the brute off to a police officer – they were all corrupt and useless. What, then, was left? Violence? Was that the resort of a good man? Was the violence he had done to Bidaut right or wrong? Did it all come down to perspective?

It had never been this hard before. Erik had always acted as his conscience (or whatever it was he had possessed in its place) had dictated. A year ago, he would have let the Punjab lasso take care of this lout, choking the life from him – or at least the consciousness. What good was it to add sin atop sin? Did any of it matter?

The man hastened his steps, getting closer to the woman as they approached another alley that would be a perfect spot to rob her. Erik acted, darting ahead and snatching the man by his collar.

"Get off me!" the man yelled as Erik hauled him backward. The intended victim jumped and turned around, looking more scandalized than grateful.

"Nothing to worry about, Madame," Erik said politely as he pulled the man aside by scruff of his neck. The woman rushed off, the sound of her fleeing steps mixing with the man's grunts.

Erik commended himself for the gentleness with which he shoved the man against the nearest doorframe; it would barely leave a bruise and his captive could still breathe. He was being so merciful. This was what a good man would do, wasn't it?

"A bit early in the evening for a robbery," Erik drawled.

The man struggled, reaching rather obviously for a pocket.

"Let me help you." Erik fished in the man's coat and pulled out the switchblade. "You really should take better care of your weapons. They could fall into the wrong hands."

"I'll kill—" the man began, but that was enough for Erik to tighten his grip on the thief's windpipe, tutting as he did. He wagged the knife in front of the man's bulging eyes before tucking it into his own pocket.

"You will not kill me, sir. Nor I you, as I'm feeling charitable. In gratitude for that, I'd like you to not rob anyone else tonight. Maybe try and make something better of your life."

The man's only reply was a further reddening of his face. Erik sighed and threw the pathetic figure against the wall, knocking his head just enough to disorient him, and then kicked his legs out from under him so he crumpled to the ground. That was sufficient.

Erik fled quickly, leaving the man on the ground without looking back. He'd be a fool to pursue, but his steps were loud and Erik would catch him if he did. Luckily, no footsteps followed Erik through the street.

Soon enough, he was at the door of Adèle's townhouse. He looked up towards the golden light in the windows and smiled. He'd done well, if he did say so. He had helped someone with minimal damage to another human. Christine would be annoyed at Erik risking his person for such an endeavor, but he hoped she was proud.

Months ago, nearly a year ago, he had done something close to this when he had followed Christine through the streets on Christmas. Then he had been willing and ready to kill the man who had attempted to rob her. She'd never known about it. Maybe he would tell her now, as an example of how she had changed him. However, that might raise more questions. At least now he didn't have to wait outside on the street, looking up at warmth from which he was excluded. At least now he could go to her and be the one to take her home.

Or back to their rented bed. The idea of home came back to him often, especially now as he ascended the stairs to Adèle's door. Even Christine's old friend had more of a home in this strange city than they did. Perhaps that was something that needed to change.

The maid let Erik in and led him to the parlor. The sight that greeted him was as pleasant as it was hard to believe. Christine was beautiful in green, her smile broad and her eyes full of light. His wife – his wife! – rushed to him and embraced him in the presence of a friend, who also smiled to see him. Adèle had every reason to resent them or be wary, but there was welcome in her face too.

"You're late," Christine admonished with a grin, guiding Erik to a seat as he took off his layers of concealment.

"I had a minor adventure on the way," Erik said. It wasn't a lie, but it drew a stern look from Christine that was quite delightful. "What counts is that I'm here."

"Yes, though it will cost me a pound," Adèle sighed. "We had a bet and I was foolish to think your wife didn't know you."

"She knows me more than anyone," Erik replied.

"Speaking of, I have not heard back from Shaya, before you ask," Adèle said. Erik tried not to let that worry him. Letters were slow and there could be any number of reasons for the delay. "This business with someone lurking about the Opéra must infuriate you."

"Annoys, more like," Erik replied, folding himself onto Adèle's couch next to Christine with his hand in hers. "I worked hard to create my legend and reputation. I can't just let anyone take it."

"You let me and Julianne take it easily enough," Adèle corrected.

Christine smirked. "I can't say I'm not jealous. I always wanted to know what it was like to lurk about the Opéra frightening ballet rats."

"There was more to it than that," Erik grumbled.

"There's a real ghost at Covent Garden," Adèle said, picking up a cup from the side table and pouring fresh tea into it from a porcelain pot, as English as could be. "More than one, I think."

"Well, it's a proper theater then. Any building with a stage needs a resident spirit," Erik said, taking it.

"You told me you heard things in the cellars, felt things," Christine added, shivering. "I felt it too, I think. Restless dead things. None of them took boxes though."

"The Opéra certainly has reason to host such spirits," Adèle said, then frowned to herself. "Though I think a few of them would be better served in hell."

She meant Antoine, who truly deserved to rot in those haunted cellars and writhe in hell. Erik could see the same thought flash through Christine's mind. He saw her eyes become distant and her face pale, as memory overtook her. Erik grasped her hand, hoping to hold her in the present.

"They do," Christine whispered, blinking back to life and meeting Erik's eyes.

"Are you alright for money?" Erik asked Adèle.

"What? I'm paid well, if that's what you mean," Adèle replied suspiciously.

"There was an inheritance and if anyone deserves it—" Erik began, but Adèle stopped him with a glare.

"You don't owe me compensation, or any legacy of his. He's dead, and that's enough," Adèle said with unquestionable steel in her tone.

Erik nodded. "Very well."

"That money is for you to start a life," Adèle went on. "Which I really think you two need to get around to at some point. Unless your plan is to simply wander the great cities of the world until you expire."

"I'm sure the thought has crossed my husband's mind," Christine muttered, and Erik felt a stab of guilt at her tone. "We did try, in the Alps, but—"

"It was too remote and backward," Erik cut in. "I'm not suited for village life."

"Then stay here, in London. There's music and amusement enough," Adèle said. "Or is it too close to Paris?"

"There's not much we could do without attracting attention when it comes to music," Christine said.

"You could compose under an assumed name," Adèle suggested. "Not that the English have much in the way of opera. There are a few symphonists that are promising – Elgar, Grieg – but they have yet to produce a composer of their own capable of the true grandiosity required of the stage. Perhaps one day. Or perhaps you."

Erik looked between the two women as he considered it. "Such an idea had never occurred to me."

"Because all your life, you wanted acclaim in your own right as revenge," Christine said simply and Erik gaped at her. "You've passed that now though. Matured. I think a pseudonym is worth pursuing."

"I'd still need to meet with producers and conductors and..." Erik sighed, shaking his head. "It would fall apart."

"There could be a way," Christine said. "Don't let go of it so fast."

"We were talking about something else though, weren't we?" Erik said as he sipped his tea. "An idea that offends both my Irish and French blood."

"Staying in London among the English," Christine laughed. "Would it be so terrible?"

"No," Erik said and saw the surprise on Christine's face. "It's why I was going to ask how Adèle went about acquiring such a house and if there was a solicitor she might introduce us to."

Though Erik had doubts and reservations about the idea, the delight on Christine's face was worth the worry. Maybe they had found a place to stay.

# Paris

The *Salon du Danse* was a forest of bodies, and all of them were taller than Meg. The space behind the stage was always a madhouse after a performance, but tonight, it felt particularly overwhelming. It was an odorous jungle of gowns and black suits. It didn't help that the floor was raked at the same angle as the stage, making the place all the more disconcerting to navigate for someone so small. Meg would need to jump to see over the crowd. She was ready to do it too if it meant finding Monsieur d'Amboise.

She settled for rising *en pointe*, which was easy, as she was still in her white tulle skirt and pointe shoes. Everyone would know she was a dancer this way, and the patrons enjoyed seeing girls in their revealing clothes – even if, for Meg, it was little more than the uniform. Surely she could find him...

"What are you doing here, Meg Giry?" someone hissed in her ear, making her jump. She spun to see Rochelle, looking thunderous, with Jammes beside her.

"I was looking for—" Meg stopped herself. Rochelle had kept her from seeing d'Amboise before. "Blanche."

"Oh, she's far too popular right now to be bothered with her real friends," Rochelle sneered. "With all the stories she has to tell."

"Thanks to me!" Meg squawked, noting how Jammes rolled her eyes. "Isn't that old news now?"

"A secret marriage and child? Hardly," a voice said at Meg's elbow. It was Marie. She looked much like Meg in her tutu, hair up and tied with a silken ribbon. She was the very image of her statue, right down to the proud upward tilt of her chin.

"They aren't even patrons anymore," Meg muttered, wondering if the story was being shared around them now, whispered from person to person, spreading the same way colds tended to among the dancers.

"I don't think ruining the de Chagny family name will do well for Blanche's ambitions to be the next Comtesse," Rochelle said with an air of world-weary annoyance.

"As if anyone will ever compare to the great Christine Daaé," Jammes said, finally deigning to speak. "I know the Comte well enough to tell you that. He was obsessed with that witch like everyone else."

"Speaking of old stories," Rochelle said, rolling her eyes. "Next will you tell us how it was you who alerted Raoul about Buquet?"

Jammes gave Rochelle a glare then turned it on Meg, eyes narrowing. "I do know him better than most of you and Blanche. Why didn't you ask me to go with you, Meg?" Jammes demanded.

"Probably because you're a miserable shrew and she's terrified of you," Marie said without any hesitation, nor did she seem bothered when Jammes gave her a horrified look.

"I was going to say we aren't very close," Meg stammered. To her shock, Jammes looked more hurt than angry. "I apologize."

Jammes's face hardened again. "I don't care," she said, her gaze shifting to the milling crowd. "There are better ways to gain a patron."

"I was hoping to see Monsieur d'Amboise," Meg said unsteadily, avoiding a look from Rochelle in favor of looking penitently at Jammes. The grin she gave Meg was as troubling as one of her glares.

"Oh, I know where he is," Jammes said and took Meg by the hand. Meg found herself led through the crowd to a corner of the salon. Lo and behold, d'Amboise was there with his friend Clermont.

"Ah, Mademoiselle Giry!" d'Amboise exclaimed. He looked particularly oily today, as if he'd added a fresh coat of lacquer to attend the Opéra. Clermont beside him was much more handsome, if only by comparison.

"You know our dear, young Meg?" Jammes said with a saccharine smile. "You're so lucky to catch her tonight without her mother in tow; she's usually chaperoned."

"I told her I was going to supper with Blanche," Meg said and the men's faces lit up. It was fine. This was part of the plan.

"We are fortunate indeed to have such lovely company," Clermont said. He gave Jammes a look from toe to nose, his eyes pausing at her chest so that he didn't see the disgust on her face. Meg could feel d'Amboise looking at her the same way.

"Does that mean you're free for supper?" d'Amboise asked, touching Meg's elbow. Warnings old and recent about the patrons rang in her head and her skin crawled at the touch. She wasn't like Rochelle or Jammes or the other dancers; she wouldn't give up her virtue for a few francs and a chance of elevation. She would get what she wanted instead.

"Can we not converse as friends first? Or walk the Opéra? I'm sure the Grand Foyer is lovely this time of night, now that the crowds have gone," Meg said as coyly as she could manage.

"Of course," d'Amboise said with a grin. "It would be my pleasure."

"Cécile can entertain your friend," Meg added with a smile and took d'Amboise's offered arm. He smelled of cologne over sweat, Meg noted as they made their way out of the *Salon du Danse*. She caught sight of Rochelle, looking furious, and turned her attention back to d'Amboise. "Tell me, Monsieur—"

"You must call me Étienne," the patron interrupted. "And I will call you Meg and we will be the best of friends."

Meg swallowed and forced a new smile. "Étienne, of course. I must confess my ignorance. How long have you been a patron of our great National Academy of Music?"

"And dance," d'Amboise added. "I believe it is dance that makes the Paris Opéra great. You and your sisters are the heart of all beauty and art in this city, the perfect flowers in our garden."

"You flatter me, Étienne," Meg said, though she felt more queasy than flattered. "But you—"

"My patronage! Yes!" he crowed as they made their way through the stage door and into the lobby proper. It was uncrowded now that the performance was over, though not empty. The mosaic floor was cold through Meg's slippers, and she suddenly felt extremely exposed walking about in the public spaces in her tutu, though she had just danced for two thousand people in the same outfit.

"I have had the privilege of supporting the Opéra for over two years now," d'Amboise said proudly. "I have seen many great talents rise and fall. I have an eye for potential."

"Oh, really?" Meg asked, trying to bat her eyes the way someone like Blanche would and not look like she was going blind. "So you must have known all the managers?"

"Well, there have only been the four," d'Amboise corrected her. Meg got the impression he liked doing so.

"Did they listen to your ideas as a patron?" Meg asked. "I heard Monsieur Richard especially was very close with the patrons."

D'Amboise frowned at that and Meg worried she had said something wrong. "Richard showed a definite preference for certain opinions. Men who made themselves hard to ignore and were great beasts about it."

So he was jealous of more important men like Antoine and Raoul. "Were you a supporter of Carlotta or Daaé?" Meg asked, turning to the main controversy of Richard's tenure. "Such nasty business that was."

"Oh, I was for Carlotta at first, but only as a favor to more invested friends," d'Amboise laughed, guiding Meg into the jewel box of a lobby and down the *grand escalier*. "But as I said, I favor dance, and I wasn't in Richard's preferred circle."

"Did anyone speak up when he was ousted?" Meg asked, hoping to sound innocent. "You haven't even said who this circle was."

"Oh, no one spoke up," d'Amboise said. They had come to the foot of the stairs where twin muses of bronze held up flickering candelabrum. "Soon, they will replace these with electric lights, you know," d'Amboise said of the quavering flames.

"Like the chandelier."

"Richard took all the blame for that disaster, however unfairly," d'Amboise sighed. "What a ghastly thing to happen. I was lucky to make it out alive."

"Surely a man such as you wasn't sitting in the stalls?"

For the first time, her escort looked nervous, but he laughed it off, leading Meg down now, below the stairs to the rotunda reserved for patrons and subscribers. "It was a close thing but let us not talk of such dark times."

Meg froze as d'Amboise slid his arms around her waist and twirled her so her back was pressed to his chest. They were beneath the stair with the little fountain of Pythia, another nubile young woman in gauzy clothes displayed for the amusement of the audience. Of men. Meg suddenly, horribly, felt exactly like her.

"Who – who was in Richard's corner that betrayed him?" Meg asked, voice shaking as the heat from d'Amboise's hands seeped through the fabric of her bodice. She tried to ignore the similar heat from his body behind her. All she needed were names.

"Oh, Tremblay was a great supporter, the fool. He'd do anything to keep free reign to pluck sweet flowers like you from the garden," d'Amboise whispered against Meg's neck and that was enough for her. All of this was enough.

"I think I must get back," Meg nearly yelped when his lips brushed her skin, all her idiotic confidence and curiosity replaced by terror. "My mother—"

"Don't worry, my dear," d'Amboise said, and again he was laughing as his arm tightened around Meg's waist. Why was this man always laughing? Did it amuse him to have trapped a girl like her? Was this sport? "We will be back soon."

"What does that mean?" Meg asked, suddenly unable to breathe. She thought of Rochelle and Hermine and so many other girls who had gone off with patrons and how they had been changed and used. Why had she believed herself above such a fate? "I want to leave," Meg almost whispered. Like a prayer.

"But my dear, you asked—" A huge clang cut off d'Amboise's words – metal clanking and crashing from somewhere by the ticket offices. The man jumped in shock, releasing Meg as he did.

Meg didn't look for the source of the noise to find who to thank. She did that in a silent prayer, instead, as she rushed away from d'Amboise quick as her legs would carry her. She knew it was a shadow that had saved her, causing chaos as a diversion for her escape. The same chaos he always had caused that sometimes hurt and sometimes helped. Tonight, the ghost had helped her.

She was breathless when she made it backstage, the shock finally hitting her, mixed with relief that she had evaded a fate she should not have tempted. Her nerves were shot, even so, and she found herself shaking as she panted in the dim hall.

The hand on her wrist made her scream, and she couldn't be blamed for it. Rochelle looked as terrified as Meg when she turned to see her in the hall.

"It's just me, Giry, you ninny!" Rochelle snapped. "I was coming to make sure you didn't do anything too stupid."

"You're too late for that," Meg shot back. She felt so ashamed at how Rochelle was right. She was stupid and she had almost ruined herself because of it.

"What happened?" Rochelle's voice cut through her thoughts, and to Meg's shock, there was real worry in her friend's face. "Did he take you so quickly?"

"No," Meg answered and Rochelle sighed in clear relief. "But he was going to try."

"Why would you go with him? You know what those men are like," Rochelle asked, now sad. "You've never been foolish enough to trifle with them, and I always admired that about you."

Meg felt another bubble of shame from deep in her stomach, rising like bile. "I thought he might know something useful," Meg confessed. "About the men who have been targeted by the ghost."

"You're still on that?" Rochelle squawked.

"It's important!" Meg cried in return. "People are being hurt and—"

"Jesus Christ in heaven, Giry, don't you understand it yet?" Rochelle exclaimed, throwing up her hands. "The men who have been hurt and the ones on that bloody list all have something in common if you ask the right people!"

"That's what I've been trying to do!" Meg balked. "But you—"

"They hurt girls the same way d'Amboise tried to hurt you." Rochelle cut her off.

Meg gaped at Rochelle, blinking in horror at the revelation and her own continued idiocy. "I... I didn't realize."

"That's how they get away with it!" Rochelle went on. "Tremblay wasn't kind to me, nor was Sabran to Hermine. I've heard rumors about De Lancey and the others, as well. They all do very ungentlemanly things to the dancers they ensnare, and no one cares or sees because girls like us don't matter. We're just playthings to them."

"But the ghost..."

"Whatever the ghost is doing, you shouldn't try to stop it. He warned you and you're being a fool," Rochelle said, sounding sad and so many years past her age. "You should let it happen because these men deserve it."

Meg stared at her friend, feeling like the greatest fool in the world. If this was true, was the list only the beginning?

"I still don't understand why it's happening now," Meg said aloud, and Rochelle looked confused. "The ghost never cared about these things before. He annoyed singers and made accidents happen. Why go after loathsome patrons now?"

"I don't know, maybe getting rid of that monster de Martiniac gave him a taste for it," Rochelle replied. "Or maybe he found God or something."

"Or maybe he was hurt too," Meg whispered, though that didn't seem right either. Everything and nothing made sense. Meg knew more now than she had an hour before and that was something she could bring to Shaya, but she wasn't sure this knowledge was worth the cost.

# London

Perhaps it was the music, perhaps it was the ale, but Christine felt like she was among her people for the first time in months. Adèle had taken them to the pubs, and Letitia and Howard had joined; Howard even brought a letter from Jack with news that nothing concerning had happened in Lucca or Florence.

What she felt was more than friendship. It was more than having Erik beside her, tucked in their corner of the pub, even though it filled her heart with joy to have him out and about beside her. It went even beyond her recent dreams of green gardens and overgrown walls, without a single fire or disaster marring the peace.

No, the joy brimming inside Christine came from how familiar people were, though she had never met them before tonight. They were musicians and travelers, the sort of folk her father and she would meet on the road, in a village tavern, or at a fair. People who lived closer to the wild and the earth than the rich men in their fancy houses, people who knew the old songs and were ready with a welcome and an invitation to play. They were like theater people too, the kind that became your comrade as soon as you sang with them.

Christine didn't know the language completely or recognize the songs, but they both knew how to join in harmony singing praises to the ale. The group of drinkers and companions had taken her, Erik, and their friends in tonight.

Christine was deliriously happy to finally be singing with others. It felt so good to let her voice be heard, she thought, as she took another sip of nut-brown ale and squeezed her husband's hand. The night had started quietly and grown more raucous as new people had joined the singing, each taking turns to lead the assembled drinkers in song.

Part of Christine – the soprano part – had taken some pride in the way heads turned when she harmonized and sang along, adding high descants a few times and reveling in the thrill. Erik had not been so ostentatious, and she had not minded that either. If he had started singing – really singing the way no one but him could – it would have stopped the whole night and caused a sensation. They still didn't need to attract that much attention.

Now the singing was over, and she and Erik had taken a place by the fading fire. It was cozy and inviting, made all the more so by the cool, black night outside. Erik looked relaxed, as much as he could be in a public setting where his mask was noticeable. People had been kind enough not to ask about it. As a couple, they were learning ways to divert attention from it. A vague story about being hurt in 'the war' would often suffice. No one ever asked which war, for there always had been one somewhere. Maybe that made him relaxed or maybe it was the ale in his hand. It made Christine feel warm to see that, too.

"This could be our life," Christine said aloud, gazing at the man she loved by the fire. "If we stayed here. This could be normal."

"And you'd like that?" Erik asked back, a sparkle in his eyes that reminded her of the stars in the most wonderful way.

"I would. Wouldn't you?" Christine answered. "We could find our people here. I think we already have."

Erik turned and looked out at the crowd. Adèle had fallen into conversation with Howard and a friend of hers from the theater. Letitia was regaling the barmaid with a tale, perhaps ready to invite her to the next salon. Erik took it all in. "I didn't think I'd ever have people. The kind that kept me or stayed. Then I had you..."

Christine smiled as he turned to her, even as her chest tightened. "I shouldn't be the whole world."

"You are, to me, but I understand your meaning," Erik sighed. "It's not so bad, I guess. Having people like this."

"London is a city that can keep you occupied," Christine pressed. "We can visit other places from here. Ireland, maybe?"

"Not there," Erik grumbled, bristling.

"If we have a house, we can do more," Christine tried, and he relaxed. "The noise wouldn't bother anyone."

Erik gave her a mischievous smile. "What exactly do you intend for us to do that would make so much noise?"

"I meant music, you wicked man," Christine scowled through her blush. It did give her ideas though. She had been waiting for a complaint from someone in another room near theirs in the hotel and she was tired of dampening her pleasure in pillows. "We could have a piano. I could have a garden even."

"A garden?" Erik asked with infinite warmth. "Do you like gardens, Mrs. Gilbride?"

"I do." Christine felt a flutter in her chest, a hope that had kindled there as soon as he had started talking about houses back at Adèle's.

"What are we talking about? You look disgustingly happy," Letitia purred. Christine turned to see where she and Howard had accosted them.

"Does this have something to do with you looking for a house?" Howard said with a grin. "Madame Valerius told us the news."

"That was not hers to share," Erik said with a hint of disapproval. Christine sent him a look reminding him to behave himself. Or perhaps she wanted him to misbehave – she saw the gleam in his eyes and it gave her rather delicious ideas about what she could do this evening.

"I traded her for some gossip about a baritone she needs to avoid," Howard replied with a hand wave. "What a delightful woman she is. I'm quite in love."

"I don't think she has the instruments that you're looking for, my dear," Letitia said, plopping into a chair next to Christine and giving Howard a smirk.

"I think, of all women, you'd be aware of what sort of instruments a resourceful woman might have at her disposal," Howard quipped back with a wink.

Christine looked quizzically between her friends and then at Erik, who was chuckling, as well. "What does that mean?"

"Oh, dear. It seems we have more to teach this sweet, young thing." Letitia grinned, and Christine's mind started racing.

"I think I can handle such education in this case," Erik said. It made something curious stir in Christine as the courtesan and her husband held a knowing beat of eye contact.

"Back to the matter of a house. I have an agent I know," Letitia went on. "Howard would use him if he wasn't destitute and useless."

"We will consider it, of course," Christine smiled back. "There is much to consider and we're still not sure—"

"We'd like something new and modern with all the latest luxuries," Erik said to Christine's delight.

"My husband is a terrible snob, you see. He practically built his last home himself," Christine shot back.

"I am sure that somewhere with a garden will be harder to find," Erik countered, and Christine couldn't help but grin.

Adèle approached, looking satisfied and amused. "Are you smiling like that because you're talking about your new residence?" she asked. "It better be close to mine. Not that I'll always be there. I have an offer from the opera in Nice in the spring."

"We are considering it," Erik replied with an overly serious tone. "I still don't know if my pride can take living in this city."

"Your pride be damned," Adèle clucked. "I know you. If your wife demands it, you will do it."

Erik opened his mouth in protest, but Christine cut him off. "He is rather indulgent of me. Obedient, even."

"That's my girl," Adèle said.

"You're starting to sound like Letitia," Howard laughed.

Letitia nudged Christine with her shoulder. "She's a good student. One whose cup is woefully empty! Let us help with that."

Before Christine knew it, the glass was out of her hands, and Howard followed towards the bar with Adèle on his arm. Once again, she and Erik were alone.

"So, will you make me wait to educate me on what Letitia was talking about?" Christine asked, biting her lip. Whatever they were talking about had the air of desire about it.

"Oh, well, I don't want to scandalize you," Erik chuckled, his eyes glinting gold as he looked across the pub to where Letitia and Howard were now bickering. "You're an intelligent woman. You can surely put it together when you think of how a man who enjoys the company of men... achieves that enjoyment."

Christine's cheeks would have reddened had the ale not already given them color, but her shock still must have shown on her face. Erik gave a low, warm laugh at her expense. He had told her, after some prodding on her part, what could be involved in the act of love between two men. The idea had stuck with Christine for many days, then their business in Geneva and beyond had banished the fascination. Now it roared back.

"Letitia said instruments," Christine muttered as she glanced once more at the fascinating woman. "She meant instruments of..."

"Of pleasure. They exist in all sorts of forms and have for centuries," Erik confirmed as if it was obvious. Maybe it was to him, but it was a revelation to Christine. "And they have been used by all people, men and women and those that don't fit those labels."

"Oh," was all Christine could exclaim. Certain pictures formed in her head, so vivid and lewd that she almost choked on her tongue. "Oh my."

"It's a delight to still be able to shock you, I must say," Erik drawled.

"I'm not shocked," Christine countered, indignation rising. "I'm intrigued. There's a difference."

The look Erik gave her, however sidelong and fleeting, was pure fire. It made something molten bubble in Christine's chest and quickened her heartbeat. Suddenly, she very much wanted to be back in their room and their bed.

"A woman could use these devices," Christine said with a smile that Erik matched, "On a man that enjoyed such things?"

"She could—"

"I want it back!"

The voice was accented and slurred, and in English, but Christine understood the demand. They turned to see a patron of the tavern, a new one if Christine wasn't mistaken, swaying in front of them.

"I beg your pardon, sir," Erik said stiffly. Christine felt as if she had missed something, but Erik was alert and tense.

"You took something from a friend of mine. Give it back," the man said, much to Christine's confusion. He was a rough spun sort of character, with sallow skin and eyes that didn't fit in his face. Christine didn't like the way he licked his gums as he looked over both of them and he focused on Erik's mask. "Give it back and I won't tell no one about the mask."

Christine gripped Erik's hand, heart pounding. They had known someone commenting on the mask was a risk when they came out, but she didn't want this to sour Erik from nights like these.

"Why would I care about what you say about my choice of attire?" Erik asked slowly.

"Please, leave us be," Christine added in her best English, and the man, strangely, grinned.

"Oh, that's right. They said you was French," the man replied with a hiccup. "*Pardonnez-moi, mam'selle.*"

"What are you talking about?" Erik demanded, rising, though Christine tried to pull him back. Christine noted that their friends had grown quiet where they stood a few feet away, watching the confrontation. Howard was holding Letitia's arm and Adèle looked ready to strike.

"You're famous on the streets since yesterday, masked man," the man slurred. "There's a reward. Five pounds for word of a man in a mask, maybe with a pretty lady. French. Burt was after it too, but you had to brain him and steal his knife."

Christine's blood froze, instinct born of meeting too many men like this and finding herself at their mercy electrifying her with fear and the need to run. He knew them and he was here on purpose. They had been found.

"I'm sure you're mistaken," Erik said slowly, even as Christine felt like she was falling.

"No, mate," the man said. "Now you give me back Burt's knife, and whatever coin you have to cover the reward I won't get, and I won't say a word to good Mister Bidaut."

Time slowed as panic seized Christine. Echoes of all the times before when they had been forced to fly to safety only to have it disappear. All the exhaustion and loss and uncertainty that she couldn't evade fell back upon her like chains of iron. All the consequences and scars she couldn't avoid burned in her and filled her ears with their awful sounds. Gunshots and screams and tearing flesh. All of it flooded her in a single moment, tearing her away from the hope and joy she had felt just a second before.

Somehow, they had been found again. Everything was about to be torn away from them again. Christine looked to her friends and the husband she loved, who had given everything for her. The man who she had made to kneel and beg before her, who had trusted her with his soul.

He was worthy of more than her panic and so was the life they wanted.

"No," Christine whispered, gripping Erik tight as she straightened her spine and pushed her panic away like a cocoon; a prison that had held her for too long. "No," she repeated, because she had found happiness and hope tonight and she was ready to fight for it.

## Paris

The office of the managers – well, manager – was a surprisingly restrained space, given the ostentatiousness of the rest of the Opéra. Shaya had seldom been there before now, so he took his time to take in the details. He noted the mahogany desks (still two, though one was being used as a receptacle for piles of scores and ledgers), the plastered walls made gold by the gaslight, and the red carpet matching that of the boxes. Shaya craned his head, wondering if he would be able to make out the outline of the trap door Erik had used to torment the managers for so many years.

"I'd offer you a drink, but I know it would be in vain," Armand remarked as he stepped inside after Shaya. "I hope you don't mind if I partake. I need to fortify myself before I head back into the fray."

"I didn't think you disliked mingling with the patrons so much," Shaya clucked as Armand poured himself a generous glass of brandy.

"Sometimes I feel as if begging for their money is my entire job and they've been understandably antsy these past few weeks, so they need more flattering and fawning than usual," Armand replied with the weariness of a man who had not slept for a month. "At least Robert promised to meet me after, so that's something to look forward to. Did you enjoy the performance?"

"I couldn't concentrate on it much," Shaya confessed.

"Too busy keeping an eye out for ghosts and robbers?" Armand said, flopping down in his chair. "I can't blame you. Meyerbeer is a bore, but he brings in the audiences."

Shaya shrugged. "I did like the horses."

"At least this ghost hasn't been borrowing them," Armand sighed and took a swig. "That was him, wasn't it? I can never keep track of what was rumor and what was real."

"It was real. He liked them," Shaya murmured.

The manager gave a weak smile. "Please tell me you have hopeful news on that front?"

It was Shaya's turn to heave a sigh. "I have news, but none of it is hopeful, and I have a suspect that doesn't quite make sense. That's why I wanted to talk with you."

"I don't like the sound of that at all," Armand said, face falling. "Well, out with it."

"Have you heard from your former counterpart at all?"

"Richard? No. I don't even know if he's in Paris," Armand replied with clear alarm. "Whatever does he have to do with this?"

"At the culmination of the business with the Phantom, Richard was working in league with Antoine de Martiniac. You know this," Shaya began, and Moncharmin took a long drink of liquor. "De Martiniac was, like our specter now, lurking about the Opéra in the guise of the ghost for his own ends and as a sort of agent for Richard. He plotted with him, all the while being engaged to the sister of Raoul de Chagny."

"For her money," Armand replied.

"Money that Philippe de Chagny only gave the appearance of having, it seems," Shaya went on, drawing a raised eyebrow from Armand. "Maybe Antoine knew that. I'm not sure, but he was after another fortune as well. One he nearly killed for."

Shaya didn't want to get into the complicated details of the scheme, or his part in ending it. Luckily, Armand was following. "A scheme he made promises to Richard about. He was invested in it."

"Yes. He was owed a debt, first by de Martiniac, and now, by his widow," Shaya confessed, and Armand's lips fell open. "His *pregnant* widow." At this, Armand's jaw dropped entirely.

"How do you know this?" Armand gasped.

"I had a hunch and I sent an agent of mine to confirm it. Unfortunately, she enlisted the help of someone with no discretion, so I'm sure the rumor is spreading as we speak." Shaya didn't like that this was out of his control and might wake a tiger he didn't want to deal with. "I sent this agent to investigate someone who was spying on me. They were working for Sabine and Richard as well."

"Sabine de Chagny – or de Martiniac, I guess? – and Firmin Richard have people watching you? Why?" Armand asked.

Finally, Shaya could say to someone what he couldn't confess to Meg. "They think I will lead them to Erik. It's he that possesses the money they seek and more."

"The Opéra's money, you mean," Armand scowled.

"I hate that we remain haunted by de Martiniac, even now." Shaya had dreamed of the man for the past few nights. Of him and Sabine, confronting Shaya for taking the life of her child's father... Or thanking him.

"At least Adèle got away from him," Armand said with a smile. "You know, I've just had a letter from her! Where did it go?" Armand jumped from his seat and rushed towards an untidy pile of correspondence. "Here we are!"

He fished out a letter from the stack and opened it. Shaya watched in interest as the man pulled out the letter and another sealed envelope, marked with handwriting Shaya would recognize anywhere. "What is that?" Shaya asked breathlessly.

"It's addressed to you," Armand whispered, eyes darting between the letter and the unopened envelope. "Oh my god, she's – she's found them."

Shaya snatched the letter from Armand, hands shaking as he looked over the scrawled address: For Shaya Motlagh, care of friends.

"Erik and Christine both?" Shaya asked, amazed. "Where?"

"She's in London, at Covent Garden," Armand said aloud as he read his letter. "They found her there. What does yours say? It's from him, is it not?"

Shaya broke the seal of the letter, at last, breath shallow as he did. This meant that at least they were alive and safe, something he had not been able to admit he feared wasn't true until now. Slowly, he read.

*Dearest Daroga,*

*I hope that this letter reaches you in good health, thanks to the help of our heroic Madame Valerius. Encountering her here in London has been a blessing, and a surprise, as is our presence in this city. We came here from Florence by way of Lucca with the assistance of friends – and evading the pursuit of enemies. It seems someone is intent on claiming the de Martiniac inheritance I recently came into and has sent agents across the continent to do so. They found us through Monsieur Tissot in Geneva. This is why I have been remiss in replying to you, as they held onto your letter to him with these ridiculous suspicions of me returning to my old haunts, as they say.*

*I'm appalled you would ever think I would return without alerting you first, if only because doing so would make you have the seasick expression on your face you think makes you look irate and intimidating – the one you're probably making now. I would not miss that expression for the world.*

*No, I am not engaged in any new activities at the Opéra, as I am too busy trying and failing to find some peace outside of Paris. Perhaps London will offer some, but at least it offers some familiar faces.*

*I confess that I miss your face, Daroga, and your usefulness. I think you would be of immense help in enlightening me as to who is after us and why. These methods hardly match those of the young Comte, but I cannot count him out. The man who found me goes by the name Bidaut and may have found himself slightly stabbed in the alleyways of Geneva (don't look at me like that, Daroga, I was defending myself and my wife. Christine has been very dutiful in her punishments for that transgression). If you could find out if he lived and who he worked for, it would be quite a boon. I'm sure you're bored and need entertainment. I can't imagine this imposter ghost is as interesting as the real thing.*

*Finally, I apologize for the redundancy of this letter. I don't trust the mail at this point, so this is, indeed, the second letter of the same contents I have sent you. If you have already received the first, I hope reading this one made you doubt your sanity.*

*Please reply only to Adèle and with as much secrecy as possible.*

*I remain, as ever, your obedient servant.*

*- E.*

Shaya read and reread the letter, connecting pieces in his mind, his anxiety and guilt rising.

"What is it? You've gone rather ashen!" Armand asked, peering at the letter over Shaya's shoulder.

"Erik was found, as I suspected he might have been, but he fled," Shaya replied. "Unfortunately, I think he will be found again. The men who have been watching me – they've been getting into my mail somehow."

"Is that legal?" Armand scoffed and Shaya glared at him. "Of course. They wouldn't care."

"They followed my letter to Geneva and found Erik that way, I think," Shaya confessed. "His other letter never reached me. This was sent as insurance. He must have suspected, but that means his enemies know Erik is in London."

# London

Bidaut's name hung like a curse in the air. He had found them. The how didn't matter, though Erik could guess at it. What mattered more was the consequences they were facing right now.

"So your friend was following me," Erik mused. He hated it when his paranoia was correct.

"Burt thinks he's so smart," this new rogue declared. "Tried to throw you off going after that biddy, but you had to make it complicated and go thieving. I told him to let ol' John take care of it."

"I don't think it counts to steal from another thief," Erik intoned. Out of the corner of his eye, he saw Christine's brow furrow as she tried to translate. Her English was improving but John's cockney accent and slang were no doubt baffling. Even so, she looked as furious as Erik felt.

"Don't matter. I want my reward, and I'll take it any way I have to," John spat.

Erik weighed his options. John would be easy to subdue in a fight, easier than Burt had been, considering his inebriated state. Erik very much wanted to make this fool suffer, but their friends were watching. Adèle knew what kind of monster Erik was, but Howard and Letitia didn't know the ugliness that lurked in his soul or his face. He didn't want them to see any of that and he didn't want to disappoint Christine more than he already had, yet his hands still itched to give this man back his friend's knife by plunging it into his throat. That was not the thought of a good man.

As if sensing the murderous intent rising in him, Christine pulled Erik back an inch. "Give him what he wants and let him go," she whispered, shaking her head in disgust. "He's not worth it."

Howard came up behind the man, clapping a hand on John's shoulder. "I think it's time you leave, sir."

The man shrugged Howard off roughly, fixing Erik with a glare. "Not until I get what I want. Or I run to tell where you are as fast as I can."

"Hasn't your friend already done that?" Erik asked back. That was the rub, wasn't it? They might contain this man's threat, but others awaited. Erik had been so sloppy... "Maybe I want you to give Bidaut a message for me. Tell him I won't be as merciful with him if he tries to find me again."

"Erik, no," Christine hissed. "Just let him go!"

"I'd listen to your lady, *Erik*," John warned, hand twitching over his pocket. So he was armed. Damn. Erik hated this – he hated giving in when he wanted to fight, but Christine was right. His blood was worthless.

"Fine, have your friend's little blade," Erik sighed. He threw the knife to John, who caught it clumsily.

"Don't forget the money," John hissed.

"Five pounds, was it?" Erik muttered. Maybe this would buy them time. Or maybe he was getting swindled by a lout who would go running to Bidaut no matter what they did. Still, the relief on Christine's face when Erik produced the coins was worth it. He held them out and the man approached, reeking of whiskey. "I doubt this will last you a day."

"Oh, it will," John said with a smile that curdled Erik's blood. He was too close and Erik couldn't move because Christine was holding onto his arm so tightly. "When I add that to the ten I'll get for giving him this."

Of all the things Erik had suspected the man to do when he lunged forward, tearing off his mask wasn't one of them. A blow or a stab he could have endured, but not this. Not the horrible feeling of cool air against his skin or the sickened gasp someone gave when the mask clattered to the ground.

"Jesus Christ!" John screamed, eyes like saucers, the same disgust Erik had come to know for decades flooding his eyes. But it wasn't John's horror that hurt, it was that of the strangers Erik had sung with just hours before jumping from their seats and fleeing. It was the way Howard looked at him in utter shock, his cheeks pale and his mouth slack. The way Letitia covered her mouth to dampen her cry. The noise of despair Christine made because she knew it was over.

It was the ruin of it all. So familiar and so terrible.

"Erik!" Christine screamed, but it was too late. His hands were around John's throat and the man was on the ground with Erik above him. "Erik, stop!"

"Did Bidaut not warn you?" Erik growled, his muscles like iron as Christine tried to pull him off the stupid, useless criminal who didn't deserve to live. There were other hands upon him, Howard perhaps, trying to wrench him away, but Erik was too strong, too determined. Then there was a hand around his own throat forcing him to look into a face full of fury and terrible beauty.

"Erik, I order you to *stop*." Christine's voice was that of a goddess of wrath and Erik obeyed before he could even comprehend the words. It was like a flame inside him had been snuffed out, leaving only the smoking remnants of his rage as Christine pushed him away from the fray.

He kept his focus on her, on his Christine, his wife and world. There was anger in her face, and horrible disappointment, but there was also love and mercy. Or he hoped there was after he had ruined it all again. Erik stared at her as John scrambled to his feet and fled. Howard comforted his friends and kept his distance from the monster that had been revealed.

"We have to go," Christine said, stricken and furious at the same time. "We have to run right now."

"Where?" Erik asked back, the heat of the room hitting his face and making him desperate for his mask. "Where? Where do we go?"

Christine looked at him with such disappointment because she had been expecting him to know, hadn't she? She had expected him to have a plan or a place all along and now he had nothing. Not even an idea. Even his apologies and pleas for forgiveness stuck in his throat.

"My flat is not far, we can go there."

They turned in shock to Letitia, though Erik hid his face immediately at the way she winced. She surely couldn't mean it...

"You're too kind. Thank you," Christine said for them. Erik kept his eyes on the floor. Where was the mask? God, had that bastard taken it like he said? Fuck. "Howard, would you please escort Adèle home safely?"

"I don't need an escort," Adèle replied. "I can help."

"You don't need to be involved in this, I promise. You've been through enough," Christine replied firmly. She didn't want Adèle to know that it was Antoine's ghost that had ruined it all. She didn't deserve that.

"Take care of yourself," Adèle sighed. Erik didn't look at her or anyone as Christine guided them out into the night, following after Letitia. He at least had the presence of mind to wrap his face in his scarf so he wouldn't frighten passersby.

When did it get so cold? Was that why he was shaking? Where were they supposed to go now? Bidaut was out there and soon enough, he'd be coming after them, maybe with that awful Pauline;

both of them out for revenge as well as a fortune. Where were they supposed to hide when the past kept finding them?

# Paris

The last place Meg wanted to go was home. She knew as soon as she was back in their flat she'd feel safe, that her mother would embrace her and make sure she was fed and warm. She always showed her care, but Meg didn't feel like she deserved it. She had made an awful choice and only a ghost had saved her. Her mother would be mad about that too.

Meg lingered, instead, trying to take up as little space as possible in the Opéra's halls, half-heartedly looking for some intriguing clue. There was little new to be seen, but what Meg did see felt like a revelation after talking to Rochelle. For the first time, she looked without flinching at the way men fondled the young dancers, drew them into corners, and licked their lips at their prey. She watched as young singers forced themselves to flirt with old men, elbowing one another aside. She hated it all.

What Meg wasn't expecting to see was Shaya emerging from a staircase. In a blink, she was blocking the hall in front of him.

"I think we were wrong," Meg blurted out before she saw that Shaya wasn't alone. None other than Moncharmin was beside him, looking chagrined. Maybe it was fine, Meg hoped. Maybe he knew she was part of this now.

"Mademoiselle Giry?" Moncharmin asked in confusion, immediately proving her wrong. "What are you talking about? Do you know Monsieur Motlagh?"

Meg frowned, her embarrassment flaring. "I assumed he informed you."

"Armand, I told you I had an agent helping me at the Opéra," Shaya grumbled.

"And you wanted it to sound more mysterious and important than a ballet rat," Meg sniped back. "I see how it is."

"I'm sure you've been very helpful," Moncharmin said in that condescending, overly kind tone that parents use for a child who has shown them a cake made of mud.

"I have, actually," Meg replied. "I just had an important talk with Monsieur d'Amboise. He thinks the list was—"

"We've discussed that," Shaya cut in, pushing past Meg. She followed. "I know the men were not favorable to Richard, but there's been a different development."

"Where are you going?" Meg demanded as Shaya and the manager strode determinedly down the hall. "You can't just leave!"

"I'm afraid I must. Urgent business has come up," Shaya replied, looking over his shoulder. "I have to get to London. I may already be too late."

"London? Why?" Meg couldn't understand.

"That's not my truth to reveal," Shaya replied, casting a knowing sidelong look at Moncharmin.

"Come to me tomorrow," Moncharmin added, which Meg didn't find reassuring at all. "We'll talk through all of this and I'll hear what you have to say."

"You can visit Darius too," Shaya added. "I'll be telegramming him as soon as I'm settled."

"But—" Meg stammered, tripping to a halt. It was too late: the men were already gone and she hadn't even been able to share her theory. Or Rochelle's theory, to be more precise.

Meg dragged her feet back to the dressing rooms, her heart and conscience heavier than before. She pouted as she changed, wishing she had a dresser to help her.

Meg jerked like she had been pinched, an idea occurring to her.

One dresser in particular came to mind: Julianne Bonet, who had once helped the dancers before attending to Christine Daaé herself. She had been friends with the diva up until the very night of the chandelier disaster. Maybe she knew something about Christine and the ghost that might be of use. The only problem was that Julianne had left her employment at the Opéra after all that business. She had also been Jammes's paramour, a fact only Meg knew and had never spoken of. Maybe Jammes knew where to find her.

Meg tightened her shawl around her, determined in her course for the morning. She would talk to Moncharmin and she would also seek out Jammes and see if she could learn for herself all that Shaya wasn't telling her so that...

So that she could stop the ghost? She didn't feel like that was her quest anymore, she had to admit. Now she just wanted to know the truth, for the truth's sake, and then decide what to do with it.

Meg was deep in her thoughts when she exited the Opéra and turned up the *Rue Scribe*. It was late and it wasn't necessarily safe for a young woman to be walking home alone, but she had little choice in the matter. Their flat was thankfully not far. Maybe her mother would still be awake and if Meg was careful about what she said she could avoid an 'I told you so.' Maybe she could—

Meg yelped as she tripped over the heap of rubbish on the sidewalk. Springing back from the pile, Meg tried to make out what had been left blocking the way, for it had felt heavy and hard when she'd kicked it. The black mass was hard to make out in the flickering gaslight, but it looked very much like a pile of clothes.

In hindsight, she was too cavalier about it. She should have been cautious and should have seen how the pile was stirring. It would have at least minimized her shock when she pulled back the fabric to reveal the bruised, bloody face of Étienne d'Amboise before Meg's scream echoed against the walls of the Opéra House.

# 10. Burned

## London

"We have to make a decision." Christine didn't like how disappointed and dour she sounded, but she couldn't be bothered to pretend to be anything else. The shock of discovery and the loss of the potential of a life were a deep, throbbing ache, but she had no time or patience to attend to either. Erik was more broken than she was and it was up to her, again, to put them both back together.

Erik looked up at her from where he had secreted himself in Letitia's parlor, looking out over the dark street. It was past three in the morning; no one would be about now, but he seemed more interested in the dark than in the voice of his wife behind him.

"Did you hear me?" Christine asked, sighing in weariness that went beyond her body to her soul.

"I did," Erik replied quietly. He looked small in the corner next to the curtain. The mask he had borrowed (of course Letitia had a good store of them for salacious reasons) was black and awkward and he didn't need it with Christine, but she understood how it made him feel safer. "What must we decide?"

"Where we're going. We can't stay in London, not as long as Bidaut is looking for us here," Christine said, repeating herself from the long conversations in her head over the past few hours. "Letitia says maybe someplace like Oxford or Cardiff might suit us."

Erik shook his head. "Another city we don't know that you'll hate." He sounded utterly miserable.

"Or we can get ahead of them." Now that made Erik turn to her at last. Christine straightened up. "When I had Pauline tied up in Lucca, she made it clear where she might hunt us if we slipped her grasp. She knew the name of your mother's village. In Ireland."

"We can't go to Coolaney," Erik said, firm and sour. "No more backwaters or ignorant villagers."

"You just said no more cities!" Christine argued, aghast and confused.

"No more foreign cities we don't know," Erik corrected, eyes shining with resolve. "We can go back to France. We should go back... and face this."

"Absolutely not," Christine snapped.

Erik straightened in shock. "What?"

"We're not going back to a country where so many people want to see you dead," Christine explained, her ire rising. "It shouldn't be hard to understand."

"I said, we'll—"

"Face them?" she scoffed. "Meaning you'll drag us into more confrontations and violence? Where will it stop?"

"That's not—" Erik shook his head, at a loss for words or some other comforting falsehood.

"I know you, my Erik," Christine sighed. "I know you wouldn't seek that violence, but somehow, it would find you. Find us. At some point, we'll stop being lucky. I live in fear of the day this curse will take you from me."

"Then we should go home and hide until it's safe." Erik's voice was so sad, it hurt Christine to hear it. "I know it's not ideal, but we could make it work, somehow. Like I did before."

"You know we can't," Christine whispered, pitying him. She had spent so much time in the last months homesick for ideas of places that she could never go that she had forgotten that Erik had been forced to leave the only home and safety he had ever known too.

"I miss it, Christine," Erik said softly. "I miss my books and my organ and my piano and my bed and my opera."

"I miss it too," Christine admitted, heart and soul aching. She let herself feel it for a brief moment, that bone-deep longing for the familiar, even if it had been flawed and dark. Erik's house on the lake had been a tomb, home only to the dead. It was a place they had escaped, as much as they had left it behind. "But do you miss who you were there?"

"Sometimes," Erik answered softly. Guiltily.

"We have to leave that behind too." Christine hated to say it. Hated to tell him he had not changed enough.

"Is that really why you want to run off to my mother's cursed village on the off chance of catching that woman? Not because she hurt you, but because it's good?" Erik shot back.

Christine gritted her teeth. "Because there are innocent people in that town. People who deserve some warning about what's coming or salvation from it if she's already there."

"Why do they deserve it? What have those deluded strangers ever done for you?" There was cruelty and bitterness in Erik's voice that she had not heard in it for a long time.

"They deserve safety because they are people just like us, and we all deserve to live free of strife," Christine answered slowly.

"No one lives free or safe in this world, and most don't deserve it," Erik replied, and it made Christine ill to hear it. She had to remind herself that he was angry, rattled, and hurt. "Especially backwards fools in forgotten villages."

"Like the people in Lungern?" Christine asked, face hardening.

Erik's eyes were shocked behind his mask. "What?"

"I know some slight you won't speak of that drove us from the first place I thought we'd rest. I didn't ask because I kept hoping you'd tell me and trust me, but you never have."

"Because it was too shameful," Erik whispered back, turning away. Hiding himself from her as he so often did when he wallowed in his guilt and self-loathing.

"You never need to be ashamed with me," Christine lamented. "Haven't I told you this enough?"

"Perhaps I don't want to relive the pain of coming across a child in the woods when I was walking – like a fool – without my mask," Erik said, fists clenching. "Perhaps I don't want to remember how he screamed and ran; how he fell and cut himself when he saw my cursed face. Perhaps I don't want to go to Coolaney because the same thing will happen there when someone alerts the village of fools about the monsters at the edge of town."

"Erik," Christine sighed with equal parts pity and frustration. She pushed Erik by the shoulder to face her. "I'm sorry you had to bear that alone. I wish you had told me."

"So you could convince me to stay until some other disaster befell us?" Erik almost laughed. "Now you want me to go to the village that never welcomed me before."

"I want to go and help people because I have to be able to do something!" Christine found herself growling back with an intensity that made her husband draw back in shock. "I don't know what my life is or who I'm supposed to be anymore, but I still know what's right and what needs protecting."

Erik stared at her, and she wasn't sure if it was in horror or wonder, thanks to the damn borrowed mask. "I'm sorry," he whispered again with contrition that made Christine's heart clench.

"We are here – *I* am here – because of my choices as much as yours. We swore to face these challenges together," Christine said as she grasped his left hand with hers, entwining their fingers so their wedding bands glimmered in the light. "We have to do this. I have to do this. Please don't fight me or run away."

Erik's eyes fell on their hands, the battle raging in him evident from his shallow breath and tense shoulders. Christine squeezed his fingers, praying her touch could reach him in whatever dark place his mind had taken him to. Perhaps it worked, for his shoulders sagged as his breath left him in a defeated sigh.

"To Ireland then," Erik said at last, and Christine felt at least one knot in her chest unfurl.

"At least it will be native soil for one of us," Christine said, though she held little hope that it would be any more than a stop on this journey that never seemed to end.

# Paris

In the past, Meg had enjoyed being the center of attention in a rehearsal. Today, she hated it. She hated how her mother wouldn't let her out of her sight. She hated how she had to repeat over and over what had happened and what it had been like to speak to the police and yes, the attack on Monsieur d'Amboise was the same as the others. The assailant had struck from the dark, unseen, and the incident had left d'Amboise convinced he would never set foot in the Opéra again.

Meg didn't want to repeat that. She wanted to talk to Monsieur Moncharmin, or barring that, Jammes. She had to stumble her way through some Debussy first, then Gounod, and then assure her mother four separate times that she was fine and she could go home. Meg would be waiting in three hours at the door for Madame Giry to escort her home, she promised.

Meg hoped that was true, even though she didn't know where her adventures would take her once her mother finally relented and left. She didn't want to be home late, in all honesty. She wanted to sit with her mother by the fire and forget about Étienne d'Amboise's clumsy hands and his broken body on the street and how those things made her feel. Surely it was as wicked to have been with him as it was wicked to be happy to see her fellow man hurt.

"Have you seen Jammes?" Meg asked Blanche as they stretched in a corner.

"She was in her usual spot, of course," Blanche said idly, checking her reflection in a small mirror. She had rouge on.

"I meant since we broke," Meg sighed. "Where'd she get off to?"

"Why would I know?" Blanche shrugged. "Do you think I made a good impression on the Comte de Chagny?"

"What?" Meg squinted at her friend only to be ignored. "Never mind."

The halls were quieter than the dance studio, with the patter of toe shoes from the dark and the distant sound of the orchestra rehearsing. Meg took a moment to enjoy the calm and think how it was so rare to be alone in the Opéra. There was always someone hiding somewhere, living or dead.

Leave it to her to be so absent-minded that she turned a corner and found exactly what she was looking for. She slammed into Jammes's sturdy frame, sending the older dancer skidding back while swearing.

"Goddamnit, Giry!" Jammes hissed. "Are you so broken by finding your patron on the street that you've gone blind?"

"He wasn't my patron," Meg shot back, suddenly righteous. "And I was looking for you!"

"Why?" Jammes asked with a scowl. She was not that much taller than Giry, but she had a way of looking down her nose like she was a meter above, even so. "I hope it's not for advice on your love life."

"This is why you have no friends, you know," Meg shot back, all her patience gone now. "You're so... mean! For no good reason!"

"I have my reasons," Jammes scowled back. Meg thought back to catching Jammes at the Masquerade, to what she knew of the older girl and all the secrets she had to keep.

"I wondered if you knew where I might find Julianne Bonet these days," Meg asked carefully. Jammes's face went slack for a moment before hardening again.

"Why would I know about her?" she snapped.

"She was your friend, wasn't she?" Meg asked, feigning innocence. "She always paid special attention to you. I'm trying to find where she's working now. I have things I want to ask her."

"About me?" Jammes demanded, and Meg shook her head in surprise.

"About Christine Daaé and the affair with the ghost," Meg confessed. Maybe Jammes knew something too.

"You mean Christine Daaé's affair with the ghost." Now that was interesting, but not entirely unsuspected. "Julianne would never reveal anything about Christine to anyone again. She made that mistake before." To Meg's shock, it looked like Jammes was about to cry.

"I'd like to find that out for myself," Meg countered. "Or if you want to talk."

Jammes rolled her eyes. "Last I heard, she had taken off with Adèle Valerius after her fall from grace, but it didn't last long. I saw her a month or two ago, before she was dismissed." At that, Jammes's face darkened.

"She was dismissed?" Meg asked, truly shocked now. "I didn't know that."

Jammes looked positively ill, more and more as Meg stared at her. "I may have had something to do with it," she confessed at last. "It was so stupid. I was jealous that she and Adèle were—"

Meg raised her eyebrows wide and Jammes stopped herself. Had she been about to imply what Meg suspected? "She was working for her and you wanted her back... with the dancers?" Meg offered, hoping Jammes would take the proffered escape.

"Yes. That," Jammes said, clearing her throat. "It was unacceptable, so I, well, I talked to a patron that was showing me attention."

"Oh no, Cécile," Meg groaned.

"All he had to do was speak to the costume mistress or someone and it was done," Jammes whispered. "It was too late and she couldn't contact Moncharmin. I don't think she wanted to. She was so angry at everything."

"You mean you," Meg corrected, and Jammes gave her a glare. "Rightly so, I think."

"We had words that weren't very friendly, so I have no idea where she's gone off to," Jammes barked. "Don't go looking for her or asking about the witch Christine. Meddling in the ghost's business never serves anyone well. You'll end up mixed up with that horrible Persian."

"You know Monsieur Motlagh?"

"I never bothered learning the villain's name." Any softness Jammes had let slip in was gone, replaced by haughty scorn. "But if you mean the Persian who forced me to be his spy, then yes. He had me passing his notes and forced me to—"

Jammes face turned fully to stone and she peered coldly at Meg. "What is it?" Meg asked, suddenly afraid of the woman's wrath.

"Don't trust him, whatever he wants you to do," Jammes said. "He did awful things to track down the ghost and then left it all behind. For all I know, he's the one who brought down the chandelier."

"I don't think—"

"You're a child, Meg Giry, of course you don't," Jammes said with finality and stalked away down the hall.

Meg didn't know what to say or think. She had even more questions now than before, and even less of an idea of where to find the answers. She wished Shaya was still here to question or that she could get a moment with Armand Moncharmin. Maybe Darius would tell her something? Though he was loyal to a fault. Meg was beginning to fear that the only people who knew the truth about who the ghost had been were either long gone or would take their secrets to the grave.

# Liverpool

They had traveled separately, by train and carriage, for more than a day. Erik was tired down to his bones, but even so, he couldn't bring himself to take the last steps to the foggy dock. He knew Christine was waiting there with all they had to their name, waiting to board the ship that would take them to Dublin. It wouldn't be a long voyage – a day only – but it was just the prelude to more trains and carriages to carry them to county Sligo and an uncertain fate.

Erik knew he would feel better – or at least human again – when he saw his angel, and more so when they were alone and he could fall at her feet, but he didn't know if he deserved that. He chanced a few steps closer anyway, feeling like the cold, wet air was weighing him down.

"He should be here soon," came the sound of Christine's voice through the mist. Quiet. Apprehensive. She was waiting for him.

Erik froze.

"I'll wait with you until he comes," Letitia's voice answered. "The train back isn't until tomorrow and I have a room at the inn."

She wasn't alone, that was good. Wasn't it? Erik had been glad of the idea for Christine to travel with her friends old and new to avoid detection. Bidaut and Pauline would be looking for them to travel together or separately: it was much easier to blend in with a group.

"Thank you. For everything," Christine replied. Erik imagined her smile. It was easy to do; he'd spent months listening to her through walls and from the shadows. Imagining her beauty and perfection. Before he had ruined it. "It was good to laugh."

"I'm sure you'll make good use of the advice," Letita replied, her voice warm and seductive. "And everything else."

"Thank you for taking in Adèle as well. I promise it will only be for a—"

"Don't mention it. We'll have a lovely time," Letitia hummed back. That should have consoled Erik too, but it only weighed upon him more.

Christine had been insistent about sending word to Adèle that she might be in danger. She had been the one to make the full confession to her friend and proclaim that she had to stay with Letitia in safety for a while. Adèle, for her part, had declared that she didn't need protection from detectives, but she'd at least promised to indulge Christine for a while. It didn't make Erik feel any better. Of all the people their pursuit had endangered, Adèle deserved it the least. She had suffered because of them already and deserved peace.

"I'm sure you will," Christine laughed in a warm, suggestive way that made something in Erik squirm. He inched closer.

"I'll truly be sad not to have you at my next salon," Letitia replied and again, there was filtration in the tone that Erik couldn't understand. Or didn't want to.

"Maybe when things settle down, we can still—" Christine's voice caught with emotion, and Erik winced at the guilt stabbing him in the gut. She was crying and it was his fault. At least his guilt made him move.

He unfurled himself from the dark and appeared. Christine saw him first and he didn't deserve the light in her face. In a heartbeat, Christine was there, pulling him into her arms. Erik was so shocked that it took him a moment to hug her back. Was she genuinely happy to see him? Why? His whole body felt tired and stiff, but it was still bliss to melt into her, to feel her against him. He let out a shaking breath as he was finally made whole, though he deserved to remain broken.

"You're late," Christine muttered into his shoulder.

"We knew you'd arrive in the most dramatic way," Letitia added. Erik met her eyes over Christine's head and she gave a soft smile. It confused him as well. This woman had also seen him. Wasn't she appalled now?

"I'm sorry," Erik said automatically, the easiest words that seemed to come to him.

"I'm glad you're here," Christine sighed. She was so kind. "We should board. They've already taken our things."

"I—" Erik began to protest, but there was no fight left in him against this path. "Thank you, Letitia, for taking care of her for me." Not that he was particularly good at it.

"She takes care of herself quite well. I just kept her company," Letitia corrected, and rightly so. Erik already felt seasick.

"Safe journeys. I do hope to hear from you soon, my loves, somehow," Letitia said with a wink. "Good luck."

"Thank you. The same to you," Christine replied. Letitia gave Christine one more knowing look before squeezing her shoulder and leaving them alone.

Erik was happy to let Christine guide him from there. She always took the lead when they traveled, and he was always thankful for it. The ship was small and would get them to Dublin fast enough, carrying a few English travelers and money to return with Irish beef and other goods to sell. Leaving little for the people that had made and raised those goods.

Soon enough, Christine had presented their tickets, and a crewman showed them to the cabin where their things were waiting.

It was a small wooden box with a lumpy bed in a corner and a porthole looking out to sea. Hardly comparable to some of the finer places they had stayed or ways they had traveled, but it felt appropriate.

"You should rest," Christine said as Erik's gaze remained on the bed. "I know you haven't slept since London."

"I've dozed," Erik muttered. He took the order to heart, even so, stripping off his cloak and mask and then flopping onto the miserable mattress. It was hard and smelled of mildew, but the pillow was soft enough. Soft too were Christine's arms around him.

"You can stop torturing yourself, you know," Christine whispered in his ear. He had to be dreaming it. "You're angrier at all of this than I am right now."

"It shouldn't be like this," Erik argued, exhaustion already dragging him down. "You deserve better."

"I'll decide that, my love," Christine sighed and pulled him close to her, her back against his chest, a comforting solid heat. "I do still love you. Even when I'm mad at the world or even you. Love doesn't turn on and off like that."

Erik shut his eyes on tears – hoping he could hide the weakness, but she knew. That thought comforted him into sleep.

It was the cold, perhaps, that woke him. The cold of Christine being gone from the bed. Erik lingered a while at the edge of sleep, letting the rocking of the boat soothe him. Finally, he cracked his eyes open enough to see that it was night outside, but Christine had lit a candle in a glass and was seated in the wooden chair next to the small brazier they had for heat. She was half undressed, stripped down to her underthings with a shawl around her shoulders, its red color a contrast to the alabaster of her skin. The candles lent a golden glow to the place. Christine was golden too, the light warming her cheeks and catching in her auburn hair. So beautiful and warm. Erik stood out like a stain. A shadow on the sun.

"How are you so beautiful, even now?" he found himself asking aloud.

Christine looked up and smiled, though it was a tired sort of look. "Flatterer."

"I'm—"

"Don't say you're sorry," Christine ordered, and Erik bit his lip. "It stops meaning something when you say it all the time."

"Even when I need to?" Erik asked back, rising stiffly from the bed. He felt marginally more alive now with some rest, though his mind was still clouded with sorrows.

"What awful thing are you thinking right now?" Christine asked, and Erik couldn't tell if she was sad for him or sad she had to go through such a discussion again.

"The same as the last day or so," Erik shrugged. "That I brought this on us and I'll bring more sorrow and pain on you and your friends."

"Our friends," Christine corrected. "Mine and yours."

"Even after what they saw?" Erik met her eyes, feeling the heat on his bare face and fighting the urge to hide its ugliness, even now.

"You know very well that more people than me have seen what you look like and still cared for you," Christine argued gently, coming towards him.

"The monster they saw was more than my appearance," Erik whispered back. He pulled Christine to him, selfishly and indulgently, burying his face in her chest and savoring the softness. "You saw it too."

"I did. And I saw how you stopped when I told you to," Christine countered. Erik recalled that moment: the clarity her voice had given him. The peace he had been able to find, being hers to command. It felt so distant now.

"You shouldn't have had to," Erik said. "I should have behaved."

"Violence is a terribly hard way of life to unlearn," Christine said, calm and gentle and simple, as if it wasn't one of the more profound bits of wisdom she had ever shared. Erik looked up at her, at the compassion in her face that had driven away the sadness and disappointment. Or maybe he had imagined them.

"It's also hard to unlearn the idea that I will always be hated, in the end. Always left," Erik murmured back.

"Not by me," Christine replied. "I'd chase you down if you tried."

Erik let out a long breath, tension leaving his body, at last, as he made himself believe her, at least for now. He let his cheek fall against the soft skin of her breasts again. She smelled of the rain and faded lavender perfume. Erik nuzzled the yielding skin, his lips forming a kiss almost of their own volition. It felt good – for the first time in days, something felt good. He kissed her again, and again, his mouth exploring the mounds of flesh bound by her corset, and it made her sigh. It made her happy because it felt good to her too.

"Get this off me," Christine murmured, just as Erik began to undo the front fastenings of the garment. He'd become adept at this in recent months, enough so that he freed her in no time before impatiently pulling her left breast from her chemise.

The boat swayed and groaned as he took her hard nipple and then more into his mouth, devouring as much of her as he could. He licked and sucked, savoring the taste and sensation of her skin against his lips and tongue.

"That's good, yes," Christine whispered as she knit her hands into his hair. Then yanked, pulling him away. "Now the other."

Erik obeyed, lavishing the same attention on her other breast, his mind spinning with adoration and hunger. This he knew how to do right, this he wanted to keep more than anything. Even though he didn't deserve this pleasure.

He pulled back, guilt hitting him like a wave as the boat rocked and jostled them. He had to make himself breathe slowly, and bring himself back. He could do this.

"What do you need?" came Christine's voice, cutting through the storm.

Erik looked up at her, lost, unable to articulate through his shame that he needed her to see or deny him or...

"I see," Christine said, a glint in her eye that made Erik's dizzying thoughts slow. "Lay down, my love."

Erik obeyed, struggling to take his place on the cabin bed as Christine undressed fully before him. She approached with clear purpose and unbuttoned his shirt, kissing him gently as she did. Soon enough, she had him bare, his belt in her hands.

The sound of the sea faded when she bound his arms above his head. The world softened. His mind stilled.

"Close your eyes," she whispered and he did. He was at her mercy now, naked and hardening as she stroked him, utterly exposed.

He whimpered when she stopped but received no blow or admonition. Her absence from his side was punishment enough. He kept his eyes closed, ears straining to make out her movements, trying to sense where she was. He heard a clink, then felt heat as she returned. Warmer than before...

Searing, slicing, beautiful pain spread from his chest and he cried out in shock and pleasure, eyes flying open against his will. He looked up to see his Christine smiling, holding the candle she had taken from its holder, poised to drip more hot wax onto his skin.

"Don't make too much noise. We don't want to alarm the other passengers," Christine said with a smirk. "Or must I gag you?"

"No, please," Erik panted. He hated the idea of being denied the taste of her lips or any other part of her in any way. "I'll be good."

"You will," Christine whispered, and it made his cock throb. With another glorious, devious smile, she tipped the candle, and a stream of hot wax fell on his stomach, burning for an incandescent moment before easing into simple warmth. Erik bit his lips to not cry out from pleasure or pain and earned a nod of approval for his efforts.

Another smile from his love – his lady and mistress and torturer – and more wax dripped onto him, this time on his nipple. The heat was a beautiful agony that made him writhe in his binding before it dissipated into bliss.

"You're quite lovely like this," Christine purred, and Erik didn't fully understand. He did understand what he felt though, the delicious touch of her lips to his skin, close to where the wax now cooled, then the scratch of her nails down his side. He only realized his eyes were closed when he opened them to see her straddle his legs, candle poised and ready above his stomach – or his groin.

He waited, breathless as the heavenly creature who chose to pleasure and punish him nuzzled his dripping cock with her cheek. Was that her next target? He didn't care. He would submit to anything for her. She tipped the candle and darted out her tongue at the same time, licking him from root to tip as wax dripped onto the juncture of his hips.

It was a herculean effort not to scream at the combination of sensations, but he did it. He was panting now, lost in the mix of desire and hurt, encompassed by heat and care. His vision swam, his heart raced, and yet, he found himself almost floating when she did it again, holding back both his voice and his climax for her. He failed the third time, letting out a long moan as she stroked him, and more wax splashed on his skin, but she only laughed.

She was beautiful above him. So beautiful in her compassion and cruelty as the instrument of Erik's repentance flickered in her hand. She held it steady even as she maneuvered her body and his cock and began to sink on him, taking him in gradually as wax dripped on him in a steady, slow stream. The heat on his skin and the heat of her around him was pure heaven. He was utterly lost.

"Don't come," Christine commanded as his body began to tense. He nodded weakly, forcing himself to breathe as she raised the candle to her lips and blew it out. "I need you first," she sighed in the darkness as she began to ride him, unrelenting and savage as she chased her pleasure.

"Use me," Erik moaned back. "Use me and make me good."

"You are," Christine whimpered, and he felt her hand between them, where they were joined, adding to her pleasure with frantic speed. "You did so well. You're so beautiful when you give in and obey. You make me feel so strong and so—" Her voice cracked, body shuddering above him. "Fuck. I... *fuck.*"

He watched her in the shadows above him, throwing back her head in ecstasy as the climax took her. He had no choice but to follow, shaking and shuddering with her, his mind flying and his heart utterly full.

He drifted in the shadows, his body limp as his heart slowed, untethered from time. It wasn't sleep, this quiet state of bliss and relaxation; it was something more and less at the same time, and he had no energy left to parse it. At some point, the weight on top of him disappeared, then his hands were unbound, and gentle lips kissed his cheek. There was a cool cloth against his scalded skin, cleaning the wax and making him whole.

The waves rocked them and he found himself in her arms, safe and still. There was no pain or guilt there now. Only her and the sea and the silence.

# Calais

S haya was glad to be on the ferry at last, after long days and sleepless nights. He had tried to rest, of course, but his mind had been overcome with an endless stream of worry. It had taken too long to make arrangements, too long to pack and reassure Darius, his train from Paris had been delayed by a damn cow on the tracks only for the ferry to be canceled for two days straight due to storms. The English Channel wasn't even that wide! Some madman had swum across it in a rubber suit five years ago! Shaya had been ready to swim it himself, but finally, he was aboard the ferry, under overcast skies, on the way to England.

He found little relief in his mind from his guilt as he walked the deck and stared out over the roiling seas.

How could he have been so stupid to not think they were watching his mail? It was a brilliant tactic, though risky. Shaya himself had employed it in the court of the Shah, where only fools put their plans in writing. Now he and Erik were the fools. He couldn't imagine the lengths to which Pomeroy and his cohorts had gone to watch what Shaya was writing and to whom, or who they would have had to pay off. No matter the method, the damage was done.

The ferry deck was bustling already, with merchants and travelers alike enjoying the fresh air and chitchatting in English and French. Shaya's English was passable but rusty. He had never made the trip to the Isles himself, as he shared Erik's contempt for the English. They were a scourge on Persia and her neighbors, regarding those ancient lands as nothing more than resources to be exploited. Cows to be milked for riches and access, with no regard for their people or history.

Shaya shook himself from the grim thoughts as he went back inside, where there was a small stand set up to sell papers, coffee, and food. Best to eat his fill now – he had heard nothing positive about the food in England, and he'd come to enjoy the pastries of his adopted country. Shaya took his bun and coffee out to the deck with his paper and sat down on a bench to read. He flipped to the arts section first, noting the reviews for the most recent performance at the Opéra. He hoped the positive marks for Robert Rameau were enough to keep up Armand's spirits ahead of facing the wrath of little Meg Giry. He also hoped the girl wasn't getting into too much trouble.

Shaya froze with his coffee halfway to his lips as he stared at the latest news next to the review. In bold, blaring letters the type declared: *Another assault in the streets at the Opéra!*

Shaya read as swiftly as he could, cup forgotten and suspicions rising. A helpless chill went up his spine as he read Étienne d'Amboise's name in black and white, thinking back to the mystery he had left unsolved at the Opéra. Was it foolish to go to London? Would more people be hurt if he did nothing? Meg would be snooping into this, but that wasn't much consolation. She was barely more than a child and didn't have all the facts. It was she, more than any patron, that Shaya worried about being hurt.

If this was Richard playing, he wouldn't hesitate to hurt a girl like Meg. The Opéra ran on the pain of young women, and no one even noticed. Shaya looked down at the papers, eyes widening as he read. Was that the point? This new ghost, if it was Richard, was baffling. Was he trying to get the attention of the old one? Trying to draw him back from the grave? Sabine and Richard knew, somehow, that Erik was alive, and what better way to entice him into a trap than to tarnish his legacy? Something else that Shaya had been instrumental in informing Erik of.

"Shit," Shaya whispered under his breath. This was all the more reason to get to London and sort this out. Pomeroy's men hadn't found Erik there yet, he hoped, and Shaya had to believe he was a better detective than them.

# Ireland

C hristine understood now why they spoke of this country in terms of green. It was hard to take her eyes away from the scenery passing outside the train window. She had not expected Ireland to be much different than England, but she had been wrong. There were similarities, of course. It was still damp and rugged in a way that France was not, still an island and world unto itself, but it was like a melody that had been reused in a different song, played on a different instrument in another key.

There was a wildness here, a sort of ancient, whispering magic in the hills and rivers that was all its own. It was beautiful, and more than that, it matched the visions she had seen in her dreams for weeks... Maybe those dreams had been a warning, for they could not have been a promise, as much as she wished they were.

It was autumn now, Christine realized. The hills of green were dotted with trees painted vibrant shades of orange, yellow, and red by the change of the season, standing out starkly against the slate sky. It was utterly beautiful in a way she had not seen for months. As they passed by creeks and cairns, her eyes drank in the beauty.

She admonished herself to only admire it. There was no point getting attached. She had managed that well enough in Dublin, though it had been an effort. She had disembarked from many ships and trains and carriages over the recent months. They had all started to feel the same, which was what made the exit on the dock in Dublin surprising. It was different.

She had told herself it was just an echo of how pleasurably they had spent the crossing, but the city itself had won her over with its beauty. Bisected by the River Liffey flowing into the bay, it was a modern, bustling metropolis like London, built on foundations going back a thousand years. Compared to Paris and London, it was practically new, Erik had smugly informed her.

Far more people had been leaving the port than arriving. It had made Christine sad in the same way she had been in Genoa to see so many people waiting to get on ships to leave their home shores. She had understood better after riding through the city and seeing the poor, many of them living in little alleys called 'closes,' where the buildings all seemed to lean in on one another, ready to fall. The air was like London's too, thick with soot from factories, though not nearly as bad.

They had only been there for a night after dealing with matters at a dull English bank before catching the train that morning. Only once they had left the city, heading northwest, had Christine truly begun to enjoy the views as the train cut through the morning mist.

"It feels so remote, doesn't it?" Christine asked Erik, trying to think how long it had been since they had seen anything bigger than a village from the rails.

"It's far from everything, including the civilized world, according to some," Erik replied from where he had wedged himself into the corner of their rail compartment. (Snob and misanthrope that he was, Erik had insisted on a first class, private compartment, as usual, and Christine had teased him that they would run out of money before anyone could steal it away).

"According to you? I thought you enjoyed at least part of your time here," Christine asked back, taking in her husband's appearance as she did. Since the incident with the thug in London, he'd kept himself as concealed as possible, making sure to add his wide hat and scarf to his intricate mask and keep his head low. She hated how he felt the need to make himself small and hidden, like a wounded animal cowering from a wolf. "You like wild, empty places where you can roam free."

"I do like them when they're truly empty," Erik replied with a sigh. "People always find you eventually on an island, even one this big."

"I thought you were going to tell me some story about the woods being full of fairies." Christine scooted closer to Erik and leaned against him.

"Well, that's true too." She liked the sound of a smile in his entrancing voice.

"Tell me about them."

It was an easy thing to get him to tell her a tale. He loved to paint pictures with words and she loved to listen to them, curled against him and sharing his warmth. If she could spend every afternoon like this, without the running, she would.

"You must be careful, first of all, in how you speak of them. They are 'the good folk' or 'good neighbors, 'for they take offense quite easily. They live in the mounds that dot the lands, like that one right out there." Erik gestured towards the window and what Christine had thought was an odd hill alone in the landscape. "They're old tombs, some say, or they're gateways to the fair realm. They open the doors on the great festivals, like Samhain and Beltane, and send forth frightful hosts to hunt mortals and ensnare them forever."

"Sounds like the elves my father used to talk about," Christine mused, her mind filling with pictures.

"I'm sure he warned you to be careful when you walk at night. To never follow a light in the woods or the sound of mysterious music. The good folk may lure you in and ask you to dance. It would seem like a night, but an entire year would pass and you'd be dust at the end."

"I shall try to remember," Christine intoned. "You would come after me though, wouldn't you?"

"I would. I would sack the very halls of the Tuatha dé Danann." Christine looked up in curiosity, signaling that her poet should continue his tale. "That is the noble court of the good folk. Some say they are the old gods of this land. They fought many battles over the years, against rival clans and monsters called the Fir Bolg. Their great hero was a god of fire and wisdom, called Lugh…"

## Paris

Meg felt very silly waiting outside Monsieur Moncharmin's office in her ballet clothes, but she was required back at rehearsal soon and there was no point in changing. At least she matched the new painting. Monsieur Moncharmin must have had it hung up in recent months, for Meg didn't remember seeing it before. It was one of Monsieur Degas's larger works, full of vibrant blues and whites, depicting dancers on this Opéra's very stage. Meg didn't personally like the old painter who had made Little Marie so famous and who used the petits rats as muses. He was grumpy and seemed to hate women as people as much as he loved them as subjects.

He wasn't particularly good at faces, Meg decided, continuing to admire the work. All his dancers looked alike and she couldn't tell who anyone was. She wondered if she was supposed to. The edges of the figures in the painting were blurred, like they were in water, or perhaps in an old man's memory, since he couldn't have painted it from a seat in the stalls. It didn't depict who Meg and the other dancers were, just how one man saw them – as swirling wisps of white, ever ephemeral and pure.

"Ah, Mademoiselle Giry."

She turned at the sound of Monsieur Moncharmin's voice. He looked more tired than when she had last seen him. Had there always been a bit of silver in his chestnut hair or had running the Opéra on his own aged him?

"Thank you for finally summoning me," Meg said. "I've been coming by for days."

"I know, I've been very busy," Moncharmin groaned. He tugged Meg into a corner, rather than into his office, which was odd. "Unfortunately, the situation in the cellars – as it were – is not what I called you here for."

"But I've been helping Monsieur Motlagh!" Meg protested. "I might have solved part of the case. At least the motive."

Moncharmin sighed and Meg didn't like it at all. "He's got you talking of cases and motives? How old are you?"

"I turned fifteen last June," Meg said proudly, chin held high. It took her a moment to realize this wasn't the boast she thought it was, thanks to Moncharmin's pitying look. "Shaya trusted me to help him."

"Monsieur Motlagh sent you into dangerous situations to ferret out answers he couldn't get himself, you mean," Moncharmin corrected with a sigh. "I would have asked him not to risk my employees had he consulted me, and now I have to deal with this mess."

"He's not risking me," Meg cried, but Moncharmin frowned.

"Mademoiselle, have you any idea what I've been dealing with in the last few days?" he demanded, lowering his voice secretively and glancing to the closed door of his office.

Meg shook her head. This felt like the time when she was a child and one of the nuns at her school had found Meg sneaking to the kitchen to steal the old bread and give it to a man on the street. "No, Monsieur."

"I received a remarkably interesting visit from a Monsieur Pomeroy. I think you know him."

Meg grew queasy. "I…"

"He wanted to know why a client who had engaged him was dancing in the ballet under another name." Moncharmin's face was sympathetic but his voice was serious.

"It was Shaya's idea. They were spying on him for Sabine de Chagny," Meg tried to explain, but Moncharmin looked unimpressed.

"I assured the good detective that I had no idea what he meant. He didn't believe me, but I think he was here for some other reason I can't discern, so he let it go."

"He's investigating this new ghost too!" Meg cried, and then yelped as Moncharmin covered her mouth with his hand.

"Shhh!" Moncharmin ordered. "You are to say nothing of that when you go inside. Do you hear me? You will explain that you were looking into a rumor about Sabine de Chagny on a dare from some other dancer as part of a juvenile joke."

"What?" Meg asked when he removed his hand.

"I have had to deal with the most unpleasant of visitors today, and you're going to help me make him go away," Moncharmin said as the door of his office opened.

"What in blazes is taking so long?" demanded the man who stood at the door.

Meg was sure she was the same shade of white as her tutu, because it was the Comte de Chagny glaring at her.

Of course the consequences had come now that Shaya was gone. Meg had to face this alone.

"I was just explaining the situation to Mademoiselle Giry here," Moncharmin told the Comte. He took Meg by the elbow and steered her into his office, shutting the door behind her and leaving her alone with two men decades older than her and twice her size.

"I don't see what there is to explain," Raoul declared. "This girl and her accomplice violated my household and spread vicious rumors about my sister. She needs to be dismissed."

"What?" Meg squawked, turning to Moncharmin. He looked equally as shocked by the demand as Meg. "It was a dare! I had heard from la Sorelli—"

"Of course it was that cow," Raoul muttered. "No doubt in search of more attention and compensation."

"Comp-compensation?" Meg asked.

"You dancers and artists," Raoul said like it was an insult. "You get your claws in a man and think you can command him to do anything because you offer amusement that he could easily find in a brothel. The only difference between you and the real whores is, for some reason, my peers think it holds cachet to bed your kind."

There was such hatred in the man's face that Meg was speechless. Christine Daaé had not only broken Raoul's heart when she left him; the loss had curdled his soul.

"Monsieur, please," Moncharmin protested, stepping between Meg and the Comte to block his righteous gaze. "These were the actions of a young, foolish girl. It's my impression that the other one was the source of the gossip."

"No, don't blame Blanche," Meg said, panic rising. "She needs this job. She was only there because of me."

Raoul scoffed, but Moncharmin placed a consoling hand on Meg's shoulder. "No one will be let go. Mademoiselle Giry simply must apologize now that the situation has been explained."

"Now, see here—" Raoul began, but Moncharmin raised a hand to silence him.

"No. Monsieur," the manager cut in, voice dire. "You barge into my opera months after withdrawing your patronage and expect to be treated like you still have a stake in anything that goes on here. You insult my employees and demand their dismissal merely because, through them, the truth came out. Yes, the truth, Monsieur le Comte. You and your sister have other affairs to attend to and you have no rights here. Please leave."

Raoul glowered at the older man, and Meg decided that whatever anger she had felt for Moncharmin in the past few days would be reduced by at least half now.

"What of my apology?" the Comte asked at last, lip curling.

"I'm sorry," Meg said. She didn't mean that she was sorry for anything she had done. She was only sorry she had not done more.

"Fine. It seems this damnable place has sunk even lower since I rid myself of its nonsense," Raoul said. "Perhaps I shall have to be more watchful."

"There will be no need," Moncharmin said firmly. He made no move to assist as the nobleman gathered his hat and gloves before storming out, slamming the door behind him. Meg sank into a chair the moment Raoul was gone, sick with worry and released tension.

"I am sorry, Monsieur," Meg exhaled. "I know this has caused you great trouble."

"I'll survive. I've dealt with worse," Moncharmin said as he slumped towards his chair and collapsed, scrubbing his hand over his face so that he disturbed his glasses.

"Thank you for not firing me," Meg added. "I don't know how I'd survive."

"I don't fire people on the whim of patrons," Moncharmin replied, sounding rather proud of himself.

Meg frowned. "What about Julianne Bonet?"

"Who?" Moncharmin asked, squinting.

"Christine Daaé's old dresser," Meg reminded him, annoyance growing.

"Yes, of course. I didn't fire her. I wouldn't have." He looked doubtful though. "I think?"

"The patron who demanded it didn't go through you and from what I hear, you didn't intervene when it was brought to your attention," Meg explained.

"I've been busy and I was under the impression Mademoiselle Bonet was taken care of or at least independent. Why are you asking?"

"No one has told me the real story of what happened to Christine and the ghost," Meg said with a sigh. "I thought Julianne might know, so I sought her out through Cécile Jammes, but she's gone."

"You mustn't go snooping into all that," Moncharmin warned, sounding more tired somehow. "Especially with the Comte paying attention."

"You don't want him to know about the new phantom, do you?" Meg asked, finally making the connection. Moncharmin shook his head mournfully.

"No. That would be a disaster." Moncharmin's brows knit. "Though it would take some of the pressure off them if he..."

"Who?" Meg asked, sure she had just been party to a thought that should have stayed in Moncharmin's head.

"Never mind. Anyway, I'm sure Mademoiselle Bonet is fine. She's resilient. What did you want to talk to me about in regard to your little case?" Moncharmin asked, straightening up. "I'm curious to hear what theories a young dancer has on this case."

Meg found herself staring at the man, taking in his condescending smile and indulgent look. "Will you really listen to me?"

"Of course, Mademoiselle," Moncharmin said, the same way a parent might tell a child they wanted to hear their fairy story.

"Shaya believes these attacks and thefts are the work of Monsieur Richard or someone working for him," Meg began, and Moncharmin gave an encouraging nod. He knew this. "Because the men who have been hurt were against him after the chandelier."

"Yes, perhaps, though we don't have a record of that yet. I have been trying to reach out to the others under threat."

"Well, I was talking to a friend – another dancer," Meg continued, swallowing uneasily. "She helped me to understand that the men who have been hurt, well, they have all done some hurting themselves."

Moncharmin looked confused. It was Meg's fault for not being clearer, but she didn't want to be indelicate. "Hurting who?" he asked.

"Dancers. Like me. They have taken advantage of the girls," Meg explained, and Moncharmin immediately shook his head.

"The relationships of the patrons with the young ladies of the ballet can be distasteful, I know, but it's how things are done."

Meg felt as if she was speaking another language, and that Moncharmin was merely indulging her. He needed the patrons. The only reason she had been saved from the wrath of the Comte de Chagny was because he no longer was one, not because she didn't deserve it.

"Of course, it was a foolish fancy," Meg muttered. "I won't trouble you any further."

"Do come to me if you hear anything of more note," Moncharmin said, and she knew he meant it as kindness. Meg nodded and showed herself out.

The halls were empty as she walked back towards the rehearsal salons; devoid of life in a way that made Meg lonelier with each step.

She was of no use, was she? She'd made trouble for the manager and bothered him with her hairbrained ideas. Shaya had only cared about her as much as he could benefit from her connections. She'd been used and discarded, and that was something she was expected to tolerate in her position. She kicked a knot in the floorboards with the toe of the ballet slipper in annoyance, like the child she was seen as...

"Meg."

She looked up at the sound of the whisper to find the hall empty, and a chill ran down her spine.

"Who's there?" Meg demanded, gooseflesh rising on her arms.

"I think you know," the voice replied from somewhere Meg couldn't see. The voice of a ghost – husky and intimate.

"You," Meg whispered.

"You're on the right track, young Meg," the voice went on. "Which is why you must turn back. Don't make any more trouble for me."

"I can't though," Meg replied, excitement and terror filling her in equal measure. "I need to know."

"You'll be hurt." Meg could make out no details about the speaker from the voice, only that they seemed to entirely lack a body and knew what she had been doing.

"So will you, if you're caught," Meg found herself saying.

"You don't want that?" the ghost asked as if it was surprised.

Meg paused, as she had with Moncharmin, thinking back to all she knew of this ghost at its mission. No, its righteous cause.

"I don't want to be used anymore, by anyone," Meg declared at last. "I want to help."

The hall echoed with potent silence as Meg's heart picked up speed. Had she spoken wrong? Had she revealed too much?

"And help you shall. For now, be silent, and we will see what more you can be."

Meg knew the moment that the speaker left; she felt the energy go out of the room and she had to lean against the wall to steady herself.

She had spoken to the phantom – whatever or whoever it was that had taken to the Opéra halls now. She had bared her soul, in a small way, and been rewarded. Or damned. She wasn't sure which. But she knew now, with certainty, whose side she was on.

# 11. Temptation

## Sligo

Their lodgings in Sligo could be called a hotel as much as Sligo might be called a city, in Erik's opinion. Which was to say: only by the greatest stretch of the imagination. The Oak and Ash was a bustling inn at best, just as Sligo was barely more than a large town. It had a rail station and a sizable church (as well as dozens of smaller ones), held the county seat, and was, in general, the center of life in the coastal county of the same name, tucked away in the far west of the country. The inn was central to the city, with a large common hall on the bottom floor serving food and drink, where musicians were currently in session.

The space – all worn, caramel-colored wood and plaster – was full of people even at this late an hour, and the music was as lively as the fire crackling in the great stone hearth. Christine had insisted on staying to listen, much to Erik's distress. The whiskey he found in his hand didn't do much to tame the anxious creature inside him that wanted to be anywhere but here.

"Do you know any of these songs?" Christine asked as the fiddler on the makeshift stage in the center of the room flew through a solo, accompanied by a bodhrán drum and penny whistle.

"A few," Erik replied, attempting to sound mysterious and unmoved. The spell Christine had cast with her candles and kisses on the ship had worn off, leaving him antsier and angrier than before that he was here. He could still feel the smart of the red marks on his skin under his shirt, but the echoes of the pain weren't enough to ground him or keep his dark thoughts at bay anymore.

"You could at least pretend to enjoy yourself," Christine admonished.

"You know how I feel about being here, but I'm here," Erik said, taking another slug of whiskey on the chorus.

"I do, but what I don't know is why you're trying so hard to dislike even the pleasant bits."

Erik peered over at his wife. She seemed utterly charmed by everything around them and had been all day. Her eyes were hopeful and expectant, and Erik hated himself for how annoyed that made him. He wanted to pull himself back to her – why was it so difficult?

"I'm still cross that we have to do this," Erik muttered.

"No. You're afraid of something. You always turn your fear into anger," Christine countered. Erik was glad the mask concealed the thunderstruck look he gave her. Sometimes it was quite troublesome how well she knew him. "Are you afraid of these people more than others?"

"Yes," Erik said, almost against his will. It was pointless to lie to her, even if he could lie to himself. He looked around the common room from where they were stationed in a dark corner. He felt like he was back at the Opéra, a ghost cut off from a world he so wanted to influence and belong to. A world he longed for, despite knowing it wasn't meant for him, even if he had a claim.

"Because your mother's country is special."

"The people here aren't like others we've had to endure. And I do still hate to endure people," Erik began, swirling the whiskey in his glass and letting the smell of smoke and peat waft through the air. Like everything here, it triggered something familiar and sad in his memories. "I have roots here, however distant, and that creates...

expectations. Or perhaps hopes." He felt silly saying it, but he was glad she'd got it out of him.

"You don't want them to disappoint you." Christine's eyes were kind and knowing in a way that made Erik feel marginally less embarrassed by his fears. "Maybe they won't, if you give it a chance."

"I've given humanity enough chances."

"And some of them turned out well," Christine countered. "Or have you forgotten who you're here with?"

*The poor woman I have ensnared and dragged across the world in my shadow*, Erik wanted to answer. Christine took his hand before he could, forcing him to look at her. "Your wife, who loves you, you fool. Who wants you to give something a chance."

Erik wasn't sure that was possible, given the circumstances that had brought them here, but he was out of excuses. "I'll try," Erik whispered.

Christine's eyes narrowed. "You'll succeed. Because I want you to," Christine replied in a tone that gave Erik a chill.

"Yes, my love," Erik breathed.

"Finish your drink, listen to the band, and come up to the room when you're done," Christine ordered, rising with a twinkle in her eye. "I'm going to see what I can find in terms of a bath, so take your time. I'll be in our bed when you're ready."

Erik did like the sound of that, and the way Christine smirked at him before walking away. He watched her go as he sipped the whiskey, the warmth of the liquor burning down his throat as even warmer ideas of what he'd like to do to her later seeped into his mind.

The band finished one song and began another, the leader singing of robbing Captain Farrell on Kilgary mountain. Erik had to smile just a bit. He did know this one, and he raised his glass for another sip.

"*Musha-rin-durin dah, whack for the daddy-o, whack for the daddy-o there's whiskey in the jar,*" the whole crowd sang with the band and Erik sighed, closing his eyes to let the music reach him. He'd been trying to keep it out, but maybe Christine was right. Maybe he could give it a chance.

"*He counted out his money and it made a pretty penny, I took the money home and I gave it to me Jenny,*" the men on stage sang over the drum and pipe, their voices rough and reedy, carrying a tune old as the hills. His mother had sung this song once when she was in a fair mood; when the sun was shining and she thought no one could hear. Her father had sung it to her, and his father to him, and so on. Who knew where it came from...

"*She sighed and she said that she never would deceive me, but the devil's in the woman and I never will be easy.*"

"A violent song, though not inaccurate."

Erik's eyes flew open. There before him, seated where Christine had just been, was Pauline, with a look of pure delight in her grey eyes.

"I'm sorry, I didn't mean to surprise you," Pauline said, leaning towards him. She was dressed more fashionably than he had ever seen before, wearing a dark blue dress with a low-cut neckline edged in lace. Her spectacles were gone and her hair was up in the same sort of style Christine had favored lately, with a few ringlets loose at the base of her neck – had she changed the color somehow to look more auburn too?

"The only surprise is seeing you so soon," Erik drawled, affecting an air of disinterest. "Have you been lurking here waiting for me?"

"You do think quick," Pauline replied. "When I received word from Monsieur Bidaut that you had fled London with your tail between your legs, I knew you were on your way. You've given us quite a merry chase – the trick about America was genius. To find you so easily now is truly a delight."

"The delight will be mine when I leave you a bloody pulp out in the alley," Erik said with a sneer that was met with a mock gasp of horror and a grin.

"You'd threaten a woman? I thought you were reformed, or some such nonsense. I guess you're the killer I have heard so many things about," Pauline tutted. "And don't say I don't know you, Erik. Because I do. I'm a scholar of all things about you if I do say so myself. Your dedicated student and aficionado."

"That can't be very satisfying," Erik muttered. "There's not much to learn."

"You'd be surprised what an enterprising detective can uncover." Pauline looked so proud of herself, it would have been comical if not for the madness in her eyes.

Erik waved a thin hand. "What do you want?"

"This is a parlay before the battle begins. A courtesy offer."

"You want something in exchange for the surrender of my fortune?" Erik was almost ready to give it to her. Being chased down for such a petty reason was truly beneath him.

"Oh. No," Pauline said sweetly. "That exchange will come later. When I decide whether or not to burn your mother's crumbling old village to the ground."

The mask concealed the expression on Erik's face, but not the fire that must have sparked in his eyes, for Pauline grinned, smug and infuriating.

"Why would I care?" Erik bluffed. "Or believe you would do something so flashy and foolish? You and Bidaut have been subtle so far."

"I don't mean literally, silly man." Pauline giggled like she was flirting, a profoundly disturbing affectation. "I mean I'm going to own that town – plans are already in motion – and destroy it, bit by bit. I'll evict the useless farmers, and close down whatever godforsaken hovels they have on their main street. Drive everyone away one by one in misery. There's so much you can do with a little finesse and a vulnerable old fool."

"And money. Which your employer doesn't have or they wouldn't be after mine," Erik scoffed, though the thought was chilling.

"We've learned from you how easy it is to make people believe in ghosts and lies," Pauline replied with a shrug. "But you're right. Bidaut thinks it's too complicated. He's planning on finding someone to kill if you don't comply. Maybe our friends from Lucca? Howard or dear Giacomo. Jack to you. Or that whore in London your own strumpet was seen with? Or perhaps Adèle Valerius? That would be poetic."

Erik forced himself not to take the woman by the throat right here, audience be damned. All Erik could hope was that this was a bluff, and he had not done the thing he wished the most not to do – or that Christine had taught him to not want to do – endanger friends, old and new. Bring more people under the shadow of his curse.

"Be careful wasting all your threats now, someone may begin to doubt your honesty in making them." He kept his tone light and annoyed, even though he was seething.

"I think you know how serious we are," Pauline trilled. "But, as I said, this is a parlay. I have an offer for you and you alone."

There was something wild in the woman's eyes, something that had become untethered from reason since the last time Erik had encountered her. Maybe he could exploit that.

"I'm listening," Erik muttered.

"I will tell Bidaut, our employer, and anyone who will listen that I lost you; to give up the ghost, as it were, if you do one, simple thing for me." Pauline's face was bright with excitement as she inched closer and slid her hand across the table to grip Erik's. It made his stomach turn and his nerves go on high alert. "Something not entirely unpleasant."

"What are you suggesting?" She couldn't possibly mean what Erik feared she did, but she batted her lashes and looked at him with what he assumed was meant to be an expression of seduction.

"I think you know," Pauline purred, but Erik was silent. "If you insist on clarity: I want you to fuck me."

"Why?" Erik asked, holding in his horror and the impulse to pull his hand away. This wasn't the time to deliver any sort of rejection to a madwoman.

"This case – you. You've changed me," Pauline answered breathlessly. "The more I learn about you – how ruthless you are, how monstrous – the more it captivates me. I think about how you choked me in that cellar when I'm alone at night; the heat of you behind me and—"

"That's quite enough," Erik cut in, growing ill as he looked to the exits of the room. He tried to pull his hand back but Pauline snatched it in an iron grip, her eyes wide and feral.

"Oh, not enough at all," Pauline whispered urgently. "I can give you things that a simpering soprano would never dream of. I will let you ruin me and ask for more. I want you to be a monster and destroy me."

She looked as if she was ready to climb on him right there, which was disturbing in and of itself, but combined with her offer – her blackmail – it was worse.

"You think you can give me something she can't," Erik asked, stalling.

"I think that fool who gave up glory and gold wants you to be a lamb when you're a lion," Pauline replied. "All I ask is one night."

"A night you think will win me over to you, so I will leave my wife behind," Erik finished for her. "If she doesn't turn me away when she finds out."

Pauline shrugged, not denying it. "We'd be unstoppable, the two of us. We could burn the world down and dance among the ashes and corpses. With me, you'd be free. Would you rather keep up a war you know you will lose over a fortune you don't need for a boring life with a wilting flower?"

"You make it sound so enticing," Erik whispered, and Pauline's mad eyes grew brighter. "Let us discuss this upstairs in my room."

# London

It was odd for Shaya to be at the opera and not the Opéra. It was also disconcerting that this version of Verdi's *Don Carlos* was in Italian and not in French, as he had heard it before, and omitted the first act and the ballet. At least that meant it was a shorter affair, especially considering the abruptness of the ending – as if the librettist had grown bored with the dramatics and simply decided to end the story mid-sentence.

Shaya was out of his seat before the curtain fell, rushing to the stage door he had scouted before the performance. He hadn't wanted to gain admission then and disturb Adèle, but he couldn't afford to miss her now. He'd been searching for her fruitlessly for days, unable to find her at any address she was associated with, and for a few hours, he had been worried beyond reason that he had been too late to protect her. Again.

The stage door was two doors actually. One leading to a small antechamber where a man was sitting behind a podium with a list, guarding the actual door inside.

"Sir? Are you here to see someone?" the attendant asked as Shaya entered the first door. He couldn't hear the orchestra or applause anymore, which meant curtain call was over and he had limited time. Perhaps he was nervous because one too many sopranos had disappeared from under his nose after operas.

"I'm an old friend of Adèle Valerius," Shaya replied, noting how the guard was taking in the color of his skin and his hat with some suspicion. He probably assumed Shaya was Indian, given the empire that Britain held there.

"You're not on the list," the man said after a beat.

"How would you know when you haven't asked my name nor looked at your list?" Shaya replied, trying to remain calm.

"Madame Valerius was clear that she wanted no visitors. At all." The man seemed honest, as far as Shaya could tell. This, combined with how hard it had been to find Adèle, meant she was being cautious, which made Shaya's need to see her all the more urgent.

"Sir, on my honor, I'm an old friend of hers. If you take my name to her, she will admit me. It's a matter of great importance that I see her." Shaya didn't know if this stranger would care about the honor of a foreigner he had never met, but he looked at least interested.

"Wait here," the man said with a sigh and rose to stick his head through the second door. He yelled: "Oi, Jim, come here!" Through the glass in the door, Shaya saw a burly man approach.

"What? I got places to be," Jim asked.

"I need to get a message to Mrs. Valerius. Tell her that— what did you say your name was?"

"Shaya Motlagh," he replied, daring to feel some smidgen of hope.

"Shy-a mouth-lot – or something like that – is here and insists he's got to see her. Foreign chap," the guard said. Shaya fought against rolling his eyes. This was something. Adèle would say yes.

The man returned to his post, looking dubious and waving Shaya out of the way into a corner as another guest entered and approached the podium. Shaya made himself as unobtrusive as possible out of pure habit and observed the man.

"Good evening, has Mrs. Valerius left yet?" the new visitor asked, and Shaya's eyes flew to the man's face. It was one he recognized. He had seen this man go into Pomeroy's office when he had sent Meg in. The day she had learned they were searching for Erik.

Shaya signaled as subtly as he could from behind the man, trying to get the guard's attention. The man made a face as he met Shaya's eyes and Shaya shook his head vigorously, mouthing "Say yes" as clearly as he could.

"Uh... yes. She was quick about it," the guard stammered. "Wasn't takin' callers anyway, so, best you're on your way."

Shaya spun away when the man turned around, making a show of checking his watch. He felt the other detective's gaze linger upon him as he stepped out of the door without further questions. The moment he was gone, the door guard jumped from his perch.

"Now, what was that about?" the man asked, clearly not amused. "I went along with ya 'cause Miss Adèle said no men in glasses. She was very specific about that, but what—"

"She'll see him straight away!" Jim's booming voice interjected. Shaya didn't wait for a second more before rushing to the inner door and following the larger man through the backstage corridors. They came to the dressing room and the door burst open. Shaya was pulled inside and into a hug before he knew what was happening.

"Shaya!" Adèle cried, slamming the door behind them in poor Jim's face. "What are you doing here?"

"I came to warn you and – perhaps our mutual friends – that they have been discovered to be in London," Shaya answered. "Because of me."

"So they were tracking our mail," Adèle sighed, to Shaya's surprise. He felt like he was joining a conversation already in progress. "They were worried even something I sent might be caught, but I assured them it was fine. That must have been how the bastards knew to set up a snare here."

"They've been discovered?" Shaya asked, heart seizing. "Where are they?"

"They left the night they were discovered. The detective that's after them is a man named Bidaut. He set up a reward among the cutpurses and petty thieves for word of a man in a mask," Adèle explained. "It was unfortunate how they were found. They had started to like London."

"But they're gone now?"

"Yes," Adèle sighed. "Too fast."

"But you're still in hiding." Shaya took a moment to look over Adèle. She seemed healthy and in one piece, if perhaps tired from her performance.

"I haven't been in hiding, I've just been avoiding the public, celebrity that I am."

"Another man was trying to get in to see you!" Shaya exclaimed. "I recognized him – I saw him in Paris. He works for the men who were spying on me."

"The man with glasses," Adèle said grimly. "Damn."

"Who is he?" Shaya asked, eager to put a name to a nemesis.

"That was Bidaut! He's ruthless," Adèle answered, taking a seat at her vanity. She looked worried, which troubled Shaya: she wasn't the sort of woman to worry lightly. "I don't want to know what he wants with me."

"We intend to threaten your life in exchange for a fortune."

Adèle sprang up and Shaya jumped in front of her, placing his body in between her and the man who stood in her dressing room door. The very man they had been discussing.

"Monsieur Bidaut," Shaya intoned, furious at himself for not coming armed, but not about to let this man guess that.

"Did you really think I couldn't bribe my way in here, Monsieur Motlagh? Especially after noticing your presence," Bidaut said as he stepped into the room, closing the door ominously behind him.

Shaya could feel Adèle's tension, and it made him helplessly furious that she should be in such a situation again because of him and this mess. "There's no need to involve the lady."

"I don't think that's the right term for this one," Bidaut sneered over Shaya's shoulder towards Adèle – then blanched at the unmistakable sound of a pistol cocking.

"You would do well to address me with some respect, you odious piece of shit," Adèle growled. Shaya stepped back as she raised her gun and pointed it at the man who had sought, stupidly, to intimidate her. "Did you think I wouldn't be prepared for you?"

"Perhaps I was misinformed on your formidableness," Bidaut said slowly, raising his arms.

"I wouldn't be surprised, given the woman who employs you and her associates," Shaya said with a smirk. "Adèle, you should know this man works for the alleged widow of a certain Baron. Sister to a certain Comte."

Adèle's face grew even darker and she stepped closer to Bidaut. "I should shoot you on principle for bringing that monster to mind."

"That wouldn't stop her," Bidaut replied, his veneer of calm wavering only a little. "She's quite committed to this."

"Enough to threaten murder?" Adèle scoffed. "What a spine she has grown."

"Your refusal won't change the strategy," Bidaut went on. "We'll find other friends. We have other plans. Eventually, the ghost will have to give up what he's stolen."

"Why must it always be the innocent that get hurt in these bloody fights for riches," Adèle hissed, but Bidaut looked unmoved.

"Take me," Shaya said, surprising himself with how calm he was.

"Shaya, no," Adèle exclaimed immediately, but didn't drop her guard. "You don't have to do this."

"I do," Shaya whispered, holding her gaze for a long moment. "I am the reason for so much of this. I cannot let it harm you again, or anyone else. I'll be fine."

"Shaya," Adèle sighed, but he had already turned to Bidaut.

"Is this agreeable?" Shaya asked him. "I'll be your hostage in your nefarious negotiations, as long as you promise not to hurt or threaten anyone else."

"If you run, there will be consequences." Bidaut sounded as if he were discussing a business deal.

Shaya nodded in understanding.

"Be careful," Adèle whispered as Bidaut opened the door and indicated that Shaya should follow. He had no idea what he was bound for or if he would survive. He had some faith in Erik, at this point, and much more faith in Christine, but that was not what gave him a feeling of peace. He'd kept someone safe who he had failed before. That was worth the peril he now placed himself in.

# Sligo

Christine didn't want to be annoyed. She didn't know why she had thought it would be easy to find a bath at this hour in a place like this. She'd been informed by the yawning man at the front desk that she would have to pay, and the tub and hot water were not available now, but she could use the pump. Or that was what she hoped she had been told. She had been studying her English and making Erik practice with her, but she was still very much at sea.

She didn't want to pout as she made her way up the creaking stairs toward the room. She needed to be cheerful and optimistic amidst all this, if for no other reason than to keep Erik from slipping into an even darker mood. She hoped he was trying, though she honestly didn't know what she wanted him to try or why. They couldn't stay here more than they could stay anywhere else while they were being hunted. Not that Erik wanted to stay anywhere, except in the past.

She paused at the door, sighing as she set the key into the lock and resting her head against the wood.

She was so tired. Or maybe she had been tired for a very long time and she just wanted a place to rest that wasn't some rented room or train car. She wanted to rest, or at the least take a long bath, and then order her husband to ravish her. She'd have to settle for only the last one, though right now she just wanted to be in his arms, no matter what they were doing. He was her home now.

Their room was cold and dark. Empty of any light, no fire burning in the hearth. That left it to her to kindle it and light the candles. At least it was a larger room, with a fair-sized bed and a modest screen to conceal the washbasin and chamber pot. She didn't like having to use that but it was better than sleeping in the woods. She had to light the damn fire before she did anything.

Christine knelt by the cold hearth and pulled a few pieces of kindling from the bundle of wood that rested beside it in a metal basket, ready to be used. Soon enough, she had a pile ready and pulled a match from the jar next to the firewood. She struck it and fire filled her vision just as a voice sounded outside her door.

"I could be bringing you here to kill you, you know."

Erik's tone was dark, with only the barest hint of humor. The deadly kind he reserved for those he truly hated or meant to mock. It sent a chill through Christine's blood.

"You could, but I think we both know you're not that foolish," a female voice replied, flirtatious and familiar.

"Why? Because your compatriot will avenge you?" Erik replied with an audible sneer. "I know you came here alone, Pauline. I know you're disposable in this operation."

Christine hissed as the match burned down to her fingers, the pain snapping her out of her horror and confusion. Erik had said the name on purpose. He was stalling at the door because he wanted Christine to know who was with him and give her some sort of warning.

"You don't want the mess of another murder," Pauline replied in a tone that made Christine's skin crawl. What the hell was that bitch doing here now? They had thought to thwart her in Coolaney.

"You might be worth it," Erik replied.

"Wouldn't your saint of a wife be upset?" There was derision in Pauline's voice that made Christine want to throttle the woman herself.

"She would never have to know. She's not here, as I told you."

Christine understood. She jumped up and hid herself behind the dressing screen, stooping down in the corner and holding her breath as the door creaked open.

"I guess it would be a delicious way to die," Pauline sighed as they stepped into the room, only her footsteps audible as Erik walked silently behind her. Christine imagined him looming like a predator and wondered why he hadn't struck already. "Promise you'll use those lovely hands on my neck either way."

"Apologies for the cold," Erik said, dismissive of the bewildering words. "The maid must have been distracted while lighting the fire."

He's seen the wood and matches. He knew she was there.

"I'm sure I'll be warm enough." That was seduction in Pauline's voice; it was unmistakable. Christine twisted her head to peek through a hole in the screen in time to see Pauline slide a hand up Erik's arm before he winced away. That wince – and biting her lips hard – was all that kept Christine from screaming.

"I want details of this transaction before anything begins," Erik said, voice dire and posture aloof. "How do I know you even have the power to call off Bidaut?"

"Because we have someone to answer to, like everyone. Well, everyone but you," Pauline began with a smile. "I'll telegram dear Monsieur Pomeroy and let him know you've died or fled to Greenland or something. It will certainly be easier to convince him if you leave that baggage behind."

"Careful now," Erik hissed. "I gave up everything for her."

"And what did it get you? A life on the run? A madwoman after you for a fortune you won't ever even use?" Pauline laughed. "Sounds like a bad deal."

"Back to ours." Erik backed a step away and Pauline followed, a glimmer in her eyes and a grin on her face. Christine hated it.

"I will contact everyone once the deed is done, and you'll be free. As I said," Pauline replied with a shrug. Erik looked unconvinced. Christine, for her part, was both furious and bewildered.

"Will you tell me now who employed you in the first place?" Erik was doing his best to sound bored and dispassionate, but Christine knew him. This was a trap. It had to be.

"When we're done, I'll tell you everything."

"And what exactly will be required of me?" Erik asked grimly.

"Oh. You mean to ask if you can get away with a few quick thrusts and be done with me?" Pauline sniggered, and Christine's jaw dropped. Surely she couldn't mean... "No. I want you to well and properly fuck me. You have to make me come and you have to finish too."

She did mean it. Christine didn't care about the why or how of it, she was too angry and incensed in a way she had never been in her life.

"That may be difficult," Erik drawled as if he were bored.

"Will it though?" Pauline whispered, approaching Erik again. This time, he didn't step back. She slid a hand up his chest, making an absurd face she surely thought was alluring, and batting her lashes. "You can pretend I'm her. I want you to. I don't want you to only fuck me. I want you to make love to me the way you do to her. To your angel. You can even call me Christine if you like. Just make me feel it."

"How are you to replace her if she is the one I'm imagining?" Erik asked, voice dispassionate and spine straight. "How will I burn the world down with you if all I can think of is her?"

Pauline's smile faltered and her hand froze. "I'll be better than her. I know I'm better than a weak, delicate thing like her," Pauline tried, and Erik gave a knowing laugh. "I'll let you do things to me she's never dreamed of. Never heard of."

"You know, for all that you think you know about the woman I love, you're quite mistaken about her," Erik said calmly. "She's more formidable and vicious than you could ever imagine."

Christine didn't want to think about what it made her feel to hear him say that. Was she proud or ashamed? Was she ready, right now, for them to both embrace the darkness they had left behind or was she the weak, sweet fool Pauline assumed her to be?

"But that doesn't surprise me, Pauline," Erik went on. "You're not very smart. You think you are, but alas, you're too in love with your masks. I'd know. I used to think I was powerful and unstoppable too. Until her."

"What—" Pauline stammered, and Christine was sure she could feel the way Erik smiled.

"While our lives may not be all we want yet, you must understand, Christine is everything to me," Erik nearly sang, and Pauline's insipid, round face went pale. "I'd do anything for her, including delivering a gift to her to beat senseless if she sees fit."

"No—"

Christine moved without thinking. She felt the handle of the pitcher from the wash basin in her hand before she even decided to grab it. She had it raised before Pauline turned to her in shock and horror. The woman made a noise of protest, raising her hands to defend herself, but she was too late because Christine's rage was faster.

The pitcher shattered against Pauline's skull and the woman crumpled to the floor, clutching her ear and weeping.

"You could never be her, Pauline," Erik said with a smile as Christine let the handle of the pitcher drop to the ground. "You're a weed. A bramble. My Christine is the forest itself, in all its beauty and power."

"I was going to say you're an idiot for thinking you could seduce my husband," Christine spat, another flare of possessive jealousy sparking in her chest. "But he's more poetic."

"Fuck you, you stupid bitch," Pauline sputtered. Was there blood in her mouth? Christine found herself hoping she'd lost a tooth.

"No. I'll be fucking my husband," Christine was shocked to hear herself say. "In ways you couldn't imagine."

Pauline rose, preparing to pounce on Christine, but looking nothing but pathetic with her gashed face and bloody grimace. "Now you'll never—"

"Please shut her up, my love," Christine ordered calmly and savored a moment of pure excitement as Erik gripped their nemesis by her throat.

Pauline struggled, of course, the way people often did when Erik began to cut off the air from their lungs. Christine had seen it enough times now that it wasn't even horrifying. She found herself looking at the woman who had thought to supplant her with clinical interest, noting how her face grew red and her hands became rigid claws, trying to gain purchase on Erik's sleeve.

"Shall we dispose of her?" Erik asked, and Christine didn't know if that was a bluff or not. For a moment, she didn't care. She wanted to destroy the thing that continued to rob her of her happiness, the person that had stalked and manipulated her, only to try to be her in the most insulting and inept way possible. How embarrassing for her.

"No. Send her to sleep," Christine sighed. "Her pathetic life is punishment enough. For now."

More impotent rage flared in Pauline's eyes before they rolled back in her head and she went limp. This time, when she fell in a heap on the floor, she didn't stir.

"What do we do with her?" Erik asked, regarding the mess with some satisfaction. "We can't leave her."

"We won't. Go tell the front we have an ill friend who needs the room next to ours," Christine replied calmly, striding to the bags she had left beside the bed. She found what she was looking for quickly enough, making sure to close up the bag it had come from so nothing else would be seen too soon.

She enjoyed the look of terror and awe Erik gave her as she approached. "Why do you have shackles in your bag?"

"Letitia had extras," Christine said simply and clamped the first cuff around Pauline's wrist. It was oddly satisfying to restrain this awful woman in such a way. "How long will she be unconscious?"

"With the way you hit her, a long while," Erik muttered, watching as Christine finished restraining Pauline. "What will we do with her?"

"Make her live up to her word," Christine said with a shrug. "Or something like it. I haven't decided. Now go."

Erik quickly complied, letting the door slam behind him as he left Christine with the unconscious body of her would-be rival.

"You believed you could have him," Christine whispered. "You and Bidaut have taken my peace from me again and again, but you thought you could take my love?"

Christine didn't feel like herself, and that made her even more furious. This interloper, this stranger who didn't know her – who only hated an idea of her – had somehow taken something from her like the most adept of thieves. She'd stolen not only her happiness but Christine's very sense of who she was, fragile as it had been. Because she would never have done this to someone before... Before all this.

Maybe that was giving this pathetic girl too much credit. Perhaps many things had changed in Christine over the last year. She had seen murder and tragedy and thought she had found hope, but it kept eluding her. Because of people like Pauline, yes, but also because of Christine's own mistakes and weakness.

Erik was back quickly, and he helped Christine drag Pauline's unconscious body to the room next door. He said nothing as they attached the cuffs to the frame of the bed and Christine took a moment to gag their prisoner. They certainly didn't want her to cause a scene.

It was only when they were back in their own room, in the cold and dark, that Christine realized she was shaking. Her breath was unsteady too and she...

"You need to sit down," Erik told her, suddenly at her side and guiding her to rest on the bed. "I'll finish starting the fire."

"No," Christine gasped, grabbing his arms. "Don't leave me."

Christine was suddenly in the past, a shell of herself the night she'd seen a man die because of her. Then she was on the stage again, watching the chandelier fall and finding herself in a phantom's arms, taken by him because she had to know they were still alive.

"You need to—"

"I know what I need," Christine snapped before he could tell her to breathe or bring her back. The room was spinning so she looked into Erik's eyes behind his mask. The bitch had wanted him to take it off for her. She saw her hand on her husband's chest and wanted to scream because another had touched him in the same way and how dare she try to take what Christine had given everything for? Her dreams and her soul? "I need you."

"This isn't—" Erik tried to argue, but Christine was too fast, springing upon him. She tore away his mask, then everything else. She didn't want to think anymore, she never wanted to think and wallow in moments like this. She wanted to run because that was what they did. This ravenous thing that wanted nothing more than to be possessed and ruined was all she was in this darkness.

"Is this because she touched me?" Erik asked as Christine kissed him, straddling him and grinding herself against him so that he groaned.

"She can't have you," Christine hissed back, then bit his lip.

"She never would," Erik whispered back, twining his hands into Christine's hair and freeing it from the pins and combs keeping it in place. "Didn't you hear what I said to her?"

"Not loud enough," Christine whimpered, seeking more friction with her hips as she fumbled between them for his hardening cock. "I need you in me. I need you to prove it. I command it."

For a moment, Erik froze, some battle going on inside him that sent a wave of terror through Christine.

"Don't you want me?" she asked, hands drawing back, her voice small.

"I always want you," Erik replied instantly, kissing her cheek. "More than anything, but—"

"Then *take me*," she begged. "*Please.*"

He kissed her so hard she stopped breathing. She stopped reeling too. Stopped fearing and let herself go. She shook like a leaf as he pushed her onto the bed, roughly hitching her legs over his hip as her skirts bunched between them. Then he thrust home hard inside her and she lost all reason.

"Like that, just like that," she babbled as he drove into her so hard the bed began to creak and slam against the wall. She groped for him above her, for something to hold onto or even to hurt. Her hands, somehow, found his throat.

"Oh God," he groaned, and her grip tightened. What was she doing? Why was she careening into pleasure at the feel of his breath under the power of her hand even as his cock filled her to the brim, fucking her into a sparkling oblivion?

"Keep going," Christine panted, her body racing to meet his. "Keep fucking me like you'll never fuck another woman because you're mine."

"Yours," Erik keened, his voice hoarse and thin because Christine's hand was a vice on his throat – because she commanded his heart and soul and breath.

The knowledge made her snap. Made her break and convulse and come, letting go as she did. Erik gave a gasp and a spasm and she felt him begin to pour inside of her, savage and unmoored.

Ecstasy for a moment.

Then silence. Silence pierced only by the sound of their breath in the cooling dark.

What if all they had left was that?

# Paris

Meg couldn't fall back asleep. She'd practiced until her legs ached all afternoon because she knew herself. She had known she'd be up all night thinking about that ghostly voice, and what to do next. It had almost worked. She'd slept for a few hours, but now she was awake and had been since three o'clock. The witching hour.

The sky was growing light outside her window, and if they had lived somewhere with birds, Meg was sure they'd be starting to sing to bring the dawn. Paris only seemed to have crows and pigeons, and they were all still roosting in the Tuileries.

She crept from her bed to the low embers of the fire in the parlor. She curled herself into a ball, staring at the coals, hoping they would give her some insight.

"What are you doing up?"

Meg turned around to see her mother approaching, her face as warm as her voice. Something inside Meg uncoiled.

"I couldn't sleep," Meg confessed.

"And why is that?" Her mother sank awkwardly to the floor next to Meg, wrapping them both in her shawl, like a bird protecting her chick from the rain. "Have your adventures gotten away from you?"

"What?" Meg looked up at her mother in surprise. "I haven't..."

"Meg. You've been out and about non-stop in the last few weeks," her mother sighed. "I've been waiting for you to tell me what you've been up to, and I've been patient, but don't think I don't notice. I'm a mother – we always know when something is amiss."

Meg couldn't control the way her chin began to tremble or the moisture that sprang to her eyes. She could name it now – the crushing feeling she had endured since Shaya had left her, and even before then. Even among her supposed friends and fellow dancers, she had felt it for months – loneliness.

She fell against her mother's shoulder and wept, comforted by the embrace of someone who would never leave her. Who never had left her, all this time.

"Mama, I'm sorry, I just—"

"You wanted something of your own, I know," her mother cooed, petting Meg's hair. "Everyone wants adventure at your age, but it's a lonely thing to take it on your own, even if that's the way it must be."

Meg sniffled and nodded. Sometimes, she forgot that her mother could be wise. "I've... I've been trying to discover who the new ghost is. Or something like that. It's all gotten away from me."

"Ah, so that's where the letter went," the elder Giry chuckled.

"You're not mad?"

"Only a little. More so worried that you're putting yourself in great danger." Meg shrank into herself, remembering all the reckless things she had done and how lucky she was not to have been compromised or hurt.

"I've been so stupid, and for what?" Meg sighed. "I haven't helped anyone or discovered anything."

"Oh, I don't think that's true."

Meg blinked through her tears to look up at her mother's kind face. "You don't?"

"If you're anything like I was at your age, you've learned quite a bit about yourself," her mother said with a wry smile.

Meg paused to think those words over. Her mother, as usual, was right. In a few weeks, she had grown in ways she'd never even dreamed of. Done things that the little Meg of even a season ago wouldn't have thought possible. "Perhaps I have."

"And you didn't even have to sneak across the border into Prussia to do it like I did when I was your age," her mother remarked with an easy shrug.

"What?" Meg gaped at her mother.

"I'll tell you the story later. We're talking about you right now," Madame Giry replied as if she had not increased how interesting she was to her daughter by tenfold. "Tell me what you mean by a new ghost. I've had my suspicions about what's been going on, but I want to hear it from you."

Meg took a deep breath. If there was anyone she could tell about all of this, it was the woman who had been in the ghost's confidence as much as anyone else in the Opéra who hadn't disappeared.

"The ghost wasn't a ghost. He was a man," Meg began, and the words began to flow out of her. All she knew and suspected, all the secrets she had learned, finally confessed to a sympathetic ear.

It took her until dawn to finish the story, with the milky light of morning filtering into their parlor. Meg felt like she'd run a mile when she finished, looking up to her mother for some sign of hope or understanding.

"There is one thing in all of this that doesn't make sense to me entirely," her mother said, looking wistful.

"One thing?"

The elder Giry scowled indulgently. "I've suspected his identity. I wondered why a ghost would need somewhere to sit, honestly. But how did he bring down the chandelier when he was also snatching Christine Daaé from the stage?"

Meg blinked. She hadn't thought of that at all.

"He had help," Meg stated aloud. "He had help dropping the chandelier and turning off the gas before it fell, so there would be no fire or chaos. He was in three places at once."

"Interesting," Meg's mother murmured. "He shared secrets with someone before he disappeared. Maybe someone is still using them."

"But why?" Meg asked again.

"Why did we think the first ghost did what he did? There are only so many reasons for a man to take on such madness: love or revenge."

"It's not love," Meg said quickly, though she doubted it the moment she said it. Maybe it was that, in part. "That leaves revenge."

Her mother shrugged. "What's been done to those patrons sounds like it was something they deserved."

Meg chewed her lip, wondering where this left her, if it left her anywhere at all. "Wait. You said disappeared. I told you Shaya insists that the old ghost is dead."

"Yet he does not wish the Vicomte – pardon, Comte – who was so involved in all this to know that these attacks and hauntings have resumed," Madame Giry replied, calm and insightful as ever. "Then runs off to another country for urgent business."

Meg was thunderstruck, but it made sense. Shaya's refusal to share secrets out of supposed respect for the dead and his lack of concern for Christine Daaé. He wasn't concerned, because he knew where she was: with the man Shaya had hunted and now protected. With the ghost. Did that mean this new phantom was someone who wanted to protect them too by causing some diversion, or was it someone who wanted to draw the old phantom back?

Suddenly, Meg doubted everything.

# Sligo

When did everything become so cold? It seemed like yesterday that Erik had been going mad with the Florentine heat, but now the Irish damp was deep in his bones. He had never been one to miss the summer, but right now those days in Florence felt like a glimmer of vital life in his memory. Everything around him now bore the chill of death.

He touched his throat, letting the faint bruise there smart for a moment. It didn't bring him comfort as other mementos of penance and pleasure had. It brought him shame that he had deserved and enjoyed such a thing. He was a killer, who had been wanted by a madwoman because he was monstrous. He remained monstrous, as confined and hunted as ever, dragging an angel down into the muck with him again.

"What did she say to you?" Christine asked from across the room. She was staring at the wall that separated them from the woman they now held captive again. Who they couldn't release without risking further violence...

"What?" Erik asked back, trying to regain his bearings in the conversation they had been trying to start all morning as guilt and silence kept rearing up between them.

"Did she say anything about her plans or what she intended to do if you didn't meet her terms?" Christine looked ill as she said it, but not furious the way she had last night.

"She said she was going to burn Coolaney to the ground, metaphorically," Erik answered with a sigh. "It's a complicated scheme of some sort. She acted like she would own the town."

"How could someone own a town to destroy it?" Christine scoffed.

"The English own this entire country – well, stole it," Erik replied with a sneer. "Every village is controlled by a manor that some English family owns. Sometimes it's a rich Irish one who bowed at the right time if they're lucky."

"Does Coolaney have such a manor?" Christine asked as the same idea occurred to Erik.

"It does, though it's small, and last time I was there, it was already falling into disrepair. It was granted to a man – a knight, not even a Lord, I think. Maybe it was a punishment." Erik thought back to if he had even seen the old codger. His mother had talked about him too, so he couldn't possibly still be alive.

"Is he still alive? Who will it pass to?" Christine asked. "If Pauline had some scheme to buy it or swindle him?"

"She said Bidaut thought it was too complicated and she mentioned ghosts," Erik murmured. "It sounds vindictive enough for her."

"Then we need to go and undo it. Or something," Christine said, springing up. "We have her. We can make her tell us the details."

"Why on earth would she do that?" Erik didn't mean to sound so very condescending, but his tone made Christine freeze, then frown. "I doubt she'd even talk under torture."

"We're not going to torture anyone!"

"Yes, certainly if it won't be effective," Erik grumbled, and Christine rolled her eyes in frustration.

"That is beside the point. We have to help those people and keep them safe." Christine chewed her lip as if it would make some solution appear.

"Why though?" Erik asked with a weary sigh and knew immediately by Christine's look that was the wrong thing to say. "I know it's the right thing, but... is it? These are strangers. If we thwart her there and let her go, she and Bidaut will just go after someone else. Or us personally until we agree to their terms."

"What are you saying?" Christine asked, her face stark with a kind of shock and disappointment that made Erik's insides turn. How could he explain that he did care about people most of the time, but right now, he found it hard to care about anything? Everything felt so dark and hopeless. A world full of dead ends.

"What if we just pay them off and run?" Erik asked with a sigh.

Christine looked at him as if he'd suggested murder, which he had been proud of not doing. "You want to give up? Let them win?"

"I want peace," Erik countered. "I want to be free of this."

"What about our future?" Christine asked, something heartbroken in her eyes. "I know you never wanted that money. I know it's a burden to you, but having it means that, someday, we can finally rest and stop running."

"I know," Erik whispered back, his mind swimming with visions of domestic normalcy that made him feel like he was being choked again. A monster and freak like him, who had lived so long on the fringes and underground, couldn't belong in a life like that. He'd barely survived in this haphazard existence he'd thrown them into.

"We can't keep going like this," Christine pushed. "Erik. I can't endure this rootlessness for much longer."

"You did with your father," Erik argued automatically.

"He was running away from life," Christine snapped back, the honesty shocking Erik. "He was running from the memory of my mother and his failures, and any sort of responsibility, and it nearly broke me too. All I ever wanted was a home that lasted, and the only reason we ever came close to having one was because he got too sick to move."

"But you survived." Erik felt like he was being attacked now. Like he had to defend himself and all his choices and desires. "I lived on the road for years too."

"And you told me what you were searching for the whole time was a home – a place to stay and be safe," Christine protested, emotion rising in her voice that made Erik cringe.

"I found that place," Erik heard himself say. "And you made me leave it."

Christine blinked at him, on a precipice between fury and heartbreak. "You wanted to die there and take everything with you. I begged you to come into the light with me and live. We knew the cost."

"Did we though? This isn't..." Erik sank into a chair, cradling his skull as it pounded with confusion and hurt. "I love you and I want to make you happy, but this is so hard. You asked me to forgive, to be brave enough to let go and seek goodness. But I don't know if I can. I don't know if I'm truly brave enough to live in this cruel, greedy, confusing world."

"There's nowhere else to live." Christine's voice was small and hurt, and Erik couldn't bear to look up at her. "I know this is hard, but that's the promise we made to each other. To walk in this world side by side, through good and ill. I chose that because I love you and I'd rather face this world with you than without you."

"Even if that means falling further into darkness and depravity because of me?" Erik asked back, finally looking up. It hurt his very soul to see the tears on Christine's face. More tears he had caused her to weep. He could do nothing but hurt and corrupt.

"Stop talking like this," Christine whispered. "Or you're going to say something we'll regret."

"Christine," Erik exhaled. "I love you more than life, and that's why I hate doing this to you. If I can't give you what you want or need... If all I do is hurt you and drag you down... Maybe you should go back to London, and I should go home to—"

"I said *stop*," Christine gritted out. Erik bit his tongue as she turned away before he could indeed say something more he would regret. "I'm going to deal with her. Stay here, or I swear..."

She left without further words, and Erik stared at the door after her. He didn't understand what he had almost done. What he was still considering doing. He wanted to run, she was right. He wanted to run all the way back to Paris and hide away with his books and music and ghosts and never face these sorts of hardships or people ever again. Christine would be free and he'd be alone, like he deserved.

Was that so different from dying? The thought struck him like a blow. Would fleeing now be any different than flinging himself off a cliff? Would it hurt Christine – the woman he loved and had sworn to stand by – as much as his demise? Or would it save her? Was this what a truly good man would do when he saw someone better than him sinking into darkness? Would that temporary grief be worth it in the end if she could truly live a life of freedom... without him?

# 12. The End of the World

## Sligo

Christine stood for a long time in the hall, tears of anger and despair running down her face. She was frozen between confronting Pauline and waiting for Erik to walk out the door, attempting to flee and hide again. Somehow, after everything, after all the promises and hopes and sacrifices and words of love, nothing mattered.

Or he didn't want it to. Why would he? All he could find in life was brutality, even from her. Maybe for all she tried to be good and find a purpose, that was all she was worth. She was a coward and cruel. She was a fool and a fraud. She couldn't keep a friend close and the people she loved always left her.

She stifled a sob so Pauline wouldn't hear her and know how weak she was. Know she was right. It was all too fucking hard, and this was supposed to be the easy part. They were supposed to have lived happily ever after when they defeated the monsters and escaped the peril.

In her memory, she heard her father chuckle. When had he ever told her a story like that? His stories had been dark and dangerous, and very few heroes in them had made it to a happy end unscathed. The after wasn't automatically happy because there was no after. There was only now and a life that kept going.

Christine could certainly take some of the blame for that, for her willingness to run instead of making a stand, or, God forbid, facing a fight, whether with someone else or her husband. Why had she believed it would be easy to be a wife when she'd grown up with a widowed father and never even learned how to be on her own until it was too late? Again, she was to blame for not thinking ahead or learning more.

She imagined Pauline's laughter if she knew that was what Christine was thinking. Her laughter was also Carlotta's and so many other mean, petty, malicious voices Christine had heard all her life, none of them louder than the one in her head that said they were right. For reminding her of that alone, Christine wanted to barge through the door and make Pauline feel nothing but pain...

She thought of Carlotta and of making her croak and humiliate herself. Christine remembered the applause and the joy of revenge and saw herself triumphant on the Opéra stage. Then, in her memory, the chandelier fell.

The vision did not steal the breath from her lungs. The thought of Joseph Buquet and Antoine de Martiniac falling dead before her didn't make Christine crumble. It made her sad. Was that who she was now? Brutal and careless? She didn't want to know, and yet she had to find out.

No. She had to decide. She had to choose.

Christine unlocked the room and trudged in. Pauline was still on the bed, unconscious, and chained to the brass frame. How dare she be resting right now? At least she was still breathing, though the bruise and gash on her face were now a vivid shade of purple. Her arms probably ached too from spending the night like that.

Christine grabbed the wash pitcher from its basin and stalked back down the hall to the water pump available for guests of the inn. She felt some relief not to see Erik trying to escape, but she pushed that from her mind. She had something to do.

Pitcher filled, Christine returned to the room and locked the door behind her. She hoped the walls were thick and no one was passing by. With not-a-small amount of personal satisfaction, she took off the gag before she poured the jug onto Pauline's face.

The woman came to, sputtering and swearing as she flailed in her bonds.

"Good morning," Christine said with a smirk as Pauline looked up at her. "Please tell me you have a terrible headache."

"I'm going to skin you alive," Pauline hissed. "You stupid—"

"I really don't think I'm the one that applies to. You got cocky and creative and managed to get yourself captured a second time, on top of being rejected and beaten." Christine clicked her tongue in disapproval as Pauline glared at her, looking in every way like a doused cat.

"I don't recall being rejected." It was a weak barb, but Pauline smirked anyway. "One day, he'll see you for the pathetic thing you are."

"He already does. So do I. You don't need to remind me," Christine replied, her voice and thoughts softening. He did see her and always had. Erik saw what she could be and deserved, even when he believed he was unworthy of sharing it. "Which is why I intend to keep him."

"Good luck," Pauline muttered.

"I don't need luck – I need you to leave us alone. What will it take to get you to do that?" Christine asked, though she wasn't optimistic about getting an honest answer. It didn't hurt to ask.

Pauline, for her part, looked surprised. "It's not that simple."

"Can't it be though? We can pay you. Obviously, whatever villains employ you aren't going to keep you on after they find out how massively you've mucked things up again. We can offer you something to go away, if you'd let go of this petty vendetta against me and your obsession with my husband."

Pauline gaped up at Christine, uncomprehending. Christine couldn't blame her. This was a heavy topic for first thing in the morning with a head injury.

"I—" Pauline began, then stopped, shifting uncomfortably.

"Oh, let me help you," Christine sighed. She dug the key to the restraints from her pocket with one hand, brandishing the pitcher with the other. "Do not try anything or I will remind you of what the opera ghost has taught me."

"Noted." Pauline still stared daggers into Christine as she released her but looked relieved to sit up and have some measure of freedom. "You're an idiot if you think this false kindness is going to win me over."

"It's not false," Christine snapped back. "I know a person like you has to think the worst of someone you've decided is your enemy, so you can justify your hatred. But I know who I am, even if you don't."

Christine paused, smiling to herself, thinking of things people who cared for her had said. People like Erik and Adèle and Howard and Julianne. People who saw her light, despite the darkness.

"That must be nice," Pauline muttered. "To know who you are with such certainty."

"It's not certainty," Christine muttered. "It's a choice. I'm choosing right now to do the hard thing and not hurt you or leave you for dead. I came in here not knowing what I intended to do, but right now, looking at you... You're not worth becoming someone else."

For the first time, Pauline looked hurt. Christine knew she had struck too close to the core of this woman. Pauline was different from her, someone willing to lie to herself or others to be someone else so that she could escape her pain.

"You must be very lonely," Christine stated aloud as she realized it.

"What?" Pauline huffed.

"To be like this. I've known people like you before, people who let a lack of love turn them violent and cruel. Their loneliness made them do and believe horrible things." Christine was thinking of Raoul, but also of Erik. Perhaps Pauline saw herself in him. "You probably don't want to hear that. Or think of it, but I do see it."

"Fuck off," Pauline spat, but she looked about ready to cry. Maybe Christine was torturing her, in her own way. Maybe it would work.

"I will if you tell me what scheme you've concocted concerning Coolaney," Christine said with a shrug. "I'll feed you and let you relieve yourself and make sure you're comfortable wherever we take you."

Pauline stared at Christine, unblinking. Was she trying to will Christine into some action, or forming some plan? Or still angry? Finally, she exhaled and sagged. "I'm supposed to be there today. To get things started."

"Is that all you're going to tell me?"

"You're so smart, you'll figure it out." Pauline pursed her lips and Christine knew that was all she was going to say. She had her plans and Christine would find them out.

"I'll get your food," Christine muttered.

She didn't go downstairs when she left though. She went back to her room and let out a sigh of relief when she found Erik there.

He looked up at her, face bare and eyes stricken, and Christine's heart surged with both love and frustration.

"She has an appointment of some kind in Coolaney today. We're going in her place. I haven't decided if we'll bring her along."

Erik opened his mouth to protest, but Christine raised a hand for silence.

"I'm not letting you run away anymore. Not from Bidaut or your past, and especially not from me. I'm going to your mother's village to do some good, and you're coming with me."

"Why take me? What use will I be?" Erik asked. Christine knew he was considering all the things that could go wrong; envisioning himself run out of town by some angry mob or Christine being harmed because that was the only future he could see right now. He wanted to leave her because he loved her.

"You're coming because I need a fucking translator, and I'm going to show you that not every path leads to ruin."

## Paris

Meg felt like a different person when she was dancing. Not practicing or drilling *temps de cuisse* and *ronds de jambe*, but really, truly dancing. When she let go of thinking and criticism and simply danced, she wasn't meek, useless Meg: she was someone different.

Or maybe that wasn't it. Maybe she wasn't someone at all. She wasn't a character or a mask or some other better version of herself. When she danced, she was merely a body and music and breath and flow and... free.

Meg floated with the sounds of the orchestra, muscles straining and limbs perfectly extended as she moved as one with the rest of the corps de ballet, their delicate tulle skirts spinning around them. Nothing mattered but the movement and the music, and for a wonderful moment, she wasn't only free, she was happy. This was the reason for the hours of rehearsal and intrigue and pain: this joy.

Too bad it was only a dress rehearsal. At least, there was something of an audience, even if it was just patrons and invited guests (who the Opéra hoped to lure as patrons). They applauded when the ballet was finished, and Monsieur Bosarge turned from his podium in the orchestra to give them a nod of thanks. The dancers themselves were not afforded a bow, as La Roche was instantly onstage giving them notes as the curtain fell.

"Second Row," La Roche said as he came to Meg's side, looking at her, then Blanche, Rochelle, and Marie beside her. "Excellent. Giry, you're truly earning your place at last."

Meg wanted to squeal in excitement, but settled for turning to Blanche to grin, only to find her friend looking perturbed.

"I was good too," Blanche muttered. "I honestly don't know how he couldn't see me."

"Oh, I..." Meg faltered. Rochelle met Meg's eyes over Blanche's shoulder with a look of bewilderment that made Meg feel somewhat better.

"Maybe we won't have to run it again," Rochelle offered. "Since all of us did well."

"And they'll be wanting us to spread our charms amongst the patrons," Blanche added with a cheeky smile.

"We all know what you want to spread, Blanche," Marie teased, and without warning, Blanche leapt at her friend. Rochelle had to step in between Blanche and the little dancer to keep Blanche from scratching out her eyes before everyone exploded in laughter.

"Ladies!" La Roche called, and the commotion quieted. "If you can manage to contain yourselves, you may go mingle with the audience."

Blanche made a face and scurried off. "That girl is going to get herself hurt, isn't she?" Meg muttered.

"She is. It's up to us to protect her if anyone goes too far," Rochelle replied, and Marie frowned beside her.

"Well, us and the ghost," Marie said to Meg's amazement. "What? We've all been thinking it. It's time someone says it. The ghost has been looking out for all of us since the Opéra reopened and I, for one, am grateful."

Meg found herself looking around the stage and up to the shadowy flies, where the movement of stagehands was still visible. Where anyone, really, could be waiting and watching. Listening. "Me too," Meg heard herself say.

Rochelle harrumphed and led Marie from the stage. Meg didn't follow. Her mind was still too full of the ghost's voice and a hundred theories and hopes.

Her feet led her to the wings and then upwards, following spiral staircases and cramped halls to a place that many knew of but only employees were allowed to visit. Even then, they were not encouraged to be up here, for it was often hot and dangerous under the great copper dome of the Opéra.

It was a strange place between the ceiling of the auditorium and the dome that sat upon the Palais Garnier. At the peak of the roof was the cupola (at least, that's what Meg thought it was called) that rested like a crown atop the dome itself. During the day, it let in light through several large windows. At the moment, the morning sun shone through them onto the great chain that held up the chandelier, anchored by five counterweights. The weights themselves were not visible, only the chains and pulleys attached to them.

Meg had not visited this secret place for months. Not since the disaster. Not since every one of the chains to the counterweights had been severed one by one with violent, explosive force.

Meg drifted closer to the mechanisms. They were bright and new, whereas before they had been tarnished and greasy. The paint on the walls behind them was fresh and didn't quite match the old color. Whatever evidence existed of how the ghost and his accomplices had taken down the chandelier was gone now, but the scars remained.

"Here we are!"

Meg jumped behind the chain and pulley system when she heard Moncharmin's voice. She didn't know what sort of terms she was on with the manager, but she didn't want to be caught here, even so. Thankfully, she was small and flexible and it was easy for her to hide.

"What are we seeing here?" an older voice asked.

"The support system for the chandelier is fully repaired and safer than ever after the accident," Moncharmin replied. His voice was tense and high. It didn't inspire confidence in Meg, and she doubted it would impress the potential patrons Moncharmin was wooing.

"So it won't fall and kill anyone again?" another voice asked.

"No one died," Moncharmin muttered.

"Philippe de Chagny did. And Antoine de Martiniac if some are to be believed," the first man declared. "What about this phantom that caused that?"

"There is no phantom, Messieurs. There never was," Moncharmin said firmly. "That was merely a myth created by artists and disgruntled employees to cover up bad behavior. Like Carlotta's poisoning that made her sound like she croaked! That was no phantom, just a jealous rival."

"And you wish us to support an institution that allows such nonsense to persist?" the second speaker scoffed.

"Well, it is the national theater, Giles," the first man interjected. "It's not like it can be closed down."

"Quite right, Edouard. I hear the minister of fine arts is already looking for a new manager, or considering eliminating the Opéra entirely," Giles said with an incongruous laugh. Meg covered her mouth to keep from gasping. "No one thinks this sort of excess befits a modern state. This place was built for an emperor who was deposed, for God's sake!"

"It's the people's Opéra now," Moncharmin countered. "And the center of Parisian society. Everyone wants to be seen at the Opéra."

"Wanted to. Before people started dying!" Edouard said. Meg tried to think back to the last few performances. Had they been sold out? She could remember empty seats, but the idea of the Opéra being in danger was absurd!

"Who is saying such things?" Moncharmin asked. "I assure you they are rumors."

"Well, Raoul de Chagny is adamant about it," Giles answered. "He's the one who's been pushing the minister from what I hear, not that he has much influence nowadays with his fortune depleted, though you didn't hear that from me."

"Of course he would be saying that," Moncharmin groaned.

"If the Opéra is in such good condition, why are you soliciting us?" Edouard asked, and there was a certain cruel humor in his voice that Meg very much disliked.

"So that she can thrive, not merely survive," Moncharmin answered with sincerity that Meg admired.

"We will consider it," Giles said. "Only because I have heard from friends that you're willing to introduce patrons to your cast for *intimate performances*. The ballet dancers you put on display today were quite the delicacy."

Silence stretched out, and Meg wondered, sickly, how often Moncharmin, La Roche, or the other men who were supposed to be protecting them were called to act as pimps.

"The second act is starting soon. You should return," Moncharmin answered quietly to Meg's relief.

"Noted," Giles replied sourly. Meg listened to the retreating footsteps and slam of a door before leaving her hiding space.

Moncharmin was bent over the iron railing around the chandelier chain, looking down at the auditorium below. He seemed so sad and exhausted. Meg found herself feeling pity, despite her complicated mix of anger and worry.

"Are we really in trouble?" Meg demanded, and the man jumped in surprise at her voice. "I can see why the minister might want to sack you, but they can't close the national opera."

Moncharmin sighed as he looked at Meg. She couldn't tell if it was relief or disappointment. Maybe he had hoped she was a ghost; come to end his misery.

"You'd be surprised what politicians with grudges and no vision are willing to destroy, Mademoiselle Giry."

"Things can't be that bad! I know the audience has been slow to return, but—"

"It's not just the audience, my dear," Moncharmin sighed. "It's this new ghost. Or someone who wants to be him – I can't even tell. He's robbed us in a way that hurts, at last."

"Robbed you?" Meg echoed in horror. "Of what? His salary?"

"If only that were it," Moncharmin replied, combing a hand through his hair and leaving it a mess. "Someone has been stealing from the office directly. The box office and the management."

Meg blinked, confusion crashing through her head. She hadn't thought the theft amounted to that much. This wasn't right. This wasn't righteous like this ghost seemed to be. The phantom protected his theater, he didn't undermine it. "Why haven't you called the police? Or told Shaya?" Meg demanded.

"After all that's happened, we can't afford any whiff of scandal! I should be trying harder to keep the attacks out of the papers, now that I think of it. If anyone that I have to answer to learns how bad things have been, especially in the last few weeks..."

"It's not—" Meg bit her lip before she said more, and Moncharmin stared at her. She didn't need to debate this with him. She could and would go to the source.

"Don't you have a theory, young detective?" he asked, with a tired laugh.

"Worse: I have an idea."

# Coolaney

E rik resented the bright autumn sun as it fell on the little village of Coolaney. He resented everything he was experiencing at that moment, but the sun was of particular annoyance. His back hurt, his head ached, and the horses in front of him stank. He had thought being the one to drive the carriage to the village would make things easier. This way, they didn't have to pay someone to wait and no one would notice the gagged woman in chains they were carting around. It also meant he had an excuse not to talk to anyone as it was Christine's unfortunate job to watch Pauline.

It was hot and awkward, and Erik hated the tension between him and his wife, as well as the hard seat and deafening brightness from the sky. He'd spent the ride brooding, going through a hundred different scenarios of how to make this right and all of them ended with him absent from either Christine's life or the earth. It had not been productive. Now, the sun was glaring in his eyes as he pulled the horses to a stop outside the village his mother had fled so long ago.

The autumn light made Coolaney look picturesque and deceptively lovely. The hills around the village rose boldly from the landscape, some forming dramatic bluffs, all covered in vibrant green no words could describe. Erik knew from past experience that, on a clear day like today, if you climbed one of them, you could see to the coast, following the path of little rivers and streams to the sea. The trees were old and wise, turning gold for the season, and the village buildings were humble constructions of thatch and stone that seemed built to endure storms and centuries. It was beautiful, and Erik had learned what could hide behind beauty.

He stretched and groaned as soon as he was on the ground, the bearded mask heavy and uncomfortable in the warm day. A thump sounded behind him, then a muffled cry of annoyance. He turned in time to see Christine exiting the carriage looking smug.

"She's taken care of, for now," Christine said.

"Are you sure it's safe to leave her in there alone?" Erik asked, terrified and pleased despite himself by the efficiency with which Christine continued to deal with this threat.

"She can breathe. It will be fine." Christine paused to look over the landscape and village, a soft smile playing on her face. "It's rather beautiful."

"It's medieval," Erik countered, annoyance returning. All he saw when he looked at this town was a backwards backwater that was even worse than all the other such primitive, hateful towns because it had already disappointed him.

"Remote, though, as you said," Christine added, indulgent rather than cross.

"Let us be done with it," Erik muttered. "We should start at the pub."

"Do you need a drink so early?"

"It's the heart of any village like this," Erik sighed. He wondered if any of them would remember him from the long years past when he had journeyed here in search of family or a home. He'd found little welcome; only warnings that anyone with the name Gilbride had long departed for America or the grave. Then again, Erik hadn't been very trustworthy.

They made their way to one of the larger buildings in the town. It was two stories and bore an old wooden sign on an iron hook above the door declaring it The Harp. Simple enough, and yet, Erik paused. He was in the woods of Lungern again, or the London pub where he had been unmasked, or a hundred other places he'd been exposed and expelled. He couldn't do this. Not here.

Christine's hand slipped into his and he started in surprise, looking down at her and finding her smiling kindly at him. She looked so beautiful in the sun, it made his heart quake to look at her.

"I'm right beside you, whether you like it or not," she said softly, somehow forgiving him before he had even complained.

"Thank you, my love." The words soothed him and placated her. His wife's hand in his, he entered the pub.

It was as Erik remembered it. Or perhaps he didn't remember the specifics, but it was like many pubs he had visited over the years. It was a warm, welcoming place (or would be for most) with walls and furniture in all shades of honey and brown, worn chairs, and a large hearth. The bar was old, but looked well taken care of, and the light through the windows was thin, as it tended to be in places like this.

The people were as he expected too. They fit in a place like this, so close to the earth and the sea. They had a proud roughness about them that reminded Erik of the hills and crags and woods outside. And they were all looking at the two strangers who had just walked in.

To Erik's surprise, they didn't look entirely suspicious. There was a man behind the bar tending to work with his back turned to the room and a pair of men in a corner that looked like farmers sharing a pint. They looked at Erik and Christine like cats that had wandered in from the street – something surprising and perhaps unwelcome, but not dangerous. Beside the crackling fire, there was a middle-aged, round woman fussing over a chair full of blankets and ignoring them.

A younger woman was wiping down the long, empty central table. She smiled at them when she saw them and ran to the barkeep, whispering something in his ear.

"Already?" the man behind the bar said, turning to look at Erik and Christine. His eyes widened in a show of welcome that Erik had not expected at all. "Oh! Right you are. Sir, I think she is here! And not alone!" he called towards the fire.

The older woman turned to Erik and Christine and gave a startled cry before bending to shake the blankets on the chair.

"Sir!" the woman said softly because, to Erik's shock, there was someone in all those blankets. "Sir. Your guest."

The man revealed in the chair was sleeping soundly and looked almost as close to a corpse as Erik did. He had to be nearing a hundred and, had the woman not been addressing him, Erik would have worried that he was already expired. He snorted and bobbed his head, but didn't reply to his attendant. She gave a frustrated sigh.

"Sir Edward!" the older woman yelled in his ear, shaking him vigorously, and the old man started awake, blinking in confusion as he did.

"What's that?" Sir Edward said in a refined English accent before turning his bleary eyes to the new visitors.

"The one you were telling us about!" the maid said. "She's here! With a friend."

Christine leaned close to Erik and whispered, "Do they think I'm Pauline?"

Erik nodded tensely. This was the plan and they had to play along.

"Oh. Yes. Of course," Sir Edward said, gesturing for Erik and Christine to approach. "I apologize for resting. We were not expecting you so early. I must say, my dear lady, you're more beautiful than your words which so warmed this old man's heart."

"You're too kind," Christine replied in her careful English, and the man beamed.

"Ah, what a lovely accent," Sir Edward sighed.

"If you expect me to learn French like some fancy lady, you're out of your gourd," declared the woman who had awoken him in a thick Irish accent. It was unclear if she was talking to the old man or them.

"Oh, her English is excellent, Siobahn. You know that from reading the letters to me," the knight chided. "It's a joy to meet you at last, Mademoiselle Pauline. Oh." Sir Edward looked at Erik, noticing him for the first time, and perhaps taking in his rather odd appearance. "I thought you said you'd be alone?"

"I think there has been a mistake, Sir," Erik cut in, taking the opportunity to speak. "You seem to know my wife, but she has not told me anything of your prior correspondence. She insisted on surprising me when we arrived here."

"Oh, what a devious woman!" Sir Edward declared, then yawned so wide, Erik could count all his remaining teeth. "Your lovely wife reached out to me a month ago! Or was it two? About..." The man froze for a moment, looking to the woman beside him for help.

"I swear, the thoughts go out of your head like rabbits running from a bush," Siobahn sighed. She had russet hair and bright cheeks and looked entirely annoyed. "The lady wrote about the manor and her claim."

"My manor?" The knight looked aghast. "Siobahn, why would I write to a lady about the manor? It's falling apart and the only people who want it are dead!"

Siobahn groaned, her head falling into her hands as if the old man had said something disastrous. "Sir, don't you remember? These are good, rich lands with enormous potential." She was repeating something she had told him before, it was clear. What was not clear was who was swindling who – a dying Lord and his caretaker, or Pauline.

"There was that one woman," Sir Edward said slowly. "A French girl said she was a distant relation and was willing to take it on. She was going to visit, but she's not supposed to be here to look it over until—"

"Today! This is her!" Siobahn groaned. "And her husband. Who we must be kind to." Siobhan looked Erik over and tried to smile.

"Her husband who is confused," Erik muttered.

"You'll need to forgive our Sir Edward," Siobahn replied. "It's me who's been doing most of the writing and reading of your wife's letters. Good thing too, as the first one nearly sent him to the grave with the shock." Siobhan gave Christine a bright, grateful smile.

"I..." Christine began, and she looked entirely at sea, and Erik wished dearly he could translate it all for her, though she seemed to understand most of what was going on.

"Are you telling me my dear wife has been in correspondence with your lord here about taking on his manor?" Erik asked Siobahn directly. "And the lands?"

"She was the one who wrote!" Siobahn exclaimed. "With God as my witness, none of us went looking for a claimant. We were all resigned to the lands going back to the Queen to be doled back out to some dandy who'd let it keep rotting."

"But my wife has swooped in to help her distant relation with no other heirs," Erik stated carefully so that Christine would understand. Had he not harbored such a burning hatred for Pauline, he might have been impressed with how cruel and brilliant the scheme was. Now everything she had said about ghosts and trickery made sense – she was the ghost. A phantom of the past ready to take on a manor, and then discard it in the cruelest, most destructive way possible.

"I hope you are not so angry," Christine said sweetly to Erik, playing her part. "Of course, we would like to visit the house first."

"Must you?" Siobhan asked, looking suddenly ill. "The house isn't prepared for guests at the moment."

Erik had never been to the old manor house outside the village, even when he had visited years ago. As far as he had known then, the old knight lived there alone and did little to maintain the house or lands. It was Sir Edward's neglect that had let Coolaney keep up some old ways when it came to tradition, but he hadn't pushed the village to prosperity or progress either. That had been years ago, and Erik shuddered to think how dreadful things were now.

"Are you interested in my house?" Sir Edward asked, blinking like he had just seen Erik and Christine for the first time. "You must be quick with your offer. There's a lady coming today to sign for it straight away!"

"Saints preserve me," Siobahn sighed, looking to heaven.

"How bad is it?" Erik asked the poor woman. She didn't seem to be a born liar; more likely, she was trying to save her job and community by taking advantage of an opportunity that had been presented.

"Well, you see," Siobahn began. "It's a very large house for one old man and his maid, and so, Sir Edward has been staying in town these last few weeks, to save on heating costs. It takes an awful lot of wood to keep the fires lit in a place like that. That's all."

"We'd like to see it," Erik repeated, with what he hoped sounded like good humor. "We'll stay the night if you don't mind. Believe me, I've stayed in worse places."

Siobhan looked between Erik and Christine as if the woman she thought was on her side might help her.

"We'll pay for firewood?" Christine offered, and that brought a light to Siobahn's face.

"If you insist," Siobhan said, finally giving a nod.

"Siobhan, I want to get some rest before my guest arrives," Sir Edward declared out of nowhere, sinking into his chair again and immediately nodding off.

"Either I'll be up to let you in once I've attended to my master here, or I'll send someone," Siobahn sighed, looking down at the unconscious man she had somehow been saddled with keeping alive. "It's good to meet you, Miss Pauline and Mister..."

"My name is Christine." Both Siobahn and Erik turned to Christine in surprise and she slowly continued, looking to Erik for some help. "I did not want to use my—"

"Real name. For reasons of security," Erik finished for her. He couldn't blame her for not wanting to keep up the ruse of being Pauline; he wouldn't want to be saddled with the name of an enemy either. "And I am Mister Gilbride."

"You're Irish?" Siobahn asked in shock, looking over Erik anew. Her eyes remained uncomfortably on his mask as he nodded. "There used to be a Gilbride family in this very village."

"I'm your countryman only by descent. It's a complicated story," Erik muttered. He didn't want to tell that story or find any sort of connection with this woman or this place. This was temporary and they needed to deal with things quickly before Pauline's subterfuge was found out. "We will see you at the house."

Erik didn't wait for more questions, leaving the pub as fast as he could with poor Christine muttering apologies. She rushed to keep up with him as he slaked back to the carriage and wrenched open the door. Pauline was positioned on the floor with her feet bound and a gag in her mouth.

"It takes a rare sort of wickedness to trick a whole town. Did you really think someone as inept as you could make such an insane plan work?" Erik demanded of their hostage, taking care to speak in French in case anyone was walking by. "Did you really think I'd care?"

Pauline, still gagged, scrunched her face rudely, managing to look smug, even in this state.

"Leave her be. Let's get to our accommodations," Christine muttered, pulling Erik back before shaking her head at Pauline and closing the door.

This time, she joined Erik on the driver's seat of the carriage, her closeness both a comfort and a torture. He was delusional to think he could ever give it up, and yet, just as delusional to think he deserved this or that she couldn't do better.

"I still think you should go back to London. This can't be all they're planning," Erik finally said. It didn't feel any better to have it out in the open.

"I know you think that, but you've been overruled," Christine replied, firm and foolish. "You were overruled in that respect the moment you asked me to marry you."

Erik remembered that. The vivid knowledge in the dark under the Opéra that, if Christine Daaé agreed to not just be with him, but to be his wife, that he would be brave enough to walk in the world of light with her. They had wed among friends, he had shown his face in the presence of the divine, and sworn to her, and that should have changed him.

Now here he was, willing to run back to the dark again to save her, and she wouldn't let him, because he had shackled her with those vows. She was doomed if she didn't let go, like the poor people of this village tied to this dying land ruled by a distant queen. Would his poor Christine end up like the manor they headed towards – empty and crumbling and forgotten?

## Paris

M eg was sick of waiting to make her escape after rehearsal. There were simply too many people going back and forth, especially new and potential patrons who seemed to be everywhere.

Meg resented them more than before, and that was saying something.

"Why are you in such a tizzy?" Marie demanded after Meg craned her neck to see if the hall was empty for the fifth time.

"I need to find someone," Meg muttered.

"Everyone you know is here except your mother," Marie replied, blunt as always.

"Where is your sister? Shouldn't you be fetching her?"

"No, she's sick today," Marie pouted. "Leaving me to deal with all the attention. I honestly don't know if this fame is worth what Monsieur Degas paid me."

"At least he paid you," Meg sighed. "Where's Blanche and Rochelle then?"

"Blanche was whisked off by some patron! Taking her to dinner with someone very special!" Marie giggled. "Didn't you hear her bragging about it earlier?"

"No, I was distracted." Meg's stomach was uneasy at the prospect. Blanche was older than her by a few years, but that didn't mean much in terms of her resilience and wisdom when it came to all of this. What if she was getting herself in trouble and the ghost was needed? The ghost who might very well be a thief endangering everything Meg held dear?

"I'm going," Meg declared, unable to stand it any longer. She left Marie without another word and headed down. Down, down, down, as far as she could go, into the dark where no one would hear her but the dead. Or someone close to them.

She came to a corridor of stone, dark and ominous, brimming with thick darkness. She couldn't see beyond, but she could feel it; how the air was colder. Stiller. It carried a sense of mourning and emptiness that made Meg shiver and question the choices that had brought her here. The darkness was watching in a way she had not felt before.

"Are you there?!" Meg cried.

No response. No words, at least. Meg swore she heard something like movement in the dark, and a groan of pain. Was it her eyes playing tricks on her or was the shadow moving?

Meg screamed when a firm hand locked around her wrist, yanking her away from the abyss. She tumbled to the ground, cries stifled, thrown by her captor. Her rescuer, a looming figure in black glowering at her from behind a mask.

"Stay away from there. It's dangerous," the ghost whispered.

"I need to talk to you!" Meg blurted out.

The ghost looked surprised, as much as a phantom in a black hat, cloak and mask covering the entire face could look surprised.

"I told you to be patient."

"I can't be patient when everything is at stake!" The intensity of Meg's voice was a shock to both of them. "You have to give it all back!"

The ghost stared at Meg and fear rose in the young dancer. She had gone too far. She had been mistaken. She had...

"Meet me tomorrow at midnight. Right here," the phantom whispered, voice eerie and certain. Meg nodded and made the mistake of blinking too slowly; that was all the time the specter needed to disappear.

Meg stared after the ghost into the darkness, praying she had not made everything worse.

# Coolaney

The manor was worse than Christine had feared, and she had feared it would be terrible. It was built of stone, mostly, with a few additions of wood and plaster that looked like they had been added haphazardly in recent years. The bones of it were older, she could tell, past the swaths of ivy that covered the place, but all parts of it were crumbling. The entrance to the grounds was bordered by briars and overgrown shrubs, interspersed with twisted oaks still clinging to their summer leaves. Maybe there had been a wall, long ago, to keep the commoners out. Now, the few stones and thorns served to contain something that might have been a garden once.

There was a carriage house and stable, but it looked of dubious stability. Erik took the horses in as Christine checked that Pauline was still alive. There may have been some disappointment to find her fully intact. The woman had slept through much of the journey, thankfully, freeing Christine from more conversation had she taken off the gag.

She left Pauline in the carriage, resolving to take her into the house at some point when they found a suitably miserable corner to leave her in. Eventually, they would have to do something with the woman, but for now, she had not answered as to how much money it would take to make her disappear. Christine was beginning to worry it was an amount they couldn't afford. Or that she'd, again, demand something other than money.

Erik stood in the yard in the shadow of the main house. Maybe if Christine squinted, it would be beautiful. As it was, she wasn't looking forward to sleeping there.

"It looks haunted," Erik muttered as she came close. "It feels haunted."

"Does it?"

Christine took a moment to extend her senses beyond what she could merely see (and smell, which was mainly mildew and weeds). There was a heaviness to the house, like it was watching them and not quite empty. It reminded her of the Opéra or other great buildings like it – this place had seen years of life, and perhaps death as well. Whether there was some restless spirit inside the walls, Christine couldn't say, but it certainly had a soul, this old manor at the edge of the world.

"You think we'll sleep well here?" Erik asked. He was looking for a reason to leave.

Christine wouldn't allow it, and if that meant sleeping among the spiders and rats and ghosts, then so be it. "No, but we're going to try anyway."

Erik opened his mouth to argue more, but thankfully, the woman from the tavern who had been attending to the old knight ran up the path to interrupt them at the perfect time.

"It's better inside!" Siobhan cried, skidding to a halt before doubling over and panting. "The gardener, he's been—"

"Dead for several years?" Erik muttered, and Christine elbowed him gently.

"*Be nice*," Christine hissed in French. "*They aren't to blame for this scheme.*"

Erik gave Christine a look that she would have been happy to punish him for were it not for... everything.

"Show us in then," Erik sighed to Siobhan. She continued to speak – quick and breathless – as she led them to the door and unlocked it. Christine didn't try to understand it, only catching a few words – king, castle, family, walls. She was telling Erik about the house and its history.

As far as Christine was concerned, it spoke for itself when they entered. Siobahn hadn't been lying: it was better inside. Christine had expected rot and rats, but, while the front hall was dusty, with cobwebs in the corners and the walls held on to a distinct chill, there was a different kind of warmth there. Somewhere in the past, long ago, this place had been alive and loved.

It made Christine sad to see it now. It reminded her of the village of Coolaney, at least what she had seen of it. It was a place that once had been vital and vibrant and now sat almost forgotten. Beautiful in a way that activated her instinct to heal and repair it.

The main hall would have been grand in another life, with a proud staircase in the center leading to the upper floor. Christine was impressed to see two full suits of armor gathering dust in alcoves. Fitting for a knight. There were double doors to each side, one set leading to a drawing room that looked well-used. It was stuffed with all sorts of furniture and books and papers. There was even a bed, though it was more of a cot.

"Sir Edward has slept down here for a few years," Siobhan was telling Erik as Christine made the connection. "Too hard to get up the stairs. Now, with the cold coming back and the fireplace..."

Christine drifted across the front hall as Siobhan continued, drawn to the other set of doors that remained closed. Her rational brain told her not to open them, with visions of bats streaming out of the room filling her head. But her curiosity was stronger.

No bats flew out when Christine opened the door, only a single disturbed moth. The room was dark: the shutters closed and curtains drawn, so it took Christine a few moments to focus. The walls were curiously textured. The smell was what made her understand and cleared her vision – paper and ink.

It was a library. Well, not just a library. It was a grand collection of books, waiting on their shelves like friends she had always known yet never met. And in the corner, under a sheet, was the unmistakable shape of a piano.

Christine smiled sadly, forcing herself not to imagine anything. How could she not, though, when the sight was so familiar, like the green hills she had been among for days? Not from her waking life, but from her dreams. She couldn't be moved, she told herself. She couldn't see this place and know she was sent there because it was the last place Erik wanted to be. It was hard though, especially when she sensed Erik beside her, looking into the shadows.

"This isn't so bad," he muttered. "Siobahn says there's a clean bedroom upstairs, but no food in the kitchen."

"It's only for one night," Christine sighed. "We'll live."

"Probably."

"Is Siobhan gone?"

"Off to keep Sir Edward alive for another day," Erik replied bitterly. "Do you think it will kill the poor man to discover no one will be taking this place?"

"That's not true, is it though?" Christine better understood now. "Pauline was accelerating what would happen anyway. This manor will eventually go to some Englishman who will either keep neglecting it or suck this land dry."

"Isn't that a good reason to throw her in the stable and leave?" Erik asked, more sarcastic than hopeful. "I guess that won't solve everything."

"I offered her money," Christine confessed at last. "I asked how much it would take for her to go away. She didn't say no."

"Even if she goes away, we still have Bidaut to deal with." Christine hated that he was right. "You're still in danger. If you let me—"

"That's not an option. I'm going to see if she's decided. Maybe she can be of use if so," Christine declared, and left Erik in the hall. She felt like she was keeping him near her by the thinnest thread. If she let go or said the wrong thing, he'd be gone forever, back to the dark, where she'd never find him again.

Pauline looked asleep when Christine opened the carriage door. Christine resented her finding a single moment of peace but kept herself from shaking her too hard to wake her. She also took care not to be bitten when she removed the gag.

"Have you made a decision?" Christine asked, trying to keep herself cold and aloof. "I'll be feeding you no matter what you say, so don't worry about that."

For a second, Pauline looked relieved. Grateful even.

"It would cost quite a lot. To disappear *and* be of service," Pauline said slowly, not smirking for once. She looked... sad. "Not that I want to help."

"You couldn't just leave? I guess we could drop you somewhere."

Pauline looked up from her bonds at Christine, her customary smugness returning. "You should consider how much you're willing to pay to make me and Bidaut go away. Because he's coming."

## West of Dublin

All things considered, Monsieur Bidaut had been an accommodating hostage taker. Shaya had been allowed to sleep, rest, and relieve himself, and had not been restrained. The food had been a problem, as all Bidaut had on offer was salt pork and turnips cooked with it. Nor had Shaya been able to turn towards Mecca and pray, but he had made a note of it in his mind and said his prayers to Allah in his heart. He assumed his current predicament would earn some dispensation from the Merciful Almighty.

Bidaut had not been a particularly talkative host, which, at this point, Shaya found more boring than annoying. If he was to be hauled across two countries (was it two? He was always confused as to what the United Kingdom considered its own or a vassal), he wanted to learn something new.

They had been on the train for over an hour. Bidaut was absorbed in a paper in English next to Shaya. Nothing in it was worth reading.

"I don't suppose you intend to tell me where we're going?" Shaya asked, keeping his eyes on the scenery rolling by. He wondered if anyone would think it curious to hear the foreigner in their midst speak French.

"I'm sure you're aware of Erik's history in this part of the world, or his connections to it," Bidaut replied without looking up.

"I am. But, I must know: how did you discover it?"

Bidaut gave him a sidelong look. "Professional curiosity?"

"Of course. I did hunt the man myself for quite a while."

Bidaut considered him for a moment, then sighed and closed his paper. "Yes. I was made aware of your failures."

Shaya scowled. "By Sabine de Chagny, whose brother, I'm sure, was talkative."

"Sabine de Martiniac, if we are being precise," Bidaut corrected, though there was a look on his face that said it was a convenient fiction. "To your question, however: Erik, despite his best effort, has left some mark on the world. His mother's origins were easy enough to discern when investigating his history with the Baron de Martiniac. Easy to exploit as well."

"You lured him to Ireland?" Shaya was almost impressed. Erik was hard to manipulate.

"My assistant in these matters was useful in that respect. Her methods, however deluded and byzantine, are predictable." Bidaut stopped talking and chuckled to himself. "She'll be furious to see you in my power. All her work, reduced to a contingency."

"You think I'll be that useful to you?" Shaya scoffed back. "I wouldn't think you'd underestimate Erik after he stabbed you. Yes, I know about that."

"Impressive. Though Pomeroy let me know that you had to use – what was it? A ballet rat to do your spying. I guess it's understandable. I had pickpockets doing mine."

"Sounds expensive." Shaya was learning, though slowly, what Bidaut was willing to do and how far he would go. His associate seemed to be the dangerous one. "Desperate, even."

"We were growing impatient," Bidaut drawled.

Shaya concealed his interest. Were. Past tense. "Has Monsieur Richard been particularly helpful then? He always seemed like a serious fellow."

Bidaut gave another soft laugh and a rueful smile. "You are good. What was it you were called: Daroga?"

"Correct." Shaya paused. This might be his only chance to make an offer. "I know Erik, and I must warn you that I don't think using me will work."

"We'll see." Bidaut looked suspect but interested.

"I could talk to him." Shaya tried to sound casual. Hopeful. "I might convince him to provide some funds to your employer. Not everything, but something."

"Oh, you're very good indeed," Bidaut said with a smirk.

Shaya gave himself a moment to smile before Bidaut heaved a genuine sigh. "It really shall be a shame to kill you, when the time comes."

# Coolaney

Oftentimes, back at the Opéra and even before, Erik had gone days without eating. Not by choice, of course. Sometimes there was no food to be had, but more often, eating was a bother or a distraction. He didn't need much, and when he was in the throes of some composition or new fixation, he didn't have time. Of the many adjustments to marriage and living in the world with a relatively normal person (at least in terms of her food consumption), eating all the time had been one of the strangest.

Erik wanted to make all these points in his argument that he didn't need supper. He'd rather stay at the manor. He'd even said so, making some excuse about exploring the house. Christine had not accepted that, especially given how hazardous such an exploration might be to his health. She was hungry, so they had to go back to the pub for food, and she insisted eating would bring Erik to his senses. He didn't tell her that the real problem was he had come to his senses and saw everything clearly now. Everything in all its hopeless horror.

The village was different on foot as evening fell. There were distant lights coming from houses, warm beacons in the dark. The air was cool and fresh, carrying the smallest hint of the sea and grass.

At least he was able to convince Christine to purchase what they needed and leave. He didn't want the looks from people in the corners. He didn't want to see the curiosity in their eyes. If only they knew how much worse he was than anything they could predict or imagine. How he was a deadly thing who took pleasure in his degradation and pain...

Erik winced, new shame mixing with rancid anger and helplessness. He looked out in the dark on the road back to the manor. It wasn't too far a walk, but it felt purgatorial at this point. Erik forced himself to breathe deep, to listen to the sounds of the night, to put one foot before the other.

"Someone is singing," Christine whispered as Erik heard the voice too. It was distant, but clear. Maybe coming from a house tucked into the wood.

"Careful, might be one of the good folk trying to tempt you from the road," Erik replied, not entirely joking.

Christine smiled in the twilight and took his hand. "I know that song. You sang it to me."

"*Oh the summertime is comin',*" the unknown voice lilted. "*And the trees are sweetly bloomin', and the wild mountain thyme grows around the purple heather.*"

Music, as always, was magic. He wanted to resist, but its power was too strong. Erik couldn't help how it moved his heart to hear the song, even with the dark deepening around them and in his heart. For a second, it was his mother's voice, carrying a bit of her home in her heart. And it was also his voice, singing to the woman he loved of all he would give her if only she'd follow him. Now that she had followed him, could he give her anything?

"Has it changed much? Since you came before?" Christine asked, tightening her grip on Erik's hand as they made their way down the road, the song fading behind them. She'd been doing that all day, holding him tight and close so he couldn't escape. Couldn't free her.

"The years have not been kind," Erik muttered, his mood souring again as the air filled with the sound of crickets and frogs. "Nor has having such a useless lord."

"It reminds me of Perros," Christine remarked wistfully, which stopped Erik in his tracks. It meant something, for Christine to compare this place to the closest thing she had ever had to a home. She was still under the music's spell. Or perhaps she had been enchanted before that. "It feels ancient in the same way. Like it's part of the landscape."

"It's not as charming." Erik knew he sounded petty and judgmental, but he couldn't let her go down this path. They passed the broken old gate and entered the yard of the manor. "Look at this place. It's a ruin built by a cruel kingdom far away, stuck in a dying village on the outskirts of civilization."

"Some things are more than they look, if I recall," Christine argued lightly. Carefully. A prelude Erik couldn't let continue.

"We can't stay," he said, slow and firm. He knew she had been thinking it all day.

"I didn't say that I wanted to," she argued back, but she was avoiding his eyes, looking at the decrepit house and overgrown garden. Anything but him.

"We're strangers here. They'll turn on us as soon as they realize we're here because of a lie. When they realize what I am."

Christine spun to glare at him. "You'd say that about any place."

"Because I've been to every place, and everywhere I go, it turns out the same!" His voice was too loud and too harsh, but he couldn't help it.

"Things are different now! You have me!" They'd been over this, he knew, and he knew she was right, but it didn't feel like she was.

"But things aren't different, and they never will be." Erik spat, hating that he had to say it. "We should—"

"I can't run anymore!" Christine's voice echoed against the empty walls of the manor. "I'm tired and I'm not like you. I need a home."

"What happened to being each other's home?" Erik countered, his voice brittle and bitter. It was a cruel thing to say, but it was necessary. He had to convince her to let him go.

"Saying that and living it are different things," Christine said softly and sadly, reaching for him. "It can be true, if we choose a place to stay. It doesn't have to be here! We can go back to London and our friends."

"You want it to be here so you can help people you've never known," he sneered, pulling away from her touch. Her face hardened with resolve.

"Because I have to be something of use to the world!" Christine protested, voice breaking. "I have given up everything I wanted to walk this path with you! I did it with joy because I love you, but I need more than just that in my life."

"And you suddenly think saving a dying town that would throw you to the wolves if it suited them will give you purpose?" Erik scoffed, digging his nails into his palms with the effort of being so callous in the face of her dreams. "You've known this village for half a day. There are other places in the world to worry about."

"Then pick one! We'll go there and leave everyone else to rot!" Christine cast a look to the carriage house where their goddamn hostage waited.

"I thought you wanted to pay her off," Erik countered, as cruel as he could bear to make himself sound.

"I want to do whatever it takes to live," Christine whimpered. There were tears in her eyes already and Erik hated them. Hated that he needed her to cry them. "I want to really live."

There it was: the ultimate truth he could not escape. The one thing he could never give her. He had started this by telling her yes, by surrendering to her light and going with her, but it was so hard and he was so weak and so broken.

"Then you should not have married a thing made of death," Erik whispered back.

"What did I do wrong?" Christine asked now, her voice small and contrite. "All day you've been insisting on madness. Did I go too far last night or ask too much? I can't reach you and—"

"You did nothing wrong. That's the whole problem. You're good and you deserve a home, like you want. You shouldn't have to reach me," Erik sighed. "You shouldn't have to repair me or punish me. You shouldn't have to lower yourself—"

"Will you stop deciding what I want or need!" Christine yelled with a force that echoed off the walls of the manor into the dark of the night, shocking Erik into mollified silence as he stared at her. There was true fire in her eyes, righteous and dazzling.

"I am my own person. I chose you. I chose this. Marriage is about continuing to choose one another day after day. I choose you right now. Can't you do the same?"

A choice, once again. One he had made before and rejoiced in. One he had to make again... for love.

"I want to," Erik replied, voice rough now. "I want to, I do; but I don't know if I can. Or if I can, I don't know if I can do it right or be enough. I don't know how. I can't bear to rest. I don't know why."

"Then let me help," Christine said, taking his hand, and at last, he let her. He felt the ice he had fortified around his heart the whole day melt away the moment she touched him. "People can't heal when they're running, and both of us need to."

It was as if a thorn had been deep within a wound that she had plucked out. Erik understood, finally, not only what she needed to be happy and whole, but the work he had to do to feel the same and help her heal too. He had to stop. He had to stay.

"I'm afraid I'll fail again," he lamented aloud. "If I choose a home, I'll just lose it. Even this miserable place could be somewhere you learn to love, and what if I'm the reason you must flee?"

"We don't know that disaster will strike. We have to have hope and bravery," Christine answered, pulling closer. "Whatever we do, we do it together. That's the point."

Erik stared at her, at a loss. She was so perfect, so good, and he was tired of thinking constantly that he didn't deserve her. He wanted her and to be with her more than anything, even if it was wrong. He wanted to make her happy, and he couldn't do that by running. He couldn't fly from her and he couldn't fly with her forever. He had to come down to the earth, but what if he fell? What if he failed?

Maybe she was worth the risk. Maybe his penance lay somewhere else than in his pain. Maybe it was in the work of living.

"I want to. But I have to..." Erik swallowed. He felt like he was standing on the edge of a cliff. "I have to help too. I have to solve problems, not just cause them."

"Alright," Christine replied slowly. "What does that mean?"

Erik turned and strode towards the carriage house. Moving before his resolve could fail. "I'm going to end this chase. Once and for all."

# 13. Bargains

## Coolaney

Christine walked through the grass, morning dew gathering on her hem. It was cold and misty, closer to autumn than to summer now. Mist still lingered in the green gulleys between the hills, and the outskirts of Coolaney were so beautiful in the dawn light that it made her heart swell with sadness she couldn't linger. She couldn't stay.

At least she had slept, Christine told herself. At least she'd had one night in the old manor with Erik, held close in her phantom's arms so she didn't even think about what other ghosts lingered in the dark. She wished she had been able to linger there too.

The last place she wanted to be was trudging down this muddy path outside the village with Pauline.

"You're right: this place barely qualifies as civilization," Pauline quipped beside her, keeping her head high and her back straight as they made their way past an old farmhouse. It was long abandoned, with a gaping hole in a roof made of mud and moss. "I would have been doing the world a favor by clearing it out."

"Your plan was cruel," Christine stated, trying to keep her anger in check. None of this would work if she snapped on Pauline now.

"Yes. I can think of nothing worse than giving someone hope and dashing it away," Pauline grumbled pointedly. Christine heard Erik sigh in annoyance behind them.

"This is an odd place to meet," Christine declared as they came to the edge of a clearing. In it stood a large stone with others set around it at regular intervals. It was some ancient, sacred place.

"Well, some of us have a flair for the dramatic," Pauline sighed. "Would you please get these off me now?"

Pauline raised her wrists. There were red marks where the cuffs had rubbed the skin raw after more than a day in them, and Christine almost felt guilty seeing them. Almost. Pauline's face looked worse, with the purple bruise and cut Christine had left there. Her hair and clothes were a mess as well. "How will you explain your current state?"

"I don't want to give away the show," Pauline answered with a smile as Christine removed her restraints. "So we are clear: if you don't pay up after this is done, I will lead Bidaut and our employer straight back to your door. Or worse."

"Understood," Erik answered before Christine could. "But you don't get to change the price."

"Why would I, when you've made the deal so delicious?" Pauline gave Erik a grin that turned Christine's stomach. She hated this, but it was the only choice they had.

"There's nowhere to run out here," Christine reminded the odious woman and was answered with only an eye roll. Pauline strode to the center of the stone circle, rubbing her wrists and stretching as Erik and Christine took their place hidden in the trees to the side. "Do you trust her?" Christine asked her beloved uneasily.

"At this point, yes," Erik replied, but she could feel his tension. He was beside her, but she didn't know if it was right to reach for him.

"What did you offer her?" Christine asked softly. "You came back last night having made some sort of deal and I didn't press because I didn't want to know then. You have to tell me now, though."

"I don't want to disappoint you if it doesn't work," Erik replied, hanging his head. He had reverted to one of his more typical masks: cream-colored, plain, and comfortingly familiar. His worry and pain were familiar too.

Christine couldn't bear it any longer. She reached out and took his hands, their rough texture so familiar now. She still wanted to hold them forever. "Please. I need to know."

"You primed the pump, making her feel sentimental and sad," Erik began slowly. "I want you to know that whatever you said to make her reconsider her life mattered, but she's the sort of person who only wants to hurt others more when she's reminded of her own pain. Our Pauline isn't kind like you. Not forgiving, or even very bright, but she is petty and vindictive, enough that I could make her an offer beyond money, though she wants that too. I can give her the one thing she wants if she can't have her fantasy of me."

"And what is that?" Christine wasn't sure she liked where this was going.

"Her fantasy is part of it. She's studied me, or whatever version of me she could piece together from the years. She sees me as someone who can't be tamed or contained by normal life." Erik squeezed Christine's hands, his eyes upon the golden ring on her finger that made her his. "I think that's not entirely wrong. I leap into everything without thinking about what it means. I leapt into this life with you not knowing what it would entail."

"We both did," Christine countered, trying to sound hopeful.

"It's against my nature to stay. To rest and retreat into a small, simple life. That's how she sees me. Maybe better than I see myself." Erik took a deep breath. "So that's what I gave her as my punishment."

"What?" Christine blinked in confusion as Erik's golden eyes met hers.

"I offered her my suffering. My imprisonment in the ordinary," Erik replied, soft and sincere. "I told her I would do the thing most abhorrent to me if that pain would satisfy her vendetta. I promised her I would give up running."

Christine stifled a gasp, glancing to where Pauline stood idly in the glen, ignoring them and unable to hear what they said. No wonder she looked so pleased with herself.

"You promised her..."

"That I would stay here, in this pathetic shithole of a village, and allow myself to be forgotten. I promised to take on the punishment of trying to live in a world that hates me and that I despise in return."

Christine didn't hold back her tears. They flowed hot down her cheeks as her husband gripped her hands. "We're staying? Because she thinks it's a punishment for you?"

Erik smiled at the edge of his mask, sly and warm. "She is not aware of how much I can enjoy punishment when it's for you."

"You should have told me," Christine whimpered as she pulled him into a fierce hug. She fit perfectly against him, his chin atop her head as he wrapped her in his arms. "I've been so worried."

"I didn't want something to go horribly wrong... Fuck."

Christine pulled back to look at whatever Erik had seen, and her stomach plummeted. Bidaut had arrived, as Pauline had promised, but Shaya Motlagh was with him at gunpoint. "Fuck," she whispered as well. "We have to—"

Erik held her back from rushing into the clearing. "Wait," he hissed, gaze intent on the trio in the circle. "I want to see what she does."

Christine shook, worry vibrating in her gut as Erik's hand steadied her and they watched.

"You look like shit. What the hell happened to you?" Bidaut demanded of Pauline without ceremony.

"I ran into trouble." She touched the vivid bruise on her cheek and looked sheepish. "I may have tried to negotiate with our target on my own."

"You absolute idiot," Bidaut growled. Shaya merely chuckled beside him, drawing Pauline's attention.

"Is this who I think it is?" Pauline asked, looking Shaya over.

"He's our leverage," Bidaut snapped.

"Well, it's useless now. Erik is gone," Pauline said, and Christine held her breath. The woman was a skilled liar, but there was something in the way she said it that was too nervous.

Bidaut heard it too. "What do you mean he's gone?"

"I found him. Tried to negotiate and failed." Pauline indicated her injuries. Christine was only slightly annoyed to not receive proper credit for them. "I was lucky to escape alive, but I don't know where he disappeared to. We should go back to Pomeroy and tell him it's over."

Bidaut stared at the woman, as did Shaya. Did they know she was lying? Would this ruse work? "That's a pity," Bidaut began slowly. "I was quite sure having leverage Erik cared about rather than manipulating some old man in a forgotten town might actually get us somewhere."

"My plan was sound," Pauline sneered.

"Your plan was useless, it seems." Bidaut looked over at Shaya and sighed. "As are you. I guess if this is over, there's no reason to keep you around."

Shaya's look of relief lasted only until Bidaut cocked his pistol and aimed it at Shaya's temple.

"What are you doing?" Pauline gasped.

"Testing a theory. At least it won't be hard to hide a body in wilderness like this—"

"Stop!" Erik yelled before Christine could do the same. They rushed together from the trees, stopping short when Bidaut aimed the revolver at them.

"Ah, there you are," Bidaut smiled. "Right on time."

"I did try," Pauline muttered with a sigh to Christine. Erik stood tall at Christine's side, angling himself between her and Bidaut's weapon.

"How on earth did you get mixed up in this, Daroga?" Erik asked, casual and unbothered as ever.

"As soon as your second letter reached Armand, I knew that the people spying on me would be on their way to you. I was trying to intervene," Shaya replied with the same nonchalance. "It was good to see Adèle. She was the initial target."

"And you stepped in to be a hero," Erik grumbled.

Shaya smiled wistfully. "Well, one must try when one can."

Despite the danger, Christine found herself smiling at the man who had changed so much since she first met him.

"You consider this heroism?" Bidaut interjected.

"I consider it a chance to end this madness without further violence," Shaya said, meeting Christine's eyes and smiling sadly. "I'm glad to see you're well."

"For now," Christine replied sadly.

"You think too highly of a violent man," Bidaut said, visibly bored, and now focused on Erik. "You are cornered, Monsieur Gilbride. Do as I asked back in Geneva and let this be over. My employer may even be generous enough not to send authorities after you."

Christine wanted to intervene, to say to hell with the money: they didn't need it more than anyone's life.

"His employer is Sabine de Chagny," Shaya said, quick as a gunshot and just as shocking. Christine exchanged a look of disbelief with Erik. "Though she goes by Sabine de Martiniac now."

"What?" Christine asked, utterly stunned.

"Sabine doesn't need the money," Erik scoffed, unimpressed. Christine knew him, knew that the very mention of someone close to Raoul was guaranteed to turn him against any idea of surrender.

"Oh, she does," Pauline interjected with a cruel smile. "Big brother Philippe wasted the whole fortune, leaving almost nothing for his siblings after his debts were called in. They could barely pay us without help."

"Shut up," Bidaut hissed at Pauline. She had revealed something interesting if Shaya's pleased look was any indication. For Chistine's part, it did nothing to comfort her.

"All the better to know that family suffers. I wouldn't give them a sou," Erik sneered. "Even if we had it."

"Is this the game you're going to play? Trying to trick me again?" Bidaut snarled back. "I won't be had this time. If you don't—"

"Erik," Shaya cut in urgently. "*O hamleh est.*"

Whatever Shaya had said made Erik's eyes go wide. Christine looked between him and her husband, trying to understand what message had been delivered.

"*Mal baradram?*" Erik's voice was unsteady in a way Christine had rarely heard.

"*Beleh.*"

Erik stared at Shaya for a long moment, then Bidaut and Pauline. Finally, his eyes settled on Christine. "Trust me," his voice whispered in her ear, directed by his ventriloquist skill so only she could hear.

"They're up to something," Pauline remarked. Christine wished Bidaut would slap her, but he only sent her a look.

"As I was saying," Bidaut went on. "You will do as I asked in Geneva and—"

"And as I said, there is nothing left to give her," Erik said, vehement. "Thanks to your colleague here."

"What the hell is he talking about?" Bidaut demanded of Pauline, his anger finally showing through.

"She made a promise to the lord of this village. Well, knight, technically. Said she would buy all his lands and invest in their upkeep," Erik explained, sounding more annoyed than urgent. Christine was beginning to understand.

"What does that have to do with your stolen legacy?" Bidaut sighed back.

"We felt beholden," Christine answered, making sure to scowl at Pauline. "So we have fulfilled the deal."

"Our dear Erik has not only set his fortune on fire for this pathetic hamlet, he swore to never leave this place," Pauline added with clear relish. "That he'd rot and suffer here and never set foot on the continent again."

Now that wasn't a detail Erik had shared with Christine, and it was certainly troubling.

"And you believed him?" Bidaut asked, face bright with suspicion. "You didn't think it was some ruse to hide the funds? This place can't possibly be worth what he had."

"We kept some," Erik began cautiously. "Around a hundred thousand Francs, to sustain us."

Bidaut gave a satisfied grin and raised the aim of his pistol. It made excitement surge through Christine, not from fear, but because she knew they had him. "A hundred thousand will be more than sufficient for Madame de Martiniac's needs."

"We still need to live," Erik scoffed. Christine grabbed his arm, making a show of it as if she objected. "I will give her twenty if I can be done with you."

"Fifty," Bidaut countered, and Christine held her breath. "Final offer. Do it and our business is concluded and you can go on your way."

"How do we know you won't come after us again?" Christine asked, still terrified. "Or that you won't reveal us?"

"Because if he does, I will kill him," Erik said simply, darkness in his voice that would send a chill up the bravest spine. He advanced on Bidaut, unbothered by the gun aimed at his chest, and removed his mask. He was showing the man the face of his doom.

"Erik," Shaya whispered, sounding as worried as Christine felt.

"I will kill him slowly if he ever comes back near me or my wife again," Erik went on, and Bidaut gulped. "And I will take a lesson from him too. Before I let him die, I will hurt him. I'll find someone he loves – everyone he loves – and I will ruin them and leave them to rot. I will destroy everything he has and not feel a shred of regret."

Christine wanted Erik to be lying. She wanted that awful threat to be part of the ruse, part of the desperate attempt to win their peace, but there was a dark corner of her heart that knew it was true. She was wed to a man still capable of murder, but only if someone was foolish enough to threaten her. It should have made her ashamed, or scared, yet all the knowledge gave her was a thrill. Was this what power felt like?

Bidaut took an unsteady breath and looked at Christine, perhaps for some sign of weakness or a signal that she would keep her husband at bay. "I will be happy to help him," she added instead, and any resolve left in Bidaut's face disappeared like morning mist before the sun.

"It is agreed then," Bidaut whispered. "Fifty thousand."

"And other incidental payments and promises owed," Erik added with a look to Pauline that enticed a satisfied smile from her. He wasn't going back on their deal.

"Let us sort out the details as soon as we can," Bidaut said and finally put away his gun.

# Sligo

The bank was quiet, so late at night, though Shaya could hear a chorus of frogs echoing from some distant bog through the open window. The building itself was humble but sturdy, and Shaya could honestly not be critical, as he was pleased a town like this had a bank at all. Even so, Shaya didn't think they endured dramatic requests such as this very often.

Erik handed over the truly staggering amount of cash to Bidaut first, with nary a complaint or even a sarcastic quip. It took all of Shaya's composure to not ask if something was wrong with the man, but he kept quiet until the deal was done and the bewildered banker showed them all out into the street. Well, almost all of them. Erik lingered behind for a moment, as Shaya waited next to Bidaut and the woman called Pauline under Christine's watchful eye.

"I assume our friend is free to go now?" Christine asked impatiently, glancing to where Bidaut had his hand on his hidden revolver in his pocket.

"Our business is concluded, yes," Bidaut sighed, and raised both his empty hands.

"Praise Allah," Shaya muttered to himself and removed himself from Bidaut's proximity. It was a relief to stand by Christine instead and receive the gift of her smile.

"What of my business?" Pauline asked pointedly, as if it was a threat.

"It's being attended to now," Christine answered without missing a beat.

"You don't have to indulge her anymore," Bidaut said, sounding utterly annoyed with Pauline. "I assure you that as of now, she is no longer employed by the Pomeroy agency."

"You think I wanted to be after this?" Pauline shot back. "Idiot."

Bidaut shook his head. "Have you ever noticed how those who are aware of their own defects, yet unwilling to change themselves, tend to insult others with barbs that only apply to themselves?"

"I have noticed that," Christine replied. "But as much as I would like to stay here and discuss dear Pauline's faults, I would like to never see your face again. Please leave."

"Without a goodbye to your illustrious husband?" Bidaut smiled, then frowned as a shadowy figure emerged from the bank.

"Goodbye," Erik intoned as he came to loom next to Christine. "Never trouble us again."

Bidaut gave the couple one more circumspect look, then nodded. It was bold of him to turn his back on a man who could so easily kill him and walk away down a dark street with a small fortune in a valise, but that was his problem now.

"You seem to be on your own now," Christine quipped as Pauline turned to her with a scowl.

"Do you have it?" she demanded.

Erik held out an envelope and Pauline snatched it.

"There. Happy?" Christine said, and Shaya could feel the animosity between the women. Pauline reminded Shaya in that moment of Raoul de Chagny of all people. Blinded by a vendetta and self-deception. At least this woman was giving it up, though not without cost to her targets.

"I'll be happy knowing that you two are stuck in that hellhole, rotting away into obscurity," Pauline replied. "Remember, I have corresponded with people in that village and I will be keeping tabs. I'll know any move you make."

"Of course you will," Christine said, looking at the woman from head to toe and shaking her head. "I do hope that somehow, someday, you learn to be happy."

It struck Shaya as perhaps the most devastating insult Christine could have delivered. Shaya had known Pauline for a matter of hours, but he was quite sure she was the sort that would never truly be happy. They were too angry and too lost.

"I hope you wither up and rot in a life as barren as your belly," Pauline spat back, and for a second, Christine looked like she was ready for violence.

"Come along," Erik whispered, placing an arm around his wife. "We have a long journey home."

They turned without another word, leaving Shaya to give Pauline a final bow. "Perhaps we will meet again in Paris. I keep my eye on things there," he said, as polite a warning as he could manage.

Shaya had to trot to catch up with Erik and Christine, who thankfully seemed to know where they were going. He'd been transported to and fro in rickety carriages all day, and he had the sneaking suspicion they were bound for another one.

"Well, that was an exciting conclusion," Erik muttered. "Thank you for your assistance, Daroga."

"I hope I didn't make things too much worse," Shaya replied, and was grateful when Christine gave him a gentle smile.

"I think you helped immensely." Christine looked back and forth between her husband and the man who had once hunted him. "Though I would like to know what it was you said that changed his mind."

Shaya met Erik's eyes and saw a rare look of panic there. It had been the simplest thing, back in that glen, to tell Erik in Persian that Sabine was with child and confirm it was Antoine's. He didn't know why, but Shaya had been sure Erik would be moved to do something for the child. The poor thing was not unlike himself; the product of violence from a de Martiniac man. Erik would want to give the babe a chance. Or at least a portion of the fortune that came from his blood.

But Shaya had also noted Pauline's passing barb and had, indeed, been surprised not to find Christine in the same state as Sabine. There was a wound there, he was sure of it. Perhaps Erik didn't want his wife to know that Sabine was pregnant when Christine couldn't become so herself.

"I told him they would take a portion, not all," Shaya lied, trying to keep his voice light.

"Why is that?" Christine pushed, inherently curious. Now this, Shaya did have a theory on.

"Well, the Opera Ghost may have something to do with it," Shaya replied, and Erik's gaze snapped to him. "Not you. As I wrote to you in the first place, you've been replaced. This imposter is a much bolder thief than you and is somehow tied up in all of this intrigue."

"Do you think that getting you to alert me of this was part of this foolish game?" Erik asked, voice dripping with derision. "Or did they just want to besmirch my reputation?"

"For a while, I thought it might not be about you at all." Shaya took a moment to look around and enjoy the evening air – and annoying his old quarry. "Not everything is."

"Wait," Christine said, stopping in her tracks. "You wrote when we were already in Florence, according to the date in the letter. After Pauline had already found me."

Shaya paused too, gears in his mind clicking and whirring. "Have you heard from anyone else back in Paris?"

"I wrote to Julianne through Tissot, but I never heard back. I've been worried about her," Christine answered, face falling. "I should have tried again, but everything was so chaotic. I thought maybe she was traveling with Adèle, but she hasn't heard anything either."

"She's no longer at the Opéra," Shaya offered, but it made Christine visibly more worried.

"Will you please look in on her and tell her I haven't forgotten her as soon as you're back?" Christine looked over to Erik, whose eyes held a certain level of regret. "Since we can't go."

"Which is all the more of a torture, knowing my reputation is being trod upon," Erik muttered. Christine gave him a gentle glare that spoke volumes, and he sighed. "Which I will endure happily."

"You think you can survive in that little village?" Shaya asked.

"I don't know, honestly," Erik answered, eyes still on his wife, softening. "But for love, I shall try. I think that is the most any of us can do."

# Paris

M eg was somewhere she wasn't supposed to be, and though this was starting to become a regular occurrence, she was more nervous than ever before. She'd lied to her mother and hidden for hours from firemen and guards. Now, a clock chimed distantly to mark three-quarters past eleven. It was time for Meg to keep her appointment.

She took the backstage stairs down to the cellars to the round, empty space right below the rotunda where, sometimes, singers would practice in the echoing dark. Now, the only echo was her footsteps. She shivered and the lantern in her hand trembled too, its meager flame casting dancing light over the cold gray stone.

Even if Meg hadn't been here to meet a ghost, she would feel this place was haunted.

"I better not die here," Meg muttered to herself. Her mother would be furious about it, to start, and it would be terribly embarrassing. Maybe she should have told Darius she was going to do this, but she was still cross with Shaya for leaving her. She'd confront this phantom on her own.

This wasn't a ghost, she reminded herself. If she was right, this was a friend. Or could be.

"You're early."

Meg spun at the sound of the voice, echoing from somewhere in the shadows she couldn't see. This ghost was exceptionally good at the dramatics of it all, she had to admit.

"I didn't want to miss you," Meg replied. She didn't even try to keep her voice from shaking. What was the point?

"Of course not, you've been chasing me for weeks." The voice came from behind her now, closer, and Meg turned to see a sight that made her catch her breath, no matter how much she had anticipated it.

The Phantom stepped from the shadows. Or a version of the specter Meg and the rest of the Opéra knew. Cloaked in black with a wide-brimmed hat and a mask to match. The black mask was the only thing that was wrong with the picture, as far as Meg knew. The old ghost had always worn a white one, and it had not covered his mouth as this new ghost's disguise did. Not everyone knew that though, and this, of course, was more convenient if you were hiding one's face entirely.

"You don't need to wear that, you know," Meg said, trying to be brave. She failed and sounded mildly seasick instead.

"Because you know who I am?" The ghost chuckled.

Meg gulped. She still wasn't sure, but, even so, she nodded. "I'm sorry it took me so long to figure it out... Julianne."

Before Meg's eyes, the ghost transformed, shoulders slumping in resignation and letting out a sigh before removing the mask and revealing the face Meg knew.

Julianne Bonet looked older somehow, with the tight black ringlets of her hair now pulled back behind her head, and shadows under her eyes standing out on her brown skin. Meg had never felt so guilty seeing an old friend again. Though, perhaps she didn't have the right to call Julianne a friend after all this.

"How did you figure it out?" Julianne asked, not angry or threatening at all now, just sad and amused.

"I realized first that it was someone on our side – the dancers and girls – when I talked to Rochelle. After you helped me with d'Amboise," Meg said. "When she told me what all those men have in common."

Julianne gave a small smile. "I wondered when someone would make the connection."

"Even if someone else had, I don't know if anyone would care. Moncharmin didn't," Meg went on, frowning at the memory. "I thought he was on the side of the artists."

"As much as he would wish not to be, he is on the side of men and money," Julianne replied with a scowl. "Much to our disappointment."

"Then I considered 'Who would know enough about the ghost to pretend to be him,'" Meg continued. "It all had to do with Christine and you knew her best: even Adèle too. You were involved with nearly everyone and everything. I thought you might have the truth of the story, at least, but when Jammes told me what she'd done—"

"How she took it upon herself to punish me," Julianne cut in, hurt vividly in her expression. "I always knew she had a temper, but what she did... I don't think you'd understand why it hurt so much."

"I know about you and her," Meg said softly. "I saw you at the masquerade. I don't think you knew it was me."

Julianne tilted her head, looking bemused. "All Cécile knew was that we had been discovered again and she no longer wanted to take the risk. Her shame about us allowed her to be used, unfortunately."

"By Shaya?" Meg didn't like thinking of him being so mercenary, because it made all he had asked of her and taught her feel so cheap. Julianne still nodded. "Why was she jealous?"

"She rejected me and I found some comfort with someone else, even if it was brief." The look on Julianne's face was knowing, and for some reason that was what made Meg blush. "She was too old for me, in the end, according to her. We wanted different things and she couldn't stay. It hurt too much to be in Paris. She'd been hurt too much."

"And you don't like it when women get hurt," Meg said softly.

Julianne gave her a sidelong look. "No one should like it when girls are hurt, but that is not the world we live in. Alas."

Meg regarded the other woman. It still didn't make sense entirely. She had always been kind and lively, never the kind of person Meg would imagine beating men in the street. "What happened?" Meg asked, suddenly.

"You know what happened," Julianne replied, stiffening. "Jammes saw to it that I was dismissed. Moncharmin didn't care about me. After what he did to Cécile, I'd trust Shaya as far as I could throw him. I couldn't talk to anyone. I never even heard back when I wrote to the people who were supposed to be my friends – not even a letter of where to send their things!"

"I should have made more of a commotion when you left. I should have noticed sooner," Meg said, shaking her head in shame. "I'm so sorry."

"Thank you," Julianne said, sincere. "I needed some way to support myself and my mother, and being a ghost seemed to work well enough for—" Julianne caught herself, smirking.

"Shaya hasn't told me his name," Meg replied. "He says it's too dangerous to know, even now."

"Shaya can't be trusted in many things, but he's right about that," Julianne muttered.

"That still doesn't answer my question," Meg pushed, taking a cautious step toward the woman who had taken up the ghost's mantle. "Why start hurting those patrons? Why intervene in that way?"

Julianne gave Meg a grim look. "Maybe hiding in the walls I saw one too many of them forcing themselves on girls younger than you. Maybe I started to feel helpless being forgotten so easily. After all the slights and insults and... Maybe I wanted to show someone that I had chosen the right side and make cruel, entitled bastards pay. Maybe the first time it happened, I saw what Tremblay tried to do to a girl your age and couldn't tolerate it anymore. I don't expect you to understand it," Julianne replied. "Some days, I don't understand it myself."

Meg felt small and hopeless in the face of such quiet, seething rage. There was nothing she could say that would offer comfort that wouldn't be trite or empty, but perhaps she still had to say it. "I think you're on the right side."

Julianne gave a bitter laugh, looking down at the mask in her hand. "I thought I was too when it started. Now I'm not so sure."

"Why?"

Julianne's eyes met Meg with a look of guilt and despair. "Because it was not me that robbed the Opéra."

## Coolaney

Erik had only begun to explore the house he now – apparently – owned, and already, he had decided which rooms he enjoyed and the few he preferred to avoid. The attic was of the latter category. It was comically full of dust and cobwebs and stank of the droppings of mice and bats. The detritus of a century of neglect remained there in such a state that Erik couldn't even tell what was old furniture and what was kindling. Now it was theirs and he had no idea how to sort through it. That suited the situation.

Erik had ventured up to the top story to avoid the crowd of people who had descended on the manor all day. Some had been curious villagers, alerted by the news that the French woman and her mysterious husband had indeed taken over the manor from Sir Edward. Erik looked out a cloudy window down to the village, trying to pick out the house where the old knight now officially resided in his room near the inn. Erik was impressed the man had managed to live long enough to complete the deal.

The fiction that Christine was some distant relative had been maintained, because no one in town wanted to dispute it, and papers of dubious veracity and legality had been signed this morning. News had spread, and seemingly every person in Coolaney had come to offer some token of welcome to get a glimpse of the people who now owned the fallow lands and crumbling house. The attention had tested Erik's resolve to stay here, and he had kept to corners and avoided their eyes. Christine had been his only savior.

She had been in her element, happy to receive bread, firewood, and baskets of fruit, politely asking in her accented English if someone might help her clear out some of the fireplaces and remove the pigeon nest in the kitchen. Siobhan had been happy to help, commenting that many hands make light work. Erik appreciated that the fires were burning and that they had been treated to a real meal, but he was quite ready for everyone to be gone. At the same time, he was melancholy because Shaya had left so quickly. The Daroga had left all his things in London and his life in Paris, so it was understandable, but his old adversary and friend had been a piece of home.

From the attic, Erik watched as the sun sank into the horizon. He had thought rather naively that he might be able to see the ocean from so far up, but the view was mainly of the village and the rolling hills beyond. It was beautiful and familiar, and Erik didn't know for sure if he would be able to stand looking at it for years. That was the point, perhaps, of this strange bargain. He'd chosen the world for Christine, and now, this was the one he would have to live in.

"There you are."

He turned at the sound of Christine's voice, kind and warm and perfect as ever. Her smile was perfect too when he looked at her. For the first time in a long time, perhaps ever, he felt like he was worthy of it.

"The commotion was a little much for me," Erik demurred, picking his way through the debris to where Christine waited at the top of the stairs. "Be careful up here."

"I looked for you in the library first." She took his hand and guided him to her, all tenderness. "I assume I'll find you there often."

"I haven't even examined what sort of books are there," Erik said, squeezing her hand, and instantly warmth filled him. He hadn't noticed how cold it was in the dark, hidden part of the house. Or perhaps it was that the house itself was warmer now. While he had been hiding away from the rush of humanity, they had brought some life back to the old building. It was warm and whatever ghosts lingered seemed to have retreated. "I'm sure the piano is a disaster," Erik added with a smirk.

"It will be an excellent project for you to rehabilitate it then," Christine smiled. "If the books are nothing but old dictionaries, we can replace them. Maybe we'll hear from Shaya soon that it's safe for us to write to Julianne. She can send some of your things that she's been watching."

A cloud of worry passed over Christine's face briefly, and Erik hooked a finger under her chin. "She's fine, I'm sure. And that's an excellent idea. Though we'd need to be careful."

"You should write to Jack. See if he can visit soon and work on that symphony with you." Her smile had returned, and Erik couldn't help but echo it. "I can ask Howard and Letitia to come too when they can; maybe even Adèle."

"We will be quite a destination."

"Just because we can't go anywhere doesn't mean we're cut off," Christine said, ever the optimist. To Erik's surprise, it didn't fill him with guilt or dread to be reminded of his deal.

"I can't go anywhere. Without taking precautions," Erik countered, slyly. "You can go wherever you like."

"The only place I want to be is in my home with my husband," she whispered, voice husky and seductive as she pulled him close to her. He melted into her kiss, and the house seemed to grow even warmer. Her eyes were dark and loving when she pulled away. "The one I have chosen and will choose again and again."

"An honor I will continue to try and be worthy of," Erik replied, and let his wife lead him down the hall.

Erik felt as if he were floating when Christine pulled him into a room with a crackling fire. It was a different chamber than where they had slept last night when they had collapsed on the first bed they could find. This room was bigger and boasted a four-poster bed that was in relatively decent condition with bedding that looked clean and new.

"Courtesy of a new friend that Siobahn introduced me to," Christine explained. "They had a mattress as well. I think we'll sleep much better tonight."

"You've done well settling in," Erik remarked, proud but thoughtful.

Christine closed the door behind them and locked it, for good measure. Though they were alone in the manor, it gave Erik some sense of safety to know no one could barge in. It was security she knew he needed. "I know you're thinking that things will change."

"People tend to become less kind when they learn there's a monster living on the hill," Erik sighed. Christine shook her head and approached him. She didn't flinch when she removed his mask, and she was sweet and loving as she kissed his cheek – kissed his scars and hideousness. Kissed the bridge of his sunken nose and his forehead.

"Maybe they won't. Or they will and we will find a way to overcome it." Christine pressed her body against him and slid her hands up his chest and then around his neck. "Together."

"I don't think I understood until recently what that meant," Erik murmured, amazed by her. "What it really meant to marry you."

Christine smiled, soft and curious. "Tell me more."

"It's easy to love you. Easy to swear that I will love you until the stars are cold and we are but dust and shadow," Erik began, his voice like a song. "I thought choosing to follow that love into the light was the hardest thing I'd ever done, but it was just the beginning. It's hard, every day, to be the man you deserve and the one I want to be. It's hard to fight the darkness that's in me, pulling me down. It's hard to let go of the pain and the wounds."

"I know. It's hard for me too," Christine confessed. "But we can't heal if we don't rest and help each other. Walk side by side, through the dark, into the light."

"I couldn't do it without you. Without your support and understanding and—"

"Stubbornness?" Christine laughed. "Or – what's a good word for being willing to put you in your place and pull you back from your head?"

"Bravery, I think," Erik exhaled, and kissed her, deep and thorough. She looked beatific when he pulled back, like something in her was finally at peace. He had done that, and it filled him with joy. "You're the bravest person I've ever known, my Christine."

"Brave enough to live by your side." It was a new promise, one Erik wanted to return.

"As long as you'll have me."

A spark kindled in Christine's eye, devious and delicious. "And how, pray tell, may I have you?"

"Any way you like," Erik grinned. "Though I do think we lost those lovely restraints Letitia gifted you."

"Oh, she gifted me a few things. She's a generous and informative friend," Christine purred. Erik was almost embarrassed by the eager way his heart began to beat at her tone and the hungry, rough way she kissed him. He chased her lips when she pulled back, but she grabbed his hair to hold him at bay and clucked her tongue. "I want you to undress and await me beside our bed. Face the window, legs against the frame."

Erik's curiosity flared to new heights as he obeyed. Christine disappeared into a shadowy corner of the room where she had piled their cases of things. He took his time removing his clothes, forcing himself to breathe and be calm and not let his imagination go too wild. What she was planning, he couldn't say, but he was already half hard considering the possibilities. So much for being calm.

His belt was half undone when he made the mistake of looking up to the window she had told him to face. The curtains were only half-drawn, and it was night now. Which meant the glass of the window had been rendered into a mirror by the light inside the room. Erik found himself shocked by his own horrible reflection.

Now his heart raced for a different reason. He struggled to breathe, confronted by the awful sight of his deathly face. His scarred body. The face of a killer and a liar and an awful, broken thing.

"It's alright," Christine cooed from where she had materialized beside him. "You don't have to look. I can close it, if you like, but I don't think you should be afraid of seeing the man I love."

Erik gasped, eyes still on his reflection, as Christine's gentle hands swept up his back and she pressed a kiss to his shoulder. "I..." He couldn't speak. He couldn't answer such love.

"Close your eyes then, and wait," Christine told him, and he did.

Instantly, he was at peace in the darkness where she alone shone for him like the sun. He was compliant as she slipped her hands around him, finishing his work and undoing his belt, and he shivered as she exposed him to the air. He felt her soft breasts against his back and then... something else.

"What—" he began to ask, mind grinding to a halt as his wife took his hands and guided them behind him to touch her. First her breasts, then her ribs. Her belly, and then, a length of leather. A belt of some kind. Erik's mouth went dry in amazement as he explored the curious accessory with his fingertips, tracing where it dipped down to his wife's groin where it held a smooth, hard...

"It's an instrument of pleasure," Christine whispered, bold and amused. "I had to know what sort of weapons a woman could have in her arsenal."

"Indeed," Erik murmured, brain reeling. "And have you been instructed in its use?"

"I have, but I will need some additional direction, I think." Christine pressed against him, the shaft of her borrowed cock sliding against his ass. "I have oil too."

"Good," was all he could mutter.

He kept his eyes closed as she bent him at the hip, and he took a place on the bed. He'd been on his knees before her many times, but never like this. This was a kind of submission that was utterly different. It was terrifying and wonderful.

She was gentle as she touched him. She kissed him and caressed him for what felt like forever, easing him into a state not unlike a dream. It was pure delight when her hand found his hard member at last, stroking him slow and gentle as a mere prelude to something more. Still, he sucked in a breath in shock at the first touch of her slick finger to his entrance. To say it had been a while was an understatement.

"I'll go slow," she said sweetly. Lovingly. It bewildered him, to be given this as an act of her love. Because it was for him, for his pleasure. His mind didn't know how to accommodate that idea any more than his body knew how to respond to the way she touched him. It was a stretch, but it felt good. It felt warm and insistent and so good as she circled and pressed.

"That's... that's good..." he muttered, wondering if he'd even be able to form words soon. She chuckled in the dark above him and pressed another kiss to his spine.

"You're good. So beautiful and good for me," she cooed back, pressing deeper into him as she did. He found himself nodding, not in agreement but in acquiescence, as she kept up her work. "Tell me when you're ready."

He could only groan, his body was already taut and hot; cock dripping between his legs. She added another finger and the fullness was almost too much to bear. He breathed through it, breathed deep and relaxed for her. To be hers in yet another way.

"I'm ready," he breathed, and for a second he was empty.

Then, she pushed in, the head of her instrument slickened and warm. Erik let out a sound akin to a yell and a song, reveling in the divine pleasure and pain as his lover penetrated him. It felt like forever that she moved in and out by increments until he was stretched full, panting, and at her mercy.

"Shall we begin?" Christine asked breathlessly. Erik didn't understand, once again, because what had they been doing up until now? Why did she sound so undone, as if this gave her pleasure as well? Maybe it did. Maybe she liked fucking him this way. If so, he would let her take this pleasure too.

He nodded.

Her first thrust was not rough, but it sent lightning through Erik's body that left him trembling as she touched a place inside him that seemed made for this. Again she moved, and he gasped, eyes flying open against his will... And he saw.

He saw not only his own reflection, prone and bent on the bed, but he saw his Christine, radiant and ravenous behind him. He looked and he saw and he watched as she fucked him, her hips pumping, her breasts bobbing, each thrust sending Erik closer to oblivion.

She flattened herself against his back, grinding with her hips, and took his cock in hand as she found a perfect angle within him. He wanted to savor it, to exist in this pleasure for as long as possible, but soon, it was too much. To be seen and possessed and subsumed was all too much and he came with a fierce cry, spilling hot over her hand.

He collapsed on the bed, breathless and amazed, electricity and joy ringing through him. It was surprisingly soft, this new mattress they had found. He'd be happy to sleep here just as he was happy to linger in the afterglow. In their bed. In their house where they would stay. Where endless nights like this with his beloved awaited him.

He only stirred when he felt a soft, cool cloth against his skin. He turned to see an angel attending him, one who was beaming.

"You look pleased," Erik whispered. "Happy even."

Christine grinned sheepishly. "I am pleased. That was quite delightful. I can't even explain why, but that was what I needed too. You've made me very happy."

"I want to make you come," Erik said as the thought bloomed in his mind. Before he could think more he was moving, pulling Christine to the bed and flipping her to the mattress. "I want to make you feel as good as I do," he muttered between kisses all over her body.

"Aren't you tired?" she gasped as he kissed her belly and pushed her legs apart.

"No. I feel like I could fly," Erik sighed back before licking her thigh. "I want to taste you and serve you and ravish you until you're limp. I want to fuck you so hard you'll feel it for days. I want you to fall asleep so satisfied you won't wake until hours past dawn, and then I'll fuck you again against these walls. I'll make them ring with your cries of pleasure so that the very foundations of this house know that you belong to me, as much as this place belongs to us now."

Erik paused for one moment, looking up at her from the sweet juncture of her thighs. She looked beatific and overcome, her breasts heaving, mouth agape, and joyful tears in her eyes. "Then do it, my love," she exhaled, and that was all he needed to hear.

Erik made sure to be a man of his word. He made her come on his fingers and tongue, ecstatic at the taste of her. She made no attempt to muffle her screams, and he reveled in the way she lost control of herself and came again, even when she thought she was done. He took her on her knees when he was hard again, fucking her as hard and well as she had done him until they both collapsed and held each other until the dawn.

## Paris

Fall had found Paris in the days Shaya had been gone. Or perhaps it had followed him from the cool hills of Ireland, despite the speed of his exit from that county. There had been a part of him that wanted to stay – to learn more thoroughly what adventures had befallen Erik and Christine – but there had been too much to do. He had at least waited for a different train from

Sligo than the one his former captor would have taken. That would have been awkward.

Shaya had bid Erik adieu and begun the long journey back to London, and it was more comfortable than traveling as a hostage. Even though he had only been in Ireland's countryside for a few days, and unwillingly so, London was a heady contrast to the quiet that was now Erik's home. Or prison. Shaya was still unsure.

In London, he had also longed to rest, but that wasn't to be. His things, meager though they were, had not been thrown into the street when he didn't return to his hotel, much to his relief, and he managed to get some sleep before beginning his business. He sent telegrams and delivered letters to Adèle and, through her, various other friends that the former Opera Ghost had accumulated along the way. Shaya was particularly interested in an Italian man with an English name who had come to the city and may have entangled himself with Adèle, however briefly. Jack had spoken kindly of Erik and seemed eager to meet with him for some musical pursuit.

Shaya wasn't sure of the details. The whole affair had been a whirlwind, and soon enough, he had found himself on a succession of carriages, boats, and trains back to Paris. All that remained now was the walk up the *Rue de Rivoli* to his flat where Darius awaited, and Shaya wanted nothing more than to fall into his bed and sleep for a week.

He should have known fate wouldn't grant him such mercy. Darius was waiting in the parlor looking imperious next to, of course, young Meg Giry.

"I have been waiting for an hour!" Meg crowed, jumping up from her spot by the fire.

"You stayed because I had supper ready," Darius muttered before turning his attention to Shaya and giving him a loving smile. "Glad to see you remain alive."

"Darius won't tell me what happened, but he implied you were in danger!" Meg nearly yelped, then narrowed her eyes. "I assume you were attending to some business with Erik."

Shaya didn't attempt to disguise his shock. "How did you learn that name?"

"I learned a lot of things when I finally found someone who would be honest with me," Meg replied. "Someone who appreciated how much I figured out on my own."

Darius gave Shaya a look that told him all of this was news to him as well. Of course, little Meg had held onto this for dramatic effect. She was a performer after all.

"And who would that be? Don't keep me in suspense," Shaya asked with a sigh.

"Julianne Bonet." Meg looked quite proud of herself. "She's very cross with Christine for ignoring her for so many months."

"Christine wasn't ignoring her. Their letters were intercepted, much like mine, by Pomeroy and his men," Shaya explained, for there was no reason to keep everything secret now. "It is how they were found and why I went to London."

"Oh. That's good to know, I guess." Meg looked troubled by the news, despite her words. "Did you also know about the money that's been stolen from the Opéra? And the crisis it's causing?"

"Armand said there had been accounting issues and some funds had gone missing..." Shaya replied, looking to Darius for some confirmation. "I didn't know there was a crisis. Good heavens, what have you been doing while I was away?"

"Discovering the identity of the new Opéra Ghost for one," Meg replied with a proud smirk. "Whose motivation is exactly as I thought it was and who we needn't fear. It's the thief who is also using the ghost's mask that's the real danger, I think."

"There are two?" Shaya was too exhausted for all these revelations, but something was itching at the back of his mind.

"Yes. One ghost punishing patrons who hurt girls," Meg explained, much to Shaya's amazement. "And another motivated by money and need. That's why it's been so confusing trying to parse who's done what."

"Another ghost who is associated with Sabine," Shaya muttered. "Who may have provided her with those same missing funds. Or wanted them for himself."

"You still think it was Richard?" Darius asked, speaking the theory forming in Shaya's mind. "For his ends or hers?"

"It might be both," Shaya replied. "Sabine's situation has apparently changed. I wonder..."

"Does that mean it's over?" Darius asked, looking between Meg and Shaya. "You've found one ghost and have a clue on the other?"

"No. We have to get the money back," Meg replied urgently. "The Opéra needs it. And the Opéra needs the ghost too. To save it."

Shaya peered at Meg, assessing her. There was something more mature about her now than when he had left, more knowing and brave. She'd decided this already, and somehow, she'd involved one ghost in it. "Is this you talking? Or the phantom you have unmasked who you have yet to tell me the name of?"

Meg raised her chin defiantly, standing her ground. "This Phantom is a friend, like the old one is yours. You will forgive me for being willing to protect that."

Shaya thought back to the last few days. Of what he had been willing to do for a man he had once wished to destroy. Of what he had learned of the man Erik was becoming and what his hopes were for the future. He had been willing to protect that which he had once hated, and now Meg was protecting the ghost she had hunted.

"I think more than anyone, I understand that, Mademoiselle Giry," Shaya said. "And I am going to help you. For my friends."

# Coolaney

To go into the village alone was a particular type of adventure for Christine. First, there was the matter of being allowed to go alone. Erik not only wanted to protect her and translate for her when she went, but she had a suspicious feeling that he missed her quite terribly when she was gone. He complained jokingly that the house was haunted, but the ghosts so far were poor company. Christine had countered that they could hire a servant, and he quickly shut up.

Erik understood, however grudgingly, that Christine wanted to learn the ways and words of Coolaney on her own. Or at least practice them. She could get by well enough with her stilted English, though her one lesson in Irish had gone horribly. Erik assured her that few would expect her to learn or know it, as the English overlords had tried to snuff out the entire language. That had only made Christine more determined to learn it... eventually.

She knew the path now, down the hill from the manor and around the bend into the village proper. She knew which of the old buildings housed the baker and which hosted the cobbler who also happened to be the town's only tailor. Someone had said the baker was also a dentist, but Christine was sure she had heard that wrong. Today though, she wanted to find an apothecary, or something of the like.

As had been her strategy for everything so far, she would start at the pub. She smiled at Hugh behind the bar when she entered. He was a large man with broad shoulders and a ginger-blond beard who was quick with a kind word and a drink. He knew everyone and everything that went on in the town and if he didn't know, Connie the barmaid would. She was as enamored of gossip as a ballet rat, though Christine could barely understand anything she said. They could probably both tell Christine where she needed to go, but she decided her best bet was Siobhan, who was by the fire attending Sir Edward, as usual.

"Good morning, Mrs. Gilbride," Siobahn said as Christine approached, scrambling out of her seat and attempting something like a curtsey. Christine was unsure if Siobhan treated her like she was nobility because of mistaken identity or simply because of the status that came with owning the manor.

"Good morning. You can call me by Christine," she said carefully.

"Oh no, Ma'am. That wouldn't be right," Siobhan said, blushing. "How can I help you today?"

"I need to find a... I do not know the word," Christine began. She could have asked her husband before leaving, she knew, but he had been elbow-deep in the piano when she'd looked in on him and she hadn't wanted to disrupt his concentration. "A person who sells... *medcin*? Herbs?"

"Oh, that'll be Oona!" Siobahn cried happily, and suddenly, Christine was being herded back out the door and Siobhan was pointing to a little house at the end of the street, talking too fast for Christine to translate in her head. Something about plants and babies? Maybe Oona was the midwife.

Soon enough, Christine found herself stumbling along the street alone again, hesitant to knock on Oona's door. She didn't necessarily want to meet a midwife and have a stilted conversation about why she was childless, but she also needed more than what she could forage around her overgrown garden.

"Come in then. Don't stand around." Christine looked up to see an older woman standing at the door, smiling at her as if she'd been waiting. "I was wondering when I'd meet you."

"You are Oona?"

"And you're the new Lady of the manor," Oona replied. "Come on, get inside. Rain is coming."

Christine looked over her shoulder into the clear sky as Oona ushered her in. "Thank you. I am sorry if my English is not well. I am—"

"French, I heard," Oona chuckled. "We'll get by, love, don't worry your pretty head."

Christine smiled. Something was welcoming about the elder woman, as if she'd known her a long time. The house was welcoming too – full of herbs in jars and drying in the rafters.

"I need..." Christine held out her hands to show the raw blisters that had developed on her palms from days of work at the manor. "*Une baume?*"

"A salve – balm we also call it," Oona translated. Quick as a whip, she was rummaging through one of a dozen shelves and produced a small pot that she opened to show Christine. "Honey, tallow, and herbs," Oona explained. "It will help."

"Thank you," Christine said, fishing in her pocket for money.

"Take it as a gift," Oona said, pressing the jar into Christine's hands. "I know you will earn it."

"What? I can't..." Christine protested, but the old woman only smiled.

"You will come back and talk to me of France and what sort of adventures you have had," Oona said, confidently. "Talking is healing you now and it's the kind you need, I can tell. But not today. Today I must rest and you must get home before the rain."

"Of course," was all Christine could say, before she was once again outside, looking up at the sky. Clouds were gathering in the east.

The rain began just as Christine came inside the manor, stepping over the lumber and tools that now littered the front hall. Erik assured her they would be used very soon, and she wanted to trust that he wouldn't be distracted before that.

She knew exactly where to find him inside, for she could hear him singing.

"*If my true love will not come, I can surely find another, who'll pluck wild mountain thyme all among the purple heather.*" His voice rang out from the library, more beautiful than an angel's. Because he was mortal and unburdened, for now. Because he was happy.

"*Will ye go, lassie, go? And we'll all go together,*" he sang on as Christine quietly entered the library to watch him at work. He was bent over the disassembled piano, sleeves rolled up... mask off.

"*To pluck wild mountain thyme all around the purple heather,*" Christine sang with him, and her heart swelled when he looked up at her and smiled. In a breath he was beside her, taking her into his arms and sweeping her into a dance.

"*I will build my love a shelter, by yon crystal flowing stream,*" he sang to her, twirling her in the derelict library of the house that they could finally call home.

She sang back to him, with all her heart, "*And my love shall be the fairest that the summer sun has seen.*"

He grinned at her with such love in his golden eyes that Christine couldn't help but kiss him. She sank into his embrace as the rain pattered against the windows, music and adoration filling her soul. Christine kissed her husband, happy and content, ready to sing with him through all the day.

# Coda

H is sister did not take many visitors, not since her condition had become visible, so Raoul was surprised to hear Sabine in conversation with someone in the parlor. It was his house, and Sabine was under his supervision, so he saw nothing wrong with opening the door to discover who had breached their seclusion.

"Raoul!" Sabine cried as he entered, but he ignored her. His attention was on the man who had risen to meet him. He was exceedingly ordinary, with thinning hair, a neat suit, and spectacles. "This is private."

"What is your business with my sister?" Raoul demanded, ignoring Sabine's ire.

"Concluded," the man replied coolly.

"Monsieur Bidaut is an investigator," Sabine said. "He is the one who I tasked with the matter of Antoine's estate and he has finally come through."

Raoul felt like he had been holding the same tension for months - a cord around his neck that had slowly been tightening as their finances grew worse and worse - and suddenly it was gone. "Well, that's good news," Raoul sighed.

"And where are you going?" Sabine asked sourly, looking pointedly at Raoul's coat and the hat in his hands.

"Out. See yourself in the same direction," Raoul said to Bidaut. With a curt nod to Sabine, he left them. He could, he supposed, have stayed to celebrate with his sister, but she was difficult to tolerate lately. Raoul had never really been around a pregnant woman before and he wondered if they were all so emotional or if it was his sister's particular tragic circumstances that made things so.

He decided not to dwell on it. She'd found them some goddamn money and he was grateful. It was one less thing to worry about, thank God. Raoul had other matters to attend to, like the eager girl who sprang from the park bench to greet him. He did not like how small she was, nor was her overly cheerful demeanor endearing, but Blanche's face was nice enough to look at, and she did love to gossip.

"I was worried you'd be late, Monsieur le Comte," Blanche giggled as she reached him.

"I'm a navy man, Mademoiselle Carcaux," Raoul replied, trying to remember how to be charming. "I live and die by time."

"You'd do wonderfully at the Opéra. They're very strict there," Blanche replied. Raoul was certain she meant it as some flirtation. It was not effective.

"I doubt that," he muttered.

"Are sailors suspicious types?" Blanche asked as they began walking through the yellowing trees. "Artists are. But, of course, you know all about the Opéra."

What a tactless young thing she was, Raoul mused. "Yes. I do."

"Someone told me that every theater has a ghost," Blanche went on, blithely unaware of how deeply Raoul was frowning. He had known to expect this in conversation with her, but that didn't make it easier to be reminded of the worst days of his life and the man who had caused them.

"Luckily for everyone, yours is gone," Raoul muttered.

"Why would you say that?" Blanche asked with a laugh, and Raoul stopped in his tracks. "Ghosts don't go away."

"I'm sure the legends and superstitions continue." Raoul's throat felt tight as he forced out the words. This had been a mistake. He should have stayed away and minded his business and not let his curiosity about the Opéra lead him to this.

If he had done that, Blanche wouldn't be looking at him in wonder and bewilderment. "Haven't you heard? I guess you wouldn't have, since you've been away."

"Heard about what?" Raoul demanded, against all his better judgment.

"About the attacks. On the patrons! There have been at least four," Blanche said, sweet and naïve. She didn't know that her words were an explosion in Raoul de Chagny's mind. Even so, he could stop. He could dismiss her and let it all go, were it not for the nagging feeling that had been with him for months, The emptiness of unanswered questions. The void of suspicion and doubt that pulled him into nightmares night after night.

"What attacks?" he asked, knowing the answer might seal his doom.

Erik and Christine's story will continue in...
*Angel's Song*
2026

# Acknowledgements

As always, this new book would not exist without the support and help of so many people. Thank you to my family, especially my amazing Tamsin and my beautiful Heidi for their love and support. Thank you to my parents for their faith and to my extended family for all being there always. To Chris, who we lost in January, and your family, I send all my love.

Thank you to Ana for listening to all my ranting and raving. Thank you to Jordan for your edits and support. Thank you as well to all my readers and fans who continue to tout and support The Phantom Saga. I could not do this without you.

Finally, thank you to my furry and feathered friends, many of whom crossed the rainbow bridge before the publication of this book. Thank you to Marlon, who is still with me, for taking me on the walkies where I resolved most of my plot problems. Thank you to Lemon, Lime, and Sky, whose songs brought me such joy, and whose joyful presence is sorely missed in our home.

And finally, thank you and goodbye to Dewey Mankowski, who was in my lap or cuddled by my side for much of the drafting and editing of this book. You weren't my dog all the time, but you were still part of our family and will always have a place in my heart. I'll miss you so much, little guy. Thank you for being part of our life and thank you, Beck, for letting all of us share him.

# Don't miss out!

Visit the website below and you can sign up to receive emails whenever Jessica Mason publishes a new book. There's no charge and no obligation.

https://books2read.com/r/B-A-RZHV-GXDLG

**BOOKS 2 READ**

Connecting independent readers to independent writers.

# Also by Jessica Mason

# About the Author

Jessica Mason lives near Portland, Oregon with her wife, daughter, and corgi. She has studied opera, practiced law, and has worked as a fandom journalist and podcaster, among many varied careers. But first and foremost she has always been a storyteller. When she manages to stop writing, she enjoys gardening, travel, music, and witchcraft.

Find her on social media: @ByJessicaMason

## About the Publisher

Murmuration Books is an independent publisher bringing readers, steamy, spellbinding, spooky, sensational stories. We are committed to diverse themes, new authors, and creative takes on old ideas.

For more, visit Murmurationbooks.com